Dedications:

To my wife, Ashley, who never let me stop dreaming.

To my daughter, Lila, who will always be my dearest baby girl.

To my son, J, who will forever be my superhero.

To my family, that nurtured me to be the man that I am.

To my friend, Jesse, who empowered me to push forward.

To everyone that understands that a car is more than just an appliance.

To everyone that also believes that we all have a story to tell.

To all my fellow auto lovers that were taken too soon.

For this, loving cars is optional.

"At some point, our individual stories and struggles become one. What comes next is up to us. We are the writers, so what will we write? What is the next chapter? That is the true test of friendship."
——Agatha Peters

www.winiverse.com/projectmadtyte

- The Underground Kings –
Deluxe Edition

ISBN-13: 978-1-7349678-0-7

TUKv2.0 Series Edition

GFES 3.0.0

The Underground Trilogy

The Underground Kings
The Underground Saints
The Underground Champions

And so many more...

- The Underground Kings –
Deluxe Edition

4

PREFACE

The rhymes.

The flows.

The ability to spew poetry from his tongue at a moment's notice.

Hip hop was his passion, his connection with the soul of a movement, his gateway to sanity when it threatened to leave him. On his way home in his old two door, he cranked his music up as loud as it would go, the off-brand subwoofers rumbling so hard that the windows in his car nearly shattered. As he drove, he righted his neck and rapped along with the various artists on the radio. The movement towards classical hip hop was growing stronger. They were rebels against the common trend of tasteless, mumble-filled "hype music". Classical guys were the antithesis. They told stories. They rhymed about the misgivings and joys of life, renewing the verve in the lost art.

Jason did too, and he was good, but no one gave him any credit. He wrote his own songs, but no one cared enough to listen to them. It was nothing more than a mere fallacy, a dream that could be quickly ousted by the likes of his peers and, perhaps, his parents. In the light drizzle, he kicked the clutch and sent the tail end skittering out to the side, countering the action with just enough of a steering adjustment to hold the drift.

Rainy days were his escape. They enabled him to do what he wanted in life:

To drive, to drift, and to rap.

And there, he was back to driving straight once again, having angered an unsuspecting driver who was less than impressed with his driving antics.

"Asshole!" the man screamed from his window after he blew his horn. "Why don't you drive that old piece of shit off a cliff before you hurt someone?"

"I'll pass on that, but thanks." Jason shouted back before speeding away.

Once he cut in front of the guy and between a semi, he kicked the clutch again, harder this time, and made it a point to drift the rest of the way into this neighborhood nary any mishaps. It was always about proving a point, to that random angry guy and to himself, a point that he was at least good at *something*, even if it didn't matter to anyone else. His life was a boon, the dull repetition taxing what drive he had left, but the little red car was his personal beacon of light against the turmoil at home. Despite his heavily weighed concerns, those were the least of his current problems. Now, as he entered the door to his house, he'd have to face his new opposition.

"What happened to your face?" his mother's expression was rotten.

Boom.

There was no 'hello,' or 'how are you son' in their passive greetings. Instead, a thorough interrogation was always guaranteed.

"Got in a fight." Jason shrugged. He looked horrible, but at least he had on the fresh clothes he bought during the drive home. The original outfit was ruined during the scuffle, yet another casualty of war.

"'Got in a fight' with whom?" his father paused the movie on the television and leaned forward. He tipped his glasses down, as if he got a better view of the world this way.

Jason hated it.

"Some people that had a problem with me." he partially lied.

"What happened to them?"

"Some are in the hospital. Some are in jail."

"In the hospital?!" his mom shouted again. "What!?"

"I don't see what the problem is if I'm obviously okay." Jason stared at the carpet. "Just a little banged up, that's all."

He tried to escape when his father restarted the movie, but it wasn't that easy.

"Where do you think you're going?" he asked.

"Uh, upstairs?"

His father laughed sarcastically and pointed to the couch, "Take a seat, Junior."

Jason's mood slumped even further, but he obeyed, sitting as far away as he could. He tried to use logic, hoping to rationalize this never-ending cycle. No, they weren't overreacting. He thought of himself as a middle-aged father, admitting that he'd be frightened to see his son come home with a black eye and swollen lip. Fair. Still, it didn't leave him immune to the battering. He zoned out, nearly numb to the wild emotions of his mother. She was always upset, always on edge, a specialist of melodrama.

Jason felt drunk on the charade, the room swirling around him as he focused on breathing and slowing his heart rate. Yes, he was a slacker. Yes, he had little to no self-confidence. Yes, he had quit college because of his own inattention. These were well known travesties, yet his mother still covered them as if they were rehearsed, flailing her arms around and flinging her head about during the act. Finally, they reached the topic of the hour.

Jason summarized the story: Some kids tried to jump him and steal his car, big deal. It was a classic, a valuable construct of days past. Things normal people couldn't understand. Fortunately, the literal woman of his dreams came to the rescue with her wrist computer, filming a video long enough to spook the offenders. Embarrassing wasn't exactly the word for it, but he had no self-esteem left to ruin.

Silence.

"So fill me in." his dad finally spoke, trying to remain calm—as he had promised to work on his temper.

"On what?" Jason replied.

"What is going on with you?" his mom interrupted, her voice sharpened with distress. "Why are you running around without a care in the world? You don't care about anything! You just don't care!"

Again. Yelling, again. The brief truce was already nullified.

His dad groaned, his face reddened with frustration. Was there no feasible way to have peace in his home?

Jason scowled, "Mom, stop it!"

"Stop what?" she asked.

"Yelling! You're always yelling!" Jason exploded. "I mean, what are you even talking about?"

"You doing *this*!" she fired back. "Running out of here and not talking to us for days. We went to your grandmas to get away for a few days, trusted you with the house, and we trusted you to keep in contact and follow the rules here, but you couldn't even do that! Same thing happened when we went on vacation!"

"Mom, what are you talking about? The last time you went on vacation was *three years* ago! I was sixteen! I didn't mean to set the deck on fire! I thought we were over that!"

"Son, it took you five months to find a job." his father suddenly noted. "I mean, what is going on here? What happened to you?"

"Dad, the economy is bad. I mean, at least I have a job, right?"

"Look," his father said calmly, "I'm not trying to jump on your case, but you've *got* to pick it up, Jason. I mean, are you going back to college? Are you saving up any money? All you do is spend it on that little car."

"'Am I going back to college'?" Jason mocked. "I don't even know what to go to college for! How will I pay for it? I don't have a college fund like some of the other kids do."

"Well, we told you to get your grades up!" his mom shouted. "We told you that you'd need all the help you can get, but no, you continued to slide on by with a 'C' average that you *barely* maintained. Looks like you'll have to be like every other student in the country and work your way through school."

"'Work my way through school'?" Jason was shocked. "How do you expect me to get forty grand per year from working the register at Dealmart? That's ridiculous!"

"Student loans."

Yeah, lifelong debt. Great plan. This was his queue to zone out.

"Now, things are *rough* here for this family! You need to understand that and start picking up some slack where it's necessary. Your father and I need all the help we can get, and we can't keep wasting our time worrying about what you're doing and what the hell happens to your face every week! I mean, what the hell are you doing fighting?"

"Sometimes a kid's got to fight, honey." his father tried to mediate, fortunately flipping sides when it counted. "Your face doesn't look too bad, son. Is the other guy worse?"

"I think he's missing a few teeth." Jason smirked. "Those jab exercises are helping, I think."

"Well, we have to keep you downstairs on that bag, and you see why: Every now and then, someone out there is liable to test your resolve. I'm glad to see you're standing up for yourself."

A smile briefly flashed onto Jason's face.

"What?" Mrs. Weathers couldn't believe it. "You're okay with him fighting people? That is unacceptable! Jason, you can get put in jail for that! Your father is laid off and I'm working doubles to help us make ends meet. We can barely keep the lights on—"

Mr. Weathers had cut her rambling short there. He couldn't stand her talking about things that he deemed to be none of Jason's business. To him, their money problems were none of his concern.

"Tanya, could you please stop?" he held his hand out to signal for peace. "Please, for once?"

"No!" she pouted. "He's not going to run around thinking that everything is okay! He can't do that! This is real life!"

"Oh my god." Jason buried his face into his palms.

"I'm not going to tolerate this!" his mother continued. "He needs to know he has rules to follow, and just because he's nineteen doesn't give him the right to make his own!"

"I think he understands that."

"The hell he does!" she pointed to him. "Look at him! He's a mess! New rule, *no fighting.*"

"You can't just walk away from a guy, honey."

"Oh, right. Being the better person is too difficult!"

"He is the better person. Apparently he displayed that to the other guy with his fists."

"He's too frail for that. He just started getting meat on his bones!"

"Mom," Jason chimed in. "you know I'm sitting on the couch too, right?"

"Hush!" she cut him off, focusing her anger on his father. "I'm not just going to sit around and watch him wither away! You can't just allow this to happen!"

His father slammed his fist on the floor, the thud reminiscent of thunder, "I'm not 'allowing' anything to happen! Dammit, Tanya! Just——"

They were stopped by the desperate sobs of their son, finally bursting into tears in an outcry for relief. His mom stopped, her drive to verbally combat defeated in an instant. She looked to his father for the answer, even a suggestion on what to do.

He was stumped. Jason cried even harder, staring off into blank space. Daydreams took over, vivid ones about the go-karts, the feel of nailing a perfect apex, finally winning the league in the thrill of racing, and of course, *her*.

She was the reason he won. She had taught him how to race, how to drive, how to push the limit. Oh, god, he was a fool for her. Why was he such a fool for her?

His mother interrupted, finally embracing him with a hug.

"Don't cry, Jason." she said, on the verge of tears herself. "I'm sorry."

Jason sobbed, "Me too. I'm sorry, okay? I race go-karts all the time at the leagues. Dad knows."

"Well," his dad corrected, "I knew about the *one* time you went."

"Okay, so I go all the time. I learned how to race. I'm good at it, and that's how I got the money for my car. A couple of guys got mad that they lost their money because I beat them, so—"

The doorbell suddenly cut him off.

"Who is that?" his father peeked out of the window. "Whose loud ass car is in the driveway?"

Hers.

Jason was astounded. "Agatha?"

Everyone rushed to the door, yet his mother somehow managed to get it open first.

"Uh," she was blown away by the random girl at the door, "can I help you?"

"Hi!" Agatha smiled forcefully. "You must be Mrs. Weathers!"

"Uh huh, and you are?"

"Agatha Peters. I'm a friend of Jason." Agatha shook her hand wildly. "I work with him at the Dealmart on 5th Street. We race go-karts, too. He used to really suck at it."

Jason frowned. The misgivings of his driving past were sensitive topics no matter how far he'd grown.

"Oh, wow!" Mrs. Weathers seemed wildly interested. "You're *pretty*!"

"Mom." Jason wanted to vanish in the embarrassment. "Come on, now."

"Awww, thank you, Mrs. Weathers." Agatha seemed genuinely flattered. "I honestly appreciate that."

Jason felt his face redden. He couldn't stomach the notion of making eye contact with her. In the moments of awkwardness, he could only think of his survival instincts. Escape. Run.

"Alright, so is there anything you need in particular? We're kind of in the middle of a family discussion here." his father tried to be nice.

"Oh," Agatha giggled after winking at Jason, "just wanted to make sure Jason got home okay from our youth group retreat! It was a bit rough. He broke his wrist computer, got lost and all that."

"Oh, is that right?" Mrs. Weathers seemed interested.

"Yeah," Agatha continued. "It's my fault really. I invited him along with some more friends and we lost our cell phones at a rest stop on the way. Once we got to the youth retreat, they didn't let us use our phones! It's all about bonding and, uh, stuff."

Jason was trying hard not to laugh.

"Yeah!" he had to keep it going. "Just what I was going to say!"

"Jason, you never said anything about being on a youth group trip." his mom noted. "You told us that you had to work today, and then you started talking about some kind of go-kart league."

"I never got the chance to say anything, remember?"

Good point. For a moment, she honestly felt bad, but motherly gumption and authority could always override guilt. Nineteen or not, Jason was still her baby, and she only wanted what was best for him, whether he approved.

"Then who the hell did you get into a fight with, Junior?" his father asked. "I'm confused now."

"The youth retreat was at the go-kart league." Agatha seemed to be very good at this, using a partial truth to continue. "We teach young troubled youths how to race. Every once in a while, we get a couple of guys that like to start trouble with the kids and what not. One of these guys, uh, stole a kid's wrist computer and a lady's purse. Security came and the guys tried to get out. Luckily, we had Jason there, because he came and gave them a pretty good fight until more help arrived. We called the police while he held one of the guys down."

Nice. Mr. Weathers seemed proud, "Well, he does train for that kind of stuff. I've helped Junior out since he was four with his boxing skills."

"Broke one of their noses, too, but the rest of the guys were arrested."

"Wow!" Mr. Weathers patted his son on the back. "Well, maybe I should apologize."

"Excuse me?" Agatha was confused.

"Oh, I meant to him! We kind of got on his case when he came in. He's, you know, a young man, and they never seem to have their heads screwed on straight."

"Dad," Jason groaned, "stop it."

"Well, that's understandable, I didn't mean to intrude." Agatha was adorable. "I just wanted to check up on him and applaud his parents for raising such a noble and respectful young man. It was very courageous of him to stand up for the right thing, you know."

Jason shook his head, the urge to smile overpowering even if she was going a bit too far.

"Aww!" Mrs. Weathers seemed humble now. "Thank you! We try to raise him the best we can, but he's just so stubborn and never wants to listen. We just want him to have—"

"Okay, Mom, she gets the point." Jason stepped out of the door.

"Now don't be rude!" Mrs. Weathers huffed.

"Mom, stop."

"I'm just trying to be nice!"

"That's good Mom. K? Sweet."

Mrs. Weathers looked at Agatha and smiled, "He's just like his father. Same name for a reason."

"Sweet, Mom." Jason wanted to run. "Sweet. She's flattered."

"Oh, hush. We'll talk to you when you get back inside. I'll fix some food for you. Your favorite: SpaghettiOs and hot dogs."

"Okay. Bye, Mom. Bye."

She shut the door to let the two kids talk.

Agatha burst into laughter immediately after it shut, "'SpaghettiOs and hot dogs'? You've got to be kidding."

"So what, I like SpaghettiOs? Not a big deal."

"Jason, the only people that actually eat SpaghettiOs are five-years-old." Agatha crossed her arms. "Oh, and you're welcome, by the way."

"Couldn't thank you enough." Jason was happy. "Absolute *perfect* timing. Good at lying?"

"It was mostly true! And I knew your parents would ream you. On the way home, I figured you getting your ass kicked in front of a bunch of kids earlier was enough. Thanks, by the way."

"For what?"

"Trying to help." she folded her arms. "And for a dude who's been getting coached up on his boxing skills since 'age four,' it seems like you're always losing fights."

"I think those guys were just mad they lost a bet." Jason shrugged. "I've always hated them and vice versa. I saw them talking shit to you and the kids. The lead guy said that my car 'sucked dick,' and I told him that his little sister was pretty good at doing just that. "

"Rebecca Harmon? I thought she used to blow guys in the locker room?"

"And if you took her to see a nice movie. She's a *very* cool girl."

"That's disgusting, but that doesn't even seem like something you'd do. You're—just weird. Not one of *those* guys, but maybe one day you'll realize that having the last word isn't everything."

The reminder made him contemplate setting himself on fire. He couldn't get past the look of her face, the tiny bout of cleavage bustling in her shirt as she folded her arms, the smell of her perfume, lotion, or whatever the hell she doused herself in before stepping into the public. He wasn't one to have his way with pretty girls, but she wasn't particularly a formidable target, given her dating history. Her allure puzzled him, but he could fight it off with reality.

They had absolutely nothing in common. *Period.*

"Thanks for the reminder." he said.

"No problem. Put some ice on that eye." she winced upon getting a closer look. "It looks terrible."

She was too close. He responded by backing away.

"Yeah, thanks." was all he said.

Awkwardly, she waved goodbye and returned to her car, a particularly dull black, old Pontiac GTO. It took a few tries, but once she had it started, she backed out of the driveway and drove home. It was loud enough to shake the entire street. Jason quickly returned inside, letting his parents marvel at the fairytale painting of their otherwise mediocre son as a hero. He wanted to tell his father that he was sorry for picking at the fact that he'd been laid off for over a year, but he had shut his bedroom door.

Whenever the door was shut, you didn't disturb him.

Later, Jason sat idly at his computer desk. He yearned to find a cure. He feigned at the desire of simply rising up and whisking away the problems of his family with one swift swoop of heroism, but he cringed at the daydream.

That's all he ever did. Daydream.

Daydream about everything.

About a pretty girl, but he didn't have one.

About a nice classic car, but he an old, rotten Honda S2000.

About the moment where he'd finally amount to something worthwhile, but today, he wasn't.

Why couldn't he stop daydreaming?

"Sometimes," Jason had confessed earlier, "I find myself thinking about this girl, even though I hate her and she hates me. We have nothing in common, but I can't stop thinking about her. She's stupid, but she knows how to drive like no other. She's shallow and caring at the same time. She's brash and gentle all at once. I don't know how else to explain it, but it all makes her so wonderful. It doesn't make *any* sense."

"Love rarely does." chuckled his father.

Love? That's a strong word.

Presenting:

The Underground Kings

- The Underground Kings –
Deluxe Edition

EPISODE ONE

"Leap of Faith"

Monday June 9th, 2037.
-1:00PM-

Motivation.

Drive.

Inspiration.

It was all gone. It had all left him to wither away in lonesome. He remembered the day when he and his father had driven four hours north to retrieve an old broken-down Honda S2000 on their car trailer. His father complained about the nonsensical nature of the purchase, but that was the first time that Jason saw something that he wanted to conquer.

"Eight hundred?" Jason had to confirm before the exchange was made.

Then he had the title to his first car. His first love. His first challenge, a car manufactured 37-years-ago.

"It doesn't have an engine, Junior!" taunted his father. "You bought a car with no engine. What do you plan on doing with that? Putting one in inside the garage? How are you going to pay for it? Engines aren't cheap, especially ones in cars this old. Are you going to pick up extra hours at work? Are you going to take the time to see this through?"

"Yes." was the only simple response he needed.

His father nearly fell out of his seat, but he was surprisingly nice from that point on. Though his mother never took too kindly to the idea, Senior noted that it was good to see Junior start making goals for himself.

As he slaved away working extra hours and competing in the go-kart leagues with payouts as high as $1,000, Jason accrued the money for a new engine within weeks. The drawback was the complexity of the install, as the engine he purchased didn't originally come in the car. Determination conquered the problem. He found knowledge by trial and error, by going to the library to rummage through old mechanic textbooks, collecting each one as he went. Combined with the resources of the internet, Jason slowly worked out the kinks and mishap. The struggle of being novice went on for weeks until one fateful day, when his patience had worn thin and his anger had flared, he twisted the key one random time and the engine sprang to life.

He remembered the joy, his shouts of glee at midnight when he heard the little engine pumping away. It ran when everyone told him that he wasn't capable of getting the job done. He remembered feeding off the negativity, the empowerment that it gave him to continue forward. It was about proving the point, the point that he could, but now he had fallen stale again. It was gone. His drive to be better expired.

These days, it was back to his normal routine of getting yelled at for not working enough hours, not cleaning the dishes, not mowing the lawn, not cleaning the kitty litter, and locking himself inside his room permanently when he wasn't at the local Dealmart manning the express item cash register. The temporary solace of the go-karts came to an abrupt halt when he learned that Agatha had been forced out of mentoring the young racers. When he asked why, he was given no detailed explanation, other than she resigned.

"After that brawl, things got complicated." one of the staff told him. "But it's for the best. By the way, maybe you should wait until your face heals up. The kids need *positive* influence."

Damn.

His dad was interviewing for yet another temporary job at a local factory and his mother was busy working double shifts. He only chose to see the good in it, as that meant less pressure on him. All he needed was his wall-mounted television, his Xbox, and his wrist computer to browse the internet.

When he got bored playing Halo, he'd pull up some naughty sites, finish the deeds, and return to Halo. After a while, that cycle grew tiring. He got up and woke his wrist computer out of standby. On its desk-mounted docking station, he could project the desktop onto a display where he then checked all of the tabs open on his internet browser. A few repeated finger gestures on the tabletop was all he needed to scroll through them lethargically.

Trust Bank? Broke as usual. He had $205 to his name.

Twitter? He had two followers.

Facebook? Nothing but other people uploading photos of their happy lives. Instagram? No one cared.

But there was his private getaway, the ultimate arena, and no, it wasn't the porn. This was almost better. On occasion, he would forget his password due to the frequency that he was forced to change it, but that day his mind seemed to be spot on. Bingo. Success on the first try. The triple-encrypted login page finally welcomed him.

//Scene View v14.5.1\\

Security update: completed. We're glad you remembered your password.

Logging in. . .

Alias: [Herotits (G-4) |1:03pm; 11 June 2037|]

The United Underground. The Secret Lair.

Due to recent extensive media coverage, please be advised of your behavior in the enthusiast environment. Remember, your actions reflect upon us all. -ADMINS.

"Look at ya' boy, on his game." Jason rapped, "got a alias for these fools, so they know his damn name. Ugh. Yo. Ugh. Dammit."

Even the rhymes were hard to come by these days.

The built-in club browser automatically updated. Jason found a thread discussing one of the car shows last night in the south side of Queen City and quickly read through the posts. Within a few moments of reading, he discovered that the gathering turned into a bust when a few young G-1 ranked rookies were nabbed street racing down a major highway at rush hour.

|FordRacer13 (G-1) [12:58:41pm]|: Does anyone know what happened to those two idiots last night?

|Herotits (G-4) [1:05:09pm]|: The two kids that were racing down the Universe Turnpike at 5pm? Didn't one of them hit a minivan?

|JudgeDredd (G-2) [1:07:54pm]|: The two that hit the van are in jail probably, and the other seven participants were banned this morning.

|Herotits (G-4) [1:08:22pm]|: Damn, which one of the elites banned them?

|||13Bruiser (E-2) [1:11pm]||||: It was me. We can't have you stupid grunt retards ruining the community because you don't have brains. The next time that shit happens, I'll come in here and ban anyone that has associated with the major offenders. F*cking ricer retards racing in rush hour traffic in shitheap rust buckets. I'm surprised they got up to enough speed to cause damage.

|Herotits (G-4) [1:12pm]|: Cool story, bro.

Within minutes, Jason received a two-point infraction warning for his snarky comment. *13Bruiser* had always been an asshole, but his promotion to an E-3 moderator made that even more apparent. Quickly, he checked his user history and discovered that he still had eight points of infractions left before he got a temporary ban, but he didn't want to lose his position as a G-4. It had taken him months of hard work in the community to earn his promotion, so if it meant that he had to hold his tongue from offending some trigger-happy administrator, he'd do it.

|ThunderD (G-4) [1:15:11p]|: Jason, you're stupid LOL. I'm getting out of here before Bruiser starts handing out ban-sammiches.

|Herotits (G-4) [1:16:25pm]|: I only have two points of infractions. I'll be fine.

|||06Bruiser (E-3) [1:17:08pm]||||: Oh, Jason. So you still want to be cute? There's six more points for you. If you keep talking, I can get some more elites and admins in here to land you a 30 day ban, faggot.

|NinjaVixen (G-4) [1:17:32pm]|: This is hilarious!

"Asshole." Jason mumbled when he saw another pop up message notifying him of a six-point offense.

When more elites came into the thread, all of the grunts went running scared. Five minutes later, he had received a private message. It was an old friend from high school.

MSG |FordRacer19 (G-2)|: Hey man, did you ever get the money for that turbo kit? That Bruiser guy is an asshole. It'd be nice if you could outrun him someday.

MSG |Herotits (G-4)|: That guy's name is Chase and he's been an asshole since day one. I don't really worry about it, but this year I'm eligible for The Odyssey. I'm thinking about going.

MSG |FordRacer13 (G-2)|: LOL, don't get your hopes up too high man. Just make your car fast first. Besides, I think the requirements say that you have to have 9500 contribution points. What kind of G-4 ranked user has that many points?

MSG |Herotits (G-4)|: I do.

In total, he had 9513 contribution points.

Having grown tired of being told "no" by the people he considered to be friends, he suddenly felt signs of life in his soul. In his best moments, he had feigned on the negativity, using it to drive his ambition forward. He just wanted to have fast car, but a turbocharger kit cost four thousand dollars. These days with all the new laws up against cool things like, well, classic cars and gasoline, he could barely afford fuel and insure it the way it was. He didn't follow the government or the news, but the community was well aware of the rapidly changing legislation.

Yeah, he Googled it.

Motor Vehicle Safety Standard of 2038.

Car autonomy was experiencing a rapid swell, apparently having reduced highway crashes by 78% as told by the news. It was great news, a stupendous victory for everyone—except those that preferred to drive their own cars. The enthusiasts. The members of the United Underground.

It was about driving, a skill most cherished by a dwindling few.

Their trade was dying right before their eyes, yet here he was, still under pressure by a group of assholes that wouldn't leave him be.

"It's just a game," everyone said, "just the internet."
Too bad it seemed to bring out the worst in people.

The United Underground Scavenger Hunt "The Odyssey 2037"

Outline:
"The Odyssey is the premier annual competition hosted by the United Underground that entails a major journey around a large portion of the United States. This year, the hunt encompasses the states of Kentucky, Tennessee, Georgia, Florida, South Carolina, and select parts of North Carolina."

He scrolled through the window on the internet browser and began to read the rules, as the website had advised users to read every line *carefully*. This was odd. Normally, he would talk himself out of these wild ideas by now, but he liked the empowerment. The reminders of his past failures—all caused by an inability to finish things—pushed him forward. The excitement was difficult to contain, his eyes reading the grand prize total again, and again, and again.

"Fifty *thousand* dollars?" he repeated to himself as he read the rules. "Fifty *grand?*" ·

Jason peered blankly at the screen, wondering whether he'd really do it, whether or not he'd really have the gumption to drive for *that* long. Even after a few minutes of reasoning, he still wasn't sure. After getting through the many technicalities and rules, he narrowed it down to simpler terms.

Just him, no passengers, in his old classic car, hunting around the eastern half of the United States on some kind of mythical scavenger hunt. Gas expenses would be outrageous, calculating the estimated totals at $6.50/gallon gave him results of several hundred dollars. Shit, he'd have to max out a credit card for this.

High interest debt for fun? Meh, it seemed legit. Completely insane, but at the same time, it seemed unspeakably memorable. Well, maybe, if he actually had someone to ride with him, but he wasn't in a position where he had any friends. Most of his old ones had either moved or split off into their own ways.

Even Agatha was a no show.

In his years, learned one thing: People were unreliable.

//Scene View v14.5.1\\

Security check: completed.
[Herotits (G-4)] Would you like to confirm your eligibility?
|x| Yes | | No

Browsing through the photos of past competitions made him yearn a bit more than he usually did. It alone helped prove to him that a fast car alone wasn't a free ticket to victory, as he immediately noticed something peculiar. He saw the grand prize winners of every year back to the first Odyssey in 2002, and the hairs on the back of his neck stood up. His heart pounded as he read through their stories, their blogs, their posts, and their videos. It was something impossible to explain, but he felt it. He didn't have a nice car, but in 2007, a team won the grand prizes by driving a Nissan Maxima. In both 2015 and 2019, two other teams did it using a Camry. Family sedans. In 2025, a victory was won using a minivan, a vehicle more adept at shuffling the kids to daycare than burning up a drag strip, but in The Odyssey, speed didn't necessarily matter. The average travel mileage of the past competitions was over 4,900 miles, so perhaps fuel efficiency and reliability would matter more than anything.

Seeing the smiles of the winners, he clicked the signup link and logged in once again. After debating his decision for perhaps two minutes, Jason selected "YES" and put his name on the list of those seeking to participate. His wrist computer buzzed in response to an automated confirmation of preliminary acceptance, his heart jumping with anticipation.

Less than eight percent of the site was eligible for the competition, yet the computer system thought *he* was, without question. Hell, he could tell his parents that he was at work, or better yet, attending another youth retreat. What did he have to lose? Take a nice joy ride in his somewhat fuel-efficient roadster, find some of the target items, and possibly win some money from the ordeal. All he needed was $600 for the entry fee, and this week's paycheck plus the go-kart league winnings would give him enough for that. Today was payday, so perhaps the stars had aligned.

Overall, it sounded good enough for him. He placed his bag full of packed clothing in the space behind the seats, checked the vehicle's vital fluid levels, and headed off for work. Later that night, he'd attend one of the first preliminary meetings that could allow him to register. Call it a leap of faith or call it stupidity. Thinking that he and his car might stand a chance against the more experienced and wealthy contenders was a far cry. Either way, he was happy that for once he didn't care. Carpe Diem, perhaps. You only live once.

"YOLO." Jason mumbled to himself. He had heard the saying on some old school hip-hop. "Let's do this, son."

-9:00PM-

The customers packed into the store like zombies, rabid and soulless, in search or whatever garbage they could pack into their carts. Like a herd of sheep, they would gradually swell into a group so large that even the hardest worker could never tackle. At first, he was like any kid with the determination to make a good impression—making it a point to work as fast as he possibly could—but after six months of swiping items across the laser scanner and tallying up coupons that were usually expired or from another grocery store chain, the novelty had worn off.

Instead, he worked at the "normal," but steadily slow pace. The line would stack up for miles, but he didn't give a damn. If they wanted out of the store without the eighty-year-old security personnel threatening to call the police, they'd wait. Their dirty looks and low-volume murmurs didn't expedite the process either, as each disgruntled customer was met with the same robotic greeting that was required by the store management.

"Hello." Jason would mumble. "How was your shopping experience at Dealmart?"

"It'd be nice if you'd have more than three isles open so people could actually get out of here."

"Oh, okay."

Then he would ring the items and eventually total them.

"Those mints were supposed to be 79 cents." a customer whined.

"Oh, really?"

"They rang up at 83."

Before, he'd attempt to calm them by reassuring that the price was no mistake. Typically that resulted in a call to one of the front managers that were suffering from a plethora of anger-management issues, so to solve the problem of annoyance, he would just type in the manager code and change the price if they could show some legitimate proof.

"Is that better?" Jason would force a smile, wondering if four cents would really break the bank.

"What's my total? I want to get out of here."

"Your total is $6.77, sir."

The customers would occasionally throw the cash at him, or at worst splat down a pocket full of change that he would be forced to count. Luckily for him, most of the zombies had been using the directpays on their computers, swiping away at the counter with their wrists. It made for an easy ring-up when the NFC was working, and then it was onto the next one.

"Could you work any damn slower, Justin?" he suddenly heard Agatha's voice from behind him.

"If that was my name, I'd answer you." Jason replied.

She quickly logged into the neighboring register and directed a portion of the line towards her booth. Her hair was exceptionally curly that night.

"Justin. James. Jason. Whatever." she rolled her eyes. "They keep pulling me off of the floor to man the registers. I'm supposed to be stocking today. It's my last day, you know."

He hated the reminder. She had gotten a better job as a mechanic.

"I extend my deepest measure of sorrow to your troubles." he said.

She chuckled, ringing out two customers in the time that it took him to complete one. He begged himself to ask the question, to ask why she had been banned from the mentor league, to ask how he could still see her regularly without the excuse of go-karts or this shitty job.

Still, he couldn't work up the courage.

"So, I see you signed up for the trials." she started up the small talk.

"Trials?" Jason's voice stayed flat. These days, even a pretty girl didn't do much to curb his low work morale.

"For the Odyssey this year. So, you grew a pair. Congratulations. I'm surprised that you even meet the credentials."

"If you haven't noticed, I've been organizing events and putting meets together for the past two years."

"Oh yeah, you do all of the ricer events. Must be why I didn't remember because I forgot that no one cares about those."

"That's weird," Jason seemed irked, "because over forty percent of The Underground's population, or roughly 5,000 people, cared and showed up. There are more grunts than people in this area of Horris County, but I guess you aren't one for statistical data."

"Last I checked, didn't you always fail math in high school?"

"That was funny. So funny, in fact, that I'm wowed by your comedic skills, but yes, this is the first year I've technically been eligible. I saw that you signed up with Chase Reynolds and a few E-3 elites. Do you honestly think that's going to increase your chances?"

"They invited *me*," Agatha quickly battled back, "and I took up the offer."

"Oh," Jason's voice lowered, "so you and Chase are a 'thing' now?"

"Maybe." Agatha shrugged and continued ringing items. "Maybe not. I can't help it if he likes me and that the others said I was one of the 'coolest grunts they'd ever   met.'"

"I'm sure that there are *lots* of ways to earn cool points with those guys."

"Wow." Agatha scoffed. "And what is that supposed to mean? If you're implying what I think you are, you literally know *nothing* about me."

He had only repeated what he had heard, but then again rumors mutated like viruses. Wrong move, apparently.

"Okay, maybe that was a bit over the line and inappropriate." Jason had to admit. "Either way, I'm going to the meet tonight after work, and I'm getting off on time, whether that means I have to walk out or not."

"You can't leave a register with customers in line."

"Well, I can when a key card holder is standing at the terminal beside me." he looked over at her, just as her face turned to a frown. "Must be your lucky day as a new possessor of one of those shiny keys, eh?"

"If you don't start ringing people out faster, I will literally kill you. Speed. Up."

"'Literally' killing me is illegal."

"Jason!" she slammed her fist on the counter.

His smile gleamed as he slowly scanned another item, knowing that his plan had worked *perfectly*. BEEP! The register returned an error, a flashing message for a lack of necessary cash in the drawer. Procedure was precedent, and in the haze of beeps and chimes, all other functions were locked until a front manager arrived e to refill it and reset the trouble code. His eyes met Agatha's, the beeping register providing the perfect background crescendo as he picked up the phone to press the intercom button and say, "Code 60. Register one."

Then came the manager wobbling her way through the customer lines, her face permanently frozen in discontent. Jason greeted her, but her greeting involved a firm nudge out of the way to which he had long ago learned to accept. She checked the trouble codes, then cash drawer, pleased to actually find a legitimate problem from an otherwise honest employee. Unlike most of the others, Jason was reasonably dependable.

"What time are you off?" she asked after checking her watch.

No wrist computers here. Dial-up internet was still fresh to her.

"Nine-o-clock, ma'am." Jason announced. "I tried to keep the register going as long as possible so I wouldn't trouble you throughout the shift. I see how hard you work."

"Thank you." she said, evidently unable to discern his sarcasm from pure kindness. Her frown left for just a moment, "Just go ahead and clock out. I'll take over, sweetheart."

"Really?" he faked surprise. "Thank you! Have a good night."

Agatha's evil glare was timeless, made even more prominent by the smile on his face as he walked out the front doors. Boom. Victory. Now walking through the dark parking lot, he started a verse that had been stuck in his head all day.

"Sittin' down, gettin' paper, all my haters catch me later. Don't sweat the swag. I put the win in the bag. You and your boys are a bunch of douchebags."

Shit! He heard movement.

He froze, his freestyle stopped mid-verse. In the panic, he quickly wielded his retractable pocketknife.

"I'ma slice you, fools!" he shouted into the empty air. "Come at me, bros! I'm here! Can't stop me!"

Then, he located the source, a confused middle-aged woman who had just finished loading grocery bags into her vehicle. Her eye contact held long enough for effect. His mood changed, the Rambo voice tucked back into its hiding spot for another day. Pretending it never happened, Jason slowly moved toward his car to unlock the door before getting in. He tried starting it, but the engine simply cranked to no avail. No spark, no ignition power. To fix this, it required a reach below the dashboard and a hunt for the wiring harness. With a bit of enhanced coordination, he wiggled the knot of wires simultaneously with the 'engine start' button pressed until the car started.

Piece of cake.

He smiled, knowing the wiring problems had saved his car from being just another old classic reported stolen. Dumb luck? Nah. It was careful planning—in all, the result of a nineteen-year-old kid's poor attempt at being an electrician.

Since the realization, he considered himself to be an inventor.

Cheap and effective vehicle anti-theft. Boom.

Bathing in the success, he switched the music to a new mixtape complete with DJs blending the latest in classic hip-hop tunes. This particular mix had an up-and-coming artist named "Rod Flow," and avid spitter of the "fire" that Jason grew earnest about. He flipped on the headlights and put on a red flat billed Chicago Cubs baseball cap. It cost him fifty dollars at Hat Planet. He checked his bank account with his wrist computer, seeing that his paycheck had finally cleared. Bingo.

"I'm pimpin'. I'm stuntin'. I'm gettin' this cash." he rapped along to Rod Flow on the radio as he pulled out of the parking lot. "Your girl up in my grille, n' tonight I'm gettin' that ass!"

-10:00PM-

The initial meeting was far more involved than anticipated.

James Wrath, the founder and owner of Underground, had amassed his fortune racing in Formula 1. Dividends from his championship victories and endless franchise deals paid for a mansion the size of an average high school. Complete with more rooms than Jason could count, he fell victim to the details like wood floors deeply polished to the point where ice had more traction. His new pair of Jordans struggled here, and he nearly fell at least a dozen times walking through the expansive foyer.

"So, this is what being the world's best race car driver gets you." he said to himself. "A twenty-million-dollar house and a supermodel wife. Sign me up, please."

Daydreams. Back in reality, the only paper he could sign was a legal waiver. The fine print denied Wrath and the United Underground any liability in the case that he was seriously injured, or perhaps even died.

How morbid.

He reached the rear garden, stunned to see perhaps a hundred attending club members snidely judging him during the approach. They reeked of the one thing Jason couldn't muster: success. Exotic cars. Numerous college degrees. Extensive club history. Admin notoriety. Money.

He sat down in the back, noticing a large table filled with elites. Most of them were older, their elite rankings impossible to achieve without six to eight years of duty. Jason knew their places per the club constitution, centered upon keeping order in Underground's structure, planning club events to keep the waning culture alive. He was jealous, having yearned for that kind of recognition his entire life. Clearly out of place and made keenly aware, he still kept his shoulders high.

This was it. The preliminary meetings.

Here, he would apply for full eligibility and sign up for the vehicle testing and training course.

"What's your club alias name again?" asked one of the elites later.

"*Herotits*." Jason mumbled.

"Hero*tents*?"

"No. Hero-*tits*, as in female breasts. You know, titties."

"Interesting."

"Yeah."

"You know, you at least have to be a G-4 to be eligible, right?" the guy laughed.

"I was just promoted last week. I organized some of the local high school fundraisers for the cancer society and they turned out to be pretty good meets."

The elite was skeptical, taking his time to double-check the Scene View browser on his wrist computer. Still doubtful of the approval, he refreshed the page three times before reluctantly stamping the paper.

"Six hundred dollars, please." he asked.

"Uhm," Jason was thrown off, "don't I give that to you right before the race?"

"No." the guy was stern. "You give it to us now, we hold it while we screen you for full eligibility, and we give it back after you finish the training. After that, you either wisely decide that you don't want to do it anymore, or you compete until your piece of shit car breaks down."

Jason bit his tongue. Fighting the urge to resort to his dictionary of insults, he instead withdrew in embarrassment and drove to the nearest ATM. NFC transfers between the wrist devices were too risky for his tastes, as a hacker could exploit it and drain his funds in minutes. After emptying his bank account, he returned with the money and signed himself up.

"Is that good for you?" he asked after leaning in.

The guy laughed, took his money, and nodded.

"Tomorrow, you will either get a phone call or you won't." he said coldly. "If you do, you will follow the instructions and report to the first meeting spot for the training courses. If you fail to attend even *one* of these courses, that automatically cancels out your eligibility. Do you understand?"

"Yes."

"Good. Now go home."

He passed Agatha on the way out. Still fuming from the register ruse at Dealmart, she ignored his existence.

At least she was wearing a nice shirt.

"So you made it? Thought you'd never show up!"

Jason recognized the voice. Biff Jenkins, otherwise known by his alias "*ThunderD*", if Jason recalled correctly.

"Yeah, son." Jason smiled. "Nice to see the underdogs showing up. Got the Honda ready to roll, maybe show these assholes who's boss. You know how it is."

"Oh, you know it!" Biff agreed. "I just keep quiet. Everyone's an asshole when it makes them look good, but all these guys started somewhere. Keep your head up."

Fair point.

"You know what?" Jason seemed relieved. "I think I'm going to try that for a change."

-11:30PM-

That night, Jason arrived home to his father sitting on the couch, attentively carving out a piece of furniture that he intended to sell. Just six days ago it looked like a pile of garbage, and today it was a nearly intact ornate wood table.

"Son." he greeted lowly as Jason walked in.

"Dad." Jason returned the greeting. He removed his hat, mostly because his dad had always yelled at him about wearing them in the house.

"Did you work late tonight?" his father asked.

Oh, here it came. The interrogation. The control. The suppression of freedom.

"No, I just had some other things to do afterwards."

"Like what?"

"Dad, don't worry about it, please." Jason's voice shrieked upward. "I'm fine. Everything is fine, okay? It's something that I'm planning on doing here."

"Can I ask you a question?" his father tipped his glasses down. "Just an honest question, if you give me an honest answer. Your mother is upstairs sleeping, so this is man-to-man."

"What, dad?" Jason sighed. "What do you want? What did I do *now?*"

"Is it drugs?"

Jason's eyes nearly burst from their sockets.

"*Drugs*?!" he couldn't believe it. "You think I'm doing drugs? Are you serious? Really?"

"I'm just asking. That's all I wanted to know. It's a 'yes' or 'no' type of question."

"Dad, you've got to be kidding me! I sit at home, go to work, drive go-karts, and then come back home. When would I have time to do drugs?"

"Yes, or no?"

"*No!*" Jason emphasized. "N-O. I can't believe you'd think that I was doing drugs, Dad! I know better than that! I'm smarter than that!"

His father sighed and sat back. He regretted starting another argument, shouting was normal, the cycle repeating endlessly, now exceeding one year. Dammit, this was getting old.

"I'm not discounting the fact that you're smart, son." his father tried to keep calm. "I just know how it is to be young, I know how it is to be in your shoes. You know, my pop wasn't the best man in the world. He was never really—"

"Dad," Jason interrupted and took a step towards the foyer, "that's a really cool story, but I'm fine. I'm not doing drugs. I never will do drugs, and honestly, I'm offended to know that you'd even think that."

"So, what *really* happened to your face? Could you at least tell me that?"

"I already told you."

"I wasn't born yesterday. A 'youth retreat'? Son, you can tell me what's going on. I'll listen."

"Don't worry about it." Jason's eyes glassed over. "You've got enough to worry about, okay?"

His father scowled; his voice forced into a reluctant pause. Before, he'd yell back until Jason was left in total submission for his disrespect, but now there was little use of fighting. Talks got nowhere, even with normal voices. Without saying a word, he un-muted the television and pretended that Jason wasn't there. After a few seconds, his son got the clue to escape into his room, but he didn't.

"Sorry, dad." Jason said.

"It's alright." his father nodded. "That girl you told me about?"

"Yeah?"

"That was her at the door the other night, wasn't it?"

Jason sighed, "Yes."

"And she's why you got into a fight?"

"Yes."

It was amazing, the honesty. Reveling in the newfound trend, his father refused to change tone. There was no reason for anger, no reason to agitate their first reconciliation in months.

"What happened?" he asked, timidly.

"A couple of guys I beat in a race were talking trash to her, I guess."

"What did they say?"

"I don't know." Jason shrugged. "She won't tell me."

Three days after receiving *the* call, he was swimming freely in the hope for something new. It was a good feeling, a *great* feeling that he had nearly forgotten about until now.

//Scene View v14.5.1\\
Alias: |Herotits (G-4) [11:48pm; 11 June 2037]|

What vehicle will you be registering?

Year | Make | Model | Trim | Modification Class
2001 | Honda | S2000 | Base | [ ] None [x] Basic [ ] Moderate [ ] Extensive

Insurer | Coverage Type | Roadside Assistance?
Geico | Liability| [ ] Yes [x] No

Why not comprehensive, [Herotits (G-4)] ?

|Herotits (G-4) [4:13:11pm]|: Why is this even a question?

|ADMINS [4:14:01pm]|: We figured it'd be funny to watch you broke ass ricers get mad about it.

Just to confirm, is this information correct? Please remember that your vehicle will be inspected upon registration training.
[ ] Yes [ ] No [x] Maybe

Are you sure you're up to the challenge?
[ ] Yes [ ] No [ ] Maybe [x] Fuck off

The summertime was bliss, the keynote revival of Underground's social season. That week was filled with very warm and humid days, temperatures in the mid-nineties and scattered rain showers blundering about in the skies. The air was sticky and would've been uncomfortable were it not for the open windows and lowered top in the S2000. Any notion of air conditioning was a joke at this point. That system had failed long ago, and Jason admitted defeat when it came to fix it.

Traffic jams sucked, especially the slow crawl of the vehicles around him. It was like herded sheep in a flock, an endless sea of tall boxy vehicles towering above him on autopilot, their occupants busy fumbling away at their computers nary a care in the world. His left leg grew tired, the rummaging cycle of clutching, shifting to speed up, and clutching again to slow taking its toll. This was the stressful bane of driving, the only downside he could see in a city packed full of people. Tired of sweating, he took the risk of driving on the shoulder until he reached his exit and disembarked. Freedom. He floored the gas pedal in rebellion, oozing hooliganism, dipping through the slowpokes, speeding through the streets for only a few minutes until he found the lot guarded by Underground's finest.

It was an expansive parking lot in the Gap County wastelands, barren voids of deserted lots and old gargantuan factories left behind the trend. Already filled with the cars that had passed the first stage of entry, he learned that everyone arrived with permission of the district police precinct chief, who was an ally of the club. As the sun dipped, the towering industry skeletons kept them hidden.

Training was rough, the passing judgment annoying, but he stayed and completed the entry exam. It alone spanned the course of three days, entailing everything from basic CPR training to vehicle maneuverability coaching. The latter part was quite fun, though he did accidentally break the head off of one of the dummies used for the CPR training. Sure, he was a bit heavy handed, but at least he knew his car. The little Honda blazed through the cones with ease, it's low mass and center of gravity providing the best advantages of physics. There were no artificial enhancements. Just his automotive go-kart.

The realization warmed his heart.

"Dammit!" Agatha shouted after her GTO spun out for the third time. "Sorry!"

She was persistent in carrying excess entry speed into the last corner—an odd error considering her driving skill. He thought that perhaps the GTO was too heavy or improperly setup to attack such a course, but he had seen Agatha in her element countless times. She was a true talent, a wielder of angelic precision, yet here she was playing coy and fragile. The legacy racers rushed to her aid, providing driving tips and coaching at will. Before long, there was a single file line.

She ate up the attention, seemingly thriving from it.

God, how pathetic.

"She's not bad for a girl." noted a random contestant to his teammate as they watched.

"If you say so." Jason rolled his eyes.

It nauseated him to watch from afar, her curly brown hair blowing steadily in the wind. If he only had similar power with the ladies, life would be a boon, huh? Men flocked to her laugh, a rather sharp and arguably disruptive cackle, but he was no saint.

Who was he to judge? Another victim of her toxic presence.

Shit. Being lovesick *sucked*.

He tried telling himself that he knew a different side of her, the powerful, world-conquering side, but it was a sugarcoat. He was jealous. Plum-kicking jealous.

As the vehicle inspections began, he passed the time by rapping.

"Sittin' in the parkin' lot chillin'. Just waitin' to get my Honda on the road, wheelin'. I don't have a clique, but your girl is on my—"

Her voice interjected, stopping him mid-rhyme.

"My ears are starting to bleed." Agatha growled as she shook her head. "For the love of god, please shut up."

Everyone laughed.

Jason stopped rapping. Ah, this was the classic game of two-face.

Friendly when her friends weren't around. Asshole when they were. Nice.

He retreated to the S2000, firing up the engine after three unsuccessful tries. The idle was choppy on cold starts, the loose and worn bushings rattling in the rough harmonics. Holding his foot down on the gas pedal was the fix, highlighting the blue-tinted smoke that puffed from the tailpipes under throttle.

Valve seals. Piston rings. Maybe both?

There was no time for that, nor money. His sweaty palms gripped the vehicle controls, his left hand white-knuckled on the steering wheel, his right slipping on the shivering aluminum shift knob.

"*Herotits!*" the officiator called. "Get your shitbox over here! You're up!"

This was it. His moment of truth.

He pulled the little roadster up to the starting line, holding the engine against the launch-control. The digital tachometer bounced about nearly halfway through the gauge, the engine making a ruckus in its vigor. Jason kept his eyes on the flagger, his left foot pulling pressure from the clutch pedal just as the flag dropped.

Dry rotted tires sounded anemic under pressure, their squeals akin to whining canines. The S2000 powered forward, pausing only during Jason's shifts—second gear particularly tough to reach due to bad synchronizers. Third and fourth proved easier, letting the car stretch its legs near 100mph.

Straight-line test: Done, but he was the only one smiling.

His car ducked into the first corner, the nose peening through the cones as his mind traced the racing line. Seconds passed, an eternity in the world of competition, yet he nailed it on the first try. Everyone laughed more, but that didn't stop him. When it came time for the braking test, he watched as car after car equipped with anti-lock brakes came to a quick and quiet stop. On his turn, he slammed the pedal and locked the wheels angrily. From the outside, the little Honda came to an annoyingly loud and screeching halt.

"Is that good?" he sarcastically asked the observers. "Are you happy with that performance?"

They applauded, their sarcasm equal. He drove along and parked.

"I'm surprised this heap of bolts passed inspection." said one of the technicians. "There was a pool of people over there earlier that were placing fifty-dollar bets on your car falling apart during the preliminaries. You and the other Honda driver kid, both."

"Biff Jenkins?" Jason looked over to see him sitting on the hood of his old Civic.

"Yep, but you guys made it work. This is the first time someone this young, dumb, and broke has made it past the preliminaries."

Jason smiled, perhaps for the first time in days.

"I hoped it would." he said. "I worked hard at it."

Reading through the paperwork, he noticed something, "Why'd I only get a 83 score on the PA?"

"Oh, your Percentage Authentic?" the guy said. "Dude, your shitbox car has mismatched body panels, headlights from eBay, only two of the tires match," he pointed to one, "and the other two are so worn down that I'll be surprised if you make it 500 miles on them. I won't even get into the engine swap, junk wiring job, etcetera. 83% is the best I can do for you, and that's doing you a favor, honestly. Sorry, ricer."

"Whatever."

"Your appraised value is six grand." the guy shrugged. "That combined with this thing being 37 years old gets you a 35% tax credit per each point you earn. You came out on top, actually." he double-checked the paperwork. "You going alone? You know that The Odyssey allows for teams of up to three registered cars per team and a total of nine people."

"It's just me this time."

"Just make sure you have your safety and emergency repair kit in there by tomorrow morning. I *will* check before you leave." the guy said. "Best of luck to you, and thanks for helping me win fifty bucks. Here's your vehicle number and class declaration, and remember, think strategically. You have an old, low value car. Use that to your advantage, but low fuel efficiency and old age turn into the devil on a trip like this."

"I can manage."

"Well, at least you're helping keep a dying art alive."

"'Save the Drivers.'"

"All you got to do is drive, buddy. Never stop driving."

It was the nicest any elite had ever been to him. He took the magnetic decorations and stuck them to his car on both doors, the hood, and the full of the trunk. After he had them centered and as level as his eyes could discern, he stepped back and snapped a photo with his wrist computer.

Car #47-SPC2A

The number system was easy to understand once he read through the rules. His car was the 47th car registered in the "classic sports car" class, a 37-year-old member of the second subclass, with a measly 240hp engine that placed in the "A" subgroup.

Jason felt the relief of the victory, and that was it.

Best of luck, and he'd be on his way. Beaming with excitement, he drove home and prepared his things without telling a soul. That Thursday night, he fell victim to an anxiety-fueled insomnia. Oh, and his parents were arguing downstairs. Again. He eavesdropped, hearing that they were arguing about him, about his dad's lack of a job, about their imminent foreclosure crisis. Now at his desk, he at the item map that had been sent to him via secure email. He plotted his course, pulled up some more porn, and did the deed, finally falling asleep afterward. When he woke up following a nightmare about Agatha, he did it again while thinking of her, and fell back asleep.

Agatha's face. Agatha's hips. Agatha's legs. Agatha's breasts.

Sometimes, they were better than sleeping medication.

Nature's finest, he presumed. He wasn't a pervert, just a human.

He'd wake up the following morning and leave when the coast was clear. He couldn't tell them about this. He couldn't allow them to know, especially if he failed.

Maybe he could fix this. Just maybe.

"It's all about the light at the end of the tunnel, Son, not how far away it may seem." his father once told him. "It's about having the courage to keep chasing it. That's life."

"Dad," he had keenly prodded his father's mind about it the previous day, "if you could fix every single problem in your life, and all you had to do was drive, what would you do?"

"I'd drive until the damn wheels fell off, Junior." he chuckled.

That was the answer he needed for this. Just him, the open road, and that damn car.

-The Underground Kings-
Deluxe Edition

EPISODE TWO

"The Beginning"

Day#1:
Friday June 12th, 2037.
-5:30PM-

The lot was half full by now, clustered with oodles of the participants standing around the cars and socializing. Most were involved enough to know the others by their real name. Personal bonding. Actual friends. Jason only knew cars and aliases. There were tons of them; wondrous, beautiful cars.

"Herotits?" he heard someone holler as he rolled passed the first line of parked cars.

He fueled the fame, giving the engine a bit more throttle than most would, as making a bit of noise was his forte. If they had coined him as Odyssey 2037's "resident ricer," maybe he'd just run with the notoriety.

Jason did his best to socialize and not alienate himself. The fast car guys, elites, and administrators stuck to their own groups, making sure everyone had properly registered and received their email containing clues and locations of the items. To quell the intimidation and growing doubt, Jason reminded himself it wasn't a competition of raw speed. It was about endurance and perseverance, giving the members like him with the slower cars a fighting chance for the grand prize.

$50,000, more than enough money to get a fair share of participants.

"Defying the odds?" asked another member. Jason didn't know his name, but he knew he owned a dark gray classic S4 Audi. 2012.

[SourKraut(E-1)], he thought of his alias in his head.

"Yeah, that's me." Jason laughed. "I've always wanted to do it, and now I can."

"Oh yeah? What's done to the old Honda?"

Jason leaned against the door, proud that someone had asked.

"Just a rebuilt VTEC engine and some other 'goodies'."

There was an awkward pause, mostly because similar declarations rarely impressed anyone besides fellow nineteen-year-olds. Still, the guy nodded at the old bugger. It was a beautiful machine in its own right.

"You think it'll make it?" he asked.

"I drive it pretty hard for hours on end. It's got thousands of miles on that engine that way, so I'm hoping it'll be fine."

Jason looked around, noting cars of the newest breed, cars produced in the mid-to-late 30s. Most were relatively silent, save for the hybrid Ferraris and Lamborghinis. Even with their gasoline engines off, he knew that they had special fans that forced air through tailpipes designed to emulate the sound of a V10. The owner of this particular late model Lamborghini Heracles was bragging about the newest system, using an app on his wrist computer to manually adjust the exhaust tone for entertainment.

A bystander mentioned that running sound composers this hard would drain the onboard battery arrays, so the owner noted that aftermarket solar panels installed on the roof were more than capable of providing the power he needed.

Bollocks.

Jason turned back to view more classics, the cars that didn't have to fake it. They didn't need solar panels, or hybrid engines. They had no robotically shifted gearboxes, autopilots, or vario-tread tires to win the hearts of their fans. They existed as tools to extend the human experience, relics of a golden era that made them unique. In his mind, he lusted for them.

He saw the classic Mazda RX-7 with the turbo rotary engine, and another with the old Corvette eight-cylinder engine installed, both grafting an insurmountable crowd versus a group of new model Corvettes parked next to it. A black, fully restored Nissan 240SX was nearby with its hood lifted. The engine came out of a world-renowned Japanese supercar in the 1980s, its ritual song lush enough to invoke tears. God, he wished for one, thinking that despite the odds, what if he really won the grand prize? What would he do with the money? Would he be selfish and buy a car?

Then, he heard a few members get a bit excited.

An approaching group of cars solved the mystery, the thumping of their engines as telling as thunder.

-5:52PM-

It was the muscle car rumble, the kind that frenzied the baby boomers and their successors. He saw the crowd part like the Red Sea, people even yelling at others to clear the way. The fight or flight response was unavoidable.

The first car was *#33-GT1Z*, a late model Camaro.

Chase Reynolds.

[06Bruiser (E-2)]

He disabled the hybrid system to keep the engine running, as showing off was proving ever more difficult these days. His arm hung from the window, his left hand waving at onlookers with the grace of a true royal.

Though it shared nothing with the fabled pushrod engines of yore, the sounds piped out of the exhausts were eerily similar, only lacking the *soul* of its predecessors. Progress still had its faults, 55mpg CAFE standards be damned. It was obnoxious, its small engine rumbling so loudly that the vibrations gussied Jason's innards.

It revved, the sound composers aimed purposely at him as it reversed into a spot near the administrators. Intimidation, indeed. The engine quit, its LED headlamps switching to low power, showcasing the tall, hulking douchebag that stepped out from the driver's seat.

Oh, joy.

Up next was car *#12-GTC2B*, the familiar old Pontiac GTO rumbling along graciously, wearing its magnetic battle numbers on the doors as if it had something to prove. It sounded *amazing*, so real and authentic, the mechanical clatter of its pushrods ticking away like cicadas in the grassland.

[NinjaVixen (G-4)]

Once, Jason picked fun at the alias.

"So, '*Herotits'* is any better?" Agatha sneered. "Just stop, Jason."

The men started swooning, his distaste growing by the second.

Wait. He did the deed to the thought of her *twice* in one night.

There, he found himself standing at a crossroad between hate and attraction, toiling in the danger zone where a girl invaded his mind and emotion clouded his judgment.

People were so happy to see her.

Finally, he admitted that he was too.

So what, she was handed an old and forgotten muscle car?

Who the hell cared?!

Everyone. Yes, everyone cared, especially as she jogged across the parking lot to the check-in station. Instinctively, he watched her breasts bounce beneath her shirt. They defied all known physical laws of the universe. Jason surmised that scientists around the world remained baffled.

Dammit.

"Got a staring problem, sweetie?" Agatha taunted Jason. Chase Reynolds stood beside her with his huge arms crossed. "Looks like you saw a ghost."

"No," Jason replied, "but the ghost part seems right."

Burn.

"Hey, how about you shut the hell up, faggot?" Chase interrupted. "Shouldn't you be trying to fix up your dumb little car?"

"Dude," Jason turned towards his car and then back to Chase, "my car obviously isn't broken. You running low on insults today?"

He heard chuckles in the crowd, the comedic comeback a clear success. Embarrassed, Chase stepped forward to close the gap between them, squaring up to display his larger size. Jason didn't cower, though he was happy to see Agatha intervene.

"Why are you stopping me?" Chase looked at her, noticing her hold on his arm. "Someone has to shut this stupid kid up."

"What are you going to do?" she asked. "Beat him up like everyone else does?"

"Uh," Chase nodded, "yeah. That's the plan."

"Just leave him alone."

He obeyed, staring intently at Jason before looking away to pop the hood on Agatha's car. Things returned to normal from there.

Their team huddled over for an inspection, the crowd moving in to watch. Agatha was lathered in jubilant greetings, now with Chase ready to fend off any fanboys. Jason sat back and observed, until she caught him staring at her again. She sneered. He looked away and focused on her car. He wished that he didn't like looking at her. Her long hair blowing in the wind was hard to ignore, as was her set of brilliantly white and perfectly arranged teeth whenever she smiled, or even worse, laughed.

He found himself fighting pubescent desires, but the reminder helped.

She was just a stupid girl, Jason. He thought. *Nothing more.*

"Eyyy, ricer!" he heard Biff behind him. "It's time for the victory dance! We are here, my dude!"

"Hell yeah we are." Jason laughed, shaking his hand.

"I see you over here trying to start fights with people. You know Chase has to alpha male his way through life, man. That's the only way his brain can process shit. Chill out."

"F-ck that guy." Jason relaxed, having found someone of equal merit to chat with. "I mean look at him. He's a joke. The guy wears shit from forty years ago. Pull-up socks from *White Men Can't Jump*. Jorts Bill Clinton wore when he played b-ball with Dennis Rodman. Dude even rocks the pink shirt Ross had on in *Friends*. I mean, come on."

"You an old movie expert?"

"Hey," Jason shrugged, "my mom and dad love that shit."

"Sounds like you've become quite the hater, bro." Jenkins laughed.

"That guy just pisses me off. He's f-cking stupid and don't understand what everyone sees in him."

"Leader of the Decepticons, man. Simple as that."

Nice. Still, Biff was still somewhat of a mystery.

[ThunderD (G-4)]

He was anomaly, a skilled internet troll and peacemaker all at once, a kid that never said much on Underground forums unless absolutely needed. Biff was a tranquil and relaxed soul, a stark difference from Jason's own social anxiety.

44

"Do you play basketball?" Jason asked once.

"Is it because I'm tall and black?" Biff laughed. "Is that the real reason why everyone asks me the same damn question?"

Tall was an understatement. He was nearly a seven-footer, but cars were apparently his calling, evidenced by a thirty-year-old Honda Civic, with an original engine, no muffler, and a homemade intake pipe that he installed to give it some more sound. This was his fifth classic, all of which he promised to restore, but always fell short of the required funding. Maybe this one was different, or maybe not. Even Jenkins himself was surprised that the burgeoning rust hasn't split the car in half.

"Are you ever going to paint that thing?" Jason asked him.

"Maybe." Jenkins replied. "If I can find some junkyard body panels for cheap. Other than that, I really don't care."

And that was his attitude towards the car. He had bought it for cheap, and it was just something to screw around in for now until he found his next beater.

"Man, you kill me."

"What?" Jenkins laughed. "I'm serious. I paid six hundred dollars for that car. I don't give a shit about how it looks. It gets me where I need to go, and I love it for that. It's a great little car."

"When you put it that way, I guess that makes sense."

"And speaking of cars, I thought you were getting rid of yours so you could get something newer. I expected to see you roll up in Z32 Nissan Z or something. You know, to elevate the game."

"Ha!" Jason shook his head. "Man, I work at Dealmart as an express item register clerk. I don't have any money."

"That's true."

"Yeah, so it looks like it's just going to be me and the old S2000 for a while longer. Story of my life."

"Hey, it's a nice car. And isn't it paid off?"

"Yeah. The bank would laugh if I asked for a loan on that thing. I just saved up the money to buy it instead. I bought it with a blown engine, and then swapped in a rebuilt motor."

"So, what's the problem?" Biff continued as they walked towards the crowd centered near the moderators and elites.

"Someday I'd like to have a car that was a bit faster. Maybe over the next few years, I'd say. Before gas gets over eight bucks."

Jason grabbed his registration papers to fill them out. A tall man grinned when he saw him take the paper. Jason made eye contact and sighed,

"I didn't think you'd actually show!" the man said. "Ricer Jason!"

[The Stig (E-4)] Justin was his real name. He was one of the top elites, and a professional driver capable of driving track-prepped race cars for hours on end.

"Yeah, I figured it would be a fun trip." Jason scribbled quickly on the paper. "You know, using my car's classic class point advantage and all that. Got to keep you guys guessing."

Laughter.

"Well for once, you might actually have an advantage." Justin handed him a fabric case with a zipper. Inside was a thin slate computer, perhaps a quarter inch thick, "There's your map and instructions on the slate. Turn it on and follow the instructions. You can read, right?"

"Apparently well enough."

"Good. Scene View Deluxe and everything else you need to access the website and update your travel blog is on the slate. The rest of the paperwork is inside of the envelope in the case. I take it you've already read the online part?"

"Yeah. I'm all caught up on that."

"So, you know the rules. Like if you get arrested, or pulled over for being stupid that it's not on us?"

"I figured that part was common sense."

"Didn't know you had any of that."

Jason didn't laugh, instead snatching the case before he walked away towards his car alone. He didn't wait for Biff. Inside he opened the case, carefully removing the slate and a charger that was wrapped with a rubber band. After plugging it in, he powered it up, his face illuminating with awe like the first time he saw boobs in a health book.

Bliss. Pure bliss.

//Scene View Deluxe v13.0.1\\

Security check: completed.

Welcome to Odyssey 2037, [Herotits (G-4)]

Please place your thumb in the circle indicated on the screen to security lock this slate to your identity.

He followed the instructions and the screen flashed the Underground logo, immediately taking him to a user interface that he had never seen. His smile was undeniable, another milestone conquered. Only the important club members got access to Deluxe, which enabled more functionality than normal.

Have you read the disclosure agreement?
|x| Yes | | No

Loading. . .

Good, now look at the map. Notice that your current position is always identified by the flashing blue marker. This position is GPS accurate to one-half of a meter, as is the altitude. If at any point there is an emergency during your travels, this device can make a satellite-linked emergency call, regardless of cell phone reception. Be sure to continuously update your travel blogs, and never overlook an opportunity to acquire those coveted 'epic points' in the categories mentioned on your list. The admin team hopes that you and your team have a great time, and if it means anything, we also wish you the absolute best of luck in achieving your goals.

May the race be with you.

May you be one with your car.

May your team be one with harmony.

May you never stop driving.

— Admin Team. United Underground.

"Baller." he summed, his cheeks sore from smiling by now. Knowing the next step, his fingers quickly scrolled around the interactive map for closer study.

Map items in Scene View Deluxe were marked in blue—the first group clearly showing the beginning of the route leading into rural Tennessee. They were sorted by their point values, with the highest point items obviously being the hardest to find. On the interactive map plane, each item was located via a small beacon centered in a large circle representing the radius in which the item could be hidden. For the higher point items, Jason noticed the radii extending out beyond *twenty miles*—a huge difference versus the lower value counterparts that needed finger gestures and a zoom just to find.

There were a few that were worth tens of thousands of points, but the clues for their locations were vague. One was located somewhere in Nashville near the downtown area, its point value highlighted at 10,000— whatever it was. Strategy was apparent, as Jason saw that collecting large sums of smaller items didn't come close the value of a single large one.

Think.

Should he waste his time looking for the easier ones, or should he just focus everything on big stuff?

Taking his index finger and highlighting areas of the interactive map, he killed the last few minutes by going through the list and checking off the probable locations of the highest valued items. He figured he could follow the main route and split off towards these locations, relying on his wit to do the rest of the problem solving.

Believe it or not, he *did* have confidence in one area.

"Alright!" a voice hollered through a loudspeaker, "Everybody get your stuff ready! We'll be heading out shortly!"

The crowd quickly dissolved, the members scattering about like carpenter ants hunting for food. It was go time. Engines fired up around the parking lot, the joyful cheers of the contestants filling the air.

The sunlight gave its final bow and disappeared, but the air was still humid. Jason started his car when he saw the band of leaders beginning to file out, taking time to lower all of the windows. The driver side stuck in the middle of the track, but a swift punch freed it. His headlights illuminated once he hit the switch, with the initial flash and the glowing blue hue of the bulbs showing directly on Agatha's GTO.

Agatha squinted, with Chase riding shotgun, having put another team member in charge of his own car. He had plans, *big* plans. Jason feigned on the vendetta, their expressions humoring him enough to take his time selecting first gear.

The competitors filed out in an orderly fashion, forming a motorcade that made its way through the streets and onto the nearest highway headed south. Traversing the city in masse required careful orchestration like blocking intersections to deny access to civilian motorists. It was bold and illegal, but civilians could easily break up the line, and that was bad for the photographers.

This part took group skill, a choreography of sorts to clump together and never allow enough space for another vehicle to dive into the lane. Even at the stoplights where a left turn was required, four cars would block both sides of the intersection, the motorcade cleanly rolling through. If a stoplight changed to red, no one would stop, instead relying on the massive line of cars to keep any other vehicle—via trolling their anti-collision systems—out of the intersection. Stopped cold and powerless, the victims couldn't do more than honk.

Too bad no one cared, a tidbit Jason found quite funny.

He positioned his S2000 near the middle of the line and tried his best to keep the spot. Biff filed in behind him for a few moments until he fell back in the rotation. Their cars struggled, the problem resting in the fact that the other cars would periodically accelerate harder than they could match, sometimes creating a gap. He tried his best to keep it closed with the gas pedal floored, but the further south they got, the more the other contestants tried to switch spots to the front of the line.

Queen City and all its beautiful lights vanished behind him.

Thirty minutes after exiting the city, nearly every fast car had driven over the horizon. Jason paced himself with a small group of the slowest cars that had decided to stay together when everyone split. Taking advantage of the situation and the gaps in the thinning traffic, the small group of cars challenged each other, by slowing to a certain speed, honking three times, and trying to outrun their opponent. These races were captured on film, were they could accrue a small number of points for their actions by placing it on their travel blogs.

The S2000 surprisingly won two of the six races but was sadly outpaced by a minivan during one of the runs. Shit. They slowed down after the races, forming a line to squeeze through traffic.

Seconds turned to minutes and minutes turned to hours.

-11:18PM-

Sleep threatened to end him, the low-pitched drone of the engine lulling his eyes closed in an alarming pattern. When he realized that fighting fatigue was growing harder, he made the decision to pull off the highway at a nearby rest stop. Maybe he'd take a breather. Maybe he'd get some caffeine in his system. Leaving the group of cars, he rolled up to the building, parked, and got out. His wrist computer rang. It was his mother calling for the ninth time—a call that he forced to voicemail.

Looking around, the lot was mostly filled with semi-trucks and tractor trailers. It was still humid, but peaceful. On the toilet, he checked over the map on the slate computer, making sure that he was headed in the right direction. Now in Tennessee, the only highway that was familiar to him was I-75, where heading south was natural if it weren't for the items nearby.

//Scene View Deluxe v13.0.1\\

Item #67a
Value: 50,000pts
Beacon Radius: 30 miles

Clue: "If the shoe fits her, she's timeless."

Vague. Ridiculously vague.
If the shoe fits her, she's timeless.
This was stupid, "What is this, elementary school?" he said aloud.
What the hell could it be? A shoe? What kind of shoe? A boot? A sandal? A slip on? Velcro sneakers? Jordans? Damn. That could've been anything.
Either way, it was hidden somewhere in the Great Smoky Mountains National Park, and to add further insult, the GPS beacon had radius of nearly thirty miles.

"Great. Thirty-mile radius." Jason groaned. "It should be easy to find in the middle of a forest at night. Real easy."

He headed back to his car after grabbing a snack, wiggling the wires to start it up. The building anxiety spelled doom, but he fought back. Deep breaths. Stay calm. Think.

-11:20PM-

Uh oh. It was amazing how quickly good things could sour.

The Smoky Mountains National Park seemed like the perfect setting for a cheesy horror movie. Pitch darkness, spooky and ill-travelled roads—all combined with an unplanned adversary: fog.

She drove slowly through what seemed to be a blanket of thick smoke, the GTO's high-beam headlights ineffective at cutting through. In her stubbornness, she kept her confidence, pushing forward until visibility had all but dropped to zero. Then came the doubt, the maybes, the second guesses.

Maybe she should've waited until morning to keep going. Maybe she could find a cheap motel, but that seemed too dangerous now. After a few minutes of traveling under 20mph, the visibility range dwindled to under a few feet in front of the car. That was the final call to pull the GTO off the road.

"Yeah, this is sketchy." she spoke off-handedly to her boy toy sitting in the passenger seat. "What do you say we stop here for a little while? At least until the fog clears."

Chase smirked, knowing well what this meant, "Yeah, that's cool."

"What do the directions say?""

He held their slate in his hands. Apparently, its GPS sensor has lost its signal—or at least that's what he conveyed.

Bummer.

"We're up in the mountains and shit." he replied. "No signal, apparently."

Their wrist computers suffered the same fate.

"Do you think we're safe right here?" Agatha looked around, but the fog was too dense to see much.

The radio stations were nothing but country music, but each one had their own state-mandated fog warning playing intermittently.

"Well, you hear the warnings on the radio." Chase said. "They're telling people to stay off the roads, so I don't think we have to worry about that. There's no one out here. It's just me and you, sweetheart. We can backtrack to that parking lot from earlier. That'll be safe enough."

Agatha folded her arms, admittedly frightened by now.

When she hesitated, he said, "Tell you what, I'll drive. Okay?"

And she let him, riding along with the rush of uncertainty until they reached the secluded lot and parked by the park ranger light. The doors were locked, the radio left on. Outside, the air was still warm and the breeze perfect for sultry recreation so long as the windows were left lowered an inch. Chase had plans, but Agatha wasn't innocent. They were two good looking people thinking very much alike. If there was a time to make a move, it was now.

Soon, the seats were fully reclined.

They talked about everything.

This went on for an hour.

"You still scared?" he smiled.

His voice was deep and powerful. She cringed, possibly from hormonal overload, wondering how a man could be so perfect.

"Sort of." Agatha replied lowly.

"There's nothing to worry about." Chase assured. "You got *me*."

Damn, he already threw the line. She was googly-eyed now.

Earlier, she had agreed to store some special drinks in the trunk inside of a cooler. It was his idea, but he was too hot to deny.

"If we'll be here all night," she shrugged, "we might as well have some drinks? They're, uh, 'special' drinks."

"You got us some happy shine, didn't you?"

"Maybe."

"I mean," Chase laughed, "it's up to you."

"We'll be up here for the entire night, right?" she was anxious.

"Probably."

"I heard it tastes good, but I've never tried it." she was hesitant.

"Trust me, it does." Chase laughed. "What flavor did you get?"

"The 'apple pie' was the only kind the guy had left. He was a pretty scary guy, you know, the one you referred me too."

"Abu? Nah, he's cool. A little shady at times, but he's good for business transactions."

"Apparently."

She paused, thinking if she needed to be drunk for this.

To get laid.

No. No, she didn't, but she'd go along with it anyway. How many times did she find herself alone in a car with a man that looked like he belonged in a Calvin Klein ad?

"Well, go get it!" she eventually directed. "I'm not going out there in the dark!"

Chase played gentleman, hopping out of the car, popping the trunk, and pulling a bottle out of the specialty drink cooler. The drink was green, its taste like a minty syrup laced with cinnamon. It was delicious, almost addictively so. They drank, downing the first two cups in a noticeably short amount of time.

She kissed him, and he kissed back. In all, Agatha thought things were going quite well. By the time she was on cup number four, her top had been removed. Halfway through the same beer, everything else was gone. He hoisted himself atop of her and removed his boxers.

The rest was self-explanatory.

Well, everything except for the lack of a happy ending.

-11:42PM-

//Scene View Deluxe v3.0.1\\

System: Herotits, you are within the beacon radius of Item #67a. Please remember to be careful during your search. —Admin Team

Clue: "If the shoe fits her, she's timeless."

Best of luck.

Somehow, Jason made it through the fog and found one of the empty parking lots of the Smoky Mountain National Park. He parked his car and wiped his eyes, wondering whether he had made the dumbest decision of his life. He considered waiting until sunup to search, but he knew that time was limited.

The facts were clear: Fifty thousand points was a shitload.

It could put him at a significant advantage, and it looked as if the competition had yet to arrive. The fog kindled nightmarish fear, even to the point where he wished for a gun.

Deep breaths. Stay calm. Think.

Instead, he opened his Odyssey Blog, taking a selfie with the slate's camera to document his whereabouts. To combat the darkness, he left the car running, using the high beams to illuminate the fifty feet or so ahead.

The air was humid and sticky, the sounds of night bombarding his senses, adrenaline briefly cancelling the fatigue. It was too dark to see very much, but the extraordinarily bright headlights on his car lit the placard in front of him enough to read. The clue book said it held further information.

"If the shoe fits her, she's timeless." Jason recited the first clue again.

The placard listed a map of the nearby trails, highlighting the resident cabins with tiny squares—the item supposedly inside or around one of them. There was at least a dozen of them, requiring a search of each location. Damn this darkness, as it was turning this into an impossible feat. He could enhance his hunt if he drove the car down each trail, but it sat far too low on its tweaked suspension. The bottom would scrape and likely wind up damaging things or at worst, get the car stuck. Being stranded in the middle of nowhere with no network signal wasn't an option, plus he wasn't apt to be the first fool on record using the emergency satellite phone.

"Well, damn." he grunted in defeat. "How the hell am I supposed to walk all the way out here and find this thing?"

Not to mention, what the hell was it?

"Rappin' the captain's log." he rhymed. "Walkin' through the fog, I feel my nose gettin' sneezy, allergic to these haters who are lookin' all sleazy."

With nothing to lose, he figured he'd check the first cabin, which could be seen faintly in the headlight beams. It was less than a quarter mile away, straight down the first trail. He grabbed a flashlight loaded with fresh batteries and put on a hoodie from the passenger seat. Hoping he was alone, he bolted off down the trail, brainstorming along the way.

Jason made the run in little time, the haste sprung from fright of spookiness. The sudden exercise took his breath away, his panting almost rabid as he checked the front door of the cabin. He endured the mental strife, half of his brain knew this was stupid, but the other half convinced him to man up. The point value. Think about the point value. The cabin didn't look to be abandoned, with the walls inside still freshly painted white for the visitors that it occasionally housed.

Then, he thought about the door. It was locked. Should he break one of the new windows, or should he knock down the door? Breaking and entering? Yeah, that was illegal—but only illegal if there was someone to catch him. In this fog? No way. Maybe the spooky ambiance was turning out to be a good cover. Jason dawned a criminal mind, and in this poor judgment, he took a large stone and hurled it towards the glass.

The window broke on the first strike, the damage far more than he had originally anticipated. It was unexpectedly loud, the glass having shattered to tiny bits of evidence ready for CSI to reconstruct.

This was it. He was a certified criminal. This is how it would all end, a spellbinding spiral into the justice system. Soon, he'd be a prisoner locked in a cell with an overweight creeper, shivering in the corner every night instead of sleeping. His skin clammed up, the blood retreating from it in the regret.

Then, something moved in the woods. He froze, hoping that it was just an innocent little animal, yet he saw nothing in the fog. Seconds of uneventful silence proved it as a false alarm, letting him return to focus. It was too late to stop the crime, so he pressed onward. To deter CSI, he shielded his fingerprints by wrapping a shirt around his hands, reaching through the broken window to unlock the door. Stepping in slowly with the flashlight on, he searched and searched, only to find nothing on the first floor. Next was the basement, an even spookier expanse akin to a dungeon.

Even worse, it smelled like old socks. Awful.

He aimed the flashlight cautiously, seeing cobwebs galore, dust in every open crevice within view. There was a layer of dust on the flood undisturbed by footprints. Dammit. This place hadn't been cleaned in years, a very humbling and disappointing fact in the grand scheme of things.

Was this the wrong cabin?

He sighed, his retreat back outside halted when two large and reflective eyes peered back at him. It was a cat—a gigantic mutant cat—that seemed very displeased by his visit, holding Jason's glare to size him up before lunging at him in attack.

Scared shitless, Jason defended with his only weapon, the metal flashlight that he used to strike it down handily. In his timidity, he yelled with a voice reminiscent to a teenage girl's, his frantic screams echoing in the night. The cat landed on the floor with a large thud, stunned from the hit, leaving a temporary respite before it attacked once again. It was enough for Jason to regroup, shuffling his feet as if they were trekking across hot pavement in preparation. In an instant, the cat was within range, but Jason's heaving kick missed and sent him toppling onto the floor.

The evil cat pounced.

"Shit!" he wailed. "Get off!"

Its claws proved sharp, tearing ridges through his clothes, gouging his skin, and roughing up the brand new Jordans he had fought so dearly to preserve. They rolled and tumbled, each strike and counterstrike peeving the war of attrition.

Dammit, this was it.

His final fate, a death sentence at the helm of an irradiated super cat. How shitty.

Then, in the last move of desperation, Jason did what he should've all along—grabbing the feline by the bulk and flailing it as hard as he could into the far wall.

It ended there, the cat finally standing back up to pay respect to its formidable foe. They held eye contact once again, this time in a share of mutual appreciation.

"We done?" Jason asked, all before realizing he was talking to a cat. Yes, he asked a cat a question.

It meowed, softly approaching to cuddle.

The change of heart was moving, its fur was gritty and rough. It purred, weak to Jason's priviness with pets. For a moment, he even considered taking it along, but it left the basement, hopping up the stairs and out the open door.

"Awesome." Jason sighed, inspecting his ruined clothing. "No item, and a deathmatch with a cat. Fuck my life."

Yet, the surprises didn't stop there.

As he scurried out of the cabin and back down the trail, he noticed something else. No way. No way there was someone standing next to his car. He blinked a few times to make sure that it wasn't part of an alternate reality.

"Seriously?" he asked himself when he noticed the figure stand up.

The window glass on the driver's side door shattered, the person now desperately trying to get the door open. Realizing that he was about become a victim of grand theft auto, Jason burst into a hellbent sprint.

"HEY!" he hollered. "GET AWAY FROM MY CAR!"

The person moved a bit faster, but that's when Jason noticed another automobile. Fresh with victory from the *Great Cat Battle*, Jason jumped straight into combat, blind sighting the intruder with a whack from the flashlight. The masked man fell back, pushing off the car to jab and miss Jason's head. Too bad the follow up swing connected, but Jason fought back. They hit each other, ducked, and weaved, this exchange persisting for a moment until he heard two doors open from the unidentified car. He looked up, seeing two more figures on a rapid approach. Shit. When he was hit in the face again, he dropped the flashlight and watched it roll out of reach.

Now outnumbered, he'd fight to the end, silently wishing his cat buddy would swoop to his rescue. Jason struck the first man as hard as he could with a swift kick to his gut, but his foe reactively hunched down before his head was hit with a barrage of fists. The second man swung to protect his partner, but the first few attempts missed. Jason was either too lucky, or too fast for that. Now frightened to the core, he fought the best that he could, knowing that this would soon turn to a losing battle.

Hitting the closest target was all that he could do before he was overwhelmed. Jason collapsed onto the ground, curling up into a fetal position in an attempt to protect his body and face from the attackers.

Here he was, in the wilderness of Tennessee, being jumped by car thieves in the dark. Maybe the fog *was* spooky, the progenitor of all things terrible from mutant kitties to classic car thievery cults.

Where was his beloved Agatha now? Man, she was beautiful.

The hits stopped. They rolled him over, cleaned out his pockets and took his wrist computer. He heard his car reverse and grind away as the thief tried his best to hustle along with the stick shift.

He laid there in the darkness, trying his best to get his breathing under control. Rolling over onto his stomach, he crawled over to a bench and pulled himself up. His mouth and nose were bloodied, but he had no severe damage, thank god. He laughed. That was pretty much the only thing he could do.

He checked his pockets. They were all empty.

At least they didn't decide to kill him, but his parents would when he came clean.

Maybe he shouldn't have fixed the bad wires under the dashboard.

"F-ck my life." he muttered. At least he still had his Chicago Cubs hat, though the fresh pair of Jordans were no longer fresh.

-The Underground Kings-
Deluxe Edition

EPISODE THREE

"Recovery"

Day#2:
Saturday June 13th, 2037.
-7:08AM-

The sunrise was picturesque, probably the only positive thing now. After it had climbed high enough in the morning sky, the dense fog began to wane away, revealing the forested wilderness that blanketed the area. The air was cool and less humid than the night before, the passing storm front left the sky clear and boundless.

Agatha was solemn, feeling the aftereffects from her previous night of binge drinking and boot-knocking with her buddy who was nowhere to be found. Despite the argument, she still wished for his return after kicking him out. Instead, she accidentally fell asleep during the wait.

"Chase?" she mumbled as she squinted her eyes. "Chase, where are you?"

She was still naked, lying under a blanket that once covered the rear seat.

"Chase!" she shouted again. The doors were still locked, and the windows were still slightly lowered. Nothing on the interior of the car had appeared to be any different than she had left it last night, but the pounding headache didn't help at all. Perhaps the moonshine part of the romance really *was* a bad idea.

She checked the ignition. No keys. But wait, she took them out and threw them in the back seat when they started drinking, just in case a policeman pulled up. Her hands felt around on the carpet, beneath the front seats, in the map pockets, yet they found nothing.

Now she was scared.

Agatha hustled back into her clothing and checked her surroundings. There was nothing around. Finally, she worked up the courage and opened the door. She stood up, supporting her weight on the car while using her other hand as a mock visor to shield her eyes from the piercing morning sun.

"Chase!" she hollered, "Chase, where are you?"

No answer.

"What the hell?" she mumbled to herself.

Was he kidnapped or something during the night? She ruled that possibility out quickly, figuring that anyone looking to kidnap someone would've taken her too.

Then, it clicked.

She checked the center console for her wrist phone and the slate computer, finding that they had vanished along with her purse. That bastard. Her father's folded flag was still safe in the glove compartment. Popping the trunk and looking in, she gasped in anger when she noticed that the fifty-thousand-point item they had collected together in the forest had vanished too. With all of clues coming together, Agatha knew that she had been set up.

How could she be *that* stupid?

Luckily, there was a spare key hidden under the paneling of the fender well, just in case she locked her keys in. In the time that she hadn't used it, the key had moved, but after a few minutes of worming her hand around, it was retrieved and still in good shape. Excellent. She hustled into the driver's seat, pressed the clutch and started the car. The trusty old engine fired right up. Even her spare sunglasses were still there. They fit her as well as ever, their mirror finish slightly tarnished from the many summers of rugged use.

"At least he didn't take the engine while he was at it." she grunted to herself as she sobbed. "Bastard. Rooked me."

Women hated her, and men seemed to love her for only one thing: her assets. Call it unfortunate that she had grown accustomed to this. In her time, while Agatha had never figured out the key factor that caused the failure of her relationships, she at least knew that it was all but guaranteed. "Boys would be boys," or so they said, but they never taught her that love and lust would be so hard to grasp. Every time, it seemed, she left the situation feeling like the one who had been used. Perhaps that's all she was, just something to pass the time, just something to conquer. Having faith for better was a dwindling strategy.

Depressing.

The self-pity continued for five minutes as she cried her eyes out, all before it was replaced by the default tough girl attitude. It was only thing that kept her consistent, and damn she was good with automobiles. She put the shifter into first gear and revved the engine, dumping the clutch to spin the tires wildly in the return onto the road. The V-8 roared and the car lurched as she shifted, hoping that she would find him nearby so she could personally kick his ass. They had spent all night sifting through those cabins in the park, looking for that stupid item, and they were going to share the loot once they reached the finish line. Chase had always been a nice guy, never coming off as too much of a jerk, but Agatha knew his type well. Selfish. Conniving. In it only for their own gratification.

And she fell for it, again.

A few miles passed as she whipped the GTO around the winding corners as fast as it would go. Each time, she would swing wide, dial in for the zone, and nail the apex to a tee. Gentle throttle application kept the rear in check, the big grand tourer pushing its way out of each bend with surprising ease. Her feet danced between the pedals, her right foot curling perfectly for the heel-toe downshifts on corner entry. It was a relief to take her anger out on the car, but sanity prevailed after she passed an oncoming motorist at 90mph. Driving this fast without a license, cell phone, or any money whatsoever was as stupid as sleeping with a guy that tried to secretly film it. Dammit. Grudgingly, she slowed the car down to normal speeds, selecting the highest gear and ruffling her hair out of her face.

She fumed with anger and disgust, noting that she had over seven hundred dollars in that purse. It was the hard-earned travel money specifically saved for the journey.

Then, something caught her eye.

Just as the car crested a hill, she saw a figure trekking through the tall grass. She sped the car up, wishing that it may have been Chase, but it wasn't. Dammit, it definitely wasn't.

Serial killer? Alien? Zombie?

No. Just a clearly recognizable face: Jason Weathers, a discovery both disheartening and reassuring all at once. In fact, it was the *last* person she wanted to encounter. Hissing with spite, her first instinct was to keep driving, but then she saw what looked like blood scattered all over his clothes.

Seeing her car, he began waving his arms, feeling as if divine intervention had personally blessed this moment. His sadness vanished when the GTO pulled off the road and drove up the dirt trail that had all but killed his ankles—and apparently, the Jordans. The door opened and Agatha got out, giving him a puzzled, but terrified look. His face was heavily bruised, his nose busted, and his lip split.

In all, she had always managed to save him from doom.

"Jason?" she asked. He could barely catch his breath, hunching over and coughing up some mucus.

"Hello?" she asked again. "Are you okay?"

"Do I look okay?" he barked.

She huffed, "Well, excuse me for being concerned, but it looks like you got attacked by a pack of wolves."

"More like a mutant cat and a pack of thieves, maybe." he stood up holding his stomach. "Then some assholes beat me up and jacked my damn car."

"Wait—you got into a fight with a cat and lost?"

"No," Jason corrected, "I didn't 'lose,' if you consider the even score."

"Who keeps score with cat fights?" she pressed. "You're going to have to tell me the entire story. I *really* need someone to laugh at right now."

The insults grew awkward over time.

"Super nice." was all Jason could say. "That makes me feel so awesome."

"And you got your car stolen? Jason, where does this stuff even happen? I don't understand how you have the worst luck in the world."

Jason rolled his eyes and laughed.

"Uh, well let me summarize: I got my ass kicked."

"Again?"

"Yes."

"I've never known someone so susceptible to ass-beatings! This is like a regular ordeal for you! I mean, you're easy to dislike with your dumb sarcasm and dark humor, so I sometimes get the urge to punch you in the face, yet in the grand scheme I'd never want to actually *hurt* you."

He'd take that as a compliment.

Positivity.

"Plus, I didn't know that so many people wanted those stupid little cars anyways! Who knew?"

"They are highly sought after, I suppose."

"So, tell me about the guys that took your car."

"Spoke Spanish," he paused, trying not to sound racist, "so I *think* they were Mexicans or of 'Latin American decent', and they jumped me outside of the Smoky Mountain National Park. I mean, nothing else to say about it really."

"Did they stab you or anything?" she examined him with her eyes, being careful not to actually touch the shirt. "Where'd all this blood come from?"

"I used the shirt to wipe my face off last night. It got kind of cold and it was the only shirt I had, so I put it back on."

"You look like a mass murderer running towards the road. You're lucky I found you and not some hillbilly."

He sneered, "I wouldn't consider myself 'lucky' to be found anywhere near you."

"Okay, asshole, should I just drive away or what?" she put her hands on her hips. "You tell me!"

"Where's Chase? Thought he was your road trip buddy."

"Ha," she scratched her head and looked away, "Chase is a scoundrel, two-timing bastard. I'm hunting him down."

"Why's that?"

"Long story short, I woke up this morning to find him gone."

"Okay?"

She looked at him as if he were crazy,

"He took of all of my shit, including an item that was worth fifty-thousand points!"

"Wait." Jason couldn't believe it. "What item?"

"The one in the park." she said. "We got there and searched for about two hours in the cabins. Found it in a hidden garage. The riddle about the shoe?"

"So, you mean to tell me I got car jacked *and* jumped over an item that had already been claimed?"

She paused, eyed him up, and then burst into laughter.

"Holy shit!" she said between cackles. "Yeah, I guess so! And don't forget about the cat battle!"

"This isn't funny. That's why they tell you to update your item roster!"

"Uh huh, but there was no cell service to do that. Sure sucks for you, though."

"I knew this whole thing was a stupid idea." he sat down on the ground. "I knew it was a bad idea as soon as I started reading those third-grade scavenger hunt clues."

Agatha recited the quote, *"If the shoe fits her, she's timeless."*

"Yeah," he rolled his eyes, "what was it anyway?"

"It was Cinderella's glass slipper. Everyone was looking for it, but Chase seemed to know exactly where to hunt."

"They had us looking for a glass slipper?"

"Uh huh. All of the items are glass figurines." she squinted in judgment. "Jason, do you read *anything* at all?"

"Shut up. So, it was just sitting there or was it hidden?"

"There was a clue card outside of the cabin buried by a little yard flag about twenty-five miles away from the GPS beacon. It said the item could be found in the cabin, but it was locked so you had to find the key first. Chase busted the window and we figured out the simple little riddle and found the slipper wrapped up in a box."

"Are you allowed to forcibly enter the cabins?"

"I don't think so, but like I said, he busted the window and walked in. He seemed to know exactly where to go, where to look, and exactly what to do." Agatha stepped closer to the car. "Everything in the cabin looked pretty modern."

It clicked.

"So, they basically have us stealing shit?"

"They wouldn't have us running around the country stealing shit from random houses. What we're doing is already borderline illegal, but it's designed to be fun. You're supposed to read the damn rules, then find the key first by reading the clues. Listen, Jason. Listen."

"I didn't pay attention to any of that stuff."

"You don't pay attention to anything," she groaned, "but if you wouldn't mind, I'd like to try and find civilization. Do you have your slate?"

Jason got up and opened the passenger door.

"No." he shook his head. "Those dudes took all of my shit."

"Awesome. You're the only person in like thirty miles that I've seen, and you're worse off than I am."

She got in and shut the door, making sure to stop Jason before he did the same.

"Could you, uh, ditch the serial killer shirt first?"

"You got something for me to wear?"

Agatha looked around inside of the car and grabbed a T-shirt.

"Whose is this?"

"One of mine," she looked his body over. "But you're small enough to fit in it."

Jason rolled his eyes.

"Sorry I'm not like built like Chase."

"Just get in."

-8:30AM-

"You couldn't have found me a shittier shirt." Jason complained as he examined the t-shirt Agatha had given him. "Like, this is the worst shirt in the history of shirts."

"It's all I have in here right now."

The shirt was pink with the word '*Pink*' inscribed on the front.

"I look like a douche wearing a pink Victoria's Secret V-neck."

"Don't sweat it," her eyes searched the horizon, "Jason, you always look like a douche. Nothing to worry about, trust me."

The conversation devolved into silence, only broken by the engine's rumble, the onrush of air from the windows, and the country music playing in the radio at low volume.

It was awkward. Painfully awkward.

"Do you have the slightest clue where we are?" Agatha asked as they passed a mile marker on the two-lane rural road. "Hello?"

Jason was sleeping. After all, it had been a long night.

"Hey!" Agatha punched his shoulder, jolting him awake. "Wake up! This isn't nap time!"

"The hell if I know. I've been walking all night."

"Great."

"Why don't you have a Scene View Deluxe slate in here?"

"I told you, Chase took it. He had an awfully badass map on his slate, though."

"What do you mean?"

"The map on his slate seemed to be much better than mine. I heard him and a few of the other elites talking about having the 'hook up' regarding the map. It was like it led him straight to the item."

"So, we he had a rigged map to cheat, and you botched your chances of winning this by somehow pissing him off. Then he jacked all your stuff and left you in the middle of nowhere, alone?"

"I trusted him."

"Seems like the feeling wasn't mutual."

"That's what happens when you think that someone likes you."

"Well, *that* was stupid."

That hit a nerve.

"Look!" she snapped. "I don't need *you* to tell *me* how 'stupid' my decisions were, coming from a lazy kid who has never finished a single thing in his life!"

That stung even worse.

"I finished my car, that got stolen last night."

"I know you did."

He peened at their bond, "And I learned how to drive."

"I know."

"And I helped kids learn to drive and not be lazy, worthless screwups like me. I paid my mom and dad's mortgage for the past year when they couldn't. The house is still getting foreclosed though."

"Jason." she sighed.

"So none of that counts?"

"Okay," Agatha backtracked, "what I said was a little harsh."

"Yeah, tell me about it. Hitting below the belt."

"I'm sorry. Just stop being an asshole. I don't need you to harp on my relationships."

"I'm just being honest."

"Well," she scoffed, "then me too."

Maybe the truth hurt. Jason looked away, spotting an object bouncing around on the floor. Despite his aching body, he reached down and picked it up to take a closer look.

"Drinking cups?" he laughed and sniffed one "That smells like moonshine! Ha! So, you and Chase got drunk, except Chase waited until *you* were passed out, then stole everything out of your car?"

"It was my idea to drink."

"Moonshine?!"

"Yes. Apple Pie Mint, with a 'kick'."

Jason's low-brow chuckle grew into a laugh.

"What's funny about that?!" she pressed.

"If it's what I'm thinking about, it's that special stuff that you can buy from the guy 'down the block on the corner,' you know? What's his name? Abu, or something like that?"

"No, I don't know his name."

"It's that 'wet-wet' juice, you know what I'm talking about. Poonshine."

"*Poonshine*?!" Agatha's voice nearly ruptured his eardrums. "You can't be serious! Who calls it that?"

"Uh, everyone? It's like the best thing you've ever drank, but you realize that you get drunk twice as fast—and you, uh—."

"You get horny." Agatha finished the statement for him. "There's a drug in the moonshine that increases libido. Feels nice. The increased heart rate, body temperature and—?"

"Arousal. Yes." Jason nodded. "Some kind of herbs, or ecstasy, or something. It 'puts the heat on,' per say."

"How the hell do you know this much about it? I didn't even know you drank. I thought you were above that."

"First off, I'm not *that* sheltered. Second off, a few old friends of mine bought a bottle of it once for like a hundred bucks. I took a sip. There was a warning label on the front of the bottle talking about limiting how much you drink due to 'adverse effects' from the additives, like babies and shit. You're hounding on me about never reading anything, yet you didn't read the warning label. Poonshine brings out the worst in people."

"Like what? Unspent desire?"

"Stupidity."

"Jesus." she rolled her eyes. "You're the most judgmental asshole that I've ever seen. I mean, what are you so mad about, Jason?"

There was another pause and Jason thought some things over,

"Wait. Didn't you just start talking to Chase like last week?"

"Uh, yeah. Why?"

"He got in your britches?"

"My 'britches'? You are seriously an idiot! I can't even believe I let you in my car!"

"That's disgusting." he scowled and shook his head. "You're *so* stupid. C'mon! Dude, you got to chill with the whole bros that bang you and then steal your belongings type. That spells unhealthy relationship."

"What the hell do you know about relationships?"

"That my partner shouldn't bang me and steal my stuff when I'm asleep."

"*You* are the one getting banged? Whoa, Jason! Mr. Receiver, eh?"

"—Okay, that's not what I meant."

"Now it makes sense. Have you ever been in an *actual* relationship?"

"Yeah." he sneered.

"Your hand doesn't count."

"What if I switch hit?"

She laughed out of instinct, not happiness. "Ew, shut up!"

"Seriously. I've never done stupid shit to be in a relationship, no. I don't want to sell myself short. That stuff is important."

"Look, I don't need you to tell me how 'stupid' my decisions were!"

"People do dumb things and then wonder why dumb things happens to them." he shrugged, trying to defend himself.

"It's called life." her voice was raised. "And with you being locked up in your house judging people all the time, have *you* ever truly lived? At all? Have you ever done anything fun? Random? Something that took bravery or courage? What do you have to show for all of your 'good' decisions in life?"

"Why do you think I'm here?" he fessed. "I guess I'm just tired of being nothing."

There. Right there, was one of few genuine understandings shared between them. Agatha's scowl turned to complacency, an expression of sudden recognition of a like-minded ally.

"I don't want to argue with you." she admitted.

"Truce." he agreed. "Let's figure this out."

Fair enough.

"Why didn't he take your keys?" Jason said after some time to think. "I guess he wasn't *that* much of an asshole, eh?"

"Oh, he did. I just had a spare on the car for emergencies."

"Wow. Nice!" Jason nodded. "One of the first non-blonde moment moves you've taken so far. I'm proud of you."

"That would be funny if I were actually a blonde."

"It was a joke? You obviously have brown hair, but if you're trying to get away from the whole lack-of-common-sense stereotype, you're clearly not fooling anyone but yourself."

Suddenly the GTO slid to halt. Agatha was livid.

"Do you want to walk?" she growled. "Because I don't have to give you a damn ride anywhere. I'm just being nice at this point."

"Well, I would thank you for your hospitality, but I'll save it."

"Then you can get the hell out of my car. Seriously, get out. You're of no real use to me anyway."

"Okay," Jason opened the door and stepped out, "you're somewhere on Route 129, which if I remember correctly, connects to Interstate 40 about ninety miles from here, but you'll need Route 8 and State Roads 30, 12, and 55, I think."

She didn't reply, so he shut the door. The GTO motored off briefly until it stopped again, illuminating its reverse lights until it rolled back to him. Agatha looked a bit desperate.

"Dude, come on." she pleaded. "I don't like you, but I'm not going to leave you walking down the road to nowhere alone."

Jason got back in and buckled his seatbelt.

"I'm not the best with directions, but I think I at least remember some of the roads."

"That's better than nothing, because I didn't pay attention at all this entire way. Not the smartest thing I've done, clearly."

"Way to take ownership."

"Thanks."

"We need to find some kind of civilization as soon as we can so I can report my car stolen."

"Do you think it's too late?"

Jason avoided morbid thoughts, "That depends on how smart the thieves were."

"They were smart enough to steal it, so does that mean anything?"

"They broke the window and jumped me. I don't think they would've gotten it started if I hadn't have left it running."

"I thought you said your car couldn't be started because of wiring problems."

"I did."

"Well, there went your theft-deterrent, smart boy."

"I didn't expect anyone to be in the middle of a damn forest that late."

"How the hell did they find you in the middle of a huge park in the fog at night?"

"Obviously followed me somehow, probably my super bright headlights. Guess I didn't notice them."

"Well, that just sucks."

"Oh, hell." Jason saw the gas gauge. The GTO was running low on fuel. Its old-school digital gauge cluster flashed a warning and played an odd sounding chime in protest.

Agatha was aware, "Yeah, I know. It's low."

"What kind of fuel mileage does this 5.7 get?"

"You don't want to know."

They had no choice but to continue, lumbering along the hilly country road for another half hour taking in the country scenery. It was oddly refreshing, the air filling their lungs better than back home, the sky bluer than they had ever seen. Surreal. In all the miles they had travelled, they had only seen two other cars. Maybe the country wasn't so bad. There was peace here, quiet, simplicity

Then, a far more dire fuel warning flashed in the old digital console. "Very low fuel," it cried, as if the car was personally offended that the other, less intrusive warning light was blatantly ignored. Further realizations of doom spurned from this point.

"You got any money on you?" Agatha asked as she slowed the GTO down and steered it into the station. Jason laughed.

"No! I told you, those guys cleaned me out. I don't have a single thing. No wallet, wrist computer, nothing."

"Shit," she frowned, "I don't have any money either."

"Chase took it all?"

"He took my purse. My wrist computer was in there."

"What an asshole! You really need to start meeting some nicer guys, Agatha." Jason opened the door and got out. "Seriously."

She ignored him, instead taking focus on the immediate troubles.

"Where are you going?" she asked.

He leaned into the window. His face was slightly swollen, but his eyes were still bright and renewed. Somehow, she could see the churning gears in his head, the wit that she had grown to know conjuring up a wild plan. She felt reassured. Perhaps, he could be trusted.

"I'm going to use the bathroom. Maybe clean up my face a little."

"What are we going to do about gasoline? We'll have to figure out something."

"What's with all of this 'we' talk?" Jason laughed. "I don't even like you."

"Ditto, you moron, but at least I show up to save your ass." she snapped. "I thought we had a truce for now?"

"Well, I'm going to the bathroom. I'll take a look around along the way and let you know what I find. Oh, and don't leave me here!"

Agatha smiled.

"I'm serious!" Jason's voice dipped.

Suddenly, she removed her shirt, catching him completely off guard. His throat dried in an instant, his eyes widening to the size of baseballs.

"What are you doing?" he croaked.

"Don't worry about it. You just get ready to pump the gas." she ordered as she changed. "Relax. It's just a bra. Oh, you probably haven't seen one of these before in person being on the high horse and all. I forgot."

"Excuse me, but instead of pointing out that your statement is incorrect, I'll just go ahead and say that I'm not used to girls that randomly remove their shirts."

"But I thought you were an up and coming rapper, with 'bitches on your dick' or whatever you were rhyming the other day? What about the 'hoes you motorboat' according to your mixtape. You should be used to boobs."

"Really?" Jason growled. "Do you always have to go for the low-blows?"

"Yes, really, but hurry up in the bathroom. I'll give you a signal."

"Are you thinking what I'm thinking?"

"Uh huh."

-9:12AM-

Agatha spotted a hot-rodded pickup truck pulling into the station with a caravan of bikers in tow. It took the younger guys mere seconds to notice her, as usual. She left her long brown hair hanging down beyond her shoulders to blow in the wind, having traded the jeans for a pair of shorts that redefined the definition of "short". Her long, muscular legs would have onlookers foaming at the mouth long before their eyes reached her upper torso.

Yes, men were easy.

Weak to distraction, and deception.

She stepped out of the car, shutting the door and fluffing her hair in the wind. Sure, the stretching of her back was a bit long and exaggerated, but it felt good. Bingo. The men inside were still watching what was likely the best thing they had seen all year. Her beauty was a striking truth, its weaponization the key to lots of unrequited favors in her life.

Being honest, Agatha loved everything about it.

Stepping into the store, she flashed a courteous smile, just as cute as she could be. Her hips rocked as she pranced along, the hypnosis-stricken men entranced to their rhythm. Rebel flags and their hinted racism provided no deterrent, her lushly deep brown skin proving exotically alluring. Maybe her assumptions about them were wrong, or maybe instinct had prevailed, after all, a melting pot woman was still a woman—even an adopted Senegalese-Irish-Latina.

Her eyes scanned the targets, picking out the most vulnerable candidate for her work. An optimal case would likely include one of the younger ones, but the older men would probably have more money. She stepped into a grocery isle, pretending to look through the magazine section and then the snacks.

Her mind wandered to Jason, about how she would notify him of the plan, if he'd catch on quickly, or if he was as smart as everyone said he was. After a few more minutes of pacing around, she finally saw him walking out to the car. She made eye contact. He nodded, loosening the gas cap before he ducked behind the car.

Go time.

Agatha smirked, seeing the first one of the brave young men coming to make a move. He was a teenager, at most seventeen or eighteen years old. His hair looked recently cut, his clothes greasy and oil stained. In her immediate judgment, she found him to be quite attractive, with a sharply contoured face and manly shoulders. His voice was the killer, nice and deep. She almost fell weak kneed when he spoke,

"That your GTO, ma'am?" his accent made him that much more attractive.

She giggled, her dreamy eyes piercing holes though him.

"Yeah it is, why?"

"It's awfully nice." he responded. "How long have you had her?"

"She's been the in the family about twenty years now."

"That's nice. "

Oddly, the conversation ended here. He spent a few moments trying his best to think of something clever to say, but instead he bailed out. Similar mishaps were common occurrence in her daily life, when men would attempt to hit on her, yet fail to keep momentum on a conversation. Topics would vary, but they were mostly about her car, as men would only take point in the things that they knew best.

Focus!

Her plans took a desperate turn, with only two real options left for quick resolve. She could either pickpocket an old man or provide enough distraction for

Jason to pump enough gasoline into the tank without notice. Both options were difficult. The first required getting into close proximity, which was still fairly gross at this point. Feeling up an old guy wasn't on her to-do list of life experiences—anymore, at least. The second option sucked because the store attendant's desk provided the perfect view of the pump. Apparently, he knew the group of men from the convoy, so the conversation had him distracted enough.

Jason was firmly in position, but how would she keep attention away from the pump? Should she spill coffee down her shirt and strip in the middle of the store? No, that would hurt. Claim to be a nudist and unveil her birthday suit whilst buying Skittles and iced tea? That might work. No one ever questioned her endless skinny dipping, and she had never been kicked out of a pool because of it. *Ever*.

Oh, god. She was infected with terrible ideas.

Through the window, she caught Jason peeking around the bumper, anxiously awaiting her signal. This was it, the time where she had to pick a plan and run with it.

Birthday suit and Skittles, or clumsy bimbo?

Yeah, time for the clumsy bimbo act. *That* was a classic. Agatha took a long step and randomly fell backward, knocking a display of sunglasses atop of her. Her body hit the floor, complemented by a bit of melodrama, but the desired effect was achieved, nonetheless.

"Owww!" she howled after the initial commotion.

It hurt more than she had anticipated, but all of the men inside of the station rushed in to be the knight in shining armor. Like ants, they swarmed the scene.

———

Jason saw the commotion inside the store, assuming it to be the signal. He lifted the pump nozzle out of the holder, selected 93 octane and stuck it in the fuel feed. Holding the pump in with his right hand, he squeezed as hard as he could in hopes that it would pump faster given the situation, but it was rather old, dating back to the 1990s—or worse.

Fuel flowed through at a steady pace, his eyes locked onto the dial showing the amount in gallons that had been pumped.

"Come on." he willed. "Come on!"

Four gallons.

Everyone in the store still surrounded Agatha. One of the men had helped her to her feet, but she faked an ankle injury. She fell again—this time *not* on purpose—and was swept up by the hunky younger fellow that had tried talking to her before. He carried her to a table and gently sat her down.

Jason couldn't believe it.

"What a bunch of morons." he laughed to himself.

Seven gallons.

If he recalled correctly, a Pontiac GTO held around eighteen gallons, so they'd need a lot more. He looked towards Agatha again, now aided with pack of ice from the freezer to soothe her wounds. Jason could see her laughing, his mind replaying her flirty cackle with haunting accuracy despite the inability to actually hear it.

The attraction was toxic, a chemical weapon of emotion to which men were left defenseless. This was good for them, very good. If she could hold this up for just another minute or so, they could make their escape.

"Shit!" Jason mumbled.

The desk clerk was walking towards the front register. This was bad, both Jason and Agatha aware of their fate if he reached the machine.

They needed an escape plan.

Jason noticed a town police car sitting behind the building, but it was horribly old. Surely the GTO could outgun it if needed.

"Porter, Tennessee?"

Yes, they were officially in the middle of nowhere.

The pump clicked and stopped, the overfill protection activated by a full tank. Jason removed the spout and placed it back into the holster, but the clerk noticed an oddity on the register's display. He looked out towards the pump number that magically had a $100 charge on it. To his surprise, he spotted Jason's head rising above the trunk lid.

They made brief eye contact, and then the guy freaked.

"HEY!" he shouted, so loudly Jason could hear him through the window.

He hustled to his feet and opened the driver's door, looking for Agatha. The nearby men couldn't react in time, the hopeless fools. She burst into full sprint, carrying a speed none of them could match. Her arms extended, her hands reaching out to push the door then—wham!

She was stopped in her tracks, the broad side of an arm catching her neck and collarbone, sending her spiraling to the ground. Her breath was gone, her vision hazy, both taken by the impact of the only quick-witted man in the place. They had turned on her quickly, none too happy to have been fooled by a pretty girl and a kid attempting to swindle some high-priced gasoline. She was surrounded again and dragged away from the door just as the clerk paced his way outside.

Shit. Jason knew what came next. He jogged towards the clerk, keeping his eyes on him as they closed in on each other. Adrenaline spilled through his bloodstream, his fists curling during the approach.

"Hey!" yelled the clerk. "You and the girlie stealing gas!"

"I was just about to pay." Jason tried to convince.

"Bullshit you were!"

The man then reached out and took a strong hold of Jason's right arm. Jason used his free hand and grappled the clerk's arm, spinning him with all his might. When he yanked through the grapple, inertia rotated the clerk away, his elbow popping clear out of the socket. Maybe the boxing and self-defense lessons his dad taught him finally paid off, or maybe he only needed the confidence. The clerk found himself dizzy, lying face up on the pavement, looking towards the sky in pain. As he came back to light, he discovered Jason on a rampage inside of the station.

"Son-of-a-bitch." the clerk loathed.

Damn youngsters and their Kungfu.

The store was the real chore. Jason seemed a bit timid at first, taking on the first challenger with ease after curling up his fists. It was the younger guy, the same one that tried his luck with Agatha earlier. He was strong sure enough, but a bit too slow. In a sense of determined faith, the kid put his heart into a few well-coordinated swings, but they missed.

Jason squared up. They circled each other, talking smack in the tradition of male hand-to-hand combat.

"It's just me and you, boy." growled the kid. "What'ya going to do? Huh?"

He swung and missed again. Jason faked with a jab and watched the kid fall for it. Now frozen in a defenseless posture, he saw his fate.

One good knuckle sandwich put his lights out.

"Uh huh!" Jason woofed. "Catch these hands, bro! Where the rest of your boys?"

"Jason!"

Focus!

Agatha wrestled with the fat guy that held onto her as if his joints had locked. She tried everything to get free, from flailing and kicking, to screaming and biting. Nothing worked, his large arm solid around her torso, constricting so hard that it started to hurt. She looked up, seeing Jason take a few hits to the face before he grabbed an end stand and bopped his opponent across the head. The guy fell in a daze, knocking down some of the grocery shelves that toppled to the floor like a line of dominos. The last two shelves fell onto the only guy, pinning under the rubble to scream for help.

Now came the final standoff.

"I reckon this is where your fun ends." the fat guy taunted, having tossed Agatha aside to begin his trot towards Jason.

She was worried about the prospect of Jason facing a man roughly two to three times his size. He stepped away, trying to keep his distance, knowing that he would be unable to contest his strength if the man got a hold of him. He waited, swearing in his mind to kick the guy square in the gonads if necessary.

This was where boxing skills and luck ran dry.

Now, the time to hit below the belt had come. Fat guy took one step forward, stopped by a once pristine condition Air Jordan shunting into jewels. He howled, his face reddened with painful stupor as he began to stumble backward. His feet danced at random, his hands reaching down to address the agony.

Son-of-a-bitch!

A metallic thud echoed through the store and the fat guy careened over. His foot stepped on the metal stand of a bubble gum dispenser, which reacted to the large load by tipping over and whacking him in the jaw. Agatha was stunned.

"Holy shit!" Jason almost laughed. "That guy knocked himself out with a bubblegum machine!"

"You bastard." she coughed, grabbing at her stomach. "Squeezed the hell out of me!"

Fat guy was on the floor snoring. Hopefully he slept well.

"Yeah." Jason wasted no time turning around and heading for the door. "Well, we have to get out of here like *now*."

Agatha hustled up behind him, bursting through the door before she suddenly stopped.

"Wait!" she shouted. "The security cameras!"

She was back inside before Jason could stop her. Wasting no time, she jolted over the counter and ran into one of the back rooms. He followed her in, fists curled just in case anyone wanted another beatdown.

Yeah, they could catch them hands again.

A+ for confidence.

The townsfolk were all in the recovery process, their sleepy minds and sore bodies slowly rebooting after the battle. His fresh status as a fugitive proved nauseating, but this could be his shot at a steamy *Bonnie & Clyde* love affair, if he had one. Oh yeah, maybe his time in the love drought had come to an end.

Surprisingly, he wasn't *that* mad about his stolen car.

Shit. The guys were starting to get up, and this was taking way too long.

"Dude," he asked after finding Agatha, "what are you doing? We have to get out of here!"

"How do you get this thing out?" she squealed. It was an archaic security monitoring system, complete with a DVD recorder shielded under a metal cage.

Blunt force was deemed a viable option.

Jason found a sledgehammer and smashed the cage, destroying not only the DVD disc, but the table too.

"Good enough!" he declared.

-9:37AM-

Reinforcements arrived.

They backtracked behind the beer cave and twinkies to flank and flee their foes. Now, their freedom relied on their on-foot prowess, a duty by which Jason found Agatha far superior. Midway through the journey, they heard a loud pop behind them. Their hearts jumped. They ducked, Jason falling flat onto his stomach in the fright. Their instincts hunted for a source, finding a middle-aged cop standing in the doorway, his face strewn with determination.

"Stop right there!" he demanded. "Police! Stop right there, you little assholes!"

His rifle fired two more times. Both shots missed, obviously intended as warning shots.

"Shit!" Jason crawled backwards. Agatha reached the car and flung open the door, guiding him over to the passenger seat.

"GO! GO! GO!" he hollered.

It was a riot, the townsfolk regrouped and running out of the store in masse. They looked angry, all part of a hive mind that turned them into zombie pursuers. Agatha didn't waste any time starting the engine.

Clutch.

First Gear. Revs.

Dump it. Full throttle.

The GTO left the gas station with its tires ablaze, the muscle car thunder pouring from the tailpipes. She grabbed second gear, then third, and then fourth. Before long, they nipped at triple-digit speeds.

Jason eyes puckered, seeing the upcoming corner as a glaring warning of his untimely death. He held on for dear life, his hand tightening on the door grip with white knuckles.

Agatha wasn't fazed.

She steered wide across the double-yellow lines and eased off the throttle, kissing the brakes a tad—all before ducking the car into the slight bend and shuffling it out the other side nary a skid.

Okay, the GTO was significantly faster than he had assumed.

"Ooooh crap!" Jason's voice was muted heavily by the wind. He was shifty now, his body turning from side to side to check both the mirrors and the narrow rear windows for the targets.

"What?"

"They're coming!" he gasped. "Right behind us!"

Agatha checked the mirrors, spotting the caravan of motorcycles speeding out of the complex after them. She checked again to make sure the mirrors weren't lying, finding them to be unfortunately honest. They rounded a bend, setting them up for an ominous turn in the pursuit.

The bandits cut them off with a shortcut, forcing Agatha to turn left and jut up a curvy hill. Having lost their speed advantage, it became a pure acceleration contest, and even their hogs were reasonably fast. She gave it hell, but it made little difference. Back on a straight away, she slammed into fourth gear and pressed over a buck-ten. Still, they reared up like missiles.

"Agatha, they're catching up! They're right on us!"

"No shit!" she wailed. "How are they that fast?"

"How am I supposed to know?"

"These guys are nuts! What are we going to do?"

The old hot-rodded truck made its grand entrance, the bikes parting like the Red Sea, all for their leader—the fat guy with sore gonads, the same gentleman knocked out with a bubble gum dispenser. A hole was cut into the hood, and through it rose a giant supercharger inhaling with the fury of a rocket.

"Pull over, assholes!" he screamed. "I'ma shoot your damn tires if you don't stop!"

He flashed a gun and swerved, making it obvious that he was either preparing to use the weapon, or ram them off the road. Vowing to let neither plan see its way into reality, Agatha preempted by slamming the brakes to send the truck flying ahead. She swerved right, causing one of the bikers to lose control and spiral into the grass. Jason screamed and white-knuckled the grab handles, his heart on the verge of arrhythmia. The GTO kicked sideways and beamed down a series of curves, its driver now keenly picking gears in the fashion of a professional.

To a true wheelman, road acclimation was mere normality.

Agatha checked the mirrors, seeing their pursuers baffled and shaken, but the truck had recovered and locked onto their heading. In her periphery, she spotted another trap: the old police car originally seen at the gas station, now trekking through the grass field ahead. The trigger-happy police sheriff focused anew, for he had fresh criminals to fill the plaguing void of excitement in recent times.

He gritted his teeth against the bumpy grass, growling like a dog in the rush of action. Porter was a small town far removed from the highway, complete with three police cars and one sheriff. Monotony spread like the fog on a summer night, making new crooks one of many things he had desired for years. Eleven to be exact, and after watching repeat episodes of *"Cops"* during the idle time in the gas station, suddenly becoming part of a high-speed chase was a dream come true. He powered the car back onto the pavement and gunned the engine.

Agatha felt the pressure mounting. Alas, she started to make slight misjudgments in the midst, entering a corner with too much speed. The tires squealed in protest, the GTO's body leaning atop its heavily augmented suspension.

"Whoa! What the hell!" Jason screamed when they nearly skidded off the road.

"Agh!" Agatha seesawed the wheel both directions, finally getting the tail end back in line. "Shit! Sorry!"

"Focus! Focus!"

"Just let me drive!"

Another death-defying skid, this one sending two of the four tires into the grass. Damn the gravel-infested pavement. Her sweaty hands slipped on the steering wheel, the brakes growing softer from overheating by the second.

All this, and she wondered if they had *really* made a difference.

"Where are they?" she inquired. "WHERE ARE THEY?"

The conclusion was a toss-up until Jason turned to look out of the rear window, finding their pursuers much further behind than they were before. Yeah, the girl *could* drive.

He heard a loud cracking sound, then a few more, all following muzzle flashes from the truck's cabin. Something ricocheted pretty close, causing them to briefly duck in fear.

"He's shooting at us!" her voice was shrill.

"No, really?" Jason's face reddened with frustration, or perhaps anger. This *Bonnie & Clyde* thing wasn't going well.

"I don't want to die!"

"Well, lose them!"

"I'm trying! Do something, Jason!"

"You got something heavy enough to throw out the window? A stone or something?"

"No! Why would I carry a rock in my car?"

Jason hunched over the center console, searching the cluttered rear seat for something of use. Then he found a box with something heavy inside.

Bingo.

"Will this work?" he showed her.

Agatha glanced quickly as he continued using the corners to hold the truck off. Superior agility was the only measurable advantage.

"Can I use this?" Jason asked, seeing a straight section coming up ahead.

"Yeah! It's a crystal ball that my grandma gave me like three days ago."

"Seems heavy enough!"

"Hold on." she switched the GTO to the left lane of the road. "I'll get you in a position to chuck that thing out the window. Wait till he's close!"

"But, he's got a gun!"

"I know that! It's a revolver and he's going to have to reload!"

The truck driver shot the weapon again and missed. Hitting the tires was much harder than in the movies. Hell. He pulled up again to for another shot, but the gun was out of ammunition.

"*We need spike strips!*" he radioed. "*I can't hit them damn tires! If I keep shooting, I'll full around and accidentally kill one of em! Don't want that!*"

"*10-4!*" the Sheriff radioed back. "*I'm taking the field all the way through. I think I can cut them off!*"

Cornering at this rate would tip the truck if he wasn't careful, but he knew these roads well. The trap was set, the Sheriff ready to pounce in just a few hundred feet ahead. Soon, the corners stopped, the road just straight enough for him to close the gap. The truck guy saw this as the last opportunity to take them down, to be the hero he always dreamt of becoming.

Imagine how the town would swoon! Finally, the recognition!

He floored it, sending his engine roaring to pull up beside the GTO. A sense of victory overwhelmed him, the giddiness of having the last move curling his lips into a smile.

Then it ended.

Uh oh.

Jason popped out of the window, "Hmmph!" he growled, launching the crystal ball with all his might.

The projectile closed in *fast*, bouncing off the hood to crash straight through windshield. It hit him square in the chest, compressing the thick layer of blubber that shielded his ribs. His wind was knocked away, his hands letting go of the steering wheel in the pain.

His truck was now a loose cannon, veering off into the grass and threatening to drive into the woods, yet he tried to fight. He caught the steering wheel and quickly yanked it to the left, an action that inadvertently sent the truck skidding further off the road. It turned sideways in the next instant, its leading wheels biting into the grass, catapulting the truck airborne, tumbling over and over.

"Oh my god!" Agatha filled with remorse. "OH MY GOD!"

Jason observed through mirror, hoping that no one had died.

"Yep, we're fugitives now." Jason kept repeating on the verge of tears. "Oh, god, we're fugitives! This was the worst idea ever!"

"Well, what should we do?" Agatha was crying hysterically by now. "Can we just pull over and talk to them?"

"What?! Are you serious?" Jason's fought paranoia. "Yeah, let's just pull over right here and so can do what, go flirt with them again? That'll work just fine. Dammit, I can't believe how stupid you are!"

"Okay, just shut up!"

The remaining bikers called off the chase, rushing in to assist their fallen comrade after the truck had finally come to rest. Now it was only the sheriff, who reappeared from the shortcut ahead of them.

"Come here, gal!" he hollered over a blaze of eighties rock music, steering the car onto a collision course. "I got ya!"

Agatha saw him, opting to slow down for maneuvering options.

A game of chicken? Yeah, this wasn't her first go-around.

She smirked, ignoring Jason's growing pleas to change course. Agatha had a plan, one that the sheriff didn't expect as he made the final approach, only to find himself outwitted but a few seconds after their merge.

It was a classic fake-out, a last moment shift to left—and then suddenly the right, all before the oncoming foe could correct. With their speed, the GTO passed the police car by the time he reacted, leaving him with little control of the spin that followed.

Luckily, he didn't crash.

"Here!" Agatha plopped a folded map onto Jason's lap. "Take a look at the map and see where the hell we are! I grabbed it at the gas station!"

He searched around as fast as he could and found Porter, Tennessee on the map.

"What's the name of this road?"

"Road 1368,' I think!"

Found it.

Jason checked the onboard compass. They were headed southwest, straight for the Georgia border.

"Find us a way out of here!" Agatha demanded.

"Just keep heading this way and make a right coming up! We'll be back on 129!"

She understood and maintained speed until she reached the intersection to turn. Once straight again, she righted her body in the seat and gripped the shifter.

"There it is!" Jason cheered. "Straight road! GO! GO!"

She had the accelerator pedal on the floor, shifting through each gear as the speed grew higher and higher. Much to its driver's dismay, the police car continued to fade into the distance behind them, but the sheriff had other means of dealing with the situation. He contemplated calling the Georgia Highway Patrol for help, but that was for losers.

Help from those guys? Screw that.

He'd catch these young assholes, even if it killed him. He had a few ex-cop buddies south of the Tennessee border anyways, and they had their connections. Those kids would head that way naturally, as the nearest interstate was a good distance away east or west.

The little city dwellers were stuck in the country, and the country was his stomping ground. He smiled, the worry easing away. Now, pleased with his own plan, he sat back and watched the GTO go. He saw his speedometer pass 120mph, but they were at least a half mile ahead, blazing toward the horizon like a bullet.

"Heck damn!" he chuckled in awe. "They're haulin' ass!"

Yes.

Yes, they were.

The wind noise grew to a deafening volume, overshadowing that of the engine. Agatha's heart pounded, her mind enraptured in the sensations of high speed. Her hands locked onto the wheel, gear six selected, the gas pedal buried to the carpet. For only a moment, she looked down at the digital speedometer.

It had stopped at 171mph.

One-hundred-seventy-one.

The raw speed tickled her gut. This was as fast as it goes.

Pursuers were nowhere to be seen in the mirrors. At some point, they entered Georgia.

They were free, for now.

-10:37AM-

The battle cry was wretched.

A million angry hornets buzzing through the hillside, a contrail of blue smoke dragging behind the tailpipe as the little car cruised. The rusty quarter panels squeaked and croaked as the dynamic load shifted side-to-side. The tires folded at will, their treads struggling on end to maintain their grip of the pavement.

Still, it was about the effort. It was about the fact that the car *tried* to be amazing, even if to most it wasn't. Personality was half the battle, which was a key point that the Honda Civic shared with its seven owners and 290,000 miles of motoring. Biff was proud of it, having restored it back to drivable condition, its little gasoline engine loud enough to grab the attention of everyone in a ten-mile radius. Noise meant everything to a machine so beyond its time, but now he needed quiet.

"Wait. Didn't I just pass this stop sign?" he asked himself.

He was lost in the middle of nowhere. Dammit.

If only he hadn't dropped his slate back in the forest—a calamity that left the screen cracked cleanly through and the GPS ruined. He had his wrist computer to pick up the slack, but something was wrong with the charging port in his car. It was shorted out, and the pungent smell of mildew serving as a stark reminder.

Maybe he should've fixed the leaky sunroof, too. Dammit.

Biff was best described as a pleasant soul. Negativity was poisonous and self-defeating, but alas, he was a human as ever. With the odds mounting against him, it was quickly growing harder and harder to dismiss. Whatever that was worth 50,000 points in the park was likely claimed by now, considering that he had seen at least thirty or so competing vehicles tearing through the countryside. Of course, none of them volunteered any help.

He was alone in this fight, but life was still good.

The air was still fresh, the breeze angelic, and the sun still glistening against the fullness of nature. So what, it was hot and humid. Sweat-soaked clothes were a factor of summer joy, part of the greatness of a season filled with life and adventure.

Huh? Was that what he thought it was?

The daydream cut short, his eyes pulled away to the rear view mirror to catch a second glimpse. Yes, a classic red Honda S2000 followed by a minivan, closing in fast and hard.

Faded paint and dented quarter panel? Check.

Slightly mis fitted front bumper? Check.

Queen City license plate atop the dashboard? Check.

Finally, an ally! Unable to contain his smile, he watched the S2000 accelerate into the opposing lane. He clutched and slid the shifter into a lower gear, preparing for a rush of hooliganism that would never transpire. Well, yes, he would surely lose any competition of speed, but that wasn't the reason he aborted the fun. Instead, it was the shock of learning that Jason wasn't driving his own car.

Finally, he made eye contact with the driver.

No. That wasn't Jason. His ride-along only confirmed it.

"Who the fu—?" he muttered to himself, clearly panicked.

The mystery driver dawned a stark smile. He revved the engine, nodding his head forward, obviously trying to goad Biff into a race.

No way.

There were two men in the minivan now directly behind him, positioned to box him in and ride close to his rear bumper. It was a ruse, the same kind he'd seen on Crime TV where the lead car stopped short and the bad guys jumped in from behind. Classic car thieves.

Feelings of fright overwhelmed him. Something was terribly wrong, and in the bluster, he went for it, gunning his engine and initially pulling away.

In a real situation, the S2000 should've come back and passed the Civic, but its mystery driver was a stick shift novice. He grinded the gears and frequently missed shifts all together, leaving him to stay back as they flew onwards.

Biff pushed as fast as he could go, blowing by rural homes and tearing through passing lanes whenever his gut saw fit. It was risky, but in his experience, instinct had never steered him wrong. Soon, he saw more buildings, more trucks, and more annoyed people. To his dismay, no one seemed inclined to help.

WELCOME TO PORTER.

There was a fork in the road, but he checked the mirror, his sweaty palms slipping against the worn leather steering wheel. The strange men pinned the old Civic as the next candidate for theft, but he'd make this one would be a bit tricky. Not today. No sir, Biff Jenkins was no helpless victim. He spun the wheel to the left, the Civic skittering onto Route 129—where he caught someone's eye.

It was game time.

1990's copstache trimmed.

Sheriff badge polished.

Aviator sunglasses cleaned.

Boots shined and primed.

Weapons safely stored and ready.

The sheriff trekked out to his cruiser, loading it with a bag full of weapons and freshly folded uniforms. Waldorf, his lifelong friend, helped him pack, still rather shaken up from crashing his truck earlier.

It was a shame, really, considering how nice the pickup was.

They stared at the mangled mess, silence leading the conference of wreckage. Still, it was a place for subtle, but well-timed humor.

"Maybe it'll buff out?" the sheriff understated.

There was damage to every body panel, the roof partially buckled, the ball joints sheared cleanly from the control arms to leave the bent front wheels flopping freely. Adding insult to the injuries, there were tree branches wedged into the grille, yet the engine remained pristine as ever.

Racecars, or in the case race*trucks*, were run on dedication.

Oh, and hope too. This would be no different than any other case he'd seen. When Waldorf didn't laugh, the sheriff caved.

"We'll rebuild it." he promised, patting Waldorf on the back. "It'll be okay, bud."

But Ford F-150 Lightnings weren't easy to come by.

"Bastards." Waldorf sneered. "I almost had em', Darwin."

"We'll get them."

"That gon' be enough for this trip, Darwin?" he asked.

"Yep." the sheriff nodded. "Shouldn't be gone too long. These kids ain't experts."

The noise interrupted them—a swarm of invading bees, growing in intensity by the second. Their bodies clenched, expecting an onrushing biblical plague or squadron of Mitsubishi Zeroes. It approached like a wall, a crescendo of opportunity, thrill, and suspense bouncing off the trees and hills behind them.

Darwin smiled. More racers. By god, today was making out to be something genuinely exciting. There, around the final bend before his home, three cars burst through the tree line, barreling down the road with fierce speed.

"What in the hell is that?" Waldorf squinted through his sunglasses. "More hoodlums?"

"Looks like it." Darwin replied, righting his sheriff hat before flinging open the driver's door. "Get in!"

Waldorf hopped in, wrestling to buckle his seatbelt. Darwin flipped on the sirens and gunned the cruiser's engine to catch up, the hairs on his back standing on end in the excitement. The hoodlums were too distracted in their own imprudence to notice the resting police car, hidden away from their view in the nearby vegetation. Biff kept his eyes on the thieves still busy trying to force him off the road.

"Hey! Esse!" the driver shouted. "Pull over! Pull over, homes!"

"Fuck off!" Biff shouted back.

He attempted to evade, swerving back and forth, knowing that his car's smaller engine couldn't outrun either pursuer. They laughed at him, pushing over into his lane with the minivan, pulling up to bump the rear end of the little Civic. The whiplash stung his neck, leaving Biff fearing for his life now, especially seeing that the men were armed with guns.

Then he looked far off into the mirror, spotting what he thought was a glimmer of flashing hope. They were fast approaching blue and red lights, a sight that lifted a load from his shoulders, his soul relieved by contact with law enforcement for the first time in his life. Maybe they were on his side this time. The thieves noticed, too, their crazy driving knocked off in an instant. Speed limits and motor vehicle laws applied again, little more than an act to play it off, but Sheriff Darwin wasn't born yesterday.

This kind of shit didn't fly in Porter, Tennessee.

He motored the cruiser up behind them at high speed, his patience for nonsense expunged roughly an hour ago. Waldorf cheered, handing his friend the microphone switched to loudspeaker mode.

"Hey!" Darwin shouted. "Hey, you three asshole vehicles! This is the Porter, Tennessee Sheriff! Pull over *now* or I will force you over under the right of the law! It is in your best interest to comply to these demands! I'm only giving *one* chance!"

Ten seconds passed with no obvious change.

"Well, I guess that's a no." Darwin shook his head. "Waldorf, my man, you might want to buckle up and hold on tight."

"Aw, shit." Waldorf groaned, anticipating the sudden swerve.

Biff hit the brakes, but the trailing minivan bumped him once more. Just when he thought the whiplash was bad, he looked in the mirror and watched the van suddenly fly off of the road and flip.

Classic PIT maneuver.

The minivan came to rest in the fields, steam pouring from its damaged radiator. The cruiser, however, was undeterred, seemingly engineering for this very action. Darwin swerved to the left of both cars and pulled alongside, showing his badge in the process. They had slowed substantially by now, allowing him plenty of space to swerve in front and slam the brakes. He stopped diagonally to block both lanes, forcing both cars to a rest.

Synchronizers grinded, the driver of the S2000 locked in a desperate attempt to select reverse. Understatement: He picked a bad day to learn to drive stick.

Darwin had already gotten out of the car, righting his rifle and aiming it fiercely. Jenkins instantly put his hands up, showing surrender, but the thieves pulled out their own weapons.

Things escalated from there.

Gunshots flooded the air, hitting the cruiser and sending Darwin and Waldorf searching for cover behind the car. Darwin was quite the marksman, quickly landing rifle rounds into the S2000's tires despite the enemy gunfire, flattening them to prohibit any further escape attempt. The thieves were well-hidden, but the rifle rounds could easily punch through the doors of the little red roadster, so making this point was a key to winning this short war of morale.

Quickly, it turned into a waiting game. Darwin's rifle held 45 rounds in one magazine, and he had only used ten. Eventually, the thieves reloaded, trying to find another way out when, suddenly, Darwin walked over towards them in the fashion of a robot. Through the mirrored reflection of his sunglasses, Darwin's index finger tickled the trigger to give them one last chance. He believed that everyone should've been given a chance to surrender, but in that progression, there was a clear red line that had already been crossed. He was an officer of the law, and despite this, these men instead chose to wield firearms and shoot at him.

Wrong choice, but he had been trying to be the better person.

"Freeze!" Darwin ordered as he continued his approach. "Don't make me fire! Drop your weapons!"

He could see their heads peeking around the rear bumper. They were obviously shaky, but otherwise noncompliant. He didn't know much Spanish, but he could recite one of the key words. "Rendirse!" he shouted clearly. "Uh, give-up-o tu armas!"

"I'm from Indiana, you racist asshole!" one of them shouted back.

"Then drop your damn weapons!"

But they didn't surrender, nor give up their weapons. In their heated debate, one of them accidentally fired a gun again in the sheriff's general direction. Darwin saw the move and dove to the ground, hearing bullets wiz over his head. During his fall, he aimed the rifle and shot through the car's metal skin, hitting the target in the kneecap. Inundated with immense pain, the guy flailed onto the ground and tossed his gun. His partner screamed, too, the mutually shared fear overwhelming him.

"I'm sorry, sir!" cried the gentleman with the shot kneecap.

"He didn't mean to shoot!" his partner wildly waved his pistol.

"I wouldn't do that!" Waldorf warned from the cruiser, having pulled his own firearm.

Darwin tried again, "Rendirse, por-favor, or I'll shoot! Drop the damn gun, for the millionth time! C'mon, man!"

"Punta!" the thief yelled in despair of his fallen friend, still waving his pistol. "He's going to die! He didn't mean to shoot!"

BANG. BANG.

He fell to the ground, grumbling now, his body convulsing as a few thousand volts of electricity peened through it. Waldorf looked at Darwin, happy that he'd saved the day.

They watched the guy flail around for a few seconds.

"Damn shame, this kid, eh?" he smirked. "That shit hurts."

"Punta?" Darwin was livid. He looked back at Waldorf and voiced his disapproval, "See what I mean? I'm out here trying my best to be the better person. Dammit, I try, you know? Giving bad men the option and second chance, but noooooo, no one takes it."

Waldorf hustled around to the other side of the car and kicked the pistol further away from the first gunman. Now immobilized and unarmed, both teary-eyed thieves were easily restrained, frisked, and stabilized on the pavement. Darwin phoned in an emergency call to the town's local ambulance service and finally released the tension broiling in his head.

"I'm sorry, sir!" the kneecap guy groaned. "I didn't mean to shoot!"

Darwin crouched down, giving him a bandage to press onto the wound, "I know." he said calmly. "I forgive you, man."

His friend stared off into space.

Afterwards, it was completely silent, but he had forgotten about something. Darwin motioned for Waldorf to check the surroundings before they realized that Jenkins was still in the other car. Confirming that the thieves were permanently out of commission, he hopped over to the S2000, diving and rolling as if he were in a battlefield. Using the cars as shelter from any more possible enemies, he finally reached the driver's door of Biff's car, popping up in front of the window and pointing his rifle inside.

"Freeze or you end up like crying like these assholes over here!"

"Okay! Okay!" Jenkins pleaded. He emphasized that his hands were in the air.

"Get out of the car!" Darwin ordered. "Keep your hands up!"

"Alright man, alright!"

Jenkins pulled the door handle slowly to make sure that nothing was misinterpreted before he stepped out foot by foot.

"Stand up!" Darwin barked with the rifle now pointing at Biff's head. He paused in deep thought as Waldorf stepped to his side.

"You gonna arrest him?"

"Yup."

Darwin suddenly shot forward, flinging Jenkins around and slamming him down onto the trunk. He clamped the handcuff onto his wrists as tight as they would go, pulled him up, and marched him to the back door of the police cruiser.

"This is some bullshit! Don't you have to read me my rights or something?" Jenkins asked as he was shoved into the back seat.

Darwin coughed and flickered his thick mustache before he suddenly perched into a completely upright stance.

"Oh!" he exclaimed. "That's right! 'You have the right to remain silent because you are now a jail prisoner of the Porter, Tennessee local police department. Anything you say or do could get your ass flung up on the rye for an ass-kickin', so I strongly advise you to keep your goddamn mouth shut, son. Capiche? You ain't done shit but speed, yet. Keep it that way. Please, for the sake of everyone here!"

"Alright, whatever. What kind of cop are you, anyway?"

Sheriff Darwin leaned into the opened window and glared at his captive. His copstache was uncomfortably thick and well-maintained, his ears pointy under the cowboy hat sitting high atop his head. Clearly, he was ex-military.

"Obviously, you didn't comprehend what I just said."

Biff, in his newfound wisdom, shut up.

Waldorf was busy tending to the wounded kid, talking to him to help ease the tension.

"You alright?" he asked.

"My knee is killing me, man!" the kid sobbed. "I swear I didn't mean to shoot at you guys. I panicked. I'm sorry. Man, I just wanted to play football, but you know, I had to like—*do* this."

"Well," Waldorf inspected the wound again, "looks like you'll have quite the limp after this, so maybe try reading a book or two instead. I tell ya', you and your buddies should probably find a more honest line of work."

The advice only made him cry more.

Waldorf turned to Darwin, who was standing silently, staring off into the distance.

"I shot a damn kid." he muttered, clearly upset. "What am I doing?"

"Your job." Waldorf answered. "They'll be alright. Sometimes we need stuff like this to change our life for the better. They seem like good kids, just caught up with the wrong people. Weren't you just talking about second chances?"

Touché.

They peered down the road at the wrecked minivan and back to the two cars stopped on the road.

"Anyone alive in the van back there? I sure hope so."

"Didn't see nobody get out."

Waldorf handed him a red delicious apple.

"Thanks." Darwin smiled and let his teeth sink in.

They paused, taking in the afternoon sun and the silken breeze. Birds chirped around them, the insects alive and buzzing in the fields. The peace revealed no one around them, but quiet days along these parts of southern Tennessee were purely normal. When they reached the wrecked minivan, they found no one inside.

"So, what are we going to do about this?" Waldorf asked.

"Call Dwight and get him to bring the tow truck out here as soon as he can. Pull that wrecked piece of shit and dump it into the woods."

"Alright."

"After we set it on fire first." Darwin shrugged. "If anyone asks, the shit blew up when it flipped. Them cars do that often, I hear. Ever play the *Grand Theft Auto* game?"

"Nope," Waldorf nodded towards Jenkins, "but what about this kid?"

"I'll put him in a holding cell and ask him some questions. You search his stupid car." Darwin sighed, looking at the thieves. "And I'll, uh, figure out what to do with these guys."

"They ain't bad kids, man."

"I know they aren't. Just caught up with the wrong people, trying to fit in. You and I, of all people, know a thing or two about that."

The ambulance pulled up and Darwin spent the rest of his time helping them prep their new patients. Unfortunately, they would have to be shipped to a hospital in Chattanooga. He had friends there to watch over them.

-11:24AM-

Sweat poured from Biff's head, the nervousness telling as he sat alone in the basement jail cell. The wait tested what little resolve he had left, the ominousness of being stuck in the boondocks ticking away with passed time.

Panic.

The odds were stacked against him, his life cut short the moment he saw the red roadster in the mirror. Now, he'd be a tidbit on the evening news, a gambit for race-baited reporting, a meme on Facebook, the helpless foster of a *Comedy Central* skit.

Damn. This went downhill quickly.

Porter, Tennessee hosted just one police station no larger than an average condo, a rather fitting quality for such a small town. There was little artificial light in the holding area, making him silently thank the heavens for the sunny summer day.

Then, he smelled the hallelujah. Sanctity.

Yes. Salvation had arrived, Waldorf and Officer Ralph carrying little boxes wrapped in foil. Darwin rushed to greet them. It felt like opening the door to an oven, the punishing heat from outdoors rushing into the lobby. Waldorf had the goods, the smell as pleasing as fine chocolate was to taste. Fried chicken and ribs, hand delivered by Nadine, the finest soul food maestro in town, if not the world.

"My god." Darwin salivated as he inspected the food.

"I swear it gets better every time I eat it." Ralph said.

And they ate like hyenas in full feast, their lips smacking loudly, the barbecue sauce and seasoning dripping onto the floor. The corn had the perfect taste bud snap, the peppers and cinnamon as empowering as cocaine.

Darwin paced as he ate, letting the Advil take set, hoping that it was enough to rid him of the headache. To him, it came down to morals.

"Find anything in the cars?" Waldorf asked him between chews.

"Sure did." Darwin smirked. "Got the kid who whooped your ass. That little red roadster is his car."

Waldorf fought between embarrassment and intrigue, his mind toiling on whether to be angry at Jason or the bubble gum machine that knocked him out. He rubbed the hickey on his head, vowing to never forget.

"We gon' get his ass?"

"Yeah," Darwin shrugged, "but the kid downstairs knows him and the girl. They're part of the same squad."

"Well how the hell do we get him to talk?"

Darwin's smile peaked. In the goodie bag from Nadine, he purposely ordered an extra 'Mr. Tasty Fried Chicken Deluxe'. The 'Spicy Hoot' sauce was included, all free of charge in the extension of generosity.

Waldorf and Officer Ralph nodded in concordance.

Darwin approached the holding cell, stopping just short of bars to let the smell marinate. It took but a few seconds for Biff's stomach to audibly groan with desire.

"So," Biff tried to play tough, "after all this illegal shit, you come down here to bribe me with fried chicken?"

"Correct." Darwin poached.

"It's because I'm black?"

Everyone laughed, except, of course, for Biff.

"No." Darwin countered, unphased. "It's because you look hungry, and you don't look like a stupid person. See, around here, anyone who turns down Nadine's chicken is an idiot. This shit is *good*."

"Oh god," Biff started to cave, "it really smells like it."

"So, what will you choose? Smart guy, or moron?"

Biff chose the chicken, which was an order of magnitude tastier than his wildest dreams. Two minutes in, he exhibited symptoms of rabies between bites. He didn't even care about the mess he made.

"I'm not a sellout!" he declared between wings.

"So, you and that red car seem to be associated with the same crew, eh?"

"Man, I really didn't do anything wrong!" Biff replied, licking the sauce from his fingertips. "I was just driving, and those assholes tried ramming me off the road!"

"You didn't answer my question about the cars."

"Man, I don't know!" Biff snapped. "Okay, the red S2000 belongs to someone I know, but I have no clue why those gangster guys were inside of it."

"I figured you two were associated. Both cars are registered to Queen City. Big city boys?"

"I guess?"

"What is," he paused to read the slate in his hand, "'United Underground'?"

"A club."

"What kind of 'club' are we talking about here?" Darwin taunted, his patience thinning faster than his hair. "You've got to be more specific. A swingers club? A poker club? A bingo club? C'mon."

Biff didn't answer. Darwin looked to Waldorf, then to Officer Ralph. In the meantime, they had spent their time toying with the captured wrist computer, reviving it with a charger before forcing Biff to override the facial recognition when it refused to unlock.

Progress!

"Appears to be some kind of street racing shindig." Waldorf deduced.

Darwin nodded and turned back to Biff, "Do you street race, son?"

"What the hell does that matter?" Biff squealed. "And on top of that, what am I even in jail for? You never read me the *correct* Miranda rights and you never told me what I'm charged with. Same with the other dude and the one kid that you shot."

Classic deflection, but Darwin was too involved in the excitement of interrogation.

"You're in jail because I say so." Darwin snipped, his voice hung with a tone implying little empathy. "Your word versus mine, as far as I can tell. Funny thing is, I can pretty much say anything I want at this point. Like I told you back in the hills, just *relax* and cooperate. There's no harm here, and we're just asking some questions."

The noisy printer finished chugging, its ancient motors whirring to spit out the completely job. Darwin retrieved the paper, eyeing it over before handing off to Biff. He looked down. It was a pixelated photo, printed in such awful resolution that Biff laughed out of instinct, if not horror.

"What's funny?" Darwin pressed.

Playing dumb was funny.

"Dude," Biff shook his head, unable to fight away the smirk, "you seriously need to upgrade your devices in here. I mean," he pointed to a large black blob with wheels, "you have to *try* to get pictures this bad."

"Funny guy." Waldorf sneered, the humor ineffective on him.

"This shit is retro, but in all seriousness, why'd you hand me this?"

It wasn't rocket science, but plausible deniability was still plausible at its core. This was a still-frame image from a police camera, Jason and Agatha recognizable inside her GTO. Though Biff was unsure why they had apparently joined forces, he surely wouldn't be the first to volunteer speculation.

"I see a blob," Biff trolled, squinting deeply to further the performance, "and a couple other blobs. Looks like someone drew this on a damn magna doodle, dawg."

Darwin hissed, still trying to be a better man, "Do you, recognize them two in that photograph?" he asked calmly. "Are those your friends?"

"I mean," Jenkins realized something was wrong, "it would be easier if you had used something better than a two-megapixel camera—"

"Look!" Waldorf slammed his fist atop the desk. "We can keep you here as long as we want, you know that? And, if the Sheriff wants, I could always put you in the center of town where I'm sure there's plenty of people that would be more than willing to rough you up a bit."

Darwin nodded, not too disagreeable to the idea.

"How's an ass-whooping sound, son?" he shrugged.

"I got rights, man!" Jenkins demanded. "I want my phone call!"

"This ain't no goddamn '*Law and Order*'! You don't get no phone call unless I say so, and right now you seem to be a person of interest in connection with two, now very wanted felons that ran through here earlier. Stole gasoline, assaulted my friends, committed vandalism, and fled from the law enforcement. Assholes even destroyed a classic truck!"

Wait. Classic truck? It was little more than a dog seeing a squirrel.

"Really?" Biff's mine refocused. "What kind?"

"F-150 Lightning." Waldorf answered, still proud of it.

Biff's voice perked, "Ooh! What year?"

"Two-thousand-one. Mickey Thompsons. VMP blower. Son-of-a-bitch would do a burnout so thick, you'd smell the rubber in Hawaii. Swear to god."

"Niiiice!" Biff grinned. "Shame it got wrecked, though."

"Waldorf!" Darwin snapped, breaking the short, but effective bond created by the tidbit. "Focus!" then he turned back to Biff. "Kid, just know that the more you answer, the more I'll be willing to let you walk out of here free."

"You're insane." Biff backed away from the bars. "Man, I didn't do *anything* but try to get help from the police when some dudes tried running me off the road!"

"Blah, blah, blah." Darwin rolled his eyes. "Well, I've now seen three of your street racer buddies in their cars roll through here just this morning. With the recklessness that y'all are displaying, I'm afraid that I'm left with no other choice but detainment, until we can figure out how to attack this problem head on."

"Three?"

"Yeah, some guy named 'Chase' blew through here earlier on a DUI charge. Took him in, gave him his phone call, and some other guy driving a Corvette came and bailed him out. Had those same 'Underground' stickers on the back window."

"What color was this Corvette?"

Darwin leaned against the bars again.

"Black, with a pair of white stripes." he smiled. "Sweet ass little car. Clean as a damn whistle and it sounded better than a porn star getting plowed."

Justin. One of the elites, but why the hell would he bail out Chase?

"Know him?" Darwin prodded.

"He's one of the 'higher up' guys, but I don't know him personally."

Good progress. Darwin was pleased, "Officer Ralph, here, is our computer whiz, but how come he can't see anything on 'United Underground'?"

Jenkins laughed and wiped the nervous sweat from his forehead,

"Obviously he's not too much of a 'whiz'. We got too many cops creeping through there, trying to bust people all the time, so it's locked out to non-members like you."

"What about this little slate computer thingy you got here? That Chase fella' had one of these things that looked identical. It had a special map on it, but I didn't think anything of it. How about you show us?"

Biff hit the power button on the bottom of the slate, smirking with a small victory once he confirmed that it didn't work.

"The battery is dead, and the screen is broken."

"Well, plug the damn thing in!"

"My charger is broken too."

Darwin looked up at Officer Ralph and sighed.

"Do we have anything that plugs into this?"

"Well, sir, it's a, uh, C-TYPE portable dock station, I believe." Ralph explained. "The problem here is that we don't have a dock here that supplies the right voltage to charge it up. I have to call around town to see if anyone's got one."

"I don't have time for that bullshit, Ralph. What other options do I have?"

"That website needs a login and password. I reckon the same stuff is on there."   ·

Darwin huffed and folded his arms, looked towards the computer, and thought deeply for a moment. He smiled again.

"Well, why don't you hop up and give us a hand at getting us access to this?" he proposed to Biff. "Maybe I can cut you a deal?"

Jenkins hesitated, but thought of the possible repercussions if he didn't cooperate. Noticing the illegal tendencies of the police, he could only imagine how rough the citizens would be.

He got up and walked towards the bars. Darwin unlocked them and opened the cell, placing a firm hold on Biff's arm before escorting him to the nearby desk that housed the computer.

"Go on," Darwin nodded, "log in for us, son."

Biff wiped the chicken residue from his hands.

His heart pounded, his mind toiling with the consequences of high treason against the Underground. The hesitation prompted Officer Ralph to get pushy, the other men growing impatient with every lost second. Finally, Biff caved, typing his login credentials to wait as the page appeared and slowly loaded. The internet service here seemed to be as primitive as the old desktop computer itself.

Warning: There is no Scene View browser installed on this machine!

//Scene View Emulator v5.4.0\\

Security update: failed. Scene View does not support Windows Vista.
Logging in using protected mode. . .
Alias: |ThunderD (G-4) [11:37am; 13 June 2037]|
The United Underground. The Secret Lair.
Please remember that during The Odyssey, the club forum will be limited to five-minute access for members not equipped with Scene View Deluxe. -Admin Team.

Time Limit = 5:00min

Finally, main forum menu appeared. Darwin took over and clicked through the site, finding various threads to browse. He identified the cars by matching alias signatures with the flashy vehicle photographs they included. Signatures appeared below every post made on the forum, and once he had found the "The Odyssey 2037" section, the clues grew warmer.

Time Limit = 2:47min

Darwin found what he needed. Scrolling through, he saw the red S2000, clicking on the profile to pull up Jason's information. Yes, this was definitely it. Agatha's profile proved equally valuable.

"So, you all are driving around the country lookin' for shit?" he asked as he browsed through the rules. "Different, uh, 'points' for these here items?"

Biff's stomach considered regifting the chicken.

He was a traitor. A boldfaced traitor.

"Can't you read?" he mumbled, hoping to stall them enough for the time limit to run out. "Says so plainly right there."

Time Limit = 0:31min

"Looks like a pretty hefty one was nearby in the Smoky National Park, eh?" Darwin laughed, looking to Waldorf as he read through some of the team Odyssey Blogs.

Now it made sense.

"Told you all them kids flying through here were up to no god damn good." Waldorf shrugged.

The countdown clicked towards zero.

Darwin printed a generic version of the item map, adding the aliases of the two felons and the other guys before the Scene View Emulator forced him to log out.

[Herotits (G-4)]

[NinjaVixen (G-4)]

[ThunderD (G-4)]

[06Bruiser (E-3)]

"Times up." Darwin hit the desk with his fist once the browser closed down. "They sure to make these websites fancy anymore, don't they?"

"It's a damn shame." Waldorf noted. "That little gal' in the GTO sure was a cutie, too."

Darwin turned to him as they walked outside to the cruiser. He loaded up his gun,

"Not so cute after she stole gas and made you crash your truck."

"Tell you what, that girl can *drive*."

"I don't need reminded. Made us look like fools. Maybe you can propose to her when we catch her."

Darwin looked to Officer Ralph, who was hovering annoyingly above them.

"Uh, what's the plan, sir?" Ralph asked.

"Simple." Darwin smiled and shoved the folded map into his pocket. "You sit here and keep patrol on the town, and we'll go get these bandits."

"You sure about this?"

102

"Well, hell, why not? Been a while since I've had something to keep me busy, aside from the town teens always causing a ruckus."

"Porter needs a sheriff willing to keep justice, uh, inside and outside of these here borders."

"Exactly." Darwin laughed. "Which is why I'm not going to let them get away with this shit. Not on my watch! Haven't had a drive-through-crook get away in fifteen years."

"Ain't breaking the record now." Waldorf chimed in as they sat down inside the cruiser's front seats.

Darwin fired up the engine and gave it a rev, switching on some heavy metal and bobbing his head to the rhythm.

"You got my cell phone number, Ralph." he smiled. "You're in charge here until we get back with the crooks."

"Yes sir!" Officer Ralph seemed honored.

"And let me know about that little slate computer thingy or that wrist device if you manage to get one of them working."

"Will do!"

The sheriff cruiser pulled out onto road, speeding off towards the horizon.

Biff was teary eyed.

- The Underground Kings –
Deluxe Edition

EPISODE FOUR

"Hunting Time"

-2:05PM-

Sheriff Darwin cruised past the Georgia border, the scavenger hunt map held tightly in his right hand. His police cruiser held steady at 90 miles-per-hour, its cruise control clearly set in a realm legal for only the law itself.

Times were great.

Old time rock blared from the stereo, the country breeze flowing through the open windows as they whizzed by semi-trucks on autopilot. Waldorf dozed off, nodding his head repeatedly before Darwin spooked him with a sudden flash of conversation.

"I don't get it!" Darwin shouted over ambiance.

Waldorf jumped, rubbing his achy head and finally opening his eyes, "Get what?"

"This 'scavenger hunt' shit." Darwin replied. "I don't understand why some of these items are located where they are. Like who in the hell put some shit out in the middle of the national park? Who has time for this?"

"Them hunts are like Easter egg hunts for little kids. They put that stuff where the kids can't find em' so it's more fun. Ain't you ever done anything like that before?"

"Not really," Darwin scratched his mustache. Memories of his childhood flashed through his mind, but nothing good arose, "but I wonder what this damn thing was if it was worth so much."

"Well, check the list! Which item is worth a bunch of points in the park that you can't find elsewhere?"

"Dammit." Darwin smacked the dashboard. "Shoulda asked that kid at the station that question!"

"Why don't you give Ralph a call and have him ask."

"Good idea."

Darwin picked up the cruiser's old-style car-mounted portable phone and dialed the Porter Police Station. It rang until the voice recorder picked up. Stunned, Darwin tried five more times with the same results.

He growled with regret, growing weary of his decision to leave the town, the phone in the cruiser began to ring. Noticing the number from the station, he answered,

"Well, do you know how to answer the damn phone, Ralph?"

Ralph sounded nervous and out of breath.

"Yes—sir."

"Well, I was driving here with Waldorf thinking about this whole 'Underground hunt' thing, and something came over my mind."

"Sir?"

"If this damn item was causing all this hooligan driving around town, what the hell was it if it was worth so damn much? What could be of any value in that forest?"

Ralph coughed a bit, but Darwin went on.

"Then, I thought I shoulda asked that Biff Jenkins kid what it was when I had him under interrogation, so I figured I'd shoot you a phone call to ask him for me."

Ralph was silent, his heavy breathing lingering on the line.

"Ralph?" Darwin seemed perplexed. "What the hell is wrong with you? Why do you sound like that? Why are you breathing so hard? Are you drunk already?"

"No—sir."

"Then, go ask that kid!"

"Uh, I can't."

"Say what?"

"I can't, sir."

"And just why-n-the hell 'can't' you ask him?"

"He's not here anymore, sir." Ralph's voice dipped. "He uh—got out."

"WHAT!"

"Now, sir—don't get mad at me."

Darwin hit the steering wheel, shouting as loudly as he could into the phone, "I left you in charge of the town for three hours, and the kid we arrested earlier today escaped from a locked holding cell? How on planet Earth does that kind of shit happen?"

"Well, he asked to use the bathroom. So, I took him out and shit, but I forgot to cuff him. Then, I got sleepy and took a nap. You know me."

"God dammit."

"Knocked out cold." Ralph continued. "I woke up and noticed that he got away."

"Shit." Darwin rubbed his head and thought for a moment. "Sneaky little bastards, those kids!"

"Yes sir, caught me completely by surprise."

"Did he take anything out of the station when he left?"

"Uh," Ralph cackled. "The hell if I know. The phone ringing woke me up."

Again, Darwin had to do the thinking. It was the staple of his entire life in Porter, the brains of the operation amid calmly minded folk content with simply living.

Biff Jenkins. He thought of every possible move the kid could've taken, but he was stumped. His hands were tied, each opportunity to gain the upper hand negated by technicality. How could he broadcast an APB if he had no real reason to arrest him? Darwin never filed an official report, which state law enforcement required in order to legally retrieve him.

Shit.

The kid was plenty smart. He'd stay light and low, making him even harder to track.

"Did he steal a car or anything to get away?" Darwin asked.

"No sir, not that I know of. I don't have any messages or any reports of stolen automobiles on the message machine."

"How long have you been knocked out Ralph? Jesus!"

"Eh," Ralph pondered, "maybe an hour or two."

Then it clicked.

"Shit!" Darwin hollered. "Check the key rack!"

"For what?"

"The keys to his *own* car, Ralph! Come on!"

Ralph put down the phone and went over to check, not seeing a single key on the rack. Ready to relay the information, he picked up the phone again,

"All the keys are gone, sir."

"Shit!" he hit the steering wheel once more. "Son-of-a-bitch is smart!"

"I'm—uh," Ralph was sad, "I'm not fully gettin' this, sir."

"He not only took the keys to his own car, Ralph, but he also took the keys to the other police cruisers too! Now you don't have a damn usable car!"

"Oh," Ralph realized that he wouldn't be able to search very well without a vehicle. "Damn, uh, sir, that *is* bad!"

"Check the impound lot and call me back! There's a cell phone in the drawer in my desk. Call me from that!"

"Yes, sir!" Ralph saluted. "Sorry, sir!"

"Oh, shut it with that sorry shit!"

"Sorry—I mean, uh, yes, sir!"

-2:19PM-

"Hey," Agatha said, clearly on the verge of sleep, "do you want to drive?"

Jason kept his answer simple and direct, "Yeah."

The GTO loped along a Georgia country road near Kennesaw, the windows down and the V-8 chugging along happily. Jason rightfully maintained the speed limit, attempting to keep attention at a minimum. By now, he and the old car were well acquainted. Its large diameter steering wheel and rather soft leather seats had lulled him into relaxation, the wind from the windows pointing out his lack of sleep. He was tired, but he stayed awake on the fading thrill and adrenaline. Still, he reveled in the face of a life that had taken a drastic upswing.

Car stolen? Meh, he was wheeling a V8 classic and there was a beautiful woman riding shotgun.

Nice.

His life was already looking up. Pretty girls, perilous danger, and fast cars. Take note that he left the felonious assault, theft, and fleeing law enforcement out of the daydream, but who cared about reality at this point? He liked the instant power, and most of all, the sounds it made, despite its collection of leaky exhaust pipes.

"You know we need to save our gasoline, right?" Agatha woke up from her nap.

"Yeah, I know?" Jason seemed thrown off. "I'm just driving."

"Well, Mr. Lead-foot, cut it out. I'm not stealing gas ever again after that mess."

"Sorry, I like how it sounds."

"Thought you were a tiny engine guy? You know, the dude who like their engines sounding like weed whackers." she smiled, her long brown hair blowing in the wind.

Jason looked away purposely. He would not be lulled by his affection for her at any cost, especially knowing her reputation. Still, he found it impossible to face the facts:

God created the heavens and the Earth.

Then, during the winning streak, he made Agatha.

"This thing isn't too bad, I guess." he said.

"Wow. Are you starting to actually like my car?" she *had* to tease him. "The guy who swears by Honda and all of its little teeny tiny hybrid engine cars, actually likes something with an eight cylinder?"

"Honestly," he smirked, "it's a really nice car. I'd never be able to afford the gasoline for it, though."

"Why do you think I only drive it once or twice a month? I can't let it sit or else it'll get angry with me."

"Your car gets 'angry'?"

"Yes. It gets jealous when I neglect to show it attention. It has feelings, you know."

"You're crazier than I originally thought."

"Aw, c'mon!" she suddenly grew loud. "Please don't sit here and try to tell me that you aren't the least bit sentimental about your stupid little red car."

"I like it a lot." Jason shrugged. "I honestly think that it was one of the best cars ever made, especially for its time."

"I'm not talking about what *Car and Driver* said about it, but I'm talking about *you* and *it* in a personal manner."

"I'm afraid I don't know what you mean."

"Yes, you do. You know that car like the back of your hand. You know its quirks, strengths, weaknesses, and most of all, you've invested a considerable amount of time and faith into it. It was an old banged up heap of shit with no engine in it when you bought it, right?"

Agatha Peters was the most amazing human being extant.

There. He finally admitted it to himself.

"Yes." Jason agreed. "I don't know. There was something about it that no one understood, but all it needed was a little time and effort. It's not a bad little car, even though everyone else hates on it. I think sometimes, a car just needs the right owner. Someone to care about it."

"See? You love the car. It's okay to admit it."

He also admitted to himself that he loved *her*.

"I'm very fond of it, yes."

"Then why are you always being a douche about everything?" Agatha rolled her eyes. "Because if what I said means anything to you, just know that I love my car too. I'm no different than you, so why pick fun at me about it?"

Jason was silenced.

Her tone softened again, "So if you could do me a favor, please try to be a little careful with my car, would you? Learn it first. It has quirks. And I like the engine, too, but being heavy on the gas pedal doesn't do much for efficiency, and we don't have an unlimited supply of fuel either. She's a very thirsty girl."

"What's its name?" Jason asked out of the blue.

"The car?"

"What else would I be talking about?"

"It's a she, and her name is 'Bernice'."

"That's worst name I've ever heard in my entire life."

"Oh my god, why do I even try to be nice to you?"

Jason ignored her.

"So, what are we going to do?" he asked. "Are we going to try and call out to somebody? Ask for help?"

"Call for help?" Agatha sat up straight and stretched. "Who would help *us*? Look around. Everyone is in this for themselves. I wouldn't trust a single person. I still can't believe my only ally is *you*."

"We don't have any money, and for all we know, we're now wanted felons!"

"Get real," she hissed, "I highly doubt those hicks even knew how to operate a radio."

"That was a sheriff at that gas station, so I'm sure he knows how to put out an APB."

"APB?"

"You haven't heard of that? 'All-points bulletin'? You hang around with a bunch of people who do illegal things all the time with cars and have never heard of an 'APB' before?"

He laughed. She scowled.

"Shut up." she sneered, folding up her arms in protest. "I just woke up, so I'm not thinking straight. How much gas do we have left?"

"Dude, what is with you and gas? I swear, if you say the word 'gas' one more time, I'm kicking you out of your own car. Swear to god."

"The hell you are!"

"Agatha, we have about a half tank." his voice recessed into a soothing, yet sarcastic tone. "This bad boy is getting like fifteen miles-per-gallon. Top notch."

"You're an asshole."

She sat up, twisting to look out in each direction.

"What are you looking for?" he asked.

"Cops." she replied non-enthusiastically. "If he put out an 'APB', he'd have Georgia cops crawling up and down these country roads."

"This is a lot of area to cover."

"Yeah, but we've been driving for hours and I have yet to see a single cop."

She was right, but why?

"I mean," Jason shrugged, "I'm not going to make fun of you, or discount your last statement—mostly because I want it to be true—but, I'll have to disagree by saying it's pretty unlikely."

"Jason." she paused, a distasteful squint plastered on her face. "I don't even know how to deal with you. You are incredibly dense and dumbfounding."

"Harsh."

"It's rare that I consider choking someone to be the best option to get the point across, but you know, I'm *really* feeling that way right now. I want to let you know that you bring really negative emotions out of me."

"Would you hate me if I said, 'me too'?"

"Yes." she smiled in an unusually genuine way. "Yes, I'd hate you."

"Good."

"Well, we need to call somebody." Agatha deducted. "Pull over here to this pay phone thing and we'll see if it works."

"I didn't even know they still have pay phones."

"Thank god the country keeps to the tradition."

Jason slowed the GTO and prepared to turn. He had to put faith in Agatha's statement about the APB, or else they would surely be recognized at a rest stop.

"I hope you're right about this cop thing." he grumbled as he turned the car off the road towards the small building.

"Either way," she reached into the back seat and retrieved a license plate, "you've been driving through the country for three hours with no plates."

"What?!"

"I took the license plates off when you went into the bathroom at the rest stop. If that sheriff put out an APB, he'd have to put it out for a black two-door, which I'm afraid would be quite common out here in the country."

She smiled. Jason did too, "I guess that was wise, but had a cop seen us driving without it, we would've been pulled over for sure."

"Good thing one didn't."

It appeared, the final location along a maze of marked directional signs with telephone emblems. The last one read "PAY PHONE," revealing one of the lone survivors of an ancient relic rarely seen outside of old movies. Alas, their hopes had come through. He found it hidden from the road, its metal stand and casing rustic and rundown.

He hid the GTO in the shade of the large trees towering over them, shutting off the engine and opening his door. His legs were tired, the big stretch admittedly welcome. Agatha followed suit, though the passenger door required a few nudges to release, evidence of a worn latch.

"Who are we going to call?" Jason asked as he helped her reinstall the license plate.

"Anyone but our parents." she answered.

"Do you remember phone numbers off the top of your head? This is going to suck because I don't remember *half* of the numbers I contact every day."

"Probably because you don't contact *anyone*."

She was right, but Jason found the comment rather rude. They stood in awkward silence.

"Okay." Agatha huffed. "You win. I don't remember any."

"Any guys you want to call up?"

"Now I know *exactly* why no one likes you."

He rolled his eyes and tried his best to think of any phone number that he could remember aside from family members. Most of them were wrong, and the same went for Agatha when she tried. Soon enough, they were running low on quarters.

"Okay, the last four quarters." Agatha sighed. "Seriously, this *has* to be a number you absolutely remember. I know you have to have at least one you remember no matter what."

"Yeah," he shook his head, "my ex-girlfriend's number."

Agatha laughed.

"Always remember those, eh?"

"Yup. What about you?"

"None worth wasting a quarter over."

Jason sat down on the curb. A few moments of silence passed until something popped into his head.

"I got one!" he sounded cheerful.

"Who?"

"Biff Jenkins. He gave me his phone number before I left."

"Are you sure you remember it?"

"Yeah, it's the weirdest and simplest number on earth." he laughed and nodded his head as he recited it. "765-4321."

"That's ridiculous." Agatha agreed. "Call him!"

The phone rang and reached the voicemail the first time. After a brief debate and a small physical altercation for the last two quarters, Jason placed a second call. This time he got through.

"Hello?—Hello?" Jenkins's voice seemed distant and hidden under the sounds of his screaming engine.

"Biff?" Jason didn't seem to be getting a response. "Biff!"

"Jason?"

"Yeah, what the hell are you doing?"

Some static and overwhelming ambient noise clouded the next few moments of conversation.

"Man, oh shit." Jenkins seemed frightened. "Oh shit."

"Biff?"

"Man, I'm a felon—I'm a goddamn felon. I escaped from a cop, stole his keys, and then stole my car from a police impound."

Jason was confused, now starting to think that Biff had gone a little crazy, "Biff, what are you talking about!?"

"Man, it's a long ass story! I can't stay on here cause they're probably tracing my cell number as we speak!"

"What? Who's tracing your number?"

"The police! I'm on the run!"

"Dude, just chill out. We need to meet up somewhere if you're up for it."

"And man, what are you doing without your car? Some gangster dudes tried running me off the road and shit in your car. I swear to god it was *your* car, man!"

"Jenkins, slow down." Jason paced. "I got car jacked by some Spanish speaking dudes back at the Smoky Mountains park. They jumped me and took my car."

"Well, those 'dudes' tried to get me, too, but I ran!" Biff gasped, clearly on the verge of tears. "Then this cop came up and shot the one dude, then arrested me. He didn't tell me the charges and shit, asked me a bunch of questions about you two, and made me log onto Underground!"

"Asked you questions about *us*? 'Us' as in me and Agatha?"

"Yeah, man, this is bullshit! I wasn't about to be hung up from a tree in that old racist ass town! I had to get out man, so I busted out, took my car from the *police impound*, and ran!"

Agatha yanked the phone from Jason and put it to her ear to listen.

"What town are you talking about?" she asked.

"The hell if I know. I don't remember, I just remember it was a sheriff."

"Well, we ransacked a town called 'Porter, Tennessee'."

"That's it! That's the name!"

"Well, where are you?" Agatha smirked at Jason as she asked the question. "Do you have your wallet?"

"Yeah. I also took the police car camera tape from his shit just in case I need to fight myself out of court." he then paused. "Wait, why?"

"Hold on. Say what?" Jason grabbed the phone back. "Repeat what you just said."

"I figured I'd need something to cover my ass with, so I took the recording from his police car camera. It was one of them little memory card things, and it shows him shooting at them gangster dudes, beating me up, and arresting me for basically nothing. That sheriff guy is a hot head, and he kept bragging about how no 'criminal' has ever gone uncaught in that shitty little town."

"So, is there more to that story?"

"Yeah, and considering that this guy prides himself in the ability to hunt down and bring justice to criminals, the funny part of the video is, he never read those gangster guys their Miranda Rights. He recited some bullshit Miranda Rights to me, right in front of the camera."

"Well, hell," Jason smiled at Agatha, "maybe we could be of good use to each other."

"Okay?" Jenkins's car started to sound rough. "Well, please explain man! I don't have oodles of time here!"

"Basically, we ran from that same crazy ass sheriff after unsuccessfully trying to steal some gas." Jason went on. "We took the gas store's security tape and ran from him. A couple of the local goons chased us, but we lost them all, including the sheriff. It seems like he's hell bent on getting people speeding through there."

"Shit man," Jenkins sounded frantic, "man if you can, come pick me up. I'm going to have to ditch my car."

"Yeah, it sounds pretty bad. Is that knocking I hear?"

"Yes. I'm uh, by mile marker 134 somewhere near," it took a moment to attempt a pronunciation, "uh, 'Oco-nee' National Forest?"

"Shit." Jason looked at Agatha. "That's like two hours away from us on these back roads."

"Well, my car is done, man!" Jenkins squealed. "I mis-shifted into second gear at like a hundred, man, just trying to run away. I blew this thing to hell. This engine won't last much longer."

"Hold on."

Jason put down the phone and covered the microphone.

"So, what do you want to do?" he asked Agatha.

"Where is he?"

"That weird 'Oconee' forest place up north where we stopped like hours ago. He's got money."

"Well, hell, do we have enough gas to make it back that way? And we've been driving for hours too. "

"Yeah, I know. It should hold out if I baby it."

"Then, let's get him. We don't really have a choice."

He put the phone to his ear again, hearing an even more frantic Jenkins shouting in the phone due to the sudden cease in response from Jason.

"Hello? Hello, man, my car is going to die!" Jenkins shouted.

"Dude," Jason sighed and rubbed his sweaty forehead. "Just find a good place to ditch that thing and stay in that forest. We'll make our way back up there."

"Okay, man, hurry the hell up. I'm wanted, dog, I'm for real."

"Yeah, see you in a couple hours."

Another ally? Only time would tell.

They hopped back into the GTO after Agatha reinstalled the license plate onto the car and headed back north towards the forest. He drove slightly above the speed limit, trying his best to stay out of the throttle to conserve what gasoline was left in the tank.

Jason had his doubts about the decision, fearing that backtracking increased the potential of further run-ins with the crazy sheriff, or worse, his friends. Pucker incidents followed.

"Cop!" Agatha was frantic.

"Shit. Shit. Shit." he groaned as they passed not one, but two cops.

Yet, there was no response. Not even a glance in their direction.

Captain Obvious delivered a message: There was no APB.

Why not?

-2:55PM-

He puked in the grass, the last remnants of his breakfast.

Disgusting, but he was free of danger—at least from the crazy cop.

Miles passed as he ran, his sprinting now reduced to a careful pace through the forests, fields, and roads of Tennessee. His broken arm ached, his battered ribs pulsing in pain with every breath, but he clutched onto a small black slate computer and kept up his jog.

They could have dogs on him, but he heard none.

Maybe it was just his paranoia, the haunting reminder that he had tried and failed to be a small class criminal, all for acceptance. Gang life wasn't his calling, clearly.

Free from the confines of town, he finally slowed his pace to barf again, all before continuing his trek until a clear sign of civilization showed. Bingo. His wrist computer had finally picked up a signal. Checking to make sure he wasn't followed, he dialed a long number and placed a call.

The phone rang twice. A man answered with a deep voice, his Spanish dialect alive with fervor, sternly questioning the boy's sudden disappearance. Yes, they had failed the initiation. Yes, they screwed up big time. Not only had they failed to steal the classic cars, they allowed the owners and key witnesses to escape without repercussion.

"¡Dime lo que pasó!" the superior repeated. "¡Dime!"

Tell me what happened! Tell me!

And the boy did, hesitantly telling the tall tale of the carjacking in the national park, the car chase for the wild man in the Civic, and the crazy sheriff shooting his fellow gang members—the last part slightly exaggerated to lessen the blow.

His superior was fuming with anger. Silence held until he spoke.

"Espera por favor." his voice had calmed.

Hold, please.

Hold? For whom?

This was one of the few times his call was transferred to the highest of the honchos.

The head of all heads.

The master of all masters.

The boss, Boss.

Yes, the idol widely known by his literal designation in the hierarchy, clearly a man that didn't take kindly to direct threats to his lovely little ring of crime.

"This better be important." Boss didn't sound very happy once the call had transferred.

There he was, the leader of the Red Devil's Mafia. The lowly kid had never spoken to the man in person. His voice was only held in the legend of folklore, the direct acknowledgments of lower-ranking members reserved for the accomplishing of impossible feats or royally screwing up. Knowing well which classification he fit (hint: #2), the kid apologized the best he could, citing that his car was flipped before he even got a chance to help out. He witnessed his buddies get shot while fleeing the scene towards the woods but fighting back would've surely spelled his death.

"Your partners die with dignity," Boss grumbled, "yet you flee like wuss?"

"But they didn't die!" said the kid. "They were taken away in the ambulance!"

"Ambulance? Where to?"

"I don't know!"

"So, why did you run? Hmm? Tell me, please."

"They would've killed me!"

"Where did this happen?" Boss inquired.

"Porter County." the kid could hardly breathe. "In Porter, Tennessee"

"Where are you now? Use the phone to get coordinates."

The gangster read the coordinates to him as Boss snapped his fingers, signaling for one of the women riding in the back seat to write down "Porter, Tennessee". There would be punishment dished for this snafu. No one failed without recourse.

Forget a jury, or better yet, a trial.

There was no habeus corpus in the Red Devils Mafia.

In a moment of drawn out silence, his mind reached a verdict.

"Boss, sir," the kid quivered with uncertainty through the hanging silence, "— I'm so sorry. I'll make it up to you, I swear to God."

"Do you know how you can make this up to me?" Boss asked with a level tone.

"No—no, sir. Please tell me. I swear. I swear, I'll do anything!"

Boss wasn't up for nonsense. Bullshit was a non-factor.

Instead he said two words and hung up. "Fuck yourself."

He was busy, having reached an important milestone seconds before the rude interruption by incompetent minions. It was time to focus, to give his best effort. Boss cracked his knuckles, wiping the sweat from his palms before shoving his hands into a pair of astute racing gloves.

The grip on the old slippery controller was necessary, for he had reached the last level of Super Mario World on the Super Nintendo. Alas, after the week it had taken to get this far, it was time for the final battle. Mario looked up at Bowser, floating in midair at the helm of his evil floating Segway.

His women watched intently, anxious to see the outcome.

"Hop your bitch ass down here, and we'll settle this!" Boss growled at his fictional nemesis.

Yes, dictators never fought fair and square. Why would Bowser leave the upper hand of his anti-gravity armor bubble? Bosses confronted adversaries from a position of power, not equal footing. Duh! He would actually have to knock Bowser out the hard way, with projectiles and ingenuity.

Lightning struck behind them, thunder clapping in the distance.

Mario squared up, in Boss' head shouting 'fuck you' to the big, ugly green turtle. Bowser flew from side to side, his grimace as telling as ever. He ducked into the bubble, tossing two mecha koopas into the mix, all apparently part of his master plan.

Boss maneuvered Mario keenly, hopping over the adversaries and knocking each one out. He held his breath, commanding Mario to grab one and hurl it into the sky towards Bower's ungainly head.

It missed.

"Shit!"

"C'mon, Boss!" one of the women cheered. "You got this!"

And he regrouped, strategizing Mario into position for another attack—this time striking Bowser clearly across the noggin. It sent him into a panic, his arms raised wildly before he swooped away off screen.

Flames fell from the heavens, yet Boss and Mario dodged the attempted immolation, finding solace at the screen's border. There, the princess shouted for help, tossing him a mushroom seemingly pulled from her ass.

Yeah, Mario somehow missed the catch.

"Shit!" Boss said again.

His gloved fingers pounded the buttons, dodging attacks ranging from more mecha koopas, to giant marbles, and finally Bowser rampaging about trying to smush Mario into a puddle. He could feel it. He was close, a mere knife edge from victory, and then it happened.

He lost, his efforts cut short when his chauffeured Cadillac Escalade suddenly hopped a curb. The jolt threw him off balance, sending his fingers pressing the wrong buttons on the controller and Mario to his doom. Out of lives, it was game over.

"God dammit!" he shouted. The car stopped.

Boss got out of the vehicle and inspected the culprit chrome wheel, which was now bent by the curb contact. He cursed at his driver, throwing his hands in the air before slapping the man across the face.

"This is the second set of twenty-twos this month!" he explained.

Men hopped out of the car behind them, clumsily filing up to check the carnage.

"Is there a problem, Boss?" the driver asked, also with a heavy accent. "Ah! Another wheel?"

"Yes! There is a huge problem, Carlos!" Boss grabbed Carlos by the neck, rotating it to point at the driver. "*Him!*"

The driver put his hands in the air and backed away in fear.

He knew what was next.

"We'll take care of it, Boss!" Carlos said before his men quickly apprehended the driver and put him in the trunk of the last car in the group.

"Carlos," Boss rubbed his head in exhaustion from the frustrating ordeal, "find me somebody who can drive my Escalade *without* grinding my twenty-twos!"

"Sure thing, boss."

There was silence, as the minions stood by.

No one wanted to volunteer at this point.

Carlos forced their hand, gesturing at his weapon for persuasion. Reluctantly, a minion got into the driver's seat and buckled in. Boss got back into the SUV and shut the door. He stared blankly at the 'game over' screen.

"It took me so long to get that far." he pouted.

"Aww, it's okay, Boss." one of the blondes rubbed his chest. "You can do it again."

"Ah, Mario." Boss accepted the failure. "Lo siento, mi hermano."

He redirected his attention back to the prior phone conversation with the minion, ordering Carlos to rehash the story. Key details of the story arose, the little roadster's owner, Jason Weathers, and the second gentleman that escaped in the Honda Civic. Both cars had the same 'Underground' sticker on the window, hinting at possible affiliation.

Together, Boss and Carlos worked their connections.

A team was dispatched to the area. The fallen minion was picked up, but he had something that would prove vital in their espionage: a slate *and* wrist computer originally collected from the S2000. For this, the youngster was spared.

"Excellent!" Boss smiled. "Tell the boy that he has almost redeemed himself."

They did.

"Carlos!" Boss peened.

"Yes, Boss?"

"Have the team start hunting them down. I want to know who these people are, and I want to know why they are expanding into *my* territory! We can't let new rivals encroach!"

"Yes, Boss!"

"Oh, and find the cop too."

Boss then hung up the phone and restarted Super Mario World.

-3:12PM-

Officer Ralph still hadn't returned the call, prompting Darwin to try again. It seemed as if no one could function without him.

"Hello, Porter, Tennessee police." Ralph answered, almost immediately after the first ring.

"Ralph!" Darwin shouted. "I thought I told you to call me back!"

"Sorry, sir, just looking up some things, sir."

"Looking up what?"

"Uh, I found some information on a break in up in the park. Some wealthy guy's cabin was reported to have been broken into. No evidence of forced entry, but the door was left hanging open. He had a 57' Vette and some other valuables there, but no one can identify what the robbers took. We can't get into contact with the owner, either."

Darwin was amused, "Oh? Is that right?"

"Yes, sir, that is right."

"Who's the owner?"

"A feller by the name of 'James Wrath'." he was pleased to announce as if it redeemed his earlier failures. "The race car driver, you know."

Darwin thought hard to associate the link. There was a key item located in that area, which explained why had seen a few fancied-up cars rolling through town to and from that direction. Then, he remembered Chase and how he had arrested him.

"Heck damn!" he shouted with glee. "Remember that 'Chase' guy that I caught doing about ninety down Main Street in one of them race cars?"

"Uh, yes—sir."

"If I recall correctly, I remember him having some kind of bag in the back of that rust bucket. I opened it up, and all I saw was a glass mold for a woman's shoe."

"Uh huh?"

"But I arrested him cause the speed limit on main street is like 35. I was only going to hold him for a few hours, but he called his buddy with that black Vette and he came and bailed him out!"

"Oh!" Ralph caught on. "I remember now!"

"Well, shit! That must've been what all them damn street racer boys was doing up in our area. Hunting for that glass shoe that was the answer to the riddle on the list."

He looked down at the map and then to the point value page before continuing, "See, that shoe was worth fifty-thousand points, which is one of the highest valued items on this list. Everyone would be hunting for it. They weren't breaking and entering, but they just had to figure out that the cabin was unlocked and that the glass slippers were hidden in there!"

"Yeah," something popped on Ralph's mind, "and sir, I got a quick question for you."

"What, Ralph?"

"When you, uh, told me to 'get rid' of that little tape recording in your cruiser, where exactly did you put that tape?"

Dammit. An overpowering sense of failure hit Darwin.

"It wasn't a tape." Darwin could feel the fail. "It was a god damn memory card that the police cruiser camera used to record. Remember when I ordered that fancy thing on the interwebs a few months ago? I put it on your desk right with the little camera machine thing. You can't miss it."

Ralph paused, remembering that his desk had been made into ruins by the escaped Biff Jenkins, "Well, uh, the guy that got out ruined my desk you see—and uhm, I don't see a memory card or tape machine 'thing' anywhere in this police station."

"WHAT!?"

"Yes, sir. I searched this whole place up and down. I remember you puttin' it down and all that, but I can't find it for shit."

"That bastard took it!"

"What's on it?"

"Oh, nothing really," Darwin was raging, "just video footage of me shooting a damn kid. You know. Not a big deal.."

"Sir, they shot at you first!"

"That doesn't matter. I could've handled it better, and I didn't exactly arrest them the way I should have." Darwin admitted. "Same with that Biff kid we took in. They were little hoodlums with them tattoos and shit on their wrists. I *hate* hoodlums. I figured I'd do the world a favor and spare their lives, but now the kid has the power to make those arrest invalid."

"How!?"

"I didn't read them their Miranda Rights."

"Well, sir, that's horseshit. Sounds like you defended yourself to me."

"That's not how a big city court judge would see it. If they saw me blasting at them boys away Rambo-style on that tape, along with not arresting them according to the rulebooks, they'd take my badge away at the *least*!"

"Oh, hell."

Darwin sat silent, so mad that he couldn't reply. He chewed his knuckles, biting down until it felt the pinch. It helped redirect his focus, the pain oddly soothing enough to help him settle down and think of the next plan. If Biff took off with the camera recordings and ruined Ralph's desk, he surely took his wrist computer. If he had his wrist computer, he'd likely call someone that he knew would be in the nearby area. Being from Queen City, which was a few hundred miles away, Darwin figured that it would be another Underground member.

"Get me the damn license plate on that black Vette that picked up Chase."

"Did we record it, sir?"

"No, but I wrote it down on my desk."

He heard some papers ruffle in the background.

"Okay, got it. It's 'C U L8TR', sir."

"Thanks."

Darwin hung up and spilled the bad news to Waldorf. After thinking for a bit, they collectively reached the decision of sending out an APB for the black Corvette. Chase had taken the bag with him once Justin picked him up, so that means the prized items were still in the car. If the crime happened in the jurisdiction of the Porter, Tennessee borders, Darwin could use his power as Sheriff to extradite them. All he had to do was claim that Waldorf was a police officer and that the crime happened on their watch.

Getting their hands on the item could possibly be a big bargaining chip for getting the tape back. If he had to do it the hard way, he didn't care. The situation had quickly escalated, now much more than a fun manhunt. It was now in the vital interest of his freedom, and his long-running career as the Porter Sheriff.

He picked up his radio and switched to the Georgia Highway State Patrol. He placed an APB for a black 2003 Corvette Z06 with Queen City license plates reading 'C U L8TR'.

It shouldn't take long to find.

-4:56PM-

On the way to Oconee Forest Park, the "low fuel" warning showed again. This time, theft was ruled out as an option. Instead, they stooped a bit lower and played a sympathy card on a nice old woman. After making up a story about needing to pick up a child left at daycare, the woman donated forty dollars to their cause.

At $6.54 per gallon, it was enough to fill the tank just over the 1/2 mark.

Jason drove as lightly as possible during the rendezvous trip, using the effort to maximize what fuel efficiency the old car could muster. It made the journey take longer, but Agatha and Jason killed the time by listening to the expansive music library linked through her wrist computer. Their musical tastes were so similar that they could sing along together. Between rap and rock, old and new, it meshed their minds, giving them solace from their immediate troubles.

For once, Agatha found herself having some genuine fun.

Honestly, it felt good. She relaxed. No implied obligation to "put out," no pressure to be pretty, no insistence that she move faster than anticipated.

"Freestyle." she randomly requested. "You're always rapping to yourself all the time, so let's hear something."

"No, thank you." Jason hissed.

"Don't be a vagina."

"I don't work well under pressure."

"Well, if you ever plan on making it big, you might want to get used to being told to freestyle."

She had a point.

Jason cleared his throat and coalesced an imaginary beat in his mind. Once he got the rhythm straightened out, he began to randomly piece together his lyrics before letting them flow. By the time he was ready to spit fire, she cut him off with a made up beat of her own. Using her mouth, she formed a surprisingly stout rhythm with a smile on her face. He couldn't tell if she was serious, yet the continuation of her beat at least implied it. To Jason, this was his moment of truth. This was the do-or-die moment that he had been preparing for.

"Psssh—psssh—pfff." she nodded to the rhythm. "Come on! Psssh—psssh—pssh—pfff."

"Ugggh, uggh," he led with a few grunts, "I'm a crook on run, takin' down fools with no gun, with the shorty on the side, like a new Bonnie n' Clyde. Uggh, yeah, I keep it real. So, tell me what's the deal? Want to stunt on me, you'll feel, the bad end of the deal, of that thing we call life. So, cross me and think twice."

Agatha's laughter interrupted his flow.

"Oh my god." she guffawed. "Is that your 'fire' that you always talk to the guys in the meat department about?"

"Yeah, I guess."

"Please, keep your day job." she *had* to pick on him. "That just made my day. 'Like a new Bonnie n' Clyde'?"

"You know what?" Jason's face reddened. "Screw you, dude. I knew you'd have something negative to say. Whatever. Just, whatever, man."

She held his hand, "Aww, Jason, did I hurt your feelings?"

"Nah. Haters will always hate." Jason shrugged. "I spit 'fire' and I know it. I don't need your confirmation."

"It wasn't that bad." she conceded. "It's just that I think that one of my civil duties is to give you shit."

She forgot to let go of his hand, riding along without notice until he abruptly pulled it away. It startled her, and she turned to see that he was flustered, even visibly disturbed. He killed the fun right there, his softened mood replaced by retreat.

"Sorry." she said.

He ignored her as they pulled into the park.

"So, where is he?" Jason finally asked after he rolled the GTO around the first circle of the forest along the automobile path. "Where's Biff?"

"I've been sitting right here with you," Agatha huffed, "and I haven't seen him either, so how the hell would I know?"

"Well, look harder. It's a beat down thirty-year-old Honda. Shouldn't be that hard to find."

"Well, you told him to hide it and didn't arrange a meeting location."

"I told him to meet us in a 'public place' in the forest."

Agatha laughed.

"What kind of public place to do you expect to be in a forest?" she asked. "A bathroom?"

"Exactly." Jason grinned and sped the car up. "Genius."

They checked all of the restrooms one by one until they reached the unit in the far northern section of the forest. Jenkins heard the GTO and ran out, waving his hands in the air, shouting joyously. Jason stopped and turned off the engine.

"Biff?" he asked while getting out. "Had a hard time finding you."

"Well, shit." Biff chuckled. "I wasn't about to sit my blown-up car out in the front of the forest for everyone to find me. So, I managed to make it back here."

"Good point."

"Nice shirt."

Jason forgot that he was wearing one of Agatha's Victoria's Secret t-shirts. She couldn't help but laugh.

"Shut up." he grunted. "It was only shirt we had available in the car, and my other one got messed up."

"So, how about that?"

"Ask the fuckboys that jacked my car." Jason rolled his eyes. "But don't mention Mexicans, or Agatha, here, might get offended."

"Is there a particular reason why you feel the need to be such a douchebag?" Agatha retorted.

"Your existence."

Biff ignored them and continued.

"Well, your car is in one piece back in the Porter impound." he told Jason. 'It might have a few bullet holes in it, though, and I'm not sure how well your transmission will work after those idiots got done with it."

"So, those guys that stole it drove it for hours *and* tried to race you?"

"Stupid, right?"

Jason saw the Honda Civic sitting behind the restroom cabin. He walked over to it, the stench of leaking oil greeting him all the while.

"Smells like it had a bad time."

"I mean, it had been burning oil for a while. The piston rings were junk from the get-go, but that valve-bending over rev was the final step."

"Will it even start?"

"It starts for a second, but if you don't keep the gas pedal floored it'll die."

"Are you going to set it on fire or something?" Agatha interrupted as she stepped closer.

Biff's expression morphed in an instant. He was in awe at the mere sight of her, admittedly a *huge* fan of her track shorts. She stood on her tall legs, her hair blowing in the wind, her body nary a square inch of imperfection.

Yeah, the rest of obvious. He remembered it all too well.

"Well, not in the forest, honey." Biff smirked. "I don't want to be responsible for a wildfire."

"Biff, it already looks and smells like the shitbox is on fire."

"Ha." Biff turned to Agatha extended his right hand. "Hello, ma'am. Nice to see you."

She scrunched up her face and kept her arms folded instead of returning the handshake. Eventually, after a period of long eye contact, she conceded.

"Hi." she said. Here came the awkwardness.

"I appreciate the rescue."

"You guys know each other?" Jason inquired.

They both said, simultaneously, "Yes."

"Sweet. No need for awkward introductions." Jason smiled, unusually happy. "This is working out rather good considering everything else! Eh?"

"Sure." she responded sarcastically. "So, where's this 'tape' that you have from the crazy cop's video camera."

"It's in the car. When I broke out of the jail, I used their computer to make like three copies of that shit. They had quite the stash of SD memory cards."

"So, it's just an SD card?"

"That's what I said, wasn't it?"

She rolled her eyes.

"Well, take all three and hide them in different places." Jason insisted. "Get a plastic bag or something and bury that stuff behind the bathroom cabin here."

"Yeah," Biff rolled his eyes, "I'll get *right* on that, captain."

"No, I'm serious. Take the other two copies and like stash them."

"One in the GTO and the other on one of us."

They stashed the memory cards and used Biff's wrist computer to view the files on the remaining card. The video could be seen and heard clearly, with the camera getting the perfect view of the shootout and Darwin's apparent assassination of the remaining gangsters.

"Damn!" Jason seemed amazed. "He did straight up blast that guy!"

"Are those the same guys that jacked your car?"

"Maybe." Jason shrugged. "I can't exactly tell by the camera and it was dark when I got jacked. Couldn't really see much."

"Oh well, let's figure out what to do with this damn car. You don't want it anymore, right? We can take those VIN plates off."

Jenkins laughed and kicked the fender.

"Nah. Like I said, it didn't cost me much." he shrugged. "Let's go drive it into that lake or whatever when it gets darker out. There aren't many people here and I haven't seen many park rangers at all."

"Sound good to you?" Jason turned to Agatha. She still had her arms folded with a frown on her face.

"I don't care." she sighed. "I guess we'll sit here and do nothing until sundown?"

Jenkins looked at his watch. They had a few hours to kill.

"Looks like it." he said.

"Sweet." Agatha sighed. "I'll just wait in the car."

She got in and slammed the door and turned up the radio. Curious to update herself on the outside world, she tried to turn on Biff's slate computer until Jason knocked on the car's fender to get her attention.

"Turn that damn radio off or you'll kill the battery."

"What about that hunk of crap Civic?"

"There's no telling that it'll even start if needed, and you've got to be quiet anyway."

"Biff," Agatha redirected her attention to his slate and its shattered screen, "do you have a charger for this thing?"

"No, honey, I forgot to steal one from the jail I escaped."

Her face dulled into a blank stare.

"For real," Biff clarified, "I was actually hoping you two had one."

"Well, there was one in my car." Jason said. "It got jacked."

Agatha loathed the time from there, as they continued to ramble about their failures and dead ends. She zoned out, distanced away from them by proxy. After a while, she fell asleep, leaving the boys to talk to themselves.

Jason froze, caught handedly in the act.

"So, man." Biff smiled as the sun set.

"So, what?" Jason kicked a few rocks.

"You like her, don't you? Someone's got a crush."

Jason scowled, "No."

"Don't lie. So, you're just gazing at her for no reason? You mean to tell me that you *haven't* enjoyed driving around with her for the past day? That's the kind of woman that'll make you sweat just by seeing her."

"She's just a stupid girl, dude." Jason shook his head. "I don't really like her."

"Are you gay?"

"No. Why the hell would you ask that?"

"I mean," Biff motioned over to Agatha who pretended to be asleep in the passenger seat, "look at *her,* dude. That shit is crazy."

"That's nice, Biff."

"If you like her, just go for it. She's a good girl, despite what you think. I've been saying that to you for months now."

"How would you know?"

"Don't judge a book by its cover. It's one of the truest things I've learned."

Jason shrugged, "Okay. I'm just saying, I don't like her. Never really have and probably never really will. Sure, she looks nice, but that only gets you part of the way, so please chill out."

"Whatever you need to tell yourself."

Jason and Biff shared a mutual laugh.

"I don't know." Jason said lowly as he straightened his hat. "Even if she *wasn't* stuck up her own pie hole, what makes you think that she'd give either one of us the slightest chance? Girls like that tend to date dumb asses with big muscles and equally swollen egotistical issues, hence her track record."

Biff stepped back, "Damn, man. Getting all technical."

"I'm just being honest. Yeah, she's incredible looking, but what else is there? Just a girl begging for attention in a car club with some old GTO that anyone else would get made fun of for."

"It's a nice car."

"Yeah, but it's probably the slowest LS engine car *ever.*" he laughed, "Tell me, if we tried signing up with an old, forgotten wannabe muscle car, we'd get laughed at every day. I mean, hell, even in 2004 when this thing was new, no one wanted it. They said it looked like a Grand Prix. Remember Pontiac? No? No one does, for a good reason. It was a fad that produced something that was great in appearance, but in the end, no one was fooled. They got the ax for a reason."

"Now, you're being a bit harsh." Jenkins shook his head. "I mean, look at the thing, it's still running strong over thirty years later. Yeah, no one cares, but does everyone have to care, or just the few that matter?"

"I think we're stepping too far into metaphorical allegories."

"Kudos for the unnecessary use of flashy vocab."

"What? An aspiring hip-hop artist can't use his expansive vocabulary provided by the public education system? Nonsense! And, we're thinking way too hard about a stupid girl and an old forgotten car."

"I never knew how judgmental you were, man." Biff shrugged. "I mean, I've heard about it, but *damn*."

Jason toiled with the realization and maybe the guilt, but he laughed, ready to lie to himself. "Everyone says I'm a douche."

"I won't go that far. You just seem like one of those people that pushes everyone away."

Jason squinted, crossing his arms in defense.

"Dude," he asked, "what are you? A therapist?"

"Nah. I'm just saying that person used to be me. Lighten up."

"I'm a realist." Jason grew more defensive. "Everyone acts happy and shit, but no one really is. I see that girl every day. I know her, and I know that everyone wants to bang her—maybe myself included—but how is she any different than the other wannabe racer girls on the site? Oh, well, maybe the fact that she's an incredible driver and mechanic, yet she pretends to be dumb."

"We all pretend to be someone we aren't."

"Damn! We are *deep* in philosophy tonight!" Jason jumped to the occasion, letting some honesty spill out in the process. "Believe me, I think she's unbelievably attractive. Like toxic attractive. Like, she's the best looking human in existence, but there's so much more than that. She's smart. She's powerful. She's *so* good at driving, I mean, dude you should've seen her blazing on that cop in Tennessee. But she doesn't let anyone see that. It's all about attention with her. The thing is, I just make sure I don't sit there and dwell on it. I know nothing good comes of that. That's what everyone else does, and that's what she wants. She feigns on that, and I'm not everyone else. I won't 'pretend' to be otherwise. I don't have time for that. I just want to do this Odyssey, but it's all messed up now. I mess up everything I touch."

"Dude, you mad?" Biff broke the tension with laughter. "Jesus, man, I'm glad you needed to get some stuff off your chest. Tell me how you *really* feel."

Jason blushed, the embarrassment setting in, "You're a troll, Biff."

"I understand what you're saying, man, but you can't judge a book by its cover."

"How do you two know each other?"

Biff kicked a few rocks, pausing to think, "Mutual friends. Why?"

"No reason."

"Uh huh, my point exactly. You got a crush."

"Who doesn't?"

"Touché."

They spent the rest of the time bullshitting about classic cars. It was a far easier and less sensitive talking point. Perhaps a dozen feet away in the car, Agatha rested against the seat cushion, fighting tears and legacy that she had wished would disappear.

Bummer.

-7:51PM-

Well, wonders never cease.

They day grew better as the sun dipped lower. Maybe it was the luck of the open road, the peeve of adventure on the horizon pushing them forward.

Darwin's phone rang, "Sheriff Loveless. Porter, Tennessee."

"Sheriff, I know this'll make you a happy man."

"Hit me!"

It was good news from the Georgia Highway State Patrol, who had diligently spotted Justin's Corvette on the highway. They pulled it over and apprehended the suspects in a local holding area in Marietta.

"You're free to extradite them if you want." they offered.

"I'm on the way!" Darwin said with glee. "Oh, and are those items I asked about in the car? Those are very important."

"Yes. We got em."

"Absolutely made my damn day!"

"We're glad to help."

Smiling, Darwin looked down at his map and realized that Marietta was roughly an hour away, near Atlanta, if he turned around now. He could cut that down to 40 minutes if he was diligent.

Waldorf woke up from his nap during the U-turn.

"Good news?"

"You bet your ass it's good news!" Darwin sounded cheerful as he headed back to the highway. "I didn't think they'd find him today, to be honest. Pretty good response time!"

"Where they at?"

The police cruiser was traveling over 100mph down Interstate 75. Eminem's most recent album blared through the stereo.

"Marietta, Georgia. It's just outside of Atlanta, and we're allowed to extradite him, as far as I know."

"What the hell are we going to do with them after we 'extradite'?"

"Who the hell knows? I'm not really worried about that."

"How far away is that?"

"Doing a hundred, maybe a half hour."

"You need your sirens for that?"

"Hell." Darwin chuckled. "Maybe I could switch em' on."

He flicked the switch, sending only the flashing strobe lights in motion. The audible sirens would grow annoying after a while.

- The Underground Kings –
Deluxe Edition

EPISODE FIVE

"Meet the Goons"

-10:02PM-

Isaac Newton was a genius, but sometimes his laws sucked.

Rolling the battered Honda grew increasingly difficult, as Jason and Biff were the only two pushing it towards the lake. The sun was gone, replaced by a boundless summer night. Stars, galaxies, and infinite space floated above them, their brilliance uninterrupted by civilization. Crickets and cicadas provided the starlight entertainment, their racket as classic as the season itself.

Humidity lingered, the dew wetting the grass and their skin, mixing with sweat to make their anguish more pronounced. The boys groaned, cursing under their breath as they pushed. Agatha smartly offered to steer, figuring that her womanly presence would get her out of the rigors of hard labor. As much as she hated pulling the woman card, sometimes it paid off, getting her free drinks, car parts, and now, it had saved her from a little strenuous work.

"This thing isn't going anywhere, guys." she leaned out of the window after the car stopped moving.

Jason and Jenkins were worn out, leaned against the back bumper panting like rabid dogs.

"Screw this, man." Jenkins couldn't catch his breath. "We're going to have to try and start it or something."

"And wake up the entire state of Georgia?"

"I'm not pushing this thing up the hill!" Jenkins shook his head wildly. "We already pushed it about a half mile down this stupid trail, man!"

"Well, you've got like another eighth mile." Agatha noted.

Jason wasn't very pleased, "You can get out and help push, too, you know?" he taunted. "At any time."

"I don't have any upper body strength." she shrugged. "I figured your boxing lessons would provide the power we needed."

"No upper body strength? No shit, because you suck at steering, too."

"Screw you, Jason!" she blurted. "It'd be nice if you'd lay off my back for once!"

Jason laughed, "Look," he stood up and walked to the driver's door, "try to turn this thing on. We'll just drive it the rest of the way."

"Should've taken the GTO with us then." Agatha rolled her eyes. "I said once we left that it was going to be a nice long walk back to it."

"Oh my god, you always have something to say!" Jason grew angry. "Would you just shut your trap and start the damn car?"

"Shut my 'trap'?" her mouth quivered as she pressed the clutch and cranked the key. The engine turned over and over, but it failed to start.

"You have to hold the gas pedal down, smarty."

She tried again, flooring the gas pedal. The engine started this time, but as soon as she released pressure, it bucked and choked out. Then, they heard movement in the distance.

"Wait, guys." Biff signaled for Agatha to stop trying to start the car. "What the hell is that?"

"Sounds like a car?" Jason listened, eventually singling out the sounds.

"I thought you said the forest closed at eight."

"It does." Biff's voice dipped.

"Cop?"

"Hell, I hope not."

They listened closer, the faint repeating booms growing clearer by second. It was a rhythm, keyed bass tones of pop music played through a shitty aftermarket stereo.

Cops didn't blast music. Crap.

Headlight beams pierced the trail, their flashy blue hue further disproving the cop theory. Then came the vehicle, its silhouette much like an alien spaceship, long, boxy, and unusually tall.

"Riced out minivan?" Biff and Jason looked at each other and said the same exact thing.

"Maybe it's a family!" Agatha denied.

"Why the hell would a family be cruising through this forest at night?"

"And alone at that. Spanish pop music?" Jason's voice held a worrisome tone. "Friends of yours, Agatha?"

Agatha wasn't amused.

"No." she answered.

"I don't know anyone that rocks that shit either." Biff shrugged, his eyes frozen in an expression of both fright and suspense.

"You got any of them gangster dudes looking for you? Specifically, gangster dudes that roll around in minivans decked out with LEDs?"

"How the hell would I know?" Biff was irked.

"I'm just asking."

The van moved quickly over the gravel road, its driver in quite the hurry. Agatha, Biff, and Jason froze to absorb the moment, their minds struggling to believe it. They weren't up for conflict, or danger. The Odyssey was the only thing they wanted so direly to return to. Maybe they underestimated the competition, silently and privately owning up to their individual misgivings along the way.

Yeah, they royally screwed up. Together, they accepted that.

The laziness of the past few hours had caught up, and as uncanny allies, now was the time to find a way out. This minivan was their last straw, their newfound adrenaline arriving to assist with the haste. Suddenly, the life in their movements returned, the crisp push of empowerment feeling like a freshly charged battery.

Their bodies were shrouded in blue, the headlights now directly on them. Spotted by the driver, the minivan changed its direction and leapt forward at full power, its electric motors whirring like a predator. It exited EV mode, its gasoline engine jumping in to piggyback full throttle.

Not good.

"Agatha."

"What!"

"Start the car."

The minivan drew closer by the second. Inside were four occupants, all male, and all on the hunt for three young kids deemed responsible for foiling their comrades. Rival gangs weren't welcome, and during territorial expansion, conflicts had to be settled quickly.

Considering this their first contact with the goons.

The Red Devils Mafia.

"Get in!" Jason ordered, his voice wrought with fear. Biff wasted no time hopping in the back, just as Jason squeezed in and shut the door.

"Start the car!"

The minivan accelerated hard toward them as the Civic's starter cranked the engine frivolously.

"Start it up! Let's go!"

"Come on!" Agatha hit the steering wheel. She was frightened now, despite her frequent dealings with physical threats.

Finally, on the third try, the engine spun to life, revving the best it could as she selected reverse and released pressure on the clutch. The Civic shot backwards down the trail, bumping along dangerously in the darkness as Agatha trying her best to keep it on the path. Again, this was her element. Her mind honed, zeroing in on the situation. The van highlighted in her consciousness, its closing rate on a clear collision course within second. She reacted and clutched, whipping the steering wheel around to spin the car while selecting first gear. The engine bucked briefly, but in her remembrance to keep the gas pedal floored, it fortunately stayed alive.

"Go! Go!" Jenkins looked out of the rear window, seeing the emotionless expressions four scary men in the tailing van. "Shit! Gangsters!"

"I can't see anything!" Agatha wailed, alternating her free hand to feel around the control binnacle. "Shit! I can't see!"

There! The headlight switch.

She turned them on, but only one worked—it alone much too dim in the pitch dark of the forest. The brights were of no help either, as Biff forgot to repair the faulty wiring.

"Just drive!" Jason tried to hold on. "Drive!"

Agatha clutched and selected second gear, accelerating the car up to speeds that turned the dirt road into a Baja 3000. None of them had the chance to buckle in, their bodies at total mercy to the conservation of momentum. Things grew downright violent as the car hopped and jolted over the terrain, throwing its unrestrained occupants around like a theme park ride from hell.

Poor little Honda. It was led through such a punishing life.

"Dammit!" Agatha wailed after she hit her head on the ceiling.

The minivan rammed the rear bumper twice before backing off. It, too, had a modified suspension and was suffering a noticeable amount of damage. Its front bumper had clipped a section of rocks and cracked, but it was obvious that the driver didn't care. He rammed Biff's car again before swerving to pull up beside it.

"Shit, man!" Biff saw them coming. "Do they have a hit out on us?"

"What did you see?" Jason couldn't believe his eyes. "Why they hell would they be after you?"

"I don't know, man! They tried to steal my car and got shot by that crazy cop! I told you that's all I saw!"

Chaos overran the conversation. Their voices overlapped.

"Who cares!" Agatha shifted gears again. "Why does your car suck so badly, Biff?"

"I told you that I blew the engine!"

"What is he doing? What is he doing, dude? These guys are insane!"

"I know that!"

"Ow, man! I keep hitting my head on the window. Can you try to *not* hit every bump?"

The van swerved and hit the passenger side door.

Bang! BANG!

"He's currently ramming us!" Jason was still sarcastic despite the turmoil. "Here he comes again!"

They felt another sharp jolt.

BANG!

"Oh, really? Get him away!"

"With what? Biff, you got any crystal balls I can throw?"

"Why the hell would I keep a crystal ball in my car?!"

"Ow!"

The little Honda hit steep dip in the road, briefly launching the car airborne. The steering wheel had a mind of its own, the rough terrain making fine control nearly impossible. Agatha did her best, futile or not.

"I can't control the car! Oh my god, I think the steering is broken!"

"Slow down!"

"Screw that!" Jenkins seemed bright. "Smoke these dudes out!"

"What?"

"The motor burns a shit load of oil and coolant! Get in front and just hold the gas and brake pedals down Smoke screen his ass!"

Excellent idea.

She checked the mirror waiting for the minivan to drop back behind her in order to miss an upcoming tree. Using both of her feet, she stomped on the gas and brake pedals, straining the critically wounded engine to the point that a cloud of smoke filled the air around the car. The fumes poured through the dashboard vents, inducing coughing spells strong enough to encourage vomiting. Their eyes watered, their throats burned, yet the pursuer nearly vanished in the engine induced smog.

The van dropped back as its driver fought to see. He opted to increase the distance between the two cars, figured he'd regroup and gain speed for another ramming attack on the side. Clever, yet his move only worked to the advantage of Agatha, who swerved left to avoid the large stone that the minivan flew into. It bounced off the rock, hopping into the air before spinning straight into the Civic's passenger side.

And there, the scene unraveled.

There was a giant crunch, the hit so hard that Jason was knocked silly. His arm and ribs burst into pain from contact with the door, the car uncontrollably yawing to the right. Agatha fought the wheel, but it was of little use. Again, Isaac Newton foretold the resultant.

Doom. Their screams erupted, each one a different tone of horror. Helpless, they watched through the cracked windshield as the car careened off of the gravel road and through a mass of trees. The front end dipped as they proceeded down the hill, plowing through anything in its way before it flew airborne and slammed down to the ground. The two front airbags hurtled out towards Agatha and Jason, hitting their faces like a wall. The mangled car continued to bounce and tumble until it finally reached a shallow pit.

Mud splashed over the remains of the hood, flying through the shattered windshield, and soaking the interior with water and dirt. Disorientation held them in place, but they came to their senses quickly.

"Owww." Jason groaned. "Everyone okay?"

"I'm still alive." Agatha grunted. "What about you, Biff?"

Jenkins held his neck. "Shit, man!"

"He's okay."

The minivan skidded to a halt, opening its sliding doors. The sound of its occupants making their way towards the hill pierced through the night air as Jason looked out the rear window, seeing two of them making their way down the hill.

"Those guys armed?"

"I figured they would've shot at us if they had the chance." Agatha saw them too. She was scared, cowering back towards the dashboard.

Breathe. Just breathe.

"Biff," Jason grabbed his hand and pulled, "let's go."

"What?"

"They're coming. Looks like we're going to have to fight them off."

"You sure they don't have guns?"

"Biff!"

He huffed and pulled himself around the back of the front seats.

"Agatha, hold my hat." Jason said as he scanned the area.

"Hold on, let me get out!"

"Stay in this car, and you don't come out unless it's for us!" Jason ordered Agatha as he climbed out of the window. Jenkins followed.

"It's sinking!" Agatha cried.

"STAY IN THE CAR!"

But instead, they would fight as one. A team. A squad.

Jason stood up, struggling to find his bearings, fighting to get his feet out of the damn mud. There was no time to plan, no means of preparation. He heard a growl, looking up to see his encroaching opponent. By now, he was used to getting beat up, but at least he'd go down swinging.

Jason Weathers was no bitch.

If he was sure of anything, that was it.

His fists curled instinctively. Hulk Mode engaged.

The first guy was coming too fast, lunging after he was within reach of his target. Biff swung at him, hitting the first time, yet missing the second due to a loss of balance in the mud. The tall and lanky attacker tried to blind side him in the temple, but Jason caught his arm.

Using his own motion against him, Jason reached around with the other hand, took a firm hold of his neck, and wrestled him until he eventually slammed his opponent's face into the rear quarter panel of the now totaled Civic. The guy fell into the mud, limited to painful groaning afterwards.

Another minion came next, landing three haphazard punches to Jason's head. Sore luck, though. Hulk mode and its adrenaline had daunting effects, notably the lack of pain recognition. His lip burst again, but the hits only angered him more. Jason stomped the guy's knee and hit him square in the face. Stunned, the minion fell into the mud.

The other minions stopped their approach.

"Aye! Aye!" shouted the bigger guy, reaching his hand out to stop his buddy. Clearly the ringleader, he had developed a backup plan in the meantime: wielding a pocketknife.

"Do you *really* want to do that?" Jason asked him. "Really?"

No, he didn't, but this fight had grown desperate. Though it started with no intent for serious harm, brash responses were great negotiation tools. Mr. Ringleader understood this, knowing that no one liked the prospect of knives nary the intended effect.

The tides of battle stabilized, both sides now under ceasefire.

He was hesitant to advance, insistent on holding his ground. The trainee minion stood behind them, still slowly creeping forward in the muck.

"He's got a knife, Jason." Jenkins said quietly, never taking his eyes off of the men.

"I can see that, but I don't think he wants to use it."

But it wasn't *his* move that broke the entente.

Unexpectedly, a fifth minion appeared from thin air—or maybe the trees—swinging away with a piece of wood that clocked Jenkins straight in the head. Jason now stood without an ally, sadly and silently preparing for a salvo of beatdown once again.

Hulk mode reengaged, marking Jason's last-ditch effort to go down giving hell. He lunged. Mr. Ringleader fell first, losing the knife in the sudden jolt of the tackle. It fell into the mud, sending the trainee scrambling for it.

Agatha screamed. Jason kicked the guy in his face. The minion fell into the mud, grabbing onto Jason's feet and yanking him off balance. He fell onto the car, once again victim to another ambush as minions buried him with punches and kicks. One of them found his way into the Civic's window, reaching in to grab Agatha.

Her voice shrieked. She backed into the other side of the interior, but he was already inside. His hands slipped on her upper torso as she slid backwards, finding grip on her shorts, pulling them down to her knees.

Instinct prevailed for her.

Juggling her legs freed her feet from the fabric constraint. Self-defense was nothing new to her, itself a skillset earned through foster hood and indifference with the world. The minion was strong, yet he was merely a man. He had the same major weakness, to which she exploited with the thriftiest power-up groin kick seen on this side of *Mortal Combat*.

It stopped him—and maybe even sterilized him, to say the least.

"Get! OFF!" she screamed, punching him as hard as she could with her puny fists.

Biff stopped counting sheep.

He rebooted, quickly getting up to help his overwhelmed friends. Powered solely by rage, he threw a minion off Jason and hammer-fisted the other's head. When the latter proved ineffective, he followed up with a full swing bitch slap. The third hit, an uppercut, finally put the guy down.

Excellent.

Seeing the commotion inside the car, Jason shifted his attention to Agatha's attacker, sliding his body through the open window and helping her inflict damage to the gangster's rancid face. His hands latched onto the guy's collar, pulling him halfway through the opening and away from Agatha. The minion never put up a fight, his throbbing gonads enough to immobilize him.

Still, Jason hit him anyways.

"You. Stupid. Asshole!" he growled between hits. "Don't. Ever. Touch. Her!"

Biff threw another guy clear over the hood, sending him tumbling into the mud on the other side of the car. He was now outnumbered, his friend halfway inside the Civic disabled by Jason's rage. Accepting defeat was the only option, looking to Jason and Biff to hear his pleas. They jumped him until he surrendered, stopping once he had curled into a ball.

Crickets returned with the peace.

Biff slumped into the mud and Jason leaned on the car. Agatha squinted, adjusting to her posture to climb out when—

"GUYS!" she screamed.

They forgot about Mr. Ringleader—the last man standing—who drew up behind Jason and locked him into a chokehold. Jason elbowed at his ribs the best he could, but he couldn't break the grip. Agatha tried to help out, but he pushed her away until a loud thud ended it once and for all.

"I think that takes care of him." she breathed heavily.

In her hands, she held the spare tire jack dutifully supplied by Honda decades ago. It was a light and rather flimsy aluminum unit, but it did the job. She stood there, gasping for air, completely covered in mud like everyone else.

Biff and Jason were stunned.

"Nice swing!" Jason wiped his mouth and laughed.

Agatha leaned onto the car's body after pulling her shorts back up.

"High school softball. Yeah, I was a beast."

"You alright, Biff?" Jason asked.

"Yeah." Biff was still filled with rage. "I'm cool. What the hell are we going to do with these wannabe gangsters?"

"Kill them." Agatha spat. "That guy yanked my shorts down!"

"Well, I think your shot to his gonads fixed that problem."

"Murder is a terrible idea." Jason shook his head. "Speaking of gangsters, we apparently have a newly risen criminal here wanting to kill people. Didn't know you were in the business of execution, Agatha."

Jenkins agreed, "I don't feel like going to jail for capital murder.

"But they attacked us!"

"Try proving that." Jason refuted. "That would take months of unnecessary agony, and none of us has the money for a lawyer."

"Okay." Agatha said. "Let's just tie these assholes up in their banged-up minivan and call the police on them. If anything, it'll give the cops something better to do than look for us."

"That's actually a great idea."

"What's up with these 'RDM' tattoos on these guys?"

"Gang identification. You've never learned anything from TV?"

"Yep," Biff sighed, "the assholes that tried to jack my car had the same tats. That sheriff was talking about it when I was locked up."

They searched the van. Agatha found a roll of duct tape. Perfect.

One of them moved. Biff lifted his head up and punched him in the face. He didn't move anymore. Biff's slate computer was still in the trunk, its screen cracked, but hopefully the innards were unharmed. Jason retrieved it and held it close for good measure.

It was the only thing keeping the hope of The Odyssey alive.

-10:32PM-

Darwin's cruiser had a bit of trouble making it through the heavy traffic towards Marietta. A multi-car accident had blocked many of the southbound lanes on Interstate 75, but police sirens fixed that annoyance with ease. Approaching the crash scene, he was stopped by a few curious Georgia patrol officers who didn't recognize the markings on the cruiser.

When they asked what the hell he was doing, Darwin simply told them. He had a prisoner that committed a crime in his jurisdiction, and he was on his way to extradite. The Georgia officers nodded and let him pass through, this time with a Georgia State Highway Patrol escort to speed up his trip. Waldorf felt important, waking up from his slumber and taking in the views of the widespan Georgia freeways as they flew by.

Finally, they arrived, pulling into the main police station at Cobb County. Darwin righted his hat, smoothed out his uniform, and opened his door. His legs were tight and cramped from the long trip. Waldorf's plump torso gave him a bit of trouble, as usual, when he went to exit, but Darwin leaned in.

"Stay here." He smiled.

"Why's that?"

"You're not 'technically' considered a police officer."

Waldorf huffed and shut the door. He hated technicalities.

"Just wait in here. I'll be back out to drive you to get another car."

"Got you." Waldorf smiled.

"Remember what we talked about on the way."

Darwin then walked into the station, locating the prisoners and positively identifying them as the suspects. The Corvette sat in the Cobb County police impound freshly doused with summer rain, the items stolen from the cabin found in the trunk of the car during the arrest.

Bingo.

Darwin filled out mounds of paperwork before he was escorted back to the holding cells to retrieve the suspects. Well, he stopped just before that. An idea popped into his head, spurred by an unshakable itch to investigate a hunch.

He turned to one of the Cobb County officers.

"You guys got facial rec?" he asked with a smile. "Would you mind looking up this girl? I'm thinking she's connected in another way to the same investigation."

"Sure!" the officer said. "What's the name?"

"Agatha Peters."

They watched as the computer paged her image with the internet database, combing through public records, social media, and every freely accessible piece of the world. Moments later, Darwin had plenty of confirmed hits.

"Whoa." the Cobb County officer blushed. "And I thought she was just a petty thief."

"Whatever floats her boat."

Darwin could get one up on her, but he wouldn't go *that* low. Instead, he combed through the printout report, finding her records and tracing the puzzle that finally confirmed his suspicions.

There, the pieces finally fit. He smiled and walked to the holding area. Cell 14E. Chase sat angrily in the corner. Justin had dozed off.

"How ya' doing there?" Darwin taunted Chase. "Happy to see me again?"

"Fuck you." he responded.

"I guess not."

The Cobb County officer opened both cells, placing the men into handcuffs and helping Darwin walk them out to his cruiser. Back on the highway, Darwin headed further south towards Atlanta.

"You got his number out of that thing yet?" Darwin asked. Waldorf searched through Jason's wrist computer that they acquired from his S2000. Apparently, the minions left it on and intact. Very unusual for carjacking.

"Kid's last name is 'Biff Jenkins,' right?" Waldorf replied. He held the contraption as if it were a tarantula. It had an unusually large foldable screen and only four buttons on the side trim.

"Yeah."

Waldorf handed Darwin the device, who read the number on the display. After a deep breath, he pressed the button on the keypad to dial it.

The network connected. It rang, and rang, and rang. . .

Voicemail. Shit.

He forced away the anger by realizing that more downtime meant more game planning. Yeah, he'd definitely need something good.

Leverage. With items they were so desperately hunting now stashed in the trunk of the cruiser, maybe he'd have a bargaining plate. If that recording ever got out to the public, Darwin knew he'd be nationally crucified for his undertakings in that gunfight. Sure, he was the arm of the law back in town, but the big cities would never understand that.

To them, cops weren't vigilantes.

Well, at least they shouldn't be.

"You going to call him or what?" Waldorf seemed confused.

"Yeah," Darwin snapped out of his trance, "I was just thinking about what I would say."

"Just be straightforward with it. No need to have a personal conversation."

"You know that Agatha girl?" Darwin said after a brief pause. "I pulled up some information on her and I'm shocked about it, both good and bad. It's a very small world, you know, Waldorf."

"I'm confused."

"I'll tell you later."

Darwin dialed the number again, but this time he got an answer.

"Hello?" an out of breath Biff answered. "Who is this?"

"Is this Biff Jenkins?" Darwin responded.

"What? Who the hell is this?"

"Son, do you remember me?"

-11:02PM-

Oh, yeah. Tension was broiling at this point.

"Who is that?" Jason asked as they continued hiking back up the trail. Biff shrugged, trying to brush the mud off of the wrist computer's display.

Agatha was still angry, defeated by her efforts to remove dried mud from her hair. She was filthy. Well, they all were.

"Ask who it is!" she demanded.

"Jason, it's your number that called."

He stopped, "Who the hell would have my phone?"

Biff put the device loudspeaker, holding it close to his face.

"I'm going to ask one more time." Biff demanded. "Who is this?"

"You know who this is. It's the Porter, Tennessee Sheriff."

Everyone paused. Their eyes widened.

"Hang up!" Jason insisted. "Just hang up!"

"What's the use of that? Dude already has the number." Agatha whispered.

"Before you hang up, I'd like to let you know of something I have that could be of great interest to you. Apparently, you all are looking for that 'high value item' out in the national park, am I right? Item #67a?"

No one responded.

"Just hang up!" Jason whispered again, lunging for the phone. Agatha took it from Jenkins, running off into the distance.

"What the hell do you want?" she asked just as Jason unintentionally tackled her to the ground during the second attempt to snatch the wrist computer.

He honestly lost balance in the sand, but that wasn't the interpretation. To prove his point of innocence, his put his hands up, but she punched him. They wrestled around for a few seconds, until he had a hold of her arms. She glared into his eyes and grunted.

"Let him talk!" she hissed between breaths. "He's got nothing on us. Remember?"

"Relax!" Biff was growing tired of them already. "Everybody chill out! We have shit to deal with!"

She stared Jason in his eyes as hers welled up with tears.

Jason let go. He pushed back up to his feet, angry. Biff stood between them, but Agatha pushed forward to square up. Yeah, this wouldn't be the first time she fist fought a guy, and it probably wouldn't be the last either.

"CHILL. OUT." Biff restrained her, but she ignored him.

"What are you going to do?" she taunted Jason, curling her fingers into fists as he retreated towards a tree. "Fight me in the mud? Come on tough guy. Is intimidating a girl your 'thing'? If you think all I'm about it attention, come get some."

"Biff," Jason shook his head, "get your girl, please."

"Agatha!" Biff said. "I swear to god, this isn't the time for your bullshit! Chill out!"

Finally, she complied. It was rare that he saw this side of her.

"Seriously." Jason looked at her, removing his hat as he leaned forward. "We're both sitting here trying to help *you* so we can get out of this collectively, and you're trying to badger *me*? This is pretty damn ironic. You know, coming from the girl who got robbed blind after being porked in the back of her car last night because she inhaled too much poonshine trying to impress some guido. Maybe you should act tough around *that* guy instead of me, but no, you're okay with being used like a rag doll as long as the guy is 'handsome'."

"What is your problem with me?" Agatha felt like crying, but she withheld. "Like, what did I ever do to *you*?"

"You quit!" Jason recoiled. "You just up and quit! We were supposed to go to the championship together with the kids, the group. Two years, Agatha. They looked up to you, and you just quit! I thought you were better than that, but I was wrong. You just abandoned those kids because you wanted attention, because that's what you do."

His eyes met hers again. In them, he could see the disparaging glare of hopelessness, the internal strife in the depth of her pupils that had widened to see in the night. He likened them to wondrously large globes, glassed over from anger and personal anguish.

It only took one look to convince him. There, Jason took a step back and held his hands up in a ceasefire position.

"*I'm* not the bad guy here!" he said. "The asshole on the other end of the phone line *is*, so please put your head on straight and think like someone more advanced than a preschooler. Come on!"

"Please," she cocked her head a bit, "drop a sweet freestyle on us to show more of your wisdom. I mean, you know so much, right? Got the keys to life. The kid with no goals, no money, no ambition, no life, no friends, and no love."

"But I loved you." was all he said.

She was stunned. It took a moment for her to process what he had admitted, "Shut up. You don't even *know* me."

"Okay," Biff sighed, "this is really awkward now."

"I thought you were my friend." he shrugged. "Both of you. That's why I'm still here, trying to figure this out."

"The only reason I even picked you up is because it would've been morally wrong to leave you walking around in the wilderness. Don't get the wrong idea."

Consider that topic covered.

Comically, after minutes of unintentional eavesdropping, Darwin spoke up, "Jesus Christ." he laughed, finding the unrequited love quite entertaining. "I called to negotiate and wound up getting a first-rate soap opera instead. You all going to fight over the phone, or should I start talking now?"

Agatha raised the wrist computer closer to her face.

"Yeah, start talking. I figure you called us for one reason."

"You'd be right there, young lady." he spoke leaving the last part of the sentence hanging as if he wanted to know her name. "You sound awfully familiar."

"As do you." she seemed to enjoy this. "Ask your pal in the truck how his chest feels. He'll be able to recall me a bit better."

"Now, now, Agatha Peters." Darwin laughed again. "Don't get *too* cocky on me."

She was startled that he knew her name. Shit.

"You're trying to bargain with a criminal? Isn't that a bad thing to do for a cop?"

"Depends on how you look at it."

"Well talk."

Darwin cleared his throat first, "I'm aware that Biff Jenkins has broken out of my jail and has taken a, uh, recording with some pretty vital information on it."

She looked up at Biff and spoke back into the phone.

"Uh huh."

"So, I'll make it simple. I'd like to retrieve that if possible, in exchange for this item that I have in my trunk. It's a glass slipper."

Agatha bit her lip. Biff was delighted, but Jason's emotion stayed neutral. Pessimism reigned with him.

"Who's to say that you actually have this item." Jason asked.

"Well, uh, judging from what I've heard lately, apparently this 'Chase Reynolds' was a good 'friend' of your little lady. I've got him in the back of my police car. I found the item with him and his friend 'Justin'."

"Oh yeah?" Agatha grew even angrier. "Let me talk to him, then."

"Fair enough." Darwin put the phone up to the rear cage in the cruiser, "Agatha would like to have a word with you."

"Agatha Peters?" Chase hollered. "Tell her to go pork herself."

Agatha winced. The judgmental glare from Jason didn't help any.

"Looks like he doesn't have much more to say." Darwin was back on the phone. "I told him I'd let him off the hook if he told me all about how he got that stuff from you, and he told me all about it. Sounded like tons of fun."

"Don't worry." she fumed. "Didn't last long."

"Oooooh!" Waldorf guffawed. "Burn!"

They could clearly hear Justin and Chase laughing in the background. She put down the phone, "This is a waste of time."

"Told you." Jason shook his head from a few yards away.

"What is the point of this, really?" Agatha talked back into the phone. "How is the exchange of that item even going to help me now that I've been wandering around with two dumb shits in the country with no map? We have less than eight hours to check into the first checkpoint, and we only have, perhaps, 4,000 points total in small items that Biff collected on his way."

"Apparently, this glass slipper is worth fifty-thousand points. Third highest of the entire list."

"Yeah, but we'd need at least two more of the ten-thousand-point items to keep us on the route to winning. Can't do that now, considering that most of the people looking for them have probably already gotten to them all."

"I can fix that."

"How?"

"I am a cop, you know?" Darwin smiled. "I can always put out an APB for all of your street racer club buddies and have the cops round them up."

"Again, what good would that do if they already have the items?"

"I could either get some of the officers to get them back for you, or I could at least give you a window of time to search without any competition. Maybe I'll throw something else special in the deal if you play nice enough."

They thought about it for a few seconds, eventually ending up at the same conclusion. Even a brief delay in the hunt could help them regain some ground.

"Uh," Jason whispered, "isn't that, like, against the rules?"

"Shhh!" Biff winked. "Let's work this."

"How could they 'get the items back'?" Agatha asked.

"I'm sure that they'll be committing crimes somewhere when they're apprehended, so that just opens the door for all that."

"I still don't have any real proof that you even have the item we're discussing."

"Want me to send you a photograph?"

"That'll work."

"Good. I'll send it when I pull off the road here soon." Darwin seemed pleased. "I'm not the kind of guy to be 'dishonest', and as you know, we've got each other by the gonads, so there's no reason to be deceitful."

"Uh huh."

"You can't go down without taking me down, and vice versa. So, let's just make this whole thing profitable for the both of us."

"Whatever." Agatha's patience had depleted. "Just send the damn picture within the next fifteen minutes. Call back after you send it and we'll talk further."

"Ha!" Darwin was happier. "You've got yourself a deal, sweet cheeks!"

The phone call ended. They got up and started walking again.

"Do you think he's bullshitting us?" Biff asked as they walked.

"No." Jason answered. "Like he said, we've got each other by the balls, and neither side can make a definite move to take down the other. He knows we want to get the item and win the hunt, and we know that he wants that video back."

"I say screw him." Agatha added. "We've got copies of it. Go get the item, run away, and mail that video to the Tennessee Capitol Building."

"Agatha, you need to chill out." Biff pointed in her face. "You're cute and all, but your little vindictive attitude ordeal is *not* going to help this whole thing out. I really don't appreciate you calling me a 'dumb shit,' either, considering that I've been nothing but nice to you. Ever."

"I'm being 'vindictive'?" Agatha seemed offended. "Yeah, I'm pissed. You want to know why? Because I just got chased off a cliff by some stupid gangsters that tried to kill me, and now I'm all covered in dried up mud in the middle of nowhere walking around in the pitch black with you stupid boys."

"Last I checked," Biff felt proud, "we were the incredible hulks that beat up those guys, you know?"

"Oh," Agata rolled her eyes, "give me a break!"

"I'll tell you what," Jason started, "let me give Chase a phone call after the crooked cop drops him off. He seems to be the type that would be *super* protective of you."

Oh, the agony of being the middleman.

Listening to these two argue would be the death of him if he didn't find a way to stop it. They were like the divorced couple he wished he'd never met. Sure, he had a headache from the car crash and fist fight, but now his ears would start bleeding any second.

Biff felt it, the billowing of his temper.

His voice deepened into the growl of a lion, his head arching back towards the sky in frustration. Finally, at the peak of his patience, he let it out. The rage. The things that should've been said.

"ARRRGH!" he slammed his fists down to his sides. "DAMMIT, WOULD BOTH OF YOU SHUT THE HELL UP!"

Jason and Agatha were too frightened to respond, each regretful that they had somehow gotten through Biff's peaceful defensive shield.

"I'm done! I'm done listening to you feud like you're arguing over joint custody in divorce court! The shit is old. It's *old*! So, stop it, or I'm bitch slapping both of you!"

"What!" Agatha was taken aback. She put her hand over her chest to dramatize the reaction. "Biff, that's no way to talk to a lady!"

"Uh huh!" he confirmed. "You too, miss. I'll slap your ass back into the 20th century if y'all don't shut the hell up!"

"Yeah," Jason followed up, "you're an independent woman of the new age, Agatha."

"God, Jason, you got some sweet jokes, bro. " she fired back. "You *always* have to have the last word, don't you? I bet your mother—"

Without warning, Agatha fell face first into the mud.

They had grown so annoying that even gravity had enough.

Following a few minutes of non-stop laughter, she got up, wrestled the hair out of her face, and scowled. Fighting the urge to smile wasn't easy, but one sprouted anyways. After a few moments of shared laughter, they continued their walk through the darkness.

"You okay, guy?" Biff toned his voice down after the boys hung back. "Everyone cool?"

"Yeah, I'm okay." Jason replied as he watched Agatha storm off ahead. "I just want to get the hell out of here and go home. Screw this stupid hunt."

"Yeah, I'm with you on that."

"Me three." Agatha agreed from ahead. Apparently, she had good hearing.

They continued until they finally reached the car. Jason took the key out of his pocket and unlocked the doors, only to be stopped by Agatha.

"Wait, wait, wait!" she shook her head. "There's *no* way we're getting in my car looking like this."

Jason stopped. Maybe she had a point.

"What do you expect us to do? Wait for the rain to wash us off?"

"That's an option, or we can find a hose or something to spray off with."

"The bathroom building has those shower stalls in it." Biff read the sign in front of the building. "Apparently it has heated water too."

"Don't they shut it off after hours though?"

"Maybe."

"I'm not taking a shower in cold water."

"Me either," Biff smiled with a conniving look, "which is exactly why I'm going first, fools!"

By the time he had finished his sentence, he had already walked into the men's shower and locked the door. Jason and Agatha beat on it with their fists.

"Open the door!"

"What the hell, Jenkins!"

"Man, I'm not taking a shower with you! Not my kind of gig, you know?"

Agatha considered it just for the hot water but changed her mind. They heard the water turn on. The women's shower door was locked.

"It's hot!" Jenkins shouted. "And they got a towel dispenser! Score!"

"Good. Then let us in!"

"Nope! I'm keeping the hot water to myself. I have to wash the annoyance off after being around both of you for too long. Give me my peace and quiet!"

-11:40PM-

Darwin stopped the car in a deserted industrial park in Mableton and turned off the engine. He got out with Waldorf and opened the back doors.

"Hi there, fellas'!" he grinned. "Looks like you two men are free to go here."

"What?" Justin couldn't believe it. "In the middle of nowhere?"

"You're in Atlanta, Georgia." Darwin unlocked his cuffs. "Take this money and wait until tomorrow to get your Corvette out."

Justin counted two hundred dollars.

"That should cover the impound fees, buy yourselves a stay at a motel, and give you enough gas money to get back to Queen City."

"Sweet."

Darwin continued, "I say give it a day because I'm going to write you two boys off for stealing that crap out of the cabin. I'll say that I had the wrong suspects and that we couldn't find any evidence to prove you're the baddies."

Justin seemed appalled.

"What?" he couldn't help but laugh. "This is by far the most illegal thing I've ever seen a cop do."

"Would you like me to turn around and take you back to Porter then? I mean, I'm sure we could at least prove Chase was there to steal the shit, and that you were an accomplice in the plan judging by that story he gave me regarding you two running off with it from that hot little girly."

Neither one of them replied, so Darwin picked up the slack as he snapped a photo of the items in the back of the police car.

"That's what I thought. So, I would just take that money, do as I say, and consider yourselves lucky that you aren't in jail over some stupid scavenger hunt."

"How the hell are we supposed to get to a motel?" Chase asked. "And where's my goddamn map?"

"Oh, you mean the 'special' map that you seem to have? Didn't find one like it on anyone else." Darwin laughed. "I'll keep it safe for you. As for the motel question, there's one about an eighth mile up the street. You two gentleman have legs. Use them."

Darwin and Waldorf got back into the car and started the engine.

"Have a safe trip!" Darwin smiled before he drove away.

"Dude," Justin was still in disbelief, "tell me that this hasn't been the craziest day of my life so far."

"Yeah," Chase smiled, "but at least we don't have to worry about charges."

"And we're still in the point lead. Is he the only one that knows about the map?"

"Agatha does, too, but it's not like anyone would believe her. I know where most of the rest of the high point items are anyways. No big deal. The cop just thinks that he's getting one over on us by being a dick."

"Okay. Well, we'll get the Vette first thing tomorrow morning, and go get some more points with Item# 88b. Considering where it is, I don't think anyone will find the damn thing on their own."

"The 'Red White and Blue' item?"

"You know it."

"Uh huh, and we probably could've gotten more points if we had arranged some way for you to join in on the festivities."

"Pssh, I've seen the videos, and I kind of wish I could have. You lucky son-of-a-bitch!"

Chase tried to be humble.

"What can I say? I'm a beast, and she's willing to do *anything* for attention."

-11:50PM-

"Okay," Agatha couldn't take it any longer, "he's been in the shower longer than I am."

"Yeah." Jason murmured. "I can *really* believe that."

"Whatever."

"Cool."

His feelings were hurt. In terms of conversation, he was prepared to give the bare minimum and nothing more. The broken slate computer provided enough distraction, as it so far refused to boot up past the manufacturer screen.

"Jason." Agatha said.

"Yeah?"

"I didn't *want* to leave the karting league." she said. "I love those kids, and I loved the joy I got working there. I didn't mean to hurt your feelings."

"That's cool."

"A few of the parents, well, they somehow found some stuff about me. Uh, I think it was one of the boys that found it. Stuff I did in the past. They said I wasn't a 'good influence' to the children."

"So, they kick you out for being a petty shoplifter and half of those kids have stolen cars or worse. Ridiculous. Such is the world. Unruly and unfair."

Who says stuff like that? Why was he so weird?

"I just figured I'd talk to you man-to-man. What you said earlier—"

Nope. There was no further discussion of the Freudian slip.

He cut her off, on purpose, "'Man-to-man'? You're a man?"

She scoffed, regretting the brief respite of hostility.

"You can't even be serious for *one* time?" she got up and stormed towards the shower door. "*One* time!"

Jason shrugged, opting to ignore her tantrum. He didn't feel like dealing with it. Not right now.

"LOGANZO!" she hollered as she beat on the door. "GET OUT SO WE CAN USE THE SHOWER!"

Suddenly, the door flew open. He was wrapped in a towel with a smile on his face, "Water's still warm, chumps."

Jason came out of nowhere and shoved him aside.

"Get out of the way." he said as he walked in, removing his shirt and shutting the door behind him, just as Agatha attempted to walk through.

"Jason!" she screamed, beating on the door. "Jason, you asshole!"

He ignored her and continued rapping in the shower.

Her heart raced. Her fingers trembled. It felt as if her head would explode at any moment, the rage threatening to undo her. She needed to calm down, as the hotheadedness had always been her biggest weakness. Years of neglect and behavioral issues stemmed in this trait, but sometimes she would get so mad that she couldn't stop. Nothing could calm her. Nothing would make it go away.

She hated it. She hated herself. She was a spiteful person.

Deep breaths. Remember the therapy. Biff was getting dressed in the distance, taking clothes from a bag he had packed for the trip. At least *he* was comfortable.

Under stress, her go-to relief was playing with her long hair. She ran her fingers through, jamming in the clumped-up mud. A towel was no help. Her anger returned, sending her racing back to the building to bang on the door more. Then, she noticed that the door wasn't locked.

"Screw it." she grunted to herself, whipping it open and walking in.

She could hear the water from the shower and feel the heat of the warm mist. Jason was in the furthest stall to the right. Figuring that she could use a shower on the other side of the room, she walked towards the one clear to the left. She undressed and turned on the shower. Finally, it was her time to relax.

At least until the warm water abandoned her.

"Dammit!" she heard Jason shout. "Biff!"

"What's the problem?" Agatha's voice burst out of seemingly nowhere.

He seemed startled, not expecting her to be inside, "Agatha?"

"Who else would it be?"

"What the hell are you doing in here?"

"I wasn't going to wait on you to use up the rest of the hot water before you came out."

"Well, congratulations. By turning on that shower, you've succeeded in using what was left of it."

He could tell that she had begun to shiver.

"Oh my god, it's cold!"

"No, really?" he was shivering uncontrollably, too, but he had almost gotten all of the mud off.

Relative silence veered over the room until Agatha spoke.

"So." she said between shivers, "are you ever going to answer me?"

"About what, Agatha?"

"About that question I asked you like five minutes ago before you ran away like a little bitch."

"You're stupid."

"Answer?"

"No." he got out of his shower stall and wrapped up in the towel as quickly as he could.

"Why not?"

"Your question, like you, is stupid." he got some water out of his ears. "I don't answer stupid questions."

She growled audibly. He could see her feet and the lower part of her legs under the stall, working furiously to clean up as fast as she could. Admiring how well-shaped her calves were was difficult to resist.

"I don't personally see how the question is stupid."

"Why are you suddenly so concerned with it, anyway?" he asked.

She finally spilled it, "Because you don't think I heard you earlier?" her voice waved. "You thought I was really sleeping, didn't you? And that you were far enough away from me to talk a bunch of shit about me without even knowing me yet?"

Shit. He knew exactly what she was talking about. His discussion with Biff, specifically about her.

"You mean when Biff kept asking me stupid questions?"

"Yeah, I guess that's what you can call it."

Jason didn't feel the need to lighten up. "Obviously you heard what I said, so what's the need to explain further?"

"I just want to hear *why*."

Her shower stopped and her towel disappeared from the stall door. Jason rolled his eyes and turned away from that direction, still choosing to stay.

"What does it matter? Seriously? Because you've never had a guy *not* like you before?"

The shower door opened, and she stepped out, wrapped in the towel, of course.

"Maybe." her hands were wrapped around her chest due to the cold. "It's kind of unusual."

"Well, I don't know really, Agatha." Jason shivered. "Maybe I just don't immediately fall penis over heels for some pretty girl in a GTO like everyone else does. I mean, I know everything in your little world always goes your way, but—"

"Hold on." Agatha growled. "Goes my 'way,' Jason? You know *nothing* about me. You think that just because you sit up in your cozy little house, borrowing gas money from your mommy and daddy to put into your stupid little car, that you can sit here and judge *me*? I mean, what's so wrong with your life? Mad because your daddy didn't buy you a new Honda instead of an old busted piece of shit one?"

"My dad is bankrupt." Jason admitted. "He got laid off two years ago and used the rest of his savings to start his own carpentry company that failed. Five months ago, he sawed through his hand trying to revive said company and racked up over eighty grand in medical bills because it costs ridiculous amounts of money to stay alive in America. My mom smokes so heavily that they fight constantly about it. Our house is about to be foreclosed on, and everything inside the house is going to be repossessed if we don't figure something out. I'm never good enough for them, no matter what I try, and my car is the only thing that I have successfully completed from start to finish. For some reason, maybe through blind hope, I thought that competing in this stupid scavenger hunt might help. I thought that maybe, just maybe, if I could win, I could fix everything. But no, I failed, again. I fail at everything I try."

Biff entered, ready to slap them both and follow up on the earlier threat to do so at the recurrence of their feud. There was a pause until Agatha finally worked up the courage to speak.

"Okay." she began. "My adoptive parents hate me. Before I left on this 'trip,' my 'mother' threatened to kick me out, saying that if I left, I would return home with all of my belongings in the front yard. So, of course, I told her that I hated her and left. So, yeah, not exactly a good way to part with the people that rescued me from a foster home after both of my parents died with no next of kin in the United States. My dad died in that stupid Afghanistan War nineteen years ago, and my mom died from complications after giving birth to me. I was an orphan until they finally found someone ballsy enough to put up with me at age thirteen, and I've strategically screwed that up over the years. The only thing I have of my dad's is a flag that he carried in his pocket, and a Pontiac GTO, you know, that car that you said is so 'stupid,' which was left sitting in a storage facility for over a decade, until I got a random note about it in the mail. Maybe I need to fix some things in my life, so I figured coming here would be a grand trip of solitude with nothing but dad's car and his flag in the glove box. Everything doesn't go my way. It rarely does."

There was silence until Jason spoke, "So what about you, Biff?"

"What?" Biff recanted. "How about a healthy dose of 'none of your business'?"

"That's not fair, dude."

"Fair?" Biff twanged, "I'm not obligated to participate in this session of Dr. Phil. I'm just ready to bitch slap the both of you. Can't say you weren't warned. This is annoying, but I'm glad you two are finally coming clean with other to make amends."

"At least I'm no longer the token douchebag of the group now."

"Douchebag'?" Biff chuckled. "No, that's not me. I just don't like getting into competitions to see who has the saddest sob story to get pity, but okay, since I want to resist being labeled a 'douchebag,' I'll summarize."

"Go ahead." Agatha said. "Everyone else has shared in this 'constructive bonding'."

"I'm in nursing school." Biff shrugged. "Yes, I want to be a nurse. I have a little brother. He's ten, and he's at the babysitter's house. I don't know who my dad is. I've never met him, and he doesn't seem to care to meet me either. Same with my mom. We were raised by my grandpa, who is currently bed ridden at the hand of stage four terminal cancer. They could prolong his life by giving him some experimental treatment, but it costs forty-thousand dollars. I told him to get the treatment, but he disagreed and instead locked the last of his money into an account that will only disperse to pay my brother's and my own tuition. I sat down for a year, studying the strategies and tactics of the winning Odyssey teams, trying to find a way to get it on my own, so I thought that doing it might— I don't know, I guess I thought I'd figured it out. But I didn't fail. Not yet. This is the only the beginning. Every time I've been pushed down, and that's been a lot, I've always gotten back up."

There was more silence.

"See?" Biff's voice echoed on the walls of the dark room. "This is constructive, but all I'm hearing is a bunch of sorry and sappy bullshit. So what, Jason, you failed at 'everything' you've tried, but only because you don't have the courage to finish it. See, what I've always seen from you was the kid that never took no for an answer, the kid that kept driving even when people told him that he couldn't. Your parents love you, dude, and they only want the best for you. Same for you, Agatha, and you aren't even their biological child, but both of you are too damn stupid to realize it! Either way, like I said before, we haven't failed yet. I'm sick of everyone arguing, and because we're sitting here loathing in self-pity, we *will* fail unless you two shut the hell up and get with the game. This is your last warning, for real, or else the bitch slappage with ensue!"

"I guess you have a point." Jason shrugged. "So, what's the plan?"

"We merge teams at the first stage checkpoint and gather up some small point items on the way to Atlanta tomorrow. My car is trash, but I had about 5,000 points worth of items in the trunk. It's old and relatively original, so I should get a bonus. I put them in the bag that I carried with me back to Agatha's car."

"That doesn't give us much of a lead in this whole ordeal."

"Yeah," Agatha chimed in, "but it's better than nothing. What do we have to lose? We have one semi-working slate, and we're meeting the cop to get the glass slipper back in the morning."

"*Now* you're talking." Biff smiled and walked out of the room.

Jason followed, and Agatha came out last. He had washed his jeans the best he could in the shower, freeing them of mud and dirt, but they were still wet. They would have to air dry over the next hour or so in the breeze, so he could only wear a towel and pair of clean boxers that he borrowed from Biff.

The tied up gangsters were alive, but pain-ridden. Just in case, they took the keys to their van after unplugging the main power source.

"Sit tight, guys." Agatha told them. "We'll have the cops pick you up in the morning."

"But I have to pee!" cried Mr. Ringleader.

"Sucks, bro. Looks like you'll have to piss your pants."

Piling into the GTO, they were finally able to get some rest for the night. At first they wondered if any more gangsters were on the way, but then an hour passed. Jenkins tried his best to get comfortable in the small back seat, fidgeting around and complaining about the lack of room until Jason moved his seat all the way up.

He looked over at Agatha, who had taken a tank top and pair of shorts from her trunk and put them on. Her hair, still wet, was beginning to curl like it did naturally. He noticed her breasts bunched up beneath her folded arms and ran his eyes along the lines of her cleavage before he looked away. When he sniffed and adjusted his position, he looked up at her, seeing her eyes punching through his face like lasers.

Caught in the act of boobage scoping. Dammit.

"Do you want me to just pull them out for you?" she asked with a sharp twinge in her voice. "Would that make you feel better?"

Yes. "No." he said. There was no use in playing it off. Jason held her glare, knowing she wanted to end him.

"Grow up, Jason."

"My bad." was all he said.

"Whatever." she turned over, smiling a little to herself once her back faced him. "Goodnight."

Maybe he had hurt her feelings, but maybe it was time that she experienced something different than what he thought she was used to.

Speaking of "maybes," maybe he needed to call his parents.

Maybe later.

- The Underground Kings –
Deluxe Edition

EPISODE SIX

"Cops and Robbers"

Day#3:
Sunday June 14th, 2037.
-8:00AM-

A new day, a new hope.

Darwin called it a night at a local Atlanta hotel, waiting for the dawn to grant him the light to continue. After submitting an APB for every Underground contestant, he ventured off to sleep. He was vivid dreamer, so much in fact that he looked forward to what his imagination would bring him night after night. Some men dreamt about cars, beautiful women, money, and fame, yet here he was, now in a world filled with Georgia cops' sirens blazing, snatching up modified classics in masse, swarming any runners, and tazing non-compliers.

It was a glorious dream. He awoke with joyful tears, reaching over to turn on his radio that was beaming with reports by now.

Yes. Tons of moving violations. Out of state classic vehicles. All of them adorned with various decals and decked out with special electronic equipment designed to evade authorities.

Darwin had created a gold mine.

He got up, readying himself with a shower and the ritualistic ironing of his uniform. After cleaning his 9MM pistols and beloved AR-15 rifle, he reloaded their ammunition magazines and got dressed. His thick and pointy mustache was trimmed, and his face was carefully shaved. Sheriff Darwin was done with his morning agenda just as the sun began to peek over the tree line.

The Atlanta News broadcasted the typical stuff: homicides, sports, weather forecasts, and traffic reports. Most of it was gibberish, but the weather was good: low nineties and humid, with a chance of some thunderstorms throughout the day. The seven-day future forecast had similar characteristics.

"Perfect summer forecast." Darwin said before he shut off the television. He walked outside, carrying his belongings and putting them in the back of the police cruiser.

Waldorf was down in the lobby eating breakfast, munching away at some bagels.

"Morning." he grinned before gulping down some orange juice.

"Morning'." Darwin grabbed a cup and filled it with coffee, adding the proper amount of cream and sugar to the mix before he sat down.

"What's on the chopping block for the day?" Waldorf asked.

"Just what n' the hell do you think?" Darwin sipped. "Catching up with these kids, getting my video back and going back home."

"Just asking."

"Yep, the news says they've got Atlanta cops crawling around this area looking for the Underground guys."

"Guess that APB worked, eh?"

"Yeah, just told them a little about what we knew. They didn't need to know much more, but apparently they've gotten a few of the contestants."

"What about the broad in the GTO?"

"They're smart, and they probably know about it anyways. Those old street racing gangs have great means of communication."

"So, I take it they called?"

"Yep, last night." Darwin liked his coffee. "They said the stuff looks authentic and all that, but we haven't discussed the 'meeting spot' yet."

"Does it matter where we meet?"

"Not really, but I was thinking about something." Darwin pulled out the folded item map from his pocket.

Waldorf looked down at it, "Yeah?"

"See this here?" Darwin pointed to a location in the downtown in the area. "It's a thirty-thousand-point item."

Item# 87b: Stars and Stripes, in harmony with the highest of heights. How daring are you, for the red-white-and blue?

"What's with this riddle shit, though?"

"Simple." Darwin laughed. "It's the American flag, dummy, but this time it's a glass prism flag. See, I was maybe going to try helping them by rounding up a few of the lesser point items myself, but this will probably solidify the deal."

"Yeah, but can't you just buy one of them prism flag things at a Dealmart or something?"

"Uh huh, but it seems as if they're referring to one that you can't exactly buy. The location is smack-dab downtown."

There was a pause, mostly because Waldorf didn't get it. Darwin sighed and decided to just spill the answer, "It's atop a goddamn skyscraper, Waldorf."

"But which one?"

"Looked up a few, and my guess would be the tallest." he unfolded another sheet of paper and sat it down on the table. "The Bank of America Tower. For that contest, they probably have it hidden in the sky lobby, according to that secret map that Chase Reynolds had in his pocket. It points straight to this area.

Waldorf seemed confused.

"But that building is like a thousand feet tall."

"One thousand twenty-three to be exact." Darwin leaned back and took another sip of coffee. "It was closed yesterday due to high winds from the storms that blew through, and none of those Underground hoodlums would likely be stupid enough to get on the top of that thing with 80mph winds whipping around them."

"True."

"And the building sky deck doesn't open today for visitors until around 10:30, and they were saying on the news that some of the windows were damaged off by the severe storms yesterday. They'll repair the ones up there before it opens, and I got a buddy that works for the Atlanta PD. Maybe we can get our hands on this glass flag, so they'll give up this stupid tape."

"But how will we get into the building?"

Darwin shrugged.

"I know a guy."

"I assume we're meeting em' there?"

"Uh huh, in about an hour or so, but you take that rental car. I'll take the cruiser."

"For what?"

"Gotta talk to a guy in building security that's going to get us the prism flag before the place opens."

Waldorf smiled, "Good deal."

But the deal only got better.

-9:39PM-

They were on the road again, headed south. The first checkpoint loomed closer and closer. All they needed was to reach the city.

Offramps increased in frequency, as with the density of traffic.

Exit 255 - Paces Ferry Rd.

Exit 254 - Moores Mill Rd.

Biff's wrist computer, which had been synced into the stereo of the car, made a sudden but surprising announcement:

"Approaching: city limits of Atlanta, Georgia! Welcome!"

Times were great now, the gas tank filled with cash recovered from Biff's tenure at the police station. Jason wound up back at the helm, Agatha at shotgun and Biff in the backseat. Both were asleep, leaving Jason to fend for himself, but again he was stricken with an undulating love for the classic car. Finally, with some peace and serenity, he was able to free his mind from the worries back home just enough to take in the scenery.

While this plan was pretty ridiculous, maybe it would work. The mafioso seemed to be more of a worry for him now. Logic agreed: If minions were sent to the park after them or Biff for some reason, more would likely to show up again, especially after the cop calling trick, leading law enforcement to their buddies tied up in their van.

Oh, hell. Speaking of vans.

He checked the mirror once more, just to confirm. No, his eyes weren't lying. In the distance behind them, he noticed a peculiar minivan of the same make and model as the one they encountered last night. The vehicle itself wasn't unusual—the prime type for every young soccer mom—but this particular example had been in the same position for the past hour. Occasionally, it would switch lanes when a slower car got in front of it, but for the most part it stayed put.

"Agatha." Jason shook her with his right arm. "Agatha, get up."

"Mmmph." she grunted. "What do you want?"

"Check your mirror. White Toyota minivan, far right lane."

She saw it, "What about it?"

"It's been back there for about an hour. Can you see who's inside clearly?"

"Tinted windows."

"The windshield isn't tinted." Jason hissed. "Is it just my eyes seeing two big dudes in the front seats wearing chains?"

"It's a minivan sitting on twenty-fours and we're in Atlanta, Georgia." she shrugged. "What's significant about any of that?"

"Sweet joke."

He slowed the GTO down to fifty miles per hour, allowing the bulk of traffic to pass him, their autopilots adjusting to keep the flow of traffic moving steadily. Some cars honked at the sudden reduction in speed, but the man in question was gaining ground. Its driver had just begun speaking into a wrist computer, but his eyes were locked onto the black coupe. Jason gulped.

"Wonder who he's calling."

"His baby momma'?"

"You a racist or something?" Biff suddenly chimed in. "And just to think, yesterday you were whining about the Latino jokes."

"I'm riding around in my car with a token black guy and a wannabe rapper that I hardly know, with no underwear, and nothing on but a tank top and a pair of old shorts because the rest of my clothes are completely ruined or stolen. I haven't been assaulted, killed, or sent into prostitution, and *I'm* the racist?"

Jenkins shrugged and laughed, scoping down Agatha's body that was stretched out in the passenger seat,

"You look nice by, the way."

"This is just temporary until I can get a pair of shorts without mud on them, but thanks, Biff. At least *someone* can be nice."

Jason chimed, "You look like a floor manager from Skanks-R'-Us, Agatha."

"You're about to get punched."

"You mad."

⸺

Boss was finally at his hotel just off the beach, relaxing through the nice back massage given by one of his many female confidantes.

Life was great. This is what he worked hard for.

Then his wrist computer rang. He didn't bother moving, mostly because he had his gangsters for that. Disturbances were unwelcome, but not entirely uncommon in this profession—evidenced by his annoyance at *fifth* ring of the phone, the last straw where he had to raise his voice.

"Carlos!" he hollered with veins bulging in his forehead. "Get the phone!"

Carlos was startled awake from his nap, hustling over to the cordless telephone. He answered, speaking in Spanish to the person on the other line.

"Boss." he said informatively. "They've got the black kid and his gangbanger homies on the highway. Black Pontiac GTO, same as our guys described in the park!"

"Give me the phone!"

Carlos obeyed, and Boss snatched the phone, acting as if the entire ordeal was a big bother to him. Patience was never one of his strong suits.

"Why are they on the highway?"

"I don't know, Boss. My guess is maybe they are headed somewhere."

Boss rubbed his thumbs against his forehead in circles, pressing inward against his skull to force the steam from his ears. Through the tension release, he let out a huge sigh, "No shit! But they should've been taken care of last night! I sent the boys after them in the park! What happened with that, Carlos?"

Then he was told that the 'boys' had been beaten up, tied up, and thrown into their wrecked minivan for the police to find. Boss found himself perplexed than angered, not knowing how the five men couldn't apprehend one kid.

When he asked how that could've happened, he got the answer.

"Apparently, he's got help."

"Help?" Boss sat up. "Help from who?"

"Don't know, but the news reports said that the boys got beat down. Yeah, Boss, they were beat up pretty damn bad."

"Who do you think this could be?"

"Looks like some karate kid gangbanger homies. The same ones in this black coupe."

"Well, take care of them!" Boss laid back down. "But stay on the line. I want to hear these puntas go down."

"Yes, Boss."

He put the phone on loudspeaker and relayed the orders.

"Take them out now."

—

"Looks like those guys are coming faster." Biff noted as he looked out of the rear window. "That van definitely isn't on autopilot."

"Yeah." Jason gave the GTO a bit more throttle. "I can see that."

"Coming pretty fast."

Finally, it happened. The minivan cut over into the left lane, accelerating at full throttle to close the distance. Once parallel to the GTO, it slowed, now directly beside them. Jason tightened his grip on the shifter and placed his foot over the clutch pedal. He wanted to be sure he was ready for anything, even if it was just a false alarm.

But it wasn't.

The van's heavily tinted window rolled down, revealing two minions of identical phenotype. Jason, Agatha, and Biff locked eyes with them. Then, out of the blue, one of the men brandished a pistol and pointed it in their direction.

Yeah, that was the final straw.

Agatha gasped. Jenkins squealed. Jason stomped the brake pedal, locking the GTO's tires and causing the SUV to overshoot its target.

Then, he released, grabbing second gear and stomping the throttle pedal to the carpet. The V-8 woke up immediately, roaring as if its bite matched its punch.

"Whoa!" Agatha held onto the door panel as the car swerved across the highway, ducking the van that attempted to meet it. "Look out!"

The van shimmied and bucked, a minion's entire upper torso outside the passenger side window, trying his best to get a clear shot. Tough luck, though, as the opportunity never showed thanks to Jason. In anticipation, he wheeled the GTO into the van's blind spot, and prepared to rocket past once he was clear.

In the midst, the van took the center lane, veering from side to side.

"Biff!" Jason shouted as he tried to anticipate the van's next move. "Are these some more of those gang dudes?"

"I think that's pretty safe to assume." Jenkins wrestled to get his seatbelt on.

"What the hell did you do to them?"

"*Me?*" Jenkins yipped. "You asshole, it's what *we* did to them. Did you forget whooping up an entire crew and calling the cops? I'd say that they're a little angry."

They played a game of highway lane chicken, the van using its size to bully the smaller Pontiac away from passing. Still, there were ways to handle this, as enough *Grand Theft Auto* video games had trained Jason very well in the art of vehicular evasion. Jason set up an old-fashioned dupe, swerving left, waiting for the minivan to do the same, all before suddenly swerving hard right. The van tipped and bobbed, showcasing its lack of crucial agility before the safety systems intervened to dampen to skid.

Now!

The GTO rocketed beyond the sliding van, Agatha wide-eyed at the impending crash. No electronic system could save it. No control input could right the wrong that had been dealt by inattention and overconfidence. She imagined the minion behind the wheel, seeing his fate as he closed quickly on a tractor trailer dawdling slowly in his lane. He was left with two options: the trailer, or the divider wall.

Well, he picked option two and yes, the result was ugly.

Boom! The front end smashed, the airbags popped, and it flipped a few times before settling in the middle of the highway.

"Holy shit!" Biff exclaimed.

"Well, that was easy." Jason tried to laugh off the fear.

He slowed back down to cruising speed, watching the Downtown Atlanta skyline come into view. Gargantuan cityscapes were fuel to his emotions. Queen City was no slouch, but Atlanta was still a different game, its steady onrush of skyscrapers headed with billboards, all primed with dancing advertisements.

Highways ten lanes wide, filled with masses of tall and bloated cars likened to air-conditioned capsules, nearly all on autopilot. Autonomous vehicles yanked away disabled cars from the shoulder, the cops too busy contending with their traffic watch to care. Aircraft zoomed low towards the Hartsfield-Jackson airport, at times looking as if they'd clip a building during descent.

It was just like home, but different all at once.

Different city. Different state. A place they'd never seen in person.

Maybe it highlighted the joy of adventure in modern America, its interlinked hugeness as breathtaking as it was frightening. Together, their hearts raced in the angst.

"Why are they still after us?" Agatha's voice was troubled as she continued hunting for any more bad guys within view.

"Why are you asking *me* that question?" Jason asked, leading further, "Here, let me pull over so you can ask the assholes in the wrecked minivan."

"These are the dumbest gangsters I've ever seen." Biff added.

"Since when have you seen gangsters?"

"Man, I live hardcore. You haven't heard?"

"Shut up, Biff."

"Jason." Biff leaned forward. "Why do you always have to be so hostile, man?"

"I'm wondering the same thing." Agatha agreed.

Jason swerved the GTO through traffic, briefly startling the other passengers who were in disbelief that the car would fit in such tight gaps. Somehow, though, he managed it.

"How am I being hostile?" he asked between swerves.

"Well," Biff gasped during another driving stunt, "because, man, you never seem to be a very friendly person. Especially over this entire trip. Last night, we all had a moment of reckoning, yet here we are, still being victimized by your hostility."

Jason laughed.

"Man, are you serious? I haven't been a 'friendly person'?"

"Well, that's," Agatha paused when they narrowly missed another car, "just an understatement. You've been a complete asshole towards me the entire time."

"Well, I'm sorry, guys, if I've been a bit dour." Jason said sarcastically as he steered the car down an off ramp. "But the past thirty-six hours or so haven't been the best for me."

"I think everyone can say that, man." Biff replied. Jason rolled his eyes.

"Where are you going?" Agatha asked when the GTO turned down a street headed opposite of their destination.

"The library." he pointed to the car's clock. "We've got an hour to kill before the first check in."

"Good, maybe I can find a pair of shorts and shirt."

"What's wrong with the tank top?" Jason joked, for the first time. "Didn't Skanks-R'-Us fire you for insubordination?"

"What is this 'Skanks-R'-Us' joke about?" Biff inquired. "It feels like I'm totally out of the loop here."

"It's a long story." Agatha insisted.

"Actually," Jason said between laughs, "it really isn't. Basically, Agatha worked at a toy store last year and got fired because she and a selection of other female employees kept wearing tank tops to work."

"Please," Biff smirked, "tell me more about why you were in a toy store so much, Jason?"

"Oh, you're going to turn on me like that?"

"Oh yes, I am. Did you work there?"

"No."

"So, how do you know so much about this?"

"I like Legos, so what?" Jason laughed as his mood was clearly lightening, "And I like seeing skanks in tank tops while buying my Legos. You mad about it?"

"See, Biff?" Agatha pointed. "I told you he was an idiot. You act like you're so much higher and better than any average guy, but you aren't. I'm glad you admitted it."

"Just because I respect women doesn't mean I don't like looking at boobs."

"*Excellent* point, sir!" Biff patted Jason on the back. "Excellent!"

"I win." Jason smirked.

"Touché, but seriously, pull into this dollar store so I can buy some shorts." Agatha smiled.

Jason obliged, parked, and even went in to buy the shorts for her.

During the wait, Agatha borrowed Biff's wrist computer and called her parents.

Still, he hoped with everything that they wouldn't answer.

-10:00AM-

Oh, yes. This was glorious.

Darwin listened to the police radio beaming with reports of more contestants dropping like flies. Twenty people had been caught racing through Atlanta alone from Underground, likely headed downtown to find the American flag.

After all their security measures, secrecy, and vows, he was still amazed that it was so easy to ruin. All it took was one small wrench tossed into the gears of a grand machine, and everything stopped.

Idioms were king.

His cruiser waited quietly, parked on the street adjacent to the building as a scout for any competition for the flag. He hoped the kids would arrive on time, but Darwin figured he'd place a phone call when time ran close. Waldorf walked up to the cruiser, opened the door and got in.

"Just a waiting game, Waldorf." Darwin smiled. "Plain and simple."

"What about that guy you said was going to help?" Waldorf was nervous. Darwin shrugged.

"He called off."

"Well hell, how are we supposed to get the flag?"

Darwin dangled a key chain with a set of electronic badges attached to the ring, "I got his security pass."

"He gave it to you?"

"Well." Darwin shrugged. "Not quite."

"You *killed* him?!"

"What!" Darwin punched Waldorf in the stomach. "You fool, hell no I didn't kill nobody! You think I'm *that* much of an asshole?"

"Sorry." Waldorf coughed while holding his stomach. "Why do you always got to punch me and shit?"

"You pansy, we been punchin' each other since we were god damn four-years-old. Grow some balls, will you?"

Waldorf huffed, "So, who's going to use the pass? They got cameras and shit in there."

"I figure I'll pay someone to do it if them kids don't want to. There's plenty of broke asses around here that'll pretty much do anything for a buck."

"Damn, I hope you're right."

Hint: he was.

-10:11AM-

Suppose it was no surprise that a Queen City GRID card was of no use in Atlanta, Georgia. Annoying, yes, but not prohibiting. Instead, Agatha used her feminine sway to woo the young librarian into giving her quick access.

They only needed a computer for a few minutes. Just enough to check Underground, to see the updates, and to pray that there was still a fighting chance in this. After all, they had done little more than commit crimes and fist fight mafioso minions—neither exactly a winning strategy in scavenger hunts.

Agatha logged into the terminal, proud to be attractive and admittedly a bit vindictive. The boys pulled up chairs behind her, anxious as they began to browse. Security protocols had changed, now requiring facial recognition atop the myriad of unique identifiers. She smiled for the built-in camera, watching as the Scene View program traced her face and calculated its authenticity.

Finally, they had access.

Forum activity was high. Non-competing spectators loitered in the viewer ring, waging speculation on the strategies, teams, and winnings. Tons of new posts centered on the hunt, each highlighted in bold with an Odyssey flag.

Minutes passed as they clicked through. Things looked different.

TommyPro, a site administrator, had shut down the signature and video features once news of law enforcement breaches were proven. The rules tightened from there where even regular members were only given ninety seconds to browse before they were locked out for two hours. Only the registered contestants were allowed up to five minutes before they too fell victim to the two-hour ban. Agatha wanted to use her five minutes wisely, choosing to select the current point roster.

Then, she noticed the oddity in the count.

"What the hell?" she blurted in confusion. Biff and Jenkins read the same thing, which disheartened them.

Jason was in disbelief, "Can someone tell me how *Chase* is the current point leader?"

"How the hell," Biff squinted to read further, "does he have 125,000 points? Looks like one of the items he got had a value of seventy-thousand!"

"That's impossible." Agatha shook her head. "I thought the highest was fifty."

"There's a seventy-thousand-point item right here on the last page of the stage one list." Jason pointed to a riddle on the back side of the list:

Item# 300: You know her, the sexy kitten. Did you know that she was an adult video vixen? Try your game, as most are shot down to shame, but its value is higher if she says your name.

They all read it and it took a moment to register. Agatha saw one of Chase's posts, which contained a URL link. Her heart sank, knowing deep down what the link hosted. Now completely devoid of her beloved pride, Jason took his fingers and gestured to click on it. It was a video and image hosting site, loading quickly on the library's fiber optic internet services, and spawning a recording from Agatha's hell on earth.

The video was lewd. Jenkins and Jason were thrown off guard as the first scene showed her head in Chase's lap. Fright clouded her eyes with tears more than embarrassment, and just as the men thought she was about to close the video down, she scanned through it more. Every time she clicked the time marker, it skipped to a different scene. In one, she was on her back against the door, with her legs up. Chase was doing pretty much what he was supposed to.

Rage compiled within her. There was no hiding from herself.

She clicked again, with it skipping to another scene. This time she was bent over, saying Chase's name like he had asked. The most shocking thing about the video was that there was no effort whatsoever to censor the nudity. She was completely exposed, though she had done this a few times before.

Biff's heart skipped. Jason's froze entirely.

Agatha had played the slutty video girl. She had done the things asked of her, and the things she liked, with multiple people, men or women, whomever she co-starred with within her comfort levels. Judge if they may, but a detailed search through Google could find her old stage name with a little determination.

So, she had done her brief stint in porn. Was she proud of it? No.

But there was a key component here that the others had missed: she volunteered for her two dozen videos. That was her consent in which to participate.

Here? In this instance? Chase had none.

Agatha cupped her hands over her mouth, beginning to break down. She had remembered telling him that it was okay to take pictures, but she thought that he was her boyfriend. He promised that he'd never share them. He *promised.* Tears ran harder and faster down her cheeks, and the heavy sobs were uncontrollable. Biff looked away from screen, still in disbelief.

Jason commandeered the machine, closing the window and making one last post under his own alias before signing out. It spilled his feelings on the situation and revealed the fact that the alcohol he and Agatha drank was loaded with drugs. Forgetting to note that he left her out in the middle of the country alone after stealing her items, he remembered and tried to edit his post, but the five-minute time limit drew nearer. Before long, he had typed a five paragraph of rant, but he deleted it and instead chose a shortened version that got straight to the point.

|Herotits (G-4) [10:04am]|: Chase Reynolds, I could explain how much of a scoundrel-ass-bitch that you really are, but then again that is readily apparent for all of Underground's users to see. I could also explain how low you have stooped by posting such an atrocious and defaming video of a woman drunk on Poonshine like it's a joke, but you'll see how low you are when you're picking yourself off of the concrete the next time I see you face to face. I tolerate your

disgusting personality for the sake of continuing with my life, but this is where I will clearly draw the line. It's you and me, asshole. Come catch these fucking hands.

Biff couldn't log in because his account had been banned, most likely for logging in from a law enforcement station. Agatha refused to give her password, fearing that anything she said in her defense would only result in even more humiliation. They couldn't get her to stop crying, and that drew the attention of the library attendants that noticed it. Moving as quickly as they could, they exited the building and made their way back to GTO.

"Agatha!" Jason ran after her. "Agatha!"

She continued to sob out of control, embarrassed to a point that she felt ill-equipped to even look at them. Jason—admittedly disgusted by the video—clearly felt bad for her. While she had always been flamboyant and flirty with men, she didn't deserve this type of public humiliation.

In fact, no one did. This wasn't even mentioning the fact that someone had actually gotten a very high reward for it.

Biff was still speechless, his wisdom somehow absent.

"Agatha come on, we have to go." Jason spoke again. This time she responded.

"Come on what?" she sobbed.

"We have to go!"

"I'm not going anywhere!" she protested. "I can't—I—"

Jason stood in front of her, "Look Agatha, yeah, that's some seriously disgusting shit, but we'll deal with that later."

"I can't deal with it later, Jason!" she hollered, her limbs trembling from the anger. "I can't do anything! I thought—I mean, I *really* thought that he was my boyfriend, but he had sex with me, videotaped it, and posted it so that everyone could see! Like I was some fucking prize! The funny thing is, I wanted to do it, but I didn't think he would ever do *that*! I know that everyone thinks that I'm a joke! I know everyone knows I've done porn!"

Uh, everyone besides Jason, who was a master of browsing nudie sites in his expansive free time. How the hell did he miss this?!

Agatha continued, "But—why would he do that? Can you imagine seeing that posted on a *public* site for everyone to see?"

179

"No." he had to be honest. It was the one thing she told him that she hated and enjoyed about their tenuous friendship, "I've never personally been in that situation."

His last statement was taken as another bit of sarcasm. Lowly, her scowl threatened to melt the skin from his face. She was tired of him, tired of his shit, and tired of trying to be friends with him with no luck. Ever since she had picked him up in Tennessee, she had never been so angry and simultaneously amazed by a single person so much in her entire life.

He was a guy, and she was a beautiful young woman. She even showered in the same room with him, and yet, he didn't even *try* to come onto her sexually. Neither did Biff. In a world where she was always the staple of sexual desire and attention, it seemed as if she met two men that respected her for who she was. She had always just been the pretty bodied bimbo that you could just walk up and grope. Guys would sometimes do that, and yeah, she'd have something to say, but it wasn't like anyone cared. She was just a pretty object, and that's all she had ever been.

So, she experimented with monetizing it.

While it was a very good and enjoyable thing in some respects, it had its bad side that fought with her mind. So, she finally met Jason, a guy who openly told her that he didn't care about how she looked, even though she was butt naked and wet, with her nudity only hidden by a towel. He was a mystery, but he was such an asshole. At least Biff had always been nice, even in the past—where she didn't expect it.

She hated assholes, even though she had a habit of dating them.

"I don't know what to do anymore." she finally admitted after some thought. "I want to go home."

"We can't." Jason shook his head. "Not yet. You heard Biff."

"Man," Biff was also shaking his head, "what Chase did was straight up wrong. I mean, of course, I know we—

Agatha cut him off, "Don't! Don't even talk about it! I don't want any reminders. Okay?"

Biff sulked and retreated, "Look. Clearly a line that has been crossed. You can't let that shit slide."

"It's not the first time." she rolled her eyes.

"That's unacceptable." Jason refused. "He will be dealt with soon, trust me. We have your back."

"No shit, Agatha." Biff brushed away his frustration. "Come on now, you can't be serious! We can handle Chase and his friends. We'll get his ass later, but don't let this stop you."

"I mean, I'm not going to sugarcoat this," Jason lead, "but is this the worst thing you've ever done? We all grew up in Horris County. We've all attended Horris County Schools and, quite frankly, we've all heard and seen some things."

She began to cry again.

"Well, thanks for the bid of confidence, you asshole!" she cried. "I know I'm a whore, so why don't you just say it!"

"That's not what I'm saying!" Jason defended. "What I'm saying is that, despite all of that stuff, you still came to school, right? You still held your head high. What people said didn't matter. Ever. You're like a superwoman. That shit just bounces off."

It took her moment to decide if that was a helpful compliment.

Yes. Yes, it was.

"No, it doesn't." she admitted. "I put on an act. I've always been good at acting. It's how you worm your way through the molds of life when you're like me. You have a deck of cards, and you play your hand."

"So, play your hand *here*." Biff suggested. "Kick his ass, and in regard to The Odyssey, that cop still has the fifty-thousand-point item for us."

"What does it matter?" Agatha retorted. "Chase hangs out with moderators and elites. Plus, he has seventy grand worth of points. Even if we got a lot of the little ones, he'd still probably have the point lead. So, basically, we've done all this for nothing, that is unless we can work to counter their lead."

"Someone else is helping him." Jason stepped forward. "That's obvious because he's collected mass of the high point items in this area pretty quickly."

"Yeah," Jason was curious, "how did you find the glass slipper so quickly? I searched all night along with a few other people I saw. You mentioned something about a 'special map' in his pocket before."

"Like I said, he seemed to know exactly where it was, and exactly what to do." Agatha recalled. "As if he had a 'special map' of some sort."

"So, you two were cheating."

Agatha scoffed at the admission, "Yes."

"Well, we need to get our hands on that map." Biff deduced.

"So, we can cheat?" Jason was perplexed.

"No. So we can take away their edge."

"By cheating, and that will get you expelled from Underground."

"Or we could always use it to prove that they were cheating. Disqualification."

"If they're friends with some of the dirty admins, who's to say that they won't just cover it up and disqualify us?"

"I didn't think about that." Biff sighed. "Well, I guess we'll deal with that later. Now, we need to work on our point count."

"Yeah." Agatha rolled her eyes. "You and Jason have found like five or six little items yourselves, right? That's what, a few hundred points?"

"What does that count for? Even with our point totals counted together, we've still failed. At the first checkpoint here in a few minutes, they'll tell us that we'd might as well just pack up and head back home. There's no way that we'll make it past Phase 1 with a count this low."

There was silence. Biff shook his head, "So, what's going on now, guys? We have, like, twenty minutes before we have to meet that stupid cop at the checkpoint." he looked at Agatha. "Are you okay now?"

"Shut up, Biff."

She rocked back and forth and looked at her watch.

"Twenty minutes." she whispered to herself.

Agatha spewed a few more remaining tears until she wiped them away. Her mind teetered amidst thoughts of desperation, "The video is valued by having me in it and by how many things I do, right?"

"Yeah?" Jason seemed thrown off. "Didn't you read that post?"

"Uh huh."

Her heart raced, but she felt sick. With her dignity already trashed and down the toilet of society, she made her offer, "If we've got twenty minutes and Biff's got the wrist computer and slate, how about we make another video?"

Biff froze in place. Jason replayed the statement in his head, and his mouth dropped open, "Whaaaaat?"

"Our point count is low because of me. We could get back in the lead if—well, if he got that many points for that video, I could—," she gulped, "—I could only imagine how much it would be with *two* guys. I'm sure we could make it work, or something."

"Whooooaaaaa." Jason shook his head over and over. "Whoa there, quicksilver. This isn't *Brazzers* here."

"What? Do you not understand what I'm saying?" she crossed her arms and held back tears again. "Let me clear it up: I'm saying that both of you can bang me, and tape it. We can find a parking garage, or a hotel somewhere, and make it happen. One at a time. Like, one of you can stand in front, and I'll—you know. I just—I'm not doing the two-at-once ordeal. Nope."

"Whoa! WHOA!" Jason waved his hands wildly in refusal. "Time out!"

"I'm sorry, but did you hear anything that we said to you a few minutes ago?" Biff asked. "I mean, what the hell, Agatha?"

"Yeah, she's gone insane." Jason ranted, backing away. "I told you she was crazy. And who the hell are *you*, Agatha? Jenna Jameson?"

She didn't verbally reply, instead raising one eyebrow.

Biff resorted to his failsafe: laughter, "Whaaaaat the hell is going on right now? Whaaaaat?"

"Well, I'm serious." Agatha opened the car door. "But I'd rather us all shower first. So, a hotel. There will be a bed too, so I won't skin my knees up on the concrete now that I think about it."

"Stop!" Jason spazzed. "Stop thinking!"

Still, she continued doing just that, "It doesn't have to be right now, but It'll easily put us in the lead. I always mess up. I mess things up for people. I messed this all up and didn't even know it. I was stupid. I can't fix it unless I do this."

"Do you have *any* sense whatsoever?" Jason was aghast. "Just when I thought I've seen it and heard it all on this shitpile of a road trip, you go off and say that? You *can't* be serious, but the sad part is that you are!"

She was crying again.

"I seriously don't care anymore." she sobbed.

"This isn't happening." Jason huffed.

"This is the one time I'll do it." she fought away more sobs and wiped away her tears. "If this happens, no one can ever talk about it again. Okay? Just this once."

"Agatha," Biff grabbed her shoulders, "please stop talking."

More silence followed. Jason battled his mind for only a split second and then got into the driver's seat. He fought away the daydreams of following through.

What? Yeah, he was human too.

After a moment, he turned on the engine.

"What are you doing?" Agatha asked.

"You're retarded, Agatha." he started to laugh. "Completely retarded."

She got in after Biff and they began to drive. Still laughing, the boys eventually cheered her up despite them making fun of her suggestion. Unfortunately, she'd be the running target for more endless jokes.

"What is so funny?" she laughed and wiped the remaining tears from her eyes.

"Whaaaaaaat!" Biff said again.

"I still can't believe that just happened." Jason added. "Like do you honestly think we'd take you up on that stupid offer? I'm not even sure if I can take you seriously right now. I think the whiplash from crashing Biff's whip into a swamp has screwed up your brain."

"What!?" Agatha laughed, silently hating herself. "Stop making fun of me!"

"You straight up offered to take on me and my boy over here, and even developed specific rules on the fly." Jason reiterated. "Just when I thought *my* self-esteem was at an all-time low, you went off and made the offer to have sex with two guys you barely know on tape. This happened just after you were crying profusely about doing a similar thing with one guy while under the influence of a cocktail of alcohol and hallucinogenic drugs a few days before. You need therapy."

She ignored most of the rant. Even if it was true.

"I'm actually surprised you turned that down, actually." she tried to play it off.

"Shit." Biff couldn't stop laughing. "I mean, don't make me reconsider."

"Well, not you, Jenkins." Agatha fired back. "I'm talking about Jason. I honestly think he's gay."

Jason pouted and shrugged off her statement.

"Like I said, you're completely retarded, Agatha. I'm by far *not* gay, but no, I'm not going to use you to get some points for some stupid sex video where I'm double-teaming you with Biff Jenkins. Even if it sounds awesome. Don't judge me for that last comment."

"Am I ugly or something?" her smile grew brighter, the sarcastic mockery of stereotypical dumb girls flowing so easily from her lips.

The leftover tears glistened around her eyes.

"Oh now, that's a classic sarcastic, attention-seeking girl statement." Jason rolled his eyes. "But why the hell would I do that, only to feel like complete hell after it's all done? Even still, I'd kick Biff out of the ordeal anyways. I don't do that two on one crap. I need to focus on the task at hand. Work my magic with the lady, you know how bad assess roll."

"Hell nah!" Biff disagreed.

"Oh, please!" she dismissed. "You wouldn't last a minute!"

"Aw, damn!" Jason scoffed.

"Whaaaaaaat!" Biff's laughter burst into a guffaw. "Roasted!"

"It's like *that*?!" Jason pretended to not actually be offended.

"All in? You'd get to five pumps, max. Tap out."

"Maybe ten." Jason mumbled. "Double or nothing."

"Whaaaaaat!"

"Ooookay, we're done." Agatha's face was red by now.

They couldn't stop laughing. It was their therapy.

"Thank you." she said, at random after a few minutes.

"For what?" Jason asked.

"Being awesome. Both of you."

"So, what are we going to do about Chase?"

"We'll call the cops or beat his ass." Biff shrugged.

"No." she quickly turned that down. "I don't need to call the cops. Let's just beat his ass, but we'll have to fight half of the elites."

"Man." Biff joked. "We're a force to be reckoned with, apparently, judging by the ordeal in the park back there. We can all whoop Chase's ass, anyway. Whoever else steps up, they can get bitch slapped too."

Jason fist bumped him, "Excellent."

"Right." Agatha fought tears again, happy with their reassurance. "Just get to this checkpoint. Piece of cake."

But things were never *that* easy.

-10:28AM- The 1st Checkpoint. Downtown Atlanta, Georgia.

"Check it out." Waldorf noted. "Looks like some more of those 'Underground' members."

Groups of fancy old cars squeaked their tires through the car garage adjacent to the skyscraper. They were loud, unforgiving, but emotionally satisfying. The sound of the old engines made both Darwin and Waldorf smile. Still, they had a job to do.

They had to get the upper hand.

"Uh huh." Darwin angled his seat back up and looked for himself. "Coming to get to that glass prism flag thingy after checking in at the first checkpoint."

"It's only 10:28, so they've got to wait a bit."

"Looks like they see us, too."

The contestants made a point to notify others of police presence in the garage, though none noticed the "Porter, Tennessee" markings on the side of the Crown Victoria. It was rule of thumb. Paying close attention could be bad. Making eye contact with a cop for too long was sure to arouse even *more* suspicion, so they played the card of ignore and disappear.

"Is that going to give us trouble?" Waldorf asked.

Darwin shook his head and kept the smile on his face, "Nah, if anything, it'll buy us cover if anyone sniffs this whole ordeal out. I'll blame it on one of them little pricks."

"Hey, Darwin."

"Yeah?"

"What did you mean last night when you said that it was 'small world,' you know, when you were talking about the girl?"

"Oh." Darwin's voice dropped low. "She's closely related to someone that I used to know."

Speak of the devil.

Finally, he saw the stealthy black Pontiac GTO. It stopped at the entrance, its passengers having found the police cruiser sitting in the dark.

Jason Weathers.

Agatha Peters.

Biff Jenkins.

From there, it accelerated into a slow creep, driving up the ramp before eventually rolling into the parking spot next to the cruiser. It sat there for a moment, its engine thumping at idle, until Agatha rolled down her window with a scowl on her face.

"Been crying, sweetie?" Darwin asked when he noticed her puffy eyes.

He immediately noticed something familiar in her face. Perhaps it was her eyes that reminded him of the war.

"Shut up." Agatha quickly recoiled. "Where's our shit?"

"In the trunk." Darwin scoffed. "Where's *my* shit?"

"You'll get your shit when we get our shit! You said you were going to 'throw something else special' in the deal if we 'played nice,' so what's going on with that?"

"You've played nice so far, so it's still 'on', but it's not going to be an easy task. It's a high-point item that I know the location of, and I'm going to help you get it, so sit tight. Besides, I've helped you all out a lot already."

Biff leaned forward, displaying hatred on his face.

"And how was that?"

"By putting out that APB for your little racer buddies in the vicinity of them items nearby this area. Ain't you heard the reports on the news about them busting a bunch of Queen City street racers on the highways?"

"Sorry." Agatha replied. "Haven't watched TV in a few days."

"Well, that's sad to hear, especially for a pretty little thing like you. Missing episodes of *'Real Housewives'* must be a killer."

"This cop dude is a real piece of shit." Jason mumbled.

"Man, get out the way." Biff shoved his way out of the car. "Let's do this."

Everyone else got out. Leaning on their cars, they faced each other and began the negotiations.

"So, can we see the item?" Jason asked. He tried his best to sound stern and assured, just like he had always seen in the action movies he wasted time watching. Instead, he looked like a grimy teenage boy that had been barbequed to a crisp by the summertime sun.

Yeah, being fair skinned wasn't a strong suit at the moment.

"Sure." Darwin popped the trunk and lifted the blanket covering the items. "There ya go."

Agatha went to grab the slipper, possibly for inspection purposes, but Darwin slapped her hand.

"Whoa, no!" he startled everyone. "No touchin' yet. Just lookin,' sweetcheeks."

"Don't touch me, you asshole."

"Oh, boo hoo!" he mocked as he shut the trunk lid. "Aw, naw! Miss Pretty Thang ain't getting what she wants! Horrible!"

"Fuck you!"

Darwin surrendered with a laugh, "Okay! Okay, calm down. You seen it, now let's get down to business. Where's my shit?"

"Man, we already told you." Biff took over, deciding to play his hand a little. "You aren't getting the tape unless you get us that other item you just spoke of."

"Okay." Darwin walked around the cruiser and spoke before getting in. "Well, why don't you go check in with zero points and then let's drive to a more 'discrete' location in the garage that your buddies can't see."

The trio agreed, getting in the GTO and driving down the checkpoint setup. There, they saw a few of the elites gathered in the rear cab of a cargo van, gesturing their hands and pointed fingers to keep the registries updated on a large electronic paper display. Behind them, more elites had pitched a tent, their wrist computers and docking stations ready to tally scores. It was busy, but United Underground prided itself on operational efficiency.

Competitors formed a single-file line limited to ten vehicles in the throughway, with each group of cars running through the tallying sequence and update within five minutes per. Raw exhaust filled the area, the stench a nose-searing reminder of the golden era long gone. Sounds of internal combustion echoed off the concrete walls.

For a few moments, they had peace again. Then, it was their turn.

"Agatha Peters." the guy greeted, withholding a grin. "I thought you were on a team with Chase."

"Not anymore." was all she said.

"Speaking of Chase, where is he?" she asked with a growl, folding her arms. "He's a got three people looking for him."

"Not here."

He looked inside and saw Jason and Biff, resulting in the urge to laugh. As he jotted down their names and the car information on his clipboard, he couldn't help but embellish in the ridicule.

"What happened to the ricers?" he asked. "Did your piece of shit cars not make it?"

"Technical difficulties." Jason replied.

"For some peculiar reason, I'm not surprised."

"I think I forgot to care."

"Uh-huh." the elite finished writing. "So, are you all part of a 'team' now? Because if you are, you must fill out the required forms on the slate and you can only do this once. When this shitbox kicks the bucket, I don't want to hear any whining. You better fix it or register a new shitbox to replace it."

Agatha looked at Jason, who then looked at Biff in the backseat.

They reached an immediate non-verbal agreement. Squad.

Jason snatched the pamphlet from the elite's hand and quickly filled it out. When he finally got down to the item tally for the first checkpoint, he wrote nothing.

"You haven't found any items?" the elite laughed. "What have you been doing for two days?"

"We've found some little things here and there." Biff was honestly tired of his attitude, but he opted to stay calm like his teammates. "Do you want us to count those?"

"Well, if you want credit for them just in case they are lost between here and the next checkpoint? Don't you kids read the rules?"

Biff took the slate, plugged it to the elite's computer, and filed in the small items on the list once the team roster had been updated via the connection. While he was relieved that the damn thing still worked, asking for a new charger would cost them 2,000 points.

//Scene View Deluxe v13.0.1\\

Security check: completed.
Welcome to the Odyssey, [ThunderD (G-4)]

Are you sure that you want to modify your team?
[x] Yes [ ] No

Please confirm your new team and vehicle status:

Team: "Three Kings"
[ThunderD (G-4)] = *Car #23-ECO2A—DECOMMISSIONED*
[NinjaVixen (G-4)] = *Car #12-GTC2B—IN PLAY*
[Herotits (G-4)] = *Car #47-SPC2A—DECOMMISSIONED*

Loading. . .

Please confirm your new team:
[x] Confirm [ ] Modify

Loading. . . Updating your team point roster. . .

1 - [Item# 04e] Glass Donald Duck - 1,500 points
2 - [Epic Points] Photos of vehicular 'weirdness'. One being a car with no doors. The other a motorcycle somehow carrying four people. - 2,000 points
3 - [Item(s)# 102d] Glass Four leaf clovers - 750 points
2 - [Epic Points] Flashing traffic cones from Tennessee - 2,000 points
1** - [DEDUCTION] Needed new charger due to being dumbasses and losing the original - 2,000-point penalty

First Checkpoint FPV (Final Point Value) Gross Total: 4,250 points

Computing adjusted FPV. . .
 Vehicle Age = 34 model years
 Percent Authenticity = 83%
 Percent Tax (based on PA) = -35%
 Correction Factor = 1.354
 Appraised Value = $6,000USD

First Checkpoint Net Total: 6077 points

"Is that better for you?" Jason asked after they had verified the items in the trunk.

"Yep." the elite nodded. "We'll take them off of your hands, and you can continue about your business, though I'd highly recommend you just turn around and drive home at his point. This score is pathetic."

Agatha looked at the electropaper display to gauge their competition, noticing many teams showing well above 30,000 total points logged.

Ouch. This sucked.

"Nah." Jason smiled. "We'll keep at it. Besides, they say you get three hundred dollars for simply crossing the finish line in Florida."

"Whatever you guys feel is logical, broke asses."

-10:37AM-

They drove away, up three levels to follow Darwin to a secluded part of the garage. Once out of the vehicle, they assumed the same positions as before, trying their darndest to intimidate.

Yet, this was all-new territory for them.

The threats. The bribes. The blackmail.

Darwin looked at Waldorf and gave a bemused shrug. He fixed the cowboy hat on his head and scratched his freshly trimmed mustache, leaning back against his cruiser to speak. He was cool, calm, collected, the AR-15 rifle hanging from a strap around his neck.

It stood out like a sore thumb. Yes, he could shoot people with it.

"Alright then." he started. "Here's the deal. That high point value item is obviously the glass prism hidden at the top of this building, which is the tallest on the continent, south of Queen City."

"Yeah, it looks like some other members have discovered that, too."

"Uh huh." Darwin cleared his throat. "Well, due to the storms last night, they had to close down the observation deck on the tower and fix the windows. That deck won't open at ten thirty. So, I don't know how you and your buddies plan on getting that glass prism without getting caught by building security. Unless they plan on running up the tower with a bunch of masks on or some shit, it just ain't happenin'. Besides, everyone else in your little competition is waiting at the door to get up there right now. How would you get through?"

"Fine. You win. So, what's your plan then?" Agatha asked.

"Well, I've got a nice security pass and a map of the building on this here wrist device thing-a-ma-jig."

Jason laughed, "And where the hell did you get *that* from?"

"Don't worry about it." Darwin winked.

"You sure are a crazy cop."

"I just do what I have to do."

Jenkins stepped in, showing his disapproval of where the conversation was going,

"Wait, wait, wait." he shook his head. "So, unless you've got someone that can pass off as an employee, or you plan on walking in there and getting that shit yourself, I sure as hell don't see how this is going to go smoothly."

"That's the thing." Darwin smiled. "It's not going to go 'smoothly'."

"Okay?"

"I mean, it's a high point value item for a reason, I suppose, and that's probably because you've either got to be connected, have a lot of balls, or just be plain stupid to try and pull this off."

"I'll tell you this." Jason put his hands up. "I'm not going up there and stealing that thing, not with my face on all of the security cameras. Most guys will just try to buy it with money or auction off their points, which is probably what the Admin Team has set up, but we don't have anything worth negotiating with. "

"Well, if you want your item, something's got to budge here."

The three bandits looked at each other and thought the same thing.

"It's not going to be us."

"Well, it looks like we're going to have us a bit of a problem then."

Growing tired of the run-around tactics, Jason stepped forward.

"Look man, it's pretty point blank. Either you or your buddy standing next to you are going to be the ones getting this shit. Not us."

"What keeps me from just kidnapping you and having you tell me where the tapes are?"

"Because we're standing in a public place for starters, and because you'd rather not have to deal with the hassle of covering up the kidnapping of three kids in a old black GTO that's pretty hard to miss." Agatha spoke up. "You might be able to get away with covering up the shooting and mismanaged arrest of three armed gangster wannabes that no one would care about, but be sure that if we went missing, there would be people that would coming looking for us."

"Oh," Jenkins, more than happy to tag-team, displayed a confirmation message on his cell phone, "look at that! I just emailed my little brother a copy of a photo that I took of your police car and of your face. See they have this app where you can make your own postcards. I told him that we've met some very nice police officers that have helped us out."

"Pretty smart kids." Darwin acknowledged, oddly not too disturbed. "And you're right. I don't feel like having to deal with any of that shit, and I don't feel like having to hurt you all because I'm honestly starting to like the three of you. Like I said before, I just want this to work out best for all of us so we can get on with our lives."

"I'm glad we have that understanding." Jason rolled his eyes. "So, who's going up to get that flag? With you guys being cops, they'd likely let you have it with little issue."

"Screw that." Waldorf disagreed. "Not happening."

Darwin chuckled, standing up off of the cruiser and looking around, trying to hide his frustration. Honestly, no one was dumb enough to go up there.

"I guess we'll go home then." Agatha sighed, letting Jenkins back into the GTO.

"Well, what about your item?" Waldorf asked. "Don't you need that?"

"Not anymore." she shrugged. "Even with it, we'd likely still be behind the current top runner."

"Chase."

"Yes."

Darwin blushed, "Saw the video. It's, uh, graphic."

"I know."

"Despite that, however," Darwin's curious voice grew, "it looks like you were quite a bit disoriented. How many beers?"

Jenkins stepped back out of the car for good measure.

"It was actually something called 'poonshine,' which is moonshine mixed with hallucinogenic additives." Agatha shrugged. "It tasted good, and I thought I'd try some, because people say that it 'puts the fire on,' if you know what I mean. Too bad he filmed it without my permission."

"Yeah, I've heard of that crap. It's produced by some of the more 'diluted' drug cartels in the south, primarily this one called the 'Red Devils Mafia.' I'd say it's unfortunately gathered quite the following with you youngins' around my locality."

"Red Devils Mafia?"

"Yep, they've been nothing more than a band of disorganized imbeciles until recently when they started to branch out. The 'RDM' tattoos on their wrists and necks gave me that inkling along with word-of-mouth cop chatter around the area. I guess they figure that stealing cars is a good gang initiation and sales tactic, along with the spiked booze business. That poonshine shit makes kids do some crazy things, but it does taste pretty damn good. You sure you're not just a lightweight?"

194

Now they were starting to understand. Jason remembered the hulk mode fight, the minions they beat up in the forest and how they were adorned in Red Devils Mafia tattoos—same as the men that stole his car and attempted to steal Biff's.

"I can hold my liquor pretty damn well," she continued, "and I only had three cups of that shit."

Darwin's eyes scanned her body. She likely weighed 110 pounds on a bloated day.

"You sure? You look pretty tiny to me."

"Believe me, I know how much alcohol I can inhale before becoming drunk off my ass. I felt like I was a horny, flying alien angel after drinking two cups. That was the last thing I remember thinking about before everything else happened."

"Can I see some I.D., miss? You don't look to be the age for drinking."

She laughed at his taunt.

"You, of all people, should know that I can get some alcohol, despite being underage. I'm nineteen, but I can walk into a corner store, show the front clerk my tits, and get whatever I want."

"I'm sure you could, because you did something similar back in my town, but it looks like Chase had you covered." Darwin rocked back onto his heels briefly. "He didn't drink any of that poonshine, did he?"

"Pretty positive he only drank a little and then made it look like he drank a lot."

"That's a goddamn shame." Darwin shook his head. "Can't get some punnani on his own, so he's got to drug the poor little girl to get his fixing. If it means anything to you, which I'm sure it does, I got some shit on him I can book him for, too. Still a shame about the videos."

"I own up to my misjudgments, Sheriff. It was my idea to drink the shit, and you have nothing that'll hold him."

"How do you think I got the items? Booked him and his Justin friend for that 'stolen' shit riding in the back of his Corvette."

"So, they're in jail?" Jason grew interested.

"Nah, I let them go just outside of town last night. Too busy making sure you assholes weren't going to try to persecute me over that goddamn video tape, so I let them go because I was dead set on the items."

Agatha sneered, "Well, what's the point in even saying anything about it then?"

"Because I'm a goddamn cop?" Darwin leaned forward. "I can just say that he knocked me out and escaped. Whose word are they going to take? Mine, or some fuckboy's?"

"Wow." Agatha seemed surprised. "Fudging stories to bury people is a nice quality in an officer of the law."

"And it's a highly functional quality, provided that there's no evidence to prove otherwise, unlike our case."

"Maybe the burglary—or vandalism could hold him if you could somehow pull his prints off of the cabin, but wait, does Porter, Tennessee even have a crime lab?"

"Yep." Darwin replied. "*I* am the crime lab."

"Well, for good measure," Jenkins reached forward handed Darwin a plastic card, "Here's the first copy of the memory card. There are two more left that we've hidden. You don't seem to be that bad of a guy, so if you help us, we'll give them all back to you fair and square."

Darwin handed it to Waldorf, who quickly verified the contents and the fact that it was a copy, as Jenkins had purposely watermarked the video image as one. With a little thought, he nodded again and adjusted his cowboy hat.

"So, you have record*ings*, you say?" Darwin asked.

"What do you think it means?" Agatha was shaking. "Do you think we'd be that stupid just to have one tape? Really? You help us out, we'll give you the other two."

"Sounds good to me." Darwin smiled. "This ain't too bad of a deal."

"And we're not usually people that operate on blackmail."

"And I'm still not going inside that damn tower."

Biff looked at the GTO's dashboard clock and sighed heavily, leaning forward in the seat so everyone could hear him

"Well, I'm sorry to break up this really touching conversation, but I'd like to inform everybody that we're running a bit short on time. Looks like the deal still isn't going on because no one has volunteered to go up there, so we're going to drive away so you can think of a better plan to get the rest of your tapes, sir."

196

Jason was surprised at the quick regression in progress, but he agreed without saying a word, getting into the driver's seat. Agatha opened the passenger side door but stopped when she heard the click.

The click of a gun being armed.

She looked to her right, seeing the barrel of an assault rifle pointed straight at her.

Everyone stopped.

Agatha gasped.

"Now, I've been pretty nice thus far with this whole ordeal, but that stops here." Darwin held the rifle very steady and robot-like.

"Whoa, man." Biff was stunned. "Put that thing away."

"I really do hate to do this." Darwin shook his head. "I *really* do, but I can't let you all leave here with those other copies. That's *my* ass."

"So, you're going to kill me?" Agatha asked.

"Maybe." Darwin thought hard. "Kill you, and your buddies."

"And find the record*ings*?"

"Yeah, I'll get the recordings out of your friends."

Biff closed his eyes, wishing it would go away, "I fully retract that statement about you seeming to be a nice guy."

He pressed the barrel of the rifle against her temple, brushing it along her soft and sweaty skin. She was overcome with goosebumps, her wit suddenly expunged in the danger.

She had no backup plan. No swift hits.

"Now, I ain't going to be having no little assholes playing tricks on me!" Darwin's voice suddenly shot up a few octaves. "Where are the goddamn tapes?"

"No one is trying to play a 'trick' on you." Jason cleanly declared. "We're just trying to get our shit so we can move on. For crying out loud, chill out!"

"Where are the other copies?"

"Wouldn't you like to know?" Agatha asked, despite having the gun pointed at her.

Jason fidgeted slowly in his seat, trying to find a way to get that rifle out of the crazy cop's hands. His buddy stood too close, however, making any type of attack too slow to quickly get the firearm out of the situation without risk of injury. He was stuck in the seat, but he saw Biff sneaking his wrist computer into view to dial a number.

9-1-1.

"WHERE ARE THE COPIES?" Darwin repeated.

"Hey!" Biff shouted. "Hey, cop!"

Darwin looked down at him briefly, making sure he wasn't too distracted from Agatha. She seemed like she'd be a feisty little lady to handle, if necessary.

"What the hell do you want?"

"Looks like the *real* cops are on the way, homie." he popped the wrist computer up to view long enough for Darwin to see the 911 numbers on the call screen.

"Don't make me blast your ass away!"

"You won't do it." Jenkins taunted, slinking back into the seat further. "You can't kill me when I'm on the phone with the police."

"Who says you've even placed the call? We're in a parking garage, boy. Can't get no damn cell phone reception in here."

"Man, I got Verizon, bitch. The network is *always* with me."

Darwin shoved Agatha away, lunging towards the open door of the car. As Jason lunged forward over the center console, he sent his right fist towards the sheriff, knocking the rifle from Darwin's hands. He tried to climb out of the car, but Darwin pushed him back inside, briefly wrestling with Jason as Agatha struggled with Waldorf.

The tight confines of the interior kept each man from gaining advantage over the other, yet a well-timed kick to the nose sent Darwin flying out the GTO and into the door of the cruiser. Jason grabbed the rifle, but Darwin wielded his backup pistol. Agatha had also gotten a gun somehow, probably from Waldorf's gun belt, but the problem was that Waldorf had *two* guns. That meant he was currently armed, too.

Shit. Together, everyone froze in place.

"Asshole!" Darwin shouted. "Busted my damn nose!"

Biff was frozen in the aim of Darwin. Jason got out of the car, too frightened to aim the rifle at anyone. Instead, he kept eye contact with Waldorf, and sat it on the ground. He was no killer. None of them were, but mutually assured destruction rarely involved the willing. Agatha found her balance and stepped behind the

GTO, keeping her grip on the revolver firm. The big guy was nervous, sweat pouring from his bulbous head in the sequence of a leaky faucet.

"Don't you raise that weapon." Waldorf growled, the uneasiness clear in his voice.

"Man," Biff's voice was very shaky, "this is one of those bullshit parts in movies were everyone with a gun just ends up shooting each other to death."

"Hopefully this doesn't end up that way." Jason sounded puny.

"Well, hell." Darwin wiped his nose and laughed. "Now, we *really* have each other by the balls. This just keeps getting better and better."

"What's your choice?" Jason reiterated, his hands jittering uncontrollably. "Put the gun down."

"Tell your friend to drop it first" Darwin sized her up. "Sweetheart, if you lift that, it'll be the wrong move, and no one wants that. We all know you don't have the gumption to shoot someone, especially a cop. "

"Just like you don't have the balls to shoot a couple of kids just trying to make a deal." Biff chimed.

"For the thousandth time, I'll give you all the copies if you give us the items." Jason's tone suddenly changed to one of negotiation. "We both can put each other away pretty good with the shit we have on each other, so why don't we keep this the way you said before."

"What'd I say?" Darwin questioned.

"How we might as well just get this all done so we can both go home happy. I don't know about you, but I don't plan on dying today. This is *stupid.*"

Agatha's gun-gripping hand trembled badly enough to need reinforcement, so she used her other hand to help brace the weapon. Still, de-escalation was her goal. In a gesture of goodwill, she stepped back.

"Easy." Waldorf reiterated. "Easy!"

"Well, if we're going to do this." her voice trembled, too. "Then, we better do this fast because we have like under five minutes now that we've wasted all this time. I don't want anyone to get hurt! That wasn't the point of this!"

"No one wants to go up there, though." Jason nodded. "And the sheriff here hasn't thought about whether or not we've told anyone about the location of the copies we made."

Darwin cringed. That was a damn good point.

His mind toiled with ways out of this. No, he wouldn't shoot anyone here. It was all a bluff, but he had no idea whether Waldorf's weapons were loaded.

"Hey, bud?" Darwin asked him.

"Yep?" Waldorf responded, never taking his eyes and aim off Agatha.

"I'm assuming them guns are loaded?"

"Unfortunately."

The script changed at that point. This was no longer about showboating or bluffing. This was about stepping too far over the line of discretion.

"Okay. Okay. I'll tell you what." Darwin suggested, making sure that his voice was steady and non-threatening. "Why don't we all just take a deep breath, step backwards, and put the guns away? We've clearly concluded that no one wants to die, and no one wants to be a killer. So, if possible, can we lower the firearms and return to our inside voices and polite negotiations? We'll work it out."

"You started it, asshole!" Agatha yelled.

"Yeah, I'm sorry. Maybe we can call this a truce?"

"Deal."

"Yeah."

"Uh huh, screw this."

"Not worth it."

Everyone lowered their weapons, the tension giving way like a cracked dam. Air returned to their lungs, the warmth to their skin, and their heartbeats to their chests.

"Whew." Darwin laughed. "That escalated quickly, eh?"

"Seriously." Jason agreed. "Every time we take one step forward, we take five steps back. This clearly isn't going to lead us to the mutual goal. What do you say, Sheriff?"

"Goddammit." Darwin wiped his nose again. "Maybe we can pay someone to do it."

"Pay?" Jenkins laughed. "Like who?"

An older model crossover caught his eye as it drove up a ramp on the other side of the garage, slightly out of view. He nodded towards it after his sharp eyes got a glimpse of the driver. The loud rap music helped with the conclusion, too. Sometimes, stereotypes rang true.

"What about that guy?"

Agatha and Jason briefly turned to look.

"A thug in a Jeep?"

"Uh huh. A Jeep with California tags and no back seats."

"Had a couple run ins with some thugs in a minivan on our way here, actually. They happened to be associated with that 'Red Devils Mafia' that you mentioned earlier." Jason noted. "What makes you think they'd do it?"

"Looks suspicious, probably selling drugs or something. They'll do anything."

"So, you're going to put all your faith in a 'thug' that nobody here knows?"

"Been a cop for over twenty years, so I can smell suspicion."

"Oh, is that right?" Jason laughed. "How will you keep him in check if your nose is right and that guy plays along?"

"There's only one way out of that tower. Down." Darwin chuckled. "Send his ass up there and wait for him at the bottom. He either comes down dead, in cuffs, or with your item."

Jason looked at Agatha, who nodded.

"Then go get him, officer." Jason smiled. "You got a plan for that?"

"I'm a cop." Darwin's nose stopped bleeding. "I don't need a plan for enticing people."

"Then have at it."

For a moment, they did nothing but stare at each other, their minds slowly settling for an inevitable, yet uneasy trust.

"Want to give me my rifle back?"

"Ha!" Jason guffawed. "So, you can turn it around and shoot me with it?"

"Nah. I'd get nothing from hurting any of you. That's not what I want. I just want those videos, and I know that a gun would only make my chances of getting them even worse."

"That's fair." Agatha agreed.

"Agreed." Biff nodded.

"Trust?" Jason reached forward, extending his hand to set their deal in stone. "That's all we have now."

Darwin checked with Waldorf, who had no opposition.

"Trust." he said with a smile.

They shook hands, firmly. This was their Treaty of Versailles.

Weapons were returned to their rightful owners without ado.

"Tell you what," Darwin added, "you keep the rifle for a little so it'll make you feel better. Eh?"

"Okay, good." Jason smiled too. "Get in your police car with your wannabe police buddy and go 'entice' him."

Darwin scoffed, but obeyed, slowly making his way back to the driver's seat. Waldorf flung open his door, plopping in with enough force to make the old car bounce on its springs.

"Damn, I really need to go on a diet." he murmured.

"Yeah," Darwin was happy he finally admitted the obvious, "that would help you out a bit, brother."

"Blood pressure's too high for this shit. These damn kids, man. Clever sons-a-bitches, eh?"

"I like them."

He started the car as Agatha stepped back, purposely turning the opposite way to avoid any type of confrontation. The men watched them retreat to their car, consoling each other in the wake of a catastrophe.

Beautiful. It was nice seeing kids so masterful at bartering.

Reluctantly, he drove up the ramp in pursuit of the Jeep.

"Me too." Waldorf processed his feelings, keeping an eye on them in the mirror. "Pretty ballsy little bastards, just like us."

"Heck dang."

············

The Jeep drove slowly towards the upper floors the garage, pacing itself as if its driver was in search of someone. His eyes hunted feverishly, his fingers tapping the steering wheel in tune with the music. It was his last drop, and it was a simple one.

Just an exchange. He'd done it a thousand times before.

Uh oh. His eyes checked twice, yet the second scan didn't erase the haunting image of a police Ford Crown Victoria turning the corner behind him. He cringed, curling his toes onto the accelerator a little to hang a quick a left, yet the trailing vehicle did the same. There was no opportunity for a hasty escape at this point.

His employers would be sorely disappointed.

Prison sucked, too. Damn, the morning had soured fast.

"¡Mierda!" he groaned.

——————

Darwin closed the distance soon enough, looking at the plate number. Coincidentally, the tags on the plates had expired just last week,

"Bingo!" he muttered as he reached for the strobe switch. "Watch my back, Wald."

"Got you." Waldorf held his pistol steady.

Darwin flipped the switch, turning on the pulsing blue and red strobe lights. When the Jeep failed to stop, he chirped the audible siren, just to further the point. The man looked in the mirror, hit the steering wheel in anger, and pulled over to the side quickly. Once it stopped, Darwin turned off the lights.

The cruiser accelerated aggressively for a split second, squealing the tires briefly before it came to an abrupt halt to block in the Jeep. If the guy decided to run, he'd have to throw it in reverse and ram him out of the way. In the back of his mind, Darwin hoped this would be enough to deter any crazy ideas. He'd hate to see his beloved cruiser harmed, but perhaps a gun to the face would give him the added reassurance.

His backup weapon was a Walther P99. Scary enough.

"Freeze right there!" he shouted after flinging open his door and dashing to the Jeep. "Don't want no moving' and shit from you!"

The driver stuck his hands out the window in compliance. He wasn't in the mood to get shot due to a misunderstanding today.

"Okay!" his voice sounded strained. "Okay!"

The telltale 'RDM' tattoos were missing from his neck. Odd.

"Yeah, 'okay' is right. Keep them hands up, son!"

Darwin reached the door, sticking the pistol up to the man's temple. He gave it a shove, solely for the added drama, before opening the door with an arrogant grin.

"What did I do, sir?" the man asked.

"Your vehicle's tags are expired." Darwin answered quickly. "Other than that, I'm asking the questions, so shut up."

"Yes, sir."

Darwin pulled out his police flashlight and turned it on, shining it inside of the vehicle's cargo areas to get a closer look.

"Where are the back seats?" he asked.

"Not in the car, sir."

"Well, no shit. What's under the blankets?" Darwin asked when he noticed evidence of concealed contraband.

The man didn't answer.

"What is under the blankets? I'm not going to ask you again, son!"

"Uh—uh—" the man seemed antsy. "Just my stuff."

Darwin rolled his eyes.

"Oh, okay. Just your 'stuff'?" he walked back to the driver's side door and opened it. "What the hell is 'stuff'? You got drugs in this car?"

"Uh—no—no, sir."

"Get out of the damn car."

The man got out. He was dressed in rather expensive clothing to be driving in an old, shitty Jeep.

"You're not going to ask for license and registration?" the man asked as Darwin handcuffed him and slammed him down onto the hood.

"I don't need your damn registration." Darwin scoffed as he opened the rear passenger doors and leaned in.

It smelled like mildew, as if the car was pulled straight from the sweaty pit between a man's toes. His nose stung, but flood cars were commonly used for transport vessels. Old appliances filled the cargo hold, forcing him to shuffle three microwaves aside to expose the dusty and smelly old cloth below. He used his right hand to lift it up, displaying a row of smashed fabric bags beneath. Bingo. Curiosity overwhelmed him and he unzipped the first one he saw, nearly losing his breath at the surprise inside.

His eyes bulged.

"Holy shit!" he exclaimed, backing away from the Jeep.

The driver groaned, his incarceration imminent now.

"You've got to be kidding me!" Darwin laughed. "Where's your ID at, son?"

The man didn't find it funny.

"I—I—don't have an ID on me." he stuttered nervously. "I left it at home."

"Bullshit."

Darwin wasn't stupid. He searched his pockets, finding his wallet which contained at least a thousand bucks and an obviously fake or stolen ID card. He also found a loaded pistol, which he stashed in his uniform belt.

Darwin *had* to laugh at the license, "Is your name 'Tyshawn Booker' from Palo Alto, California? No. You honestly think I'm *that* dumb?"

He then held the card up next to the man's face, "That doesn't even look like you!"

"Wait—wait!" the man seemed like he was going to cry. "I can explain!"

"Ha!" Darwin saw Waldorf laughing in the cruiser. "Well, I better pull up a chair and order a goddamn pizza. I'd really like to hear how a man would explain, not only a stolen wallet, and ID along with an unregistered pistol that's loaded , but also have a logical explanation for having a bazillion dollars in the back of this twenty-year-old Jeep Cherokee."

He did nothing but hyperventilate, trying his best to get words out.

"I—I—"

"You—you what?" Darwin holstered his pistol and leaned against the Jeep. Waldorf got out and walked up to check out the scene.

"Time." he pointed to his watch. Darwin nodded.

"Come on now, man." he spoke to the guy, now hunched over the hood. "I'm all ears, and you better make it quick before I radio in for some guys to come take you to lock up."

"I—I—I."

Darwin mocked him and rolled his eyes to Waldorf. Low on vital time, he figured now was the time to make the offer,

"Alright," he put his pistol up to the man's head again. "I'm going to make his pretty simple for you."

"What?!—What are you doing?!"

"Shut the hell up and let me talk!" Darwin raised his voice. "Now, I've only had you stopped for maybe three minutes and I've already got a few *big* things I can throw on you that'll send your ass *straight* to the slammer. Actually, they might throw you in the basement of the penitentiary."

He pushed the pistol into the man's temple, "Now, I'm sure you don't want to be some big fudge packer's little girlfriend, eh?"

"No—no, sir."

"Uh huh." Darwin's hidden joy continued. "So, here's what you're going to do for me, aside from letting me have a bag of that loot."

"Y—yeah?"

"Real simple." Darwin whipped a security pass, and then map from his pocket. "You can read a map and use a goddamn swipe card I assume, so you're going to take these two items into that big ole' tall skyscraper there and go to the top floor."

"Yes?"

Darwin extended his hand. The man looked down, seeing a photo of the item straight from Chase's map.

"Then," said the sheriff, "you're going to go into the maintenance room, act like a maintenance man, hunt through the observation deck, and get us this hidden glass prism. Got it?"

"O—okay."

"No glass prism means jail time." Darwin smiled. "K?"

"Yes, sir."

The man was pulled to his feet. How nice.

"Now, are you going to do what I told you to? Pretty simple, and it should be pretty empty up there. Move quick."

"Yeah."

They held eye contact, just to ensure the agreement. Darwin pointed to the cruiser's windshield, bringing the man's eyes to a small camera suctioned to the glass.

"Now, I got all of this on that there tiny camera in the cruiser. Thing is, you know it's a digital copy, so I can edit out or edit over whatever I want. So if you don't give me what I want, I'll be waiting at the bottom of this building ready to hunt your ass down."

The man gulped, holding his breath as if voluntary suffocation was the only way out. Maybe it was. Maybe it wasn't.

"O—o—okay. Okay I got it."

"If you understand the rules, you better get your ass moving!"

206

Darwin reached into the Jeep and pulled out a face mask that was squeezed between the cash bags, handing it to the man with a firm pat on the back.

"There's a face mask for the cameras. Oh, and here. . ."

He took an electropaper ink pad and pressed the man's index and thumb fingers to it. That was followed by a photograph that he took from its tiny camera, "So we got you in a stolen car, with a stolen ID, an unregistered weapon, and a zillion dollars in the back. Now I've got your fingerprints, wrist computer, and facial photo. So don't try no stupid stuff, asshole, or you'll be on the next episode of America's Most Wanted. With this missing money, your boys would probably find you first, so let's make sure this is done right. Right?"

"Yeah." the man seemed a little relieved.

"So, go." Darwin checked his watch. "You've got fifteen minutes to get in there and get back down here with my stuff."

"O—okay."

"Pull the fire alarm when you get the flag. That'll confuse the hell out of everyone in the building. Capiche?" Darwin pointed to a door about fifty yards away. "Get the hell on, I'll meet you outside that fire exit door."

"Sure!"

And he was off, dashing into the tunnel leading towards the building. Darwin knew that only the garage entrance and the main street entrance would be the only ones unlocked.

"Think he'll do it?" Waldorf asked calmly.

"Doesn't look like he's got much choice."

"What's keeping him from just running away once he gets inside?"

"He know his gang banger homies will find his ass and kill him because they'll be missing their money if that happens. They'd likely torch his family, too."

"I'd say that's some good persuasion to cooperate."

"Mhmm."

Darwin couldn't take his eyes off the money in the bags.

"How much money *is* that, anyway?" Waldorf asked.

"Looks like there's at least forty to fifty grand in each bag." Darwin observed, "And there's six bags."

"Holy shit!" Waldorf sounded giddy. "What do you think it's for?"

"Drug money, and I'm not touching it except for a few stacks here, and maybe a bag there."

"Yeah, get me some, too."

Darwin and Waldorf hustled a few handfuls of $100 bills into the cruiser, hesitated, and grabbed an entire bag of money. Screw it. Paydays like this didn't show up often, and these clowns were far too incompetent to pose a serious threat. After they both got back into the cruiser, he put it in gear and sped back to the lower floor.

Then, the thought hit him like a brick.

"Hell! Why the hell would that guy be driving through this garage with that car?"

"That's what I was trying to say."

"Shit!" Darwin hit the steering wheel. "It's a money drop! That guy I sent upstairs didn't have any 'RDM' tattoos, but he had markings that I haven't seen. This might be one of them money exchanges between two mafias in a business deal or something."

"Well, who the hell is picking up the money?"

The cruiser came to a sudden halt, the answer driving straight through the garage entrance in plain sight.

"These fellas?" Darwin nodded towards a group of conspicuously modified minivans, each loaded with passengers more in tune with RDM infantry than the United Underground.

Sunlight reflected from the chrome wheels, blinding anyone within a half mile of the beams. Insects and avian species mistook their deep pearlescent paint for nectar and pools of refuge. Darwin even saw the feathers of a stricken bird poking from the fins of the front grille, poor bastard. They rolled through in escort style, the expensive model sandwiched between two lesser trims front and rear, its lavish captain chairs swiveled for comfort.

Clearly, that was the ringleader.

Darwin reversed the cruiser behind a concrete wall to hide them from view until he figured out what was going on. He looked over at Waldorf, his eyes as big as snow globes. They had the same idea, unbuckling their seatbelts to duck under the dashboard, peeking up only enough to see.

Each van rolled by, noticing the parked police car only to assume that it was empty. The ringleader passed, with Darwin quick to notice the middle row passenger window lowered halfway. He saw over-gelled hair and a neck coated in spray tan, but no clear view of a face. That was it, nothing more than the blinking light of what was probably a wrist computer locked into a phone call.

There, Darwin asked himself the question of the hour:

How long would it take for shit to hit the fan?

EPISODE SEVEN

"Shake and Bake"

-10:50AM-

"Carlos!" Boss spoke directly into the phone, an emphasis on each syllable to stress their importance. It was as if he was orating the next great novel. "This is simple!"

"Yes, sir. We're rolling up now."

"Get the money and get the hell out!" Boss laughed. "Like a snatch and run, you dig?"

"Uh huh." Carlos replied, stretching to see out of the tinted window. "There's just a lot of people here."

"What do you mean?"

"Just a lot of people on the lower levels of the garage. Like a club or something."

"Carlos," Boss seemed annoyed, "are any of them watching you?"

"No."

"Then get the money and get out!"

"Yes, Boss."

The van stopped, its driver pointing towards the parked Jeep. Once confirmed, Carlos nodded to proceed. Go time.

"Call me back when you retrieve the money." Boss cleared his throat. "I still have a problem with those puntas from the park."

"I know, Boss. I heard the news from the boys. What's the problem now?"

"Those assholes keep taking down my men! I had a crew tailing them down the highway and they pulled some race car maneuvers and got away!" Boss shouted, his voice laden with fury. "What the hell do you think the problem is, Carlos? These people are taking down *my* men!"

"Sorry, Boss."

"Rico said they were in a really old black coupe with Queen City plates. You know, those 'Pontiac' things from back in the day, but in good shape and he said one of the passengers is a pretty luscious bonita. Legs for days and a tight ass."

"Yes, I know." Carlos smiled. "We'll find them, Boss."

"Good. Call me when you do."

⸱⸱⸱⸱⸱⸱⸱⸱⸱⸱⸱

Darwin waited until the vans disappeared beyond the ramp, counting to ten for the sake of safety. He looked to Waldorf for reassurance, a queue that his partner happily obliged in providing: A quick nod, just enough to jiggle the blubber beneath his second chin.

Excellent. It was time to go.

The cruiser drove back down to the GTO, both men at this point surprised that the car was still sitting there. They glared at each other, long enough to make it awkward. Darwin leaned out of the window,

"Got that guy to do it for us." he said just loud enough for them to hear. "But we might have a slight issue."

"Oh?" Jason was curious. "And what's that?"

"Well, when I pulled that guy over a few levels up, I found out he was driving a stolen car. Then I checked into it more and found five bags of straight up cash money stashed in the back of it."

"Say what?" Biff leaned forward, his interest piqued by the words 'cash money'.

"It's obviously a money drop." Darwin looked around. "Spotted some of the gangsters rolling up in the garage a few seconds ago. I think we might have a slight problem."

"RDM?"

"Most likely." Darwin agreed. "They fit the typical description."

Jason groaned. His mind easily connected the dots.

"Sweet. Just sweet. I mean, what are the chances that we wind up in the middle of a money drop, hosted by the gang that's been hunting us down for the past two days?"

"Hell," Biff was nervous again, "I was hoping they were low, but, I guess not."

"Guys, I think it's time we leave." Agatha suggested, clearly not up for another battle like the one in the mud pit.

"You've got to be kidding me!" Jason covered his face with both palms, the frustration threatening to melt them. "We're running from the mafia in a Pontiac GTO. Dude, how does this even happen? All I wanted was the glass slipper. That's all I wanted."

"Okay, stop crying!" Agatha nudged him before turning her attention to Darwin. "Where's the guy from the Jeep that's supposed to be getting the glass prism?"

"Hopefully up there in the tower getting the glass prism."

"Man, if those are the same mafia dudes, we need to get out of here." Biff kept shaking his head. "Like, *now*."

"Honestly," Waldorf chimed, "them guys are so disorganized that they can barely kill a fly."

"Guys, let's wait until the dude comes with the flag." Agatha insisted. "Is there some kind of secret signal that he'll send us when he's got it?"

"Yeah." Darwin replied. "He'll set off the fire alarm and come out the emergency exit where someone is going to meet him."

"Where's the emergency exit?"

Darwin pointed towards the ceiling, "Up there a few flights."

"Yeah." Jason rolled his eyes. "Right next to the Jeep loaded with drug money and surrounded by gangsters."

"Correct."

"Screw that." Jason started the GTO's engine and selected first gear. "You're the cop with the big bad gun. You go up there and get the glass prism and we'll be driving around the building looking for this guy, just in case he tries to flake."

"Fine. Whatever. I'm sending you a picture of what this asshole looks like." Darwin said as he toyed with the wrist computer. "I'll head upstairs, but I have gut feeling that this shit is going to get really stupid with those dudes here to pick up their cash."

"We'll be outside."

"If I see him, I'll call you."

"Okay."

The kids drove away towards the exit, hanging a right turn onto the adjacent street. Darwin wheeled the cruiser slowly, canvasing each level one by one until he reached the ramp near the Jeep. He stopped, seeing the mafia men crowded around the vehicle. They didn't look happy, as the discovery of missing money and a missing drop boy could sour even the best of moods.

The leader paced in circles, frantically trying to place a call.

"Shit." Waldorf knew the deal. "Looks like that money ain't insured, eh? You think he'll miss a few bags?"

"A 'few bags,' you say? How many did you lift?"

"You only win the lottery once. Don't judge me."

"Hell." Darwin cursed as he readied his rifle. "Waldorf, stay in here and keep me posted with the walkie."

"What?" Waldorf was sweating heavily. "Why?!"

"I'm gonna have to head this guy off." Darwin said after he had rolled the cruiser back behind a wall. "I didn't think the pickup guys would be here so soon! They're going to be pissed!"

"What the hell are you going to do?"

"Like I said, head that guy off. Get the glass prism, get back here, and get the hell out." Darwin opened the door and got out, "If I'm not back down here in three minutes, drive out of the garage and I'll meet you on the ground level."

"Alright." Waldorf climbed over into the driver's seat, excited that he was getting into some real action, "You be careful, you hear? Only friend I got."

"Ah, shut up, you fool." Darwin bluffed. "Leave that mushy shit at home. Just stay *away* from them damn wannabe gangster guys."

"You got it."

"Heck dang."

Darwin crept away towards the stairwell.

———

"Eh, Boss?" Carlos spoke once the call connected.

"What, Carlos?" Boss was annoyed. He hated mid-intercourse emergency phone calls.

If anything, they dulled the mood.

"We got a fucking problem." said Carlos.

Boss stopped mid-stroke, catching the lady underneath him by surprise. Her eyes opened, her breathing heavy with lust, looking up to see the issue plain and clear. There were more important things. Business. Trade. Territory. Still, she squeezed her hands on his back, willing him forward.

It only annoyed him to the point of full retreat.

What a tease.

"Mmm." he sighed. "What is it?"

"Looks like we either got jipped or set up."

"What!"

"Checked the drop car."

"Okay?"

"And there's no one in it, plus one of the bags is only half full, and three others aren't even here."

Boss was dumbfounded. His anger boiled again.

"But I don't understand! Why would they meet up if they wanted to jip us, but only leave partial payment? Is the money fake?"

"No." Carlos was angry. "One of the boys used the counterfeit pen. The stuff checks out okay. Legit Benjamins."

Boss sighed and ruffled his hair, deciding to take his anger out on the girl he was currently having relations with. He looked down at her, smiled, and advanced his way back to lovemaking. She very much enjoyed it.

"Are—you even sure—" he paused between thrusts, "those idiots—can count correctly?"

"Yes, sir."

Carlos felt odd hearing the lady in the background, their skin slapping together with each sequence. He was speeding up, drawing his performance to a crescendo.

"Carlos," Boss labored through the finale, "I don't have time for this nonsense! I'm a busy man!"

"I can hear that, Boss. My apologies."

"You nearly ruined my—ugh—conquest of femme fetale! Take care—ugh—of this!"

They heard squealing tires. Instinctively, their eyes drew to the source, seeing a large police cruiser speed off towards the ramp. That sent them all into a state of panic, rushing back to their cars and starting the engines.

"What the hell is going on?" Boss grew concerned.

"We got cops, Boss! It's a sting!"

"Ugh! Shit!" Boss punched the headboard of his bed. "Get out of there!"

Boom, he finished.

-11:08AM-

He made it into the building, gathered his bearings and headed towards the first checkpoint center. He didn't run, but he made damn sure to speed walk. Unwanted attention at this point would kill his power play, but he soon had the perfect shield for that.

Strobe lights flashed like fireworks. Audible alarms blared. A pre-recorded voice sounded earnest over the building intercom system.

"ATTENTION! ATTENTION!"

"THIS IS THE FIRE ALARM!"

"EMERGENCY EVACUATION!"

"THIS IS NOT A DRILL!"

Security guards went ballistic. Two of them hopped over the main desk, sprinting away down the hallway. Darwin stopped, knowing this was as far as he would go. There were but a few seconds of relative peace—just enough to gather his wits—before every evacuee in the building ran down the stairs, scrambling for the doors.

In theory, Sunday should've left the employee roster quite thin, yet the exodus from the upper floors likened thoughts of Moses in the Red Sea. Dozens spilled from every stairwell, looking as if they were fearing a terrorist attack. Darwin was overwhelmed in the rush, finding himself forced back out of the door.

The crowd verged on the point of stampede, the security officers nearly ineffective at calming down the fleeing people. Rumors spread like wildfire. Someone said that there was an explosion upstairs, a bomber maybe. Someone else said they heard gunfire. In reality, it was just a middle-aged man that had stolen a hidden glass prism from the maintenance area and used the fire alarm for cover.

Was this illegal? Hell yes.

Was Darwin ashamed? Well, if no one got hurt.

Darwin saw a woman on the floor, scooting across the tile to clear the crowd. He rushed over to help her up, discovering that she had twisted her ankle and was unable to walk more than a scurried limp. His Clark Kent routine shined. Like a proper gentleman—with consent, of course—he whipped her up and carried her away, dashing into the safety of the parking lot. He sat her down in one of the evacuation assembly areas, lowering her to the pavement with the grace of matador. She gazed at him, her eyes somehow caught in sequence with his.

She was beautiful, yet they little time to speak beyond cordialities.

Their moment cut short, abruptly ended by sharp thunderclaps echoing off the walls. Gunshots. Everyone screamed and hollered, diving to the floor. Darwin heard two, now three, then four shots shortly after he heard tires squealing. Instincts brought his hand to his holster, his pistol from the pouch, and his palm tightened around the grip.

Then it hit him.

"WALDORF!"

He ran as fast as he could, ducking behind the wall closest to the action area, watching as two of the gang vans peeled out and skidded past. Peeking around the corner, he saw the target standing by the Jeep with his hands up. A Red Devils minion held him at gunpoint, ready to execute, the red, white, and blue glass prism laying on the ground meters away from the door.

Darwin whirled his fingers on the wrist computer and speed dialed Biff's number. He answered,

"The guy's in here!" Darwin shouted over the commotion. "Bunch of bullshit is going on! Hurry up! I'll snatch it when I can get to it!"

"Okay, we'll be right there!" Biff confirmed as Jason sped up at full throttle towards the garage.

Darwin hung up and peeked out again, unable to find Waldorf in the cruiser. "Where the hell is he?" he asked himself, hoping that he had stayed put.

Then he heard a gunshot followed by the loud rumble of the GTO's exhaust roaring through the lower levels of the garage. He stood up, grasping the pistol close to his face and taking another look. The target was shot in the abdomen by the minion, but he managed to find a hidden gun inside of the Jeep—one that Darwin had obviously missed—and returned fire. It was a shitshow. Stray bullets hit the walls around them, as neither side displayed much aptitude in gun marksmanship. They closed their eyes and fired to cover their retreats, most of their shots off target by dozens of feet.

It only grew worse.

Along came Waldorf, following orders once the three-minute time limit had expired. He felt important, needed, and vital to this ordeal, yet this is where he made his first misjudgment. In his excitement, he took the incorrect route out of the garage, simply following the exit signs and driving straight towards the battle zone. To the warring gangsters, all they saw was a cop car rushing towards their location. Fearful of law enforcement intervention, they shot at the police car. Most of the bullets hit the body and windows, but one hit Waldorf. He hunched over, taking cover under the dashboard.

"WALDORF!" Darwin hollered, popping out from behind the wall and taking quick aim at the first two shooters that he saw.

BANG. BANG.

One shot for each target and both were down, kicking their legs in pain. It was war time, and he now had a fallen comrade on the field. He ducked below a parked car and saw the GTO heavy on approach.

Unable to hear the gunfire over the loud engine, screeching tires and fire alarms, Jason and the crew were caught majorly off guard.

"WHOA!"

Two bullets hit the car, punching holes cleanly through the outside mirror and upper corner of the windshield. They braced against the sharp turn, ducking as low as they could in instinct against the projectiles.

Jason had to find them a way out, so he searched in those critical seconds, discovering a man sneaking up behind Darwin, raising his gun to fire. No. Not today. He slammed his foot on the brake pedal and cut the steering wheel hard to the right, hitting the guy and sending him flying into the wall. Darwin viewed it as a pure save, half amazed and half thankful. The GTO reversed clear to the emergency exit.

"What the hell is going on?!" Agatha ducked.

"They're going to kill that cop!" Jason shouted.

"Get the hell out of there!" Biff hollered.

Agatha disagreed, "But someone has to get the glass prism!"

Jason advised against any further moves until he could find an unblocked way out, but Agatha—and Darwin's rifle—had disappeared out of the car before he could finish. Shit! His eyes found her ten meters away, scooping up the flag prism and tripping to the floor.

"Agatha!" he saw a Red Devils car coming from that direction.

Two of the gangster cars drove away from the rear of the group, including Carlos, who had made it to the back of his van.

"Freeze right there, assholes!" Darwin shouted as he aimed his gun. "Police!"

There were four men with guns versus just Darwin.

BANG. BANG.

He shot two of them before he was glazed by a bullet. It was a shoulder wound, which still hurt like hell, but it didn't affect him enough to dull his aim.

BANG.

He took out another, then he heard a shot behind him. The last bad guy fell, groaning on the ground, a gunshot wound somewhere in his abdomen. During his fall, his weapon has fallen well out grasp range.

Agatha had shot him.

She stood frozen, holding the smoking rifle with locked arms. Darwin turned towards her, and then a look of horror struck his face.

"Not so fast, punta!" a shaky voice seared into her ear. His strong arm clasped around her and locked their bodies together, the barrel of his 9-millimeter pistol pushed flat against her temple.

She dropped the rifle.

"Whoa! Whoa!" Darwin aimed his weapon. "Don't do anything stupid, kid!"

The minion wasn't dumb. Like his brethren, he was no stone-cold killer, but he had to plan on his feet to stay alive. Hostages were never part of the RDM operational handbook, but this was about survival. He'd let the girl go eventually, but he had to show his power to secure his fate, shielding the majority of his head behind Agatha's. Darwin had damn good aim, but he knew it wasn't *that* good.

No shot.

Another gang car rolled up, leaving Jason and Biff standing helplessly, unable to move due to the intimidation from the other minions wielding weapons in the car. They advised them to stay still, threatening to shoot if they didn't. These guys were gangsters, so they *had* to be serious.

The man dove into the van behind him, still holding Agatha in with his locked arm, and the car took off driving towards Darwin at full power. Darwin didn't flinch, arcing his neck to the side and winking one eye to get his aim. At the last second, he squeezed the trigger,

BANG.

The car sped by, and then crashed into a concrete pillar. Its driver had taken a bullet to the neck, and now the car was out of commission with the front end completely smashed up into ruins. Nevertheless, the minions exited the car in search of their closest victim, which happened to be Waldorf hiding in the police cruiser. One of them flung open the driver's door, the other assisting to toss the now immobilized Waldorf out onto the cold concrete before getting in.

BANG.

Well, he got in with a bullet in his left arm. His buddies took the other seats, with the hostage taker and Agatha occupying the back. She was as feisty as Darwin had originally thought, trying her best to put up a fight. The guy was young, probably not even eighteen, and he didn't want to kill her. He just he needed a hostage, which everyone knew was something to negotiate for.

The cruiser reversed hard, with Darwin firing into the windshield.

BANG. CLICK. CLICK.

The eight-round ammunition cartridge was out. The minions returned fire, spraying blindly in front of them until the cruiser disappeared around the corner.

"SHIT!" Darwin was fuming, angrier than ever. He rushed to Waldorf, who was groaning on the ground.

He was shot in the chest, on the right side.

"Wald!" Darwin took off his leather police jacket and stuck it on the wound. "Waldorf, you with me?!"

He coughed, but managed a slight smile, "Son-bitches shot my fat ass!"

"Hell." Darwin knew it was bad, putting pressure on the wound despite the blood. "You're a damn mess!"

220

The Pontiac reversed and wheeled around the leftover gang cars that had blocked them in. Once free, Darwin watched it sped away until it suddenly stopped. The shift linkage clicked, the reverse lights illuminating to signal its return. No, they couldn't leave Darwin and Waldorf with no help.

"Wait! Wait!" Biff shouted as he opened the door.

"Where the hell are you going, Biff!?" Jason his voice crackled, the lividness apparent, "We have to get Agatha!"

Jenkins popped the GTO's trunk, retrieved the first aid kit, and rushed to Waldorf. He pushed Darwin out of the way and looked up at him.

"GO!" he ordered.

"What?" Darwin refused.

"I said *go!*" Biff examined the wound like he actually knew what he was doing, "I got this!"

"What the hell do you mean 'you got this'?! This man is shot in the damn chest!"

"Dog, I'm training to become a nurse, man. Get the hell out of here and help Jason get Agatha back!"

Waldorf was coughing badly.

"But—!"

"I know he's your friend," Biff hated this, "but I can take care of him long enough for the ambulance to get here!"

"COME ON!" Jason wailed from the car. "COME ON!"

"Dude," Biff forced a smile, "you're a cop! Go do some cop business. I'll take care of your friend, man, if you take care of mine."

Darwin hesitated, if only for a moment.

"Go." Waldorf managed to get out. "Get em'."

Darwin pointed as he stepped backwards towards the GTO.

"You better hang in there!" he shouted to Waldorf. "You damn bastard, Waldorf, you *better* hang in there!"

Waldorf smirked, "Heck dang."

"I'll be back! I'm going to get these assholes!"

Darwin hustled to retrieve his AR-15. The car moved forward to meet him, the passenger door already open. He got in.

"What's up?" he smirked, reloading his gun.

"You better buckle up tight."

"Yes, sir." Darwin did so. "Seen you drive the hell out of this old thing before, so don't be shy with me, junior."

"My dad calls me 'junior'." Jason gritted his teeth. "And you don't have to worry about me being 'shy' either."

"I guess this is the part where shit gets real?"

Jason gripped the shifter and put it in gear. He nodded.

"You better hold on." was all he said.

He revved the engine, released the clutch, and floored the throttle. Its tires spun, the rubber treads burning, all the while flying down the remaining levels of the parking garage, careening out into the street sideways. As if it were a professional stunt, the GTO straightened out perfectly and roared ahead.

In all his years, he had yearned to dare. He had gravitated towards pressing the boundary of control, to see how far he could push, how far he could go, how fast he could bear before his luck ran dry. That he had learned to master his skill in an old jalopy made little difference. It was about the art. It was about the feeling of the steering wheel pulsing in the grip of his palms, the shifter bouncing about through the rough patch of the roads as he pitched the car sideways and held his breath, or life, in the hands of the challenge.

Everyone chastised him, because no one understood.

In the world he wanted one thing, to *drive*, and everyone asked him why. Why must he go so fast? Why must he play with his life? What reasons could justify his hooliganism? He never had a true cause aside from the raw desire, but now, things had changed. *This* was why.

Now, in these trying moments, he had something to drive *for*.

His friend. His friend was in trouble. *She* was in trouble.

And there, as he quickly closed the distance, he swore an oath to help. Just him and the damn car. All he had to do was drive. Just drive. Don't stop driving.

He needed *her*. He loved *her*.

-11:30AM- Interstate 85 Southbound. Downtown. Atlanta, Georgia.

He fixated on Agatha, the way her hands motioned to explain the dynamic forces of a vehicle during cornering. She taught him about tire contact patches, the initial flex at the cusp of turn-in, the way the vehicle responded with rotation, the slew of scenarios if the cart pushed, or tail wagged.

It was a science, one that she studied and understood with glee.

Out of her pretty girl shell, she would lecture Jason for hours at the track, pumping advice to him over hundreds if not thousands of after-hours laps.

To him, every classic car had a heartbeat. She taught him the fundamentals of reading it. The gritty harshness of the old pushrods clattering away tickled the insides of his ears. He shifted into the next gear, the old car only asking for more. At first, he was timid, worried about the prospect of crashing into an unsuspecting motorist during the escapade. He had no sirens, no lights, yet the old Pontiac was much like a police car in the way that it gathered attention. Through its widened exhaust pipes and long tube headers, the old car played a song so primal and wondrous that even the daintiest of minds grew weak.

He should've needed to honk the horn, but he didn't.

People knew that it was coming from a mile away, the *sound* it produced so telling that the warning of its impending arrival was free of mixed interpretation.

"Just drive!" she'd say. *"Feel the car. C'mon! Hold the corner! Hold it! Rotate! Rotate!—Yes!"*

And rotate he did.

Jason coursed the car through a bump at high speed, nearly sending the tires off the ground and his stomach acid into the dashboard, but with a huge thud, he was back in control with the wheel at his helm. There, through the traffic, was nothing but a cloud of gray smoke spewing from the tires ablaze and the V-8 pinned against its maximum power. The GTO slid sideways through an intersection, flying through in a fashion unseen outside of a movie screen. No one knew what to say or do when they witnessed it.

"Hold it! Add a little power!" Agatha would say. *"Not the best way through a corner! But nice drift!"*

Some honked, but most watched in awe, hearing reports coming on about some kind of attack at the Bank of America Tower downtown on their radios. They heard the sirens, tons of them whistling off in the distance. Then a few news drones flew overhead, followed by the echoing sounds of the GTO speeding through yet another intersection along the way.

"Smooth interactions, Jason!" Agatha once told him during an autocross. *"Don't be heavy-handed!"* he had dodged a cone, similar to a vehicle that pulled in front of him now. *"Guide the front end! Use your eyes!—Subtle, be subtle! Don't lose your focus!"*

The car weaved through a dense group of traffic with perfection, each successive swerve within both inches of doom and resolute control. Darwin held on for dear life, blown away by this style of raw driving. Yeah, he knew how to wheel his cruiser around with the best that Porter had to offer, but this was different. This was the shit he saw on TV. Jason's driving confidence spoke for itself. He displayed very little fear, aside from an occasional grimace at a close call with another obstacle, but in all, he remained composed and focused. He couldn't afford to break his concentration, not even for a moment. The sheriff understood as Jason white-knuckled the faded leather trim of the wheel, so he didn't dare to interrupt.

"*All units, all units.*" the police dispatcher came over Darwin's handheld police radio. "*We have a possible 10-79 and a 10-71 at 600 Peachtree. Shots fired, possible officers down, three suspects in unknown stolen police vehicle. Suspects considered armed and dangerous. All responding units, Code-3.*"

"Is that them?" Jason shouted over the loud engine.

"Yeah, looks like no one's picked them up yet!" Darwin shouted back and turned up the radio. He pressed the transmit button and spoke into it with power in his voice.

"*Atlanta dispatch, this is first responding officer Porter, Tennessee Sheriff Darwin Loveless, badge number 4-7-4-5-Alpha, over!*"

The dispatch responded back, "*Badge 4-7-4-5-Alpha, this is dispatch, state your current situation.*"

"*Uh, first responding officer on scene. Eight shots fired, one man down, one girl hostage, they have commandeered *my* vehicle, over.*"

"*Copy that badge 4-7-4-5-Alpha, is there a transponder on your vehicle?*"

"*Negative dispatch, my vehicle is pretty old! Could you give me a location on the suspects?*"

There was a brief pause before the response came through.

"*Copy that, all units, all units: suspects located in Porter, Tennessee Sheriff vehicle spotted by aerial unit. Vehicle is headed southbound, Interstate 75. All available units respond, code 10-77 high speed pursuit. Suspects armed and dangerous, one hostage in vehicle, over.*"

Jason and Darwin made brief eye contact, their thoughts in unison.

"Get on the highway here!" Darwin demanded.

Jason gauged the working area ahead, *"Apex!"* Agatha would tell him. *"Guide toward the apex!"*

"Remember," The car dipped outside before he finessed the wheel into a sharp rotation aimed squarely at the corner's apex. *You want to kiss the inside! Right there! Let the car settle!"*

The steering grew stiff and quivery, evidence of the tires at their peak grip threshold. He heard them squeal, the weight of the car shifting towards the outside. *"Good! Good! Add power! Slowly!"*

Darwin had his doubts. He squeezed the door grip, wondering whether the turn was navigable at such speed, but the GTO hunkered down and swerved right, nonetheless. The tires began to squeal in their brief protest of the maneuver, skittering sideways in a controlled fashion before Jason straightened the car's path. Once settled, he called for the V8 to accelerate down the onramp with everything it had. He shifted through the gears hard, approaching traffic near the top of third gear where he jumped to the occasion to begin his art of automotive parkour.

He pretended each car was a cone. It was easier this way, just like the autocross courses he frequented.

"This is Interstate *85* South, Sheriff!" Jason noted as he dodged them. "That lady said I-75, man."

"Don't worry!" Darwin reassured, trying not to soil his pants. "It dumps out into 75 Southbound shortly here. Just watch the traffic!"

They continued, heavy on approach towards downtown through the "corridor", which was known to have some of the worst traffic conditions south of Queen City. High in the early afternoon, the working commuters shared their part in making the maneuvers a living hell for the GTO, but Jason managed it.

He was a professional at driving like an asshole.

A ricer, as it was known.

"We need a siren!" he shouted when he was forced to slow down.

"Hell, flash your brights or something!"

Jason did that, and took turns honking the horn.

"Get out of the way!" he shouted to no avail.

During a sudden lane change, he was nearly broadsided by a crossover driven by an inattentive mother. When it drifted into his lane, Jason proactively swerved around her. Darwin was busy flashing his badge at people, but only a few paid attention. Most were locked away in their own little worlds, the shameless masses of conformity locked away in serene wheeled vaults.

But wait. Jason noticed something, the hell he played on the radar sensors aboard the pedestrian vehicles. It was easy, a cheat code courtesy of risk-averse lawyers concerned about lawsuits. The AI programs left large spaces between each vehicle, a calculated distance based on weather patterns, temperature, and vehicle type. Once the federal standards mandated such algorithms a decade prior, it became the norm.

The modern cars were cautious. They avoided everything. Always.

His plan morphed. He turned the GTO into a blockade, just one close swerve enough to trip the autopilots into evasive maneuvers. Faking them into panic mode helped the blitz, and that was nearly as much fun as having permission to wildly disobey traffic laws. Some felt people should be alert while driving, but the computers had taken over that duty. In the hilarity of watching each unsuspecting vehicle suddenly jerk its occupants back into reality, Jason saw a drone aircraft fly over them. He and Darwin had apparently managed to make the news.

The dispatch came through the police radio again,

"*Dispatch to all available units, officers in pursuit of suspects Interstate-75 Southbound, code 4-4-4 shots fired.*"

"Come on! Come on!" Darwin willed as he briefly stuck his head out of the window, his hands sweating in the grip of his rifle.

"I know!" Jason fought to squeeze through the traffic. "This is getting to be more difficult by the second."

Darwin pointed vigorously, "Take the HOV lane! Give it hell!"

Quizzically, a crossover filled with onlookers blocked his path. Children were buckled into the back seats, smashing their pasty faces against the window glass for a peek. Jason gestured for them to move over, but the children merely waved back. When Darwin showed his badge, their faces lit up with enough surprise to catch the attention of their parents up front.

"Get out of the way!" Jason screamed. "Move over!"

But the parents couldn't hear them. Instead, their bodies suddenly jerked forward as the van's collision avoidance system detected doom. In their path was a tumbling group of concrete blocks, one of which bounced up and impacted the side of the van, despite its evasive action.

"Oh hell!" Darwin yipped as the GTO split the gap between the remaining two.

"Where the hell did those come from!?" *now* Jason was growing frightened.

A tractor trailer loaded with them had clipped the retaining wall ahead and bounced into the center lane. Traffic was beginning to gridlock, but the left lanes were still free. Jason checked his surroundings, scanning the mirrors before pinpointing a clear path ahead. He aimed the car towards the escape route in the leftmost lane and pushed the accelerator to the floor. Once he cleared the wreck, he pushed their speed over 110mph.

Downtown came into view, and the blinking lights of the police up ahead highlighting the pursuit in the maze of traffic. The Pontiac closed on them *fast*, pushing through the remaining distance as if warp drives were real. Alas, they drove up behind the first pursuing squad car.

"You ready?" Jason asked, the peace short lived.

"I'm as ready as I've ever been, son." Darwin insisted. "Go around this asshole. Let's get these bastards! Yee-haw!"

"Yes sir!" Jason already had that planned. He grabbed third gear and gunned the engine. "Here we go!"

-11:36AM-

Waldorf was stabilized and loaded into an ambulance. He waved a tearful goodbye to Biff before the doors were shut. Maybe the many hours of night school training paid off. Biff felt accomplished, valued, and oddly serene. There were bigger fish to fry, but for a few seconds, this was *his* time. He sat on the curb and tried to catch his breath through all of the commotion, wondering if he had really bargained for this. During his brief meditation, his wrist computer vibrated, a plaguing reminder of his permanent link with society.

He looked down. Media notification.

BREAKING NEWS ALERT:
High Speed Chase & Hostage Situation; Downtown Atlanta.
Join now to watch live coverage! — *FOX 5 Atlanta*

A preview clip of the live footage looped on the display, showing Darwin's hijacked police vehicle on the run. Those were his friends. They needed him. Okay, the meditation was over now. Panicked, Biff ran downstairs and into the street. Electropaper billboards honed as he walked, their advertisements all custom tailored to suit a balance of both his and their needs.

Clothes. Shoes. Cars.

Things he couldn't afford, even on his best day. Well, maybe he used to, but he had straightened up. Other contestants drove by, lost in the effect of the chaos. Like roaches, Underground members scattered quickly at the sign of sudden change, the influx of cops much like a light being flipped on. Some still hunted feverishly for the high-value item, unaware that it was already claimed.

He tightened the straps on his backpack, paranoid that the glass prism flag could and would be snatched away at any moment. Not today. Not after all of this. Contestants piled into the parking lot of a convenience store and Biff followed suit. He needed a ride. He needed to help.

Walking in, he saw zombies. Everyone, including the store clerk, stared at their wrists, checking the same breaking news notification. The television on the wall automatically switched to the coverage, its base programming biased to feed important news to the masses. Only five minutes in, and every major news station in town had their aerial vehicles up and recording the event, live for everyone to see. On screen, the viewpoint focused onto Darwin's stolen police car, and in that frame, he could see Agatha furiously struggling with the man in the back seat.

"*Uh—it appears as if the woman they have taken hostage is rather young—I think she's struggling with them!*" the newscaster sounded thrilled. "*—Yes, she's fighting back—*"

"Holy hell." he muttered, seeing a line of at least twenty police cruisers chasing the gangsters down the freeway.

The camera viewpoint zoomed out, the drone's target reticule locking onto another vehicle approaching the group fast from the rear. His heart fluttered. It was the GTO.

"*—Wait—Wait!*" the newscaster's voice stumbled. "*—We have an unknown car coming into the chase! I repeat—an unknown black car here, swerving through the line of police cars in pursuit!—Oh my god! Can you get the drone to lock onto it?*"

He *had* to get out there. Now.

Biff turned around to see a group of various Underground members flocking around the television. He was chump, a ricer, a broke ass kid who'd lost his car. None of the elites were likely to help, but he had to ask. At this point, if it required stealing a car in order to catch up and help, he'd do it.

He turned to the first person that he recognized.

[TurboCoupe (E-4)]

"Can you give me a ride?" he asked him.

"Screw that." the guy replied with a laugh. A few of his teammates joined him. "I guess you need to keep better track of your team members."

He had always been a douche.

"Man, somebody give me a ride, or is every person in this 'club' an asshole?" Jenkins shouted with desperation, all in a tone never heard from him before. He was normally a nice, peaceful, and mellow guy—but today wasn't a normal day. "They took my friend! One of you motherfuckers better help me get her back!"

"Wait a minute." one of the elites stepped forward. "That *is* Agatha from Underground!"

[Slickster2JZ (E-2)]

Tony. He drove a beautiful 1994 Toyota Supra Turbo.

"Yeah, man, crazy story, and it'll take all day to tell, but I just need somebody to get me *there*!"

"Yeah, that's Agatha's stupid old GTO!" someone shouted. "That's it!"

"Will you help me?" Jenkins asked as he saw the car swerving through police cars on the television. "Please?"

"What are you going to do?" Tony asked Jenkins. "When we catch up, I mean."

"I don't know," Biff was at a loss for a plan, "but I'm sure I'd figure it out once we get there."

"*—That looks like a, uh—does anyone know what kind of car that is? No? Well, there are two occupants inside.*"

"Well, what the hell are you all doing just standing here? Let's go help out!" an administrator that he had never seen shouted. "Come on!"

That got them moving. Everyone grabbed their keys and scrambled for the door, either anxious to assist, or curious to play witness to the turmoil caused by the new and already infamous Team Three Kings. Jenkins ran with them and hopped into Tony's extremely fast Supra Turbo, speeding off in a line with the rest of the members.

The Supra Turbo fell into formation behind one of the site's fastest classic cars, a 1,170 horsepower Nissan GTR. Tony switched on the radio and discovered the news had overridden the normal music broadcasts,

"*—This is unbelievable!— Uh, and we have gotten unofficial word from the radio that the hostage is actually a visitor from Queen City—People in the garage, where the shootout occurred, claimed that her name is uh—'Agatha'—*"

The Supra followed the group onto the highway, spooling its turbocharger and rocketing down the onramp. A few old exotic cars jumped ahead to clear the way, Ferraris, Lamborghinis, and even a Pagani. The modern Corvettes stayed beside them, busy using their hybrid engine boosters to widen their reaches. In perfect formation, they pulled onto the highway to clear room for Tony and Biff, blocking traffic like a wall. The coast was clear now, the leaders ahead signaling with a strobe. A 2035 Corvette jutted into the adjacent lane, its window retreating to expose the driver. He them stuck his arm out and gave the signal.

"GO! GO!" the man shouted with a wave.

"Hold on!" Tony gunned the throttle, sending his Toyota Supra shooting down the freeway after the others. Every time he had to shift to a higher gear, their bodies would be thrown forward, only to be catapulted into the seats again once the power hit. Hands down, it was the fastest car Jenkins had *ever* ridden in.

Oh, the sounds of its straight six wailing at 8,000rpm.

Oh, the feeling of his stomach pressing into the depth of his gut.

Oh, the classics.

How wonderful they were.

"There he is!" Darwin hollered. "There he is, right there!"

"I see him! I see him!" Jason kept his eye on Darwin's swerving police cruiser.

Dispatch radioed, "*Dispatch to all cars responding to the 5-0-5-Alpha, hostage situation, suspects armed and dangerous, shots fired at police. Keep distance, repeat, keep distance.*"

"WHAT?" Jason couldn't believe the order. Maybe that explained why the grouping of cops continued to stay about twelve car lengths back from Darwin's cruiser.

"No. Screw that!" Darwin scowled. "Punch this baby up! I want a piece of these son-bitches! Assholes shot my friend!"

"Roger that." Jason agreed and floored it again. "Hold on, I'm about to do something crazy."

He maneuvered the GTO between the remaining police cars, despite their efforts to keep him from passing. One of them used the loudspeaker, warning that the men were interfering with official police business. Bollocks. Darwin flashed his badge.

"*This is being handled by the police! Please stop!*" said the voice on the loudspeaker.

"I *am* the police, bitches!" Darwin hollered back. "Get out of the way!"

Finally. They were clear to engage, the spotlight clearly on them.

The old Pontiac was an easy spot, the frightened young minions zeroing in the car like a homing missile. Darwin hoisted his rifle to aim, adding more fuel to the fire. Their eyes widened in fear. There was no plan, no discussion, and no going back. So, they did what panicked young gangsters do. Shoot first. Think later.

Bullets ricocheted nearby. Jason ducked, hearing one bounce off the car, followed by another that put a hole in the windshield in front of Darwin.

"Oh, *hell* no!" Darwin couldn't believe it. "I *know* these bastards ain't shootin' their shit at *me*!"

"Shit! Shoot back!" Jason cried. "Shoot! Shoot!"

"Hold it steady!" Darwin ordered, trying to aim the AR-15.

"I'm trying! They're kind of shooting at us!"

BANG.

A single, excellently placed shot. It hit the guy hanging out of the front passenger seat straight in the shoulder, causing his body to tense and flop out of the moving car. It would leave a hell of a road rash. Poor guy. He rolled helplessly on the ground, and Jason swerved hard to miss it.

"Ooooooooooooh!" Jason gave Darwin credit. "Nice shot!"

Traffic was too heavy to keep the car stable. Jason was forced to swerve, throwing off Darwin's otherwise impeccable aim. Instead, he wasted two, eventually managing to blow out the rear windshield of his beloved cruiser. Agatha turned to them, shouting something, the ambient noise rending it inaudible.

"Agatha!" Jason screamed to no avail. "We're coming!"

-11:55AM-

Her whole life, she had seen movies of bubbly, naive, and helpless girls taken hostage, waiting patiently as their saviors attempted the heroic rescue. It was a stoic cliché, but she never imagined being the center point of a real-life scenario. Once the shock, she realized that despite what everyone said, what everyone did, what *she* did, and how everyone always viewed her, she was not a cliché.

Not Agatha Lily Peters.

Not anymore.

Not when she was staring her captor in her face.

She was tired of being viewed as just an object, a prize of consolation, or a mere bartering piece in an impromptu hostage standoff. People were going to respect her, so long as she still lived to see another day.

The Odyssey. It was the road trip of a lifetime, where the fine details of friendship, teamwork, and the sense of unabated exploration opened the eyes of even the most experienced man or woman. On this trip, you learned many things about yourself, your friends, and the world around you.

Here, she learned about something more important: herself.

"Mmmph!" Agatha grunted, hitting the guy who had taken her hostage.

The hit knocked the gun from his hand, turning the situation into a moving death battle. He desperately tried to gain the upper hand without hurting her, but her struggle wasn't making it easy.

"Gmmph!" she kicked his groin.

He groaned, but still managed to head butt her. Blood spewed from her nose, but she ignored the wound, using her fists to pummel his face the best she could.

The guy up front was on the phone shouting in Spanish, likely to his superior, bleeding heavily from his wounded arm. Agatha understood him, of course, her Spanish as fluent as ever.

It was her heritage. Her lineage. Her history.

"Yes! The policeman—got me—" he paused as the car bounced off the retaining wall. "Get me—out of here!"

His wrist computer was on loudspeaker.

"Get them off you!" replied the opposing voice. "Then, we can help!"

"Can't!" he checked the mirror. "Got two loco guys behind me in an old coupe muscle car, swerving and shooting like lunatics!"

"What color is the coupe?"

"Black!" he looked behind him in the back seat, witness to the death match. "Jonez is fighting the girl in the back!"

"Tie her down! She is a girl!"

"He can't! I can't help because there's a cage in the way!"

"Keep driving south, use traffic to get away!" his superior said before hanging up.

Then, he saw a chemical truck in the leftmost lane, wondering what more he had to lose. He read the identifier tag. It was hauling used cooking grease. Fighting initial hesitation, he swerved towards it, using his right hand to hold the weapon.

"Lo siento." he said, sorry that it had come such desperation.

BANG. BANG. BANG.

Two tires were gone, their treads separating in the shock of depressurization. The truck jumped, its weight transferring abruptly to the front right side. Its driver tried to regain control, but along came the Newtonian killjoy, the uncontrollable momentum veering the truck right towards the wall. It hit, the crash so loud that it seared the eardrums of those nearby. The tank ruptured in the impact, spilling the grease along the roadway in cascades. Within seconds, a makeshift ice rink spanned all southbound lanes of traffic.

He cheered in rejoice, but the happiness was short-lived.

BANG. BANG.

Two shots came from the back seat, but who the hell had the gun?

"WHOA!" Jason hit the brakes hard when he saw the big chemical truck swerve out of control, but he never imagined it would contact the wall.

Damn Newton, again!

Inertia was a bitch, the GTO's dynamic controls now entirely unresponsive to Jason's inputs. Its soft, sticky tires were rendered helpless, their treads gliding over a near frictionless surface, unable to enact change in their direction. All four wheels locked. The car careened left. Jason counter steered, hoping to guide away from doom, yet the car continued into a flat spin at over 80mph.

The world around them spun, their screams hauntingly akin to the wail of a frightened toddler. Jason did all he could, fighting the steering wheel, taking turns pressing both the gas and brake pedals, but there was nothing. Just a spiral into the abyss of doom. He conceded to defeat, his budding skills outmatched.

Or maybe, they weren't.

Her voice padded his panic.

"Whenever it gets away from you," she told him once following an uncorrectable spin, *"remember to run on instinct. Sometimes you'll crash. Other*

times you won't. I figured out that the mind is astounding when you just let it run on instinct. Remember, Jason. Just drive. Drive. The. Car."

Maybe it was Agatha's teachings, his fond and profound memory of her voice, her confidence, and her resolve. Was he any different? His arms moved in ways that he didn't consciously calculate, his feet relieving their pressure on the pedals. For once, he let *himself* run on instinct.

He corrected. Somehow, yes, *somehow,* the car returned to stability.

"WOW!" Darwin guffawed. "WAHOOO! Junior, *you* can drive!"

"Oh my god—oh my god." Jason was in disbelief. "Did *that* just happen? Did that *really* just happen?!"

"Looks like it did." Darwin was still laughing. "I think I shit myself!"

"That makes two of us!"

"Holy hell, Son, that shit was *real.*"

"That was luck." Jason couldn't deny it. "Sheer luck. Oh my god, dude."

Jason gave the steering wheel a few trial tugs, checking if the tires were okay. Thank god for the renewed grip. Confident again, he sped back up, checking the rearview mirror to see a wall of mangled police cars fading behind them.

None of them made it through the grease.

Now, Jason and Darwin were the only ones left.

"*Dispatch to *any* available units, assistance requested, Interstate-75 Southbound. Multiple vehicle crash, possible injuries with officers down, repeat multiple 10-108s. 11-25 across all lanes of traffic, large vehicle obstruction, suspects still at large. *All* available units respond.*"

"Shouldn't you radio back or something to let them know that you're okay?" Jason shouted over the engine.

Darwin hesitated at first, wondering if he should put himself in the spotlight considering all he'd done.

"*Dispatch.*" he sighed. "*This is Badge 4-7-4-5-Alpha, responding to distress call.*"

"*Badge 4-7-4-5-Alpha, are you still in pursuit?*"

"*Affirmative dispatch, on these assholes like white-on-rice.*"

"*10-4 Badge 4-7-4-5-Alpha. Current orders are to keep distance on suspects and await further assistance, over.*"

"What is she talking about?" Jason was in disbelief.

Darwin looked as if he'd seen an alien, hearing a few more shots from inside the gangster-loaded police cruiser. Yes, shots fired, and dispatch wanted them to back down.

To hell with that nonsense.

"Who the hell knows?" he squinted, seeing Agatha scuffling hard with the minion in the back seat. "She's in trouble, pull up closer so I can get a good shot!"

———

Yeah, so the girl could fight, but she was alone.

All of the police cars crashed, dashing her hope of rescue.

The minion ran low on patience, pinning her against the back window to dampen her struggle. His pistol fell beneath the front seats out of reach, forcing him to resort to cruder tactics of submission—namely bashing her head against the window.

Agatha's vision distorted further with every hit, the headache growing in intensity. She reached up and clasped the width of his neck, squeezing as if she wished his throat would pop. He hit her again, but her grip persisted, throwing him off to the point where she gained a clear view of the world behind them.

Hope was approaching.

Her bloodshot eyes wandered for a mere moment, just enough to see her GTO barreling up at high speed. A tall man leaned from the passenger side window, a rifle held masterfully in his hands. Sheriff Darwin, taking names and taking aim. She knew what came next, ducking her head down and closing her eyes just before the window shattered.

One second later, her attacker was screaming, holding the side of his neck. Blood oozed through the gaps between his fingers, the wound clearly enough to change his focus. He let go of her, coughing in horror as he panicked. She was free and frozen all at once. Agatha felt the signs of shock, the ringing ears, the disconnection from reality, the temporal distortion that turned individual seconds into eons.

Gradually, she regained control of her limbs, crawling away from him towards the right-side door. Their eyes were locked. Hers were filled with empathy, while his seemed sorry, if not outright apologetic. He reached for her, for anyone that would help him, but she withdrew, looking back towards the GTO as it maneuvered to pull around. The wounded minion took hold of her foot, but she quickly kicked him away, trying to hold herself steady in the backseat. Unbuckled and completely at the mercy of forces outside her control, she slid back and forth with the lunacy of the driver.

Every time she found balance, he violently swerved, throwing her around like a toy in the cabin. Agatha screamed, but he paid no attention, his efforts solely focused on the GTO that he couldn't seem to shake.

Two men rode pressed along in the black coupe behind him.

Who were they? A cop, and a kid.

No. There *had* to be more.

He dialed his wrist computer and waited through the rings, wishing, hoping, praying that someone would answer. Finally, he heard a voice.

"Carlos!" his desperation grew with each syllable. "I don't know where to go!"

Carlos was angry, his rank now clearly in question. What kind of leader was he?

Stable? Sure.

Trustworthy? Absolutely.

Effective? Questionable.

He and his men not only botched a key money drop, but also made headline news for the entire world to see. This was the definition of *failure*. Not good when the mafia leaned towards capital punishment.

"The police still have you!" Carlos blurted.

"I know, sir, but I lost a mass of them about a mile back!" the gangster said between swerves. "But I got two gangbanger homies still chasing and shooting! Lunatics!"

"Well," Carlos tried his best to remain calm, "you're on the news Consuelo, so *everyone* can see *everything*. Lose the helicopter drones!"

"How am I supposed to do that?" he squealed when Darwin fired another shot that pierced through the front passenger window. He swerved towards the GTO but missed when it cut speed and caused him to overshoot.

The cruiser hit the wall, throwing Agatha into the front cage briefly, but the car stayed together long enough to maintain control. These old Ford Crown Victorias were obviously well built.

"Keep the car out of the damn wall!" Carlos harped. "There's a tunnel coming up about a mile ahead! Ditch the car in there but take the bitch with you!"

"O—Okay, Carlos."

-12:07PM-

"Get up closer to the car!" Darwin ordered.

"I can't exactly do that without him trying to ram us!" Jason was defiant to commit, until he saw Agatha open the door.

She hung out, desperately reaching for her car, with both arms. Her voice shouted, but the wind was far too loud. Jason locked onto her face, the movement of his mouth registering a reply that she couldn't hear.

"Hold on!" she read his lips. "We won't leave you!"

Calm swept over her disorientation, the adrenaline combining with the brief solitude enough to rid her arms and legs of sluggishness. There he was, doing what she had always promised he could:

Jason Weathers, just driving the damn car.

Another violent swerve nearly threw her from the cruiser. The door clipped a car in traffic, ripping it from the hinges. Vinyl on the door panel hit her head, dazing her again as he caught the B-pillar to avoid doom. She held on for her life, quite literally once she felt an unearthly tug against her back. It was the freed door, the fabric of her tank top caught on its remains, threatening to drag her out into the concrete.

Shit. The force was far too great, the fight against it a losing battle that Agatha clearly recognized. Still, she grappled the pillar with all her might, using her left hand to supplement as the shirt lifted to her neck like a noose.

"No, no, no!" Jason and Darwin watched in horror.

The shirt had to go. Agatha needed to free herself before it was too late, before her neck snapped, or her body tumbled into I-75, but her position drew no favor. Choking in the strangulation, she grunted and fought the best she could, feeling as if her spine would shear at any moment until the fabric started ripping across her back. Using the continuing force to her advantage, she arched her back just at the right time, giving the polyester shirt a final stretch beyond its limit.

It ripped free, her neck suddenly relieved of critical strain. She looked back, seeing the door tumbling through the traffic lanes, and her GTO leaning over on its right side.

Jason braked and cut left, missing the door before returning to his previous position. He plotted his course, figuring if he got close enough, maybe Agatha could jump onto the hood—if it weren't for the maniac minion driver.

Dammit!

The guy kept swerving, nearly losing control of the battered cruiser, but Agatha found the strength to pull herself back inside. Jason backed off, hearing Darwin holler through his radio at a pair of truckers ahead. He pleaded with dispatch, asking if they could request the truckers ahead to slow down with their AV wagon trains. It was far shot, but a moving roadblock was just what they needed.

"*Dispatch to all law enforcement and emergency vehicles: Authorities have issued an Emergency Traffic Declaration, shutting down Interstate 75 Southbound north of Exit 238. Full GRID shutdown. All sub-Class 4 vehicles pulling to the shoulders, all above-Class 4 vehicles safe stopping in perimeter lanes. Emergency vehicles use the formed partition, over.*"

Sixty long seconds passed as they zipped past oodles of vehicles pulled over to each shoulder, single-file line like ants, following the orders of Atlanta's Autonomous Vehicle GRID. All passenger cars on autopilot took the first opportunity, as they possessed far more freedom to maneuver and slow down in the declaration of a traffic emergency.

The freighters, semis, busses, and other large trucks were next.

Bingo.

It was working, their speed steadily decreasing as the minion saw the moving roadblock. Jason watched the speedometer creep below the seventy mark, then sixty, and then fifty-five. Darwin took another shot at the driver, but the bumpy highway ailed his aim—or at least that's what he blamed.

The cruiser accelerated away, the minion taking his chances to try and squeeze between the lanes that were blocked by large semi-trucks. He made it through partially, finding resistance when the drivers of two wagon trains spotted him trying to pass. They squeezed him in, swerving left to right, their AV followers mimicking each move in an effort to block the cruiser's attempt to dodge them. The seesaw motion nearly sent Agatha flying from the door again, but she grabbed onto the diving cage and fell to the floor, spotting the missing pistol from the convulsing man in the back seat.

She grabbed it, hoping it was loaded. Blindly, she pointed it up towards the driver's seat and pulled the trigger.

BANG. BANG. CLICK. CLICK

He screamed, the bullets streaming through his back and his left leg.

"AAAAAH!" it was a blood thawing yell. "Mi dios! Tú perra estúpida!"

The cruiser veered left when he let go of the steering wheel, brushing against the flatbed trailer of a semi beside it. It was an AV trailer, now triggered by the impact to the point of ignoring its route in preference of pulling over. Thankfully, the human lead drivers weren't so easily duped. Seeing the opportunity to make a move, the semi to the right of the cruiser moved left, pinning the car in between the two trucks with nowhere to go. The gangster panicked, his leg bleeding heavily, looking as if the bullet pierced his femoral artery. He grew weaker by the second, unable to do more than hold a steady speed. Knowing he was a goner, he spoke his last farewells to Carlos and pushed the accelerator to the floor, pinning it down with the floormat.

He'd go down with fury, in a ball of fire so be it.

The criminal partition kept her out of the front seat. Hearing the engine racing, she knew that the cruiser could escape at any moment, accelerating before surely hitting a wall down the road. At high speed in a vehicle *this* old? Guaranteed goner. So Agatha was proactive, climbing through the shattered rear windshield and hoisting herself atop the trunk. Jason sped up, pulling the GTO to a position as close to the trailer as possible. He was conflicted, knowing that an intercept behind the cruiser was a troubled option. The probability of being stuck in the trap wasn't worth the risk. There had to be a better way to get her out.

"What are you doing?!" he hollered to Agatha, surprised to see her.

She couldn't hear him, as she was too busy fighting to keep her balance on the mangled trunk. So she pointed, and he understood as she looked to her right, trying to gauge the distance between her body and the flatbed trailer. Darwin protested, finding her implied plan absolutely terrible. He waved his arms in a distinct "NO" pattern, but she ignored him. In the distance behind them, she spotted a collection of Underground cars approaching at high speed. Leading the group was a white Toyota Supra.

—

Biff and Tony listened to the scene from the radio. The rest of the Underground members had to make their own detour after the cooking oil spill had blocked the highway, but they were hot and heavy, still making their way to the chase. They diverted onto Interstate 88—a new north-south thoroughfare nearly parallel to I-85—and then to Interstate 20 Eastbound, knowing that it would dump back 75 South. As for the added distance? Well, they used their incredible horsepower to pick up the slack.

Besides, all the cops were busy, or crashed.

The feed continued, now a slur of hyped voices.

"*—Wow, this is insane!*" the newscaster continued, his voice deep and inspired. "*—The hostage in the back of that stolen police cruiser is now on the trunk of the car! It's uh, it's now stuck between two semi-tractor trailers that bunched up the freeway to slow down the chase!*"

"Jesus!" Biff was worried. He could see the wall of traffic ahead as they sped along. "Why'd she get out of the car?!"

"*—Uh, the man driving that black two-door is trying to motion something to her!—He can't quite pull up behind the car to get her—I think he might be telling her to jump onto that flatbed trailer that's carrying concrete piping!*"

"Can you get me up there?" Biff asked Tony, speeding past police cars and diverted AV traffic.

"What the hell are you planning on doing?" Tony was unsure about pressing their luck. "You can't get out there, are you crazy?"

"Just get up next to that damn truck!"

"*—Yeah!—*" the newscaster answered a question from another employee in the helicopter. "*—Just a few seconds ago she was hanging out of the back door, and it came off! Looks like her shirt was caught on it and we thought it was going to pull her onto the freeway, but she got the shirt off!"

"She doesn't have on a shirt now?" Tony cracked a smile.

"Dude," Biff scoffed, knowing this wasn't the time to imagine her shirtless, "would you just drive?"

Agatha positioned herself as close as she could without falling off the trunk. Her mind didn't want to jump, but she knew that her choices were short.

Do or die? Do *and* die? Don't do and definitely die.

Option one, please. She filled her lungs with air, making sure that her last breath was as full and vibrant as possible. Her eyes held focus with Jason's, watching his face as he understood what this moment truly meant.

"Aw, shit." Darwin groaned. "This girl's about to jump!"

"Yep." Jason admitted the truth. "Yep, she is."

Agatha was no bitch. She was going for it.

She leapt, as hard and as fast as she could, her body airborne for just a moment before her bare chest hit metal frame of the trailer. The deep breath of air was forced away, her ribs now riddled with jabs of awful pain beaming through her with every heartbeat. Her entire body bounced, her shoulder blades catching the fall as she rolled onto her back.

Her toes wiggled, then each foot, then each leg.

She was alive. She made it, with only a moment to spare before the cruiser bumped the trailer again, sending her toppling off the deck.

Now she held on for dear life, trying to find traction, her sweaty hands slipping on the metal surface to no avail. What little grip she mustered was quickly fading.

Yeah, maybe she should've stayed in the car.

Hindsight never failed to haunt her. Ever.

"Shit!" Jason growled, pulling the GTO's front end within inches of the trailer. "Hold on! Agatha! HOLD. ON."

Agatha reached back with her right hand, using the hood to push herself up. Then she locked her feet into the taillight rails of the trailer to assist her climb, looking back at Darwin and Jason, wondering what the next move was. Their plan was to let the semis gradually come to a halt, but she slipped again, this time falling near the helm of one of the outrageously large wheels.

In a panic, Jason tried to maneuver the GTO into a position to assist her, but there wasn't enough space to avoid crushing her. At a loss, he hoped that she had enough strength to pull up, but she didn't. Her fingers were locked around the rusty support bars of the trailers frame, her arms left with the strength of wet pool noodles.

There, she faced the prospect of seeing a dramatic end to her short run. She never knew that signing up for The Odyssey was signing her obituary.

The driver of the semis wanted to stop, but they knew that doing so would send the trapped cruiser flying into the path of the car attempting the rescue. They tried to keep their speed and positions steady, but no matter how hard they tried, they were at the mercy of luck. Repeated contact between the three vehicles kept them on borrowed time.

This wouldn't hold up much longer.

"JUMP!" Darwin screamed as he leaned out the window and motioned towards the GTO. "You've got to jump, sweetie!"

But she couldn't. If she tried, she would miss and spill into the pavement. Everyone knew it. Even Jason. Out of options, she accepted her fate—until she saw Tony's white Supra power up beside the trailer, her friend Biff hanging dutifully out of the passenger window.

With little hesitation, he jumped onto the trailer and crawled to her position, extending his hand for her to take hold. In his mind, he questioned whether he'd have the power to swing her up to the truck bed, but it was at least worth the try.

"Go on three!" Biff shouted. "One! Two!"

But she let go of frame rail and lunged for his hand. She was in his grip, but barely. Simultaneously, they confirmed Jason's position, waiting for the moment of truce.

"The truck needs to hold it steady!" Jason shook his head in disapproval. Agatha saw him, so she didn't try the jump. "I don't want her to miss the damn car. He's swerving too much, tell dispatch to tell him to keep the shit still!"

"*Dispatch this is Badge 4-7-4-5-Alpha!" Darwin yelled into the radio. "*You've got to tell that damn trucker to keep the thing steady! We're trying to get her off the trailer!*"

"*Badge 4-7-4-5-Alpha, 10-4.*" dispatch responded. "*Truckers reporting having trouble due to the road surface and the vehicle stuck between them, over.*"

"*Shit! Tell them to just smash the son-of-a-bitch!*"

"No, dude." Jason disagreed. "That'll send your police car flying straight into us!"

Then, they saw Agatha trying to say something, but they couldn't hear her voice. She and Biff used their heads to nod towards the right side of the trailer. Jason understood, moving the GTO closer to that side before matching its speed

"Good god!" Darwin couldn't help himself. "I don't know if she'll make that!"

She wouldn't. Not without further help.

Jason accepted this, taking a deep breath before he engaged the cruise control. Now was the time for risk. Then, he made the move.

"Hold the steering wheel!" he demanded.

Jason abruptly let go of the controls, giving Darwin little time to react, "I swear to god, you damn kids!" he shouted.

Now, leaning out of the driver's side window, Jason motioned that he was ready for the swing. Darwin caught on quickly, hunching over the center console, his hands locked on the pulsating wheel. With careful, but incremental movements, he got the car as close as he could.

Agatha locked eyes with Jason, giving him a faithful nod.

Yes, he loved her, but that wasn't why he felt compelled to help.

She was his messiah, the person that saved him from the doom of depression. She was there when no one else was, when his old "friends" had moved on, when his parents had retreated in their stress. Jason was a recluse, an introvert by heart. He wasn't good at making friends. He wasn't good at life, but at least this gave it meaning, even in the weirdest of ways. Wow. This was life and death, but now he had his friends. All it took was two days.

Jason reached out of the window with both arms splayed towards Agatha. He'd never forget the look on her face at that moment, the trust that it bestowed in their bond, the faith that she had in him, someone who dared to risk himself in order to ensure her own freedom. In that second that Biff swung her into the air, Jason held his breath.

Time around them slowed, her motion through the air counted in individual frames, the instant where her hands met his, clasping on for her life. Jason nearly fell out of the car, but Darwin caught his foot.

"Don't let go of me!" Agatha screamed, her feed periodically scraping the ground.

"I won't!" Jason promised. "Just hold on!"

"Don't. Let. Go."

And he didn't, combining both his strength and the help of Darwin to pull her up. Her arms wrapped around his shoulders, her legs pushing into the door panel. Somehow—he couldn't remember—his arms found their way into leverage points beneath her shoulder and opposite rib. He clasped onto her bare skin, digging in so he didn't slip, and yanked.

Three motions did the trick. Yeah, maybe the P90X paid off.

"Come on in here, sugar!" Darwin shouted with a beaming smile.

"Here ya' go." Jason said, hoisting her upper torso tightly. Now secure in his grip, he reached around to pull the rest of her in with a firm hold on her leg. "Got you!"

Agatha fell into the interior, her body stretched across the entirety of both seats. Turning onto her back, she smiled, bloody lip and all. Alas, she was safe. That was the most daring thing she'd ever done.

Inhale, exhale, each breath more calming than the previous.

"Hey there, cowboy." she greeted.

"Nice to have you back!" Jason giggled, trying not to look at her budding chest.

She sat up, adjusting herself to free the center console. Her heart pounded, the tingling in her limbs subsiding with return of her senses. The adrenaline waned as quickly as it empowered. Damn. Her ribs were royally screwed, throbbing beneath her rapidly bruising skin. It was rare to feel pain of this magnitude, but she was alive.

Spurts of agony streamed through her as she lifted her legs, preparing to jump into the back seat as the car steadied and slowed down.

"Hey there, cowboy." she greeted,

"Nice to have you back!" Jason giggled, trying not to look at her budding chest.

Trying not to. It was much harder than he thought.

She loved these people. Darwin the blackmailing, crooked cop. Jason-the-douchebag, moonlighting as the wheelman. Now, Biff-the-mellow was, in fact, the most daring person that she had ever seen. All this within a matter of seconds, then reality hit. The noise and chaos returned.

She squeezed between the front seats and folded into the rear, eventually righting herself and fastening the seat belt. Finally secure, she patted Darwin on the shoulder and smiled when he turned around,

"Nice shooting, sir."

He tipped his hat, "It's a natural gift more so than a talent, ma'am."

They all regrouped, reading for one last rescue.

"Jump!" Jason shouted to Biff.

"Man," Biff cried, "this is some bullshit!"

But his leap was much more successful than Agatha's. He squeezed his body through the window with comparative ease. For moment, she was jealous.

"Get your ass in here!" Agatha helped pull him into the back seat.

"Yeah, you're welcome." he sneered. "Man, y'all got me doing some Mission Impossible bullshit over here, leaping between cars and shit. Man, got my nerves all rattled up."

"Three Kings, son." Jason laughed. "Can't mess with the clique."

"Everyone okay?"

"Yeah."

"I think so."

"I'm good."

"Heck dang!"

Their rejoicing was short lived. Realizing the hostage was now safely back in the pursuing GTO, the semi drivers steered back into their respective lanes, releasing the pressure on the cruiser. The minion driver was nearly unconscious, unable to keep a steady speed. Free from the trap, the cruiser retreated and became fully exposed again.

Darwin took aim, hating that he'd have to do it. He loved that damn car, his pride and joy, trusty and unyielding for years. But he hated gangsters, especially hated gangsters that shot his friends, stole his car, *and* took innocent people as human shields. The severely wounded minion took one last look in the mirror. He gulped.

Darwin closed one eye and aimed for the right rear tire,

"Hasta luego, híbrido."

BANG. BANG. BANG.

It was a spectacle, seeing the police car careen into the barrier and somersault through air, tumbling endlessly before coming to rest on its top. The GTO's nose dipped, its brakes applied at full pressure, skidding sideways to an eventual halt.

Then it was done. Over. Finally, the longest thirty minutes *ever*.

Now, they would have to explain why they shut down the city.

- The Underground Kings -
Deluxe Edition

EPISODE EIGHT

"The Aftermath"

-12:30PM-

They eyed the remains of the cruiser in complete silence. Darwin got out but didn't move too far. He stood calmly by the open passenger door, holding his gun and taking off his hat. His cruiser was now nothing more than a wrecked pile of metal.

"Bastards." he shook his head.

Jason got out, seeing an entire wall of police cars advancing about half mile back. Biff climbed through the door behind him, shaking Jason's hand with a nod.

"Nice driving, man." he said.

Agatha scooted forward, but the pain stopped her. Instinctively, she looked down to inspect the damage, remembering that she was shirtless and exposed, her shirt ripped away by the door that had nearly killed her. But it didn't. She fought back and won.

Thoughts crossed her mind.

Was she self-conscious or self-confident? Society fawned to see her exposed, only to cast her victim for the exposition. Why? Why was she always stuck in the middle, wondering where she fit in the mix? Then, it dawned on her: Real people wouldn't judge, and the ones that stood with her were as real as it got.

Moments earlier, she stopped caring, the bra's strap squeezing the top of her injured ribs. With little thought, she reached back and unbuckled it, throwing the contraption to the floor. Relief. Now, she could breathe. So, what, she was topless?

Who gave a shit? None of them made it a big deal, instead focusing on the obvious. Maybe, this is what separated real men from boys.

Such a long time to discover this, poor Agatha.

"Yo, are you okay?" Jason asked as she switched hands, his voice suddenly breaking to bits. "Uh," he looked down, and quickly away, "I'm sorry."

"They're just boobs, Jason." she said. "No need to make it awkward. I don't care. Literally everyone has seen them."

"Right."

"Can you check my ribs? I can't see them. They hurt *bad*."

He checked, trying to remember that attached to these ribs, were just boobs. Just boobs. They're just boobs. The nicest boobs on Earth. Holy shrines of boobage, scrunched beneath her hands.

"Jason." she reminded with seriousness in her tone. "Ribs."

"Yeah," he gave them a once over, "they look horrible. Can you breathe okay?"

"It hurts to, but yeah."

Jason signaled for help, snapping Biff from his trance.

"I thought you said you were okay." Biff said.

"Maybe not." she sighed.

"You might want to get an ambulance on that one." he said as she spun to reveal her bare back. "You probably have a few fractures, and this cut back here, gauze pads aren't going to solve this alone. You'll need stitches."

"Don't worry, Miss Daredevil." Darwin said as police sirens echoed behind them on approach. "You'll have an EMT here in no time."

"Sorry about your car." Agatha confessed, her face slightly battered, yet it did little to take away from the beauty.

"Me too." Darwin picked up the radio. "*Badge 4-7-4-5-Alpha to dispatch, suspect is down. Repeat, suspect is down. Hostage has been rescued. Over.*"

Dispatch responded, "*10-4 badge 4-7-4-5-Alpha, assistance is close. Standby.*"

"No shit." Darwin sighed.

"You've got a damn nice shot." Jason noted. "Damn nice."

"Yep."

And they all stood there, staring off into the distance. Sirens could be heard for miles, the grinding of the city confined to a box of air somewhat far away from them. People peeked from their stopped cars, at times stepping out to view the carnage ahead. The truckers walked towards them, seeing Darwin signal the absence of any threat. Aside from the drones circling overhead, all was calm now.

"Jason," Agatha said, "could I get my shirt back?"

"Would it be selfish if I said no?" he fired back, looking at her for just a moment, his knees growing weaker by the second.

"Please?"

He removed it and handed it to her, smiling. "Here. Cover up."

"Thanks." and she did. "Hell, thank you *all*. Everyone here saved me."

"Honestly, you should've stayed in the damn car." Jason said. "The plan was to use the trucks to stop it, but you goofed it all up when you hopped on the trunk. Jesus, Agatha. You do everything the hard way."

"Yeah," Darwin shook his head, "tell me about it."

"Just had to be Spiderwoman." Biff laughed. "Just *had* to be."

"Assholes."

Doors shut behind them. Atlanta PD, finally on the scene. The officers got out quickly, rushing towards the GTO with their weapons drawn. Darwin held up his badge and they quickly stood down.

"Relax guys." he said, nodding his head towards the kids. "These three are with me."

"What about the other guys?" the lead cop asked, his arm swinging in a motion towards the Underground members bunched up in the lanes behind him. There were at least a dozen classic cars, each filled with competitors now at the mercy of the police.

Hell, at least they came to "help."

In the distance, he saw Tony waving his hands. Touché.

"Well," Biff shouted, "they're with us, too."

-12:41PM-

Carlos listened intently to the radio, cringing with every passing second of silence. His men were starkly quiet, none of them willing to say a peep as the van rolled up to a warehouse in Decatur. They got out after the garage door shut. None of them made eye contact. Taking the keys out of his pocket, Carlos walked towards a silver Porsche and opened the door. He sat down, retracted his wrist computer into free mode and dialed a number.

"Yeah." he said once the call connected. "Boss, it's Carlos."

"Carlos." Boss was quiet. "Have you reached safety?"

"Yes, Boss."

"Good."

Boss was pacing back and forth, having put his Nintendo game on pause. Thinking hard and thinking well, he needed a way to get back at those select people that had made his simple cash exchange a living hell.

"You listen to me, and you listen to me *carefully*, Carlos."

"Yes, Boss?"

"I'm putting *you* in charge of finding those lechones del martillos."

"Alright, Boss."

"And I want them here, hanging on my front porch." Boss hissed, his accent heavy. "La polica have my money now, and they've got an entire group of my men hospitalized from the parking garage. Consuelo and his boys are in critical condition! One of his men was run over by a car! This, I *cannot* tolerate!"

"Yes, Boss."

"These men lead back to *me* and *my* operations." Boss ruffled his hair. "So, this is a *big* fucking problem, Carlos."

"I understand, Boss."

"So, get your ass on the case!" Boss emphasized. "You find them, and we are talking a *big* money bonus for you, my friend."

"Got it covered." Carlos grinned. "I'm going to roll with a few of my best boys to get the cop and the three assholes in that GTO."

"Move quickly." Boss ordered. "I want this closed as soon as possible. The less witnesses, the better. Don't screw up again."

"Yes, Boss."

He hung up. One of his men then walked up, holding a slate. On the screen were web pages that displayed the information that they had acquired off of the police database,

"These are the three kids in the GTO." he explained, "They are all nineteen, and all of them are from the Queen City area. The cop riding in the car and shooting is the same cop that got the other group back in Tennessee. It was the same exact police car."

"Good." Carlos was pleased. "Well, suit up and let's go."

"Where are we going, sir?"

"The accident scene to check it out." Carlos started the Porsche. "I figure they'll still be there, if not, we'll check the hospital where that cop's friend is at."

"Yes, sir." The man signaled for the rest of the men to file out.

-12:50PM-

"I'm okay." Agatha tried to assure the paramedic as she sat in the ambulance.

"Well, I'm just doing as I was told, which was to check you out."

"I hate hospitals."

"Well that's where you're off to." the paramedic smiled. Jason hopped in, with Biff standing at the opened doors.

"Got a bump on the head?" Jason smiled.

"Yeah, along with some bruises, that's about it." she rolled her eyes. "But they're taking me to the hospital anyway."

The paramedic sighed and prepared some IVs for her.

"She's got some nice bruises along her chest, and her ribs are very tender." he countered, offended that she'd question him. "We'd like to get her checked out, just to make sure there are no fractures or internal bleeding. I have to get some more tools, so I'll be back."

He left, giving the group ample time alone.

Jason looked at Agatha and then down at her hand that was clutching her ribs, "I'm guessing you did that when you jumped onto the flatbed truck?"

"Yeah, I kind of missed."

"Almost." Jason laughed. "Thankfully there was a GTO behind you when that happened."

"Yeah, and I hope you've got the money to be buying a new hood for it."

"What?" he laughed. "The paint is fading anyways!"

"Uh huh," she laughed, but it hurt, "you've given me shit about it every moment you could."

"Well, do you need someone to ride along in the ambulance with you?" Biff seemed gleeful. "I'll be happy to volunteer."

"Get in, you loser. I guess Jason will drive my car since he apparently drives it better than I do. Damn rookies."

Then Darwin approached, knocking on the metal frame of the door and looking around, "Howdy, kids."

"Well, if it isn't Captain America." Agatha greeted. "Surprised you're still here."

"Nice to see you too, Supergirl." Darwin waited until the paramedic hopped out. "Just wanted to let you know that the police are going to need everyone to fill out a report on this nonsense."

"Oh?"

"Yeah, 'oh'." he shrugged. "I guess if you little punks want to try and rat me out, here comes your chance. I just wanted to thank Biff for helping my buddy back there."

Biff was humbled, "It's no problem, man."

"No," Darwin patted him on the back, "I've been a real asshole to you."

"I know you have." Biff squinted in the sunlight. "But that doesn't mean I'd be enough of an asshole to let him bleed to death in the garage."

"Alright, fair enough!" Darwin checked behind them, making sure the coast was clear. "So, what's our story really quick? We can cover everyone's ass then."

"Simple." Agatha shrugged. "We met you and Waldorf back in Porter, happened to see you here in Atlanta in the parking garage."

"You know that's a bunch of horse shit, right?" Darwin chuckled. "They won't believe that for anything."

"Then, what do you propose?"

"You're a teenager."

"Yeah?"

"Means you're damn good at lying. We'll go on the pretenses that I knew your father from the war, which I do. You dropped by in Porter on your little 'trip', left something, and then found out that I was in Atlanta, so you met up with me."

"Wait." Agatha was thrown off. Her smile vanished. "You knew my father?"

"Yeah." Darwin's voice lowered. "When I found out who you were, I looked up your file and found out that I served with your biological father, Tommy Garcia."

Her eyes instantly brightened, the smile on her face suddenly as powerful as ever.

"You fought with him?" she asked.

"Yes. Small world, right?" he laughed, recalling the memories. "Actually, I used to pick on him a little here and there like everyone else did. He was a small guy, but he was excited as shit when his wife sent him a picture of his baby girl."

He pulled an old photo from his wallet, displaying the image of a newborn girl,

"Said her name was 'Agatha'." he gulped. "So, we made him show it to us, then we took it. I gave it back a little later, but we always joked around about how his little girl would probably grow up to be hot and how he'd have to shoot people to keep men off you. He'd always show off your mom, I guess. God, she was a helluva woman. She'd stop you in your tracks. We poked at him. Said she had some pretty nice tits, so we figured you would. Side point: turned out to be true."

Agatha was frozen. Darwin continued.

"We told him about that shit every day." Darwin laughed and looked down at it. "He'd get so mad, but he was a good guy. When he got killed, I took the photo. Not sure why, but I always kept shit that reminded me of people I knew when I lost them. About three days after we got back to base, we got a letter saying that his wife had died, too."

"She died from a uterine infection when I was a week old. Dad died a couple weeks later, I believe. No next of kin. I was an 'anchor baby,' and my daddy smuggled momma over the border. At least that's what my adoptive parents told me. He was Special Ops. I tried getting his records, but they're 'confidential,' or whatever. It's bullshit."

"Yeah." Darwin nodded, zoning out into the distance.

"Yeah? Just 'yeah'?"

"That's right," he took a deep breath before he admitted, "it is confidential, what we did. And your adoptive parents were right about your momma, because I helped him smuggle her in. He loved her, and it's a long story I ain't got time for right now. I just know it's a small world. When I looked you up the other night, I realized exactly who you were. I can't harm you or even think about it. I apologize for what happened earlier in the garage with the guns, I'm just stuck in a rut here."

He handed the photo to her, along with an old paper note. She looked down at it, smiling.

"So, our gig's a partially true story if you put it that way." Darwin shrugged. "Didn't mean to get all Lifetime movie like with the sob story about your dead father that you never saw, but that story works for all of us, I guess. Only if *you* agree."

She hesitated, flipping the photo over and reading the handwriting on the note. In Spanish, it read:

Tommy, I don't know where you are. Maybe for good reason. I'm sorry with how things turned out. I wish they would've gone better between the family, but we can just look forward to the future when you return. Now, I'm as shocked as anyone else was when I heard the news, but I wanted to surprise you. I never planned to have a child with you gone, but she is here.

This is your baby girl. She is beautiful.
Agatha Lily Garcia. Born May 1, 2018. 12:55pm.

You be safe, Tom, and I mean that. I'm sorry. Please forgive me for the troubles you've endured. I have a new, safe, and legit life now. No more mess, so Agatha and I will be awaiting you with open arms.

Love,
Mira

He handed her another photo, displaying a group of Marines smiling for the camera in front of a military helicopter. She easily located her father, but the big surprise was a twenty-year younger Darwin standing directly to his left.

She reached up and gave him a hug, ignoring her throbbing ribs.

"Like I said," Darwin didn't want to make her cry, "it's completely up to you, or we'll have to bullshit something else."

256

"No." Agatha blinked heavily to fight away the tears building up. "That's completely fine. Wow, it's still a small world. My mom was never a legal immigrant, so I have no clue where she's even buried. "

"It's a very small world." he agreed. "Are you sure about this?"

"Totally fine." Agatha looked at the boys. "What about you guys?"

"I'm okay with it if you are." Jason mumbled, feeling awkward to hear such a sad story.

"Ditto." Jenkins agreed.

"Yeah." Darwin hiked up his belt. "They took off the addresses from letters for confidentiality. When I got back home, your mother had already been buried and I wasn't able to find her daughter again. Your adoption records were sealed. Protocol for an asylum seeking migrant."

"Mom," Agatha suddenly shook her head to correct herself, "well, my adoptive mom said I didn't come from a very good family. Something about cartels in Mexico and Columbia. They didn't want them finding me."

"Tommy said he planned on moving up north to Queen City, hell, everyone was moving there back then because it still had jobs during The Great Recession. I wanted to stay in Porter, though, so I kept the letter and the photo. It was kind of good luck whenever I had it in my uniform pocket."

"How's that?"

"Belonged to Tommy." Darwin shrugged. "He's the one who taught my stupid ass how to shoot worth a damn. Seemed like it came natural to him, and I see that runs in the family."

"Maybe it does." Agatha noticed the paramedic approaching again. "So, we'll go with that, and I'll see you at the hospital I guess."

"Yep." Darwin fixed his hat. "See you there."

Agatha handed him the photo and the note.

"Take this back." she said with a calm face. "Don't want your luck going away, do you?"

"Hell no."

"Hey, Darwin?" she said before they closed the doors.

"Yes?"

"I'm sorry for stealing gasoline from your town and tearing up that store. Gas ain't cheap these days."

"It's okay." he winked. "I promise. You only did what you had to do at the time, I suppose."

Darwin finally returned Jason's wrist computer and left.

On the screen, it displayed 58 missed calls from his house.

-1:39PM-

After a short while, they were settled into the hospital. Agatha was booked into an ER checkout room where she was looked over. Upon her arrival, the Atlanta Police Department sent some men over to file their report. Separating the participants in the fiasco, they asked their questions,

"What were you doing in the parking garage?"

"It was an odd series of events." Agatha laughed. "I was actually meeting up with a few buddies, when I realized that Sheriff Darwin was in the area."

"And how did you realize that?"

"He called me, of course."

"On your phone?"

"Oh no." she shook her head. "On my friend Jenkins' phone."

"You mean 'Biff Jenkins'?"

"Yeah."

"So, you mean to tell me that all of this is purely coincidental?"

Agatha smiled, shrugging the best she could,

"Pretty much. It's probably the biggest coincidence of all time."

"How long have you known Agatha?"

Jason thought of something quickly. They drove karts together for a year, bonded for a year, worked together, and hated each other for a year, but she had lived down the street for more than seven.

"Seven years." he replied. It was true, they had known who each other were since she first moved in.

"How do you describe your 'relationship'?"

Jason laughed, "It's not a 'relationship'. It's kind of like a 'I give her shit, she gives me shit back' kind of thing. Call it being a 'mentor of negativity'. Eventually the two negatives kind of cancel each other out and turn into positives, if that makes any sense."

The officer wrote that in his slate.

"So, you like her?" the officer asked.

"She's not a bad person."

"I guess you'd call it a 'friendship'?"

"Whatever."

"Well, no offense," the officer laughed, "but you've been driving around in her car for the past few hours. You all did come directly from Queen City, right?"

Jason knew to leave the rest of the trip's nonsense out of the story,

"Yeah." he faked a smile. "Long drive."

"You been in a fight recently?" the cop noticed Jason's face. "Looks like it."

"Had a little boxing tournament shortly before I left. My dad taught me."

The cop jotted that down, too.

"Ah."

———

"Agatha apparently says that you all are pretty good friends."

"Yeah." Biff shrugged. "Why?"

"I'm just asking. Did you know about her father?"

"She never mentioned him."

"Why not? Aren't you all friends?"

Biff scowled, "Maybe because the dude is *dead*? I don't know about you, but I wouldn't go around parading my dead ass mother and father to people. It's disturbing. What kind of question is that, man?"

The cop shrugged. Fair enough.

"True." he jotted that down. "So, what about this 'Waldorf Rosewood' guy?"

"What about him?"

"You apparently saved his life? Training to be a 'nurse' it says here in the report?"

"I put pressure on the wound and kept him calm." Biff wasn't understanding this. "It was really simple stuff. I didn't operate on him or anything."

"This guy wasn't even a cop, so what was he doing with the sheriff?"

"As far as I know, he's just dude's best friend. He was on a trip, I guess, maybe for recreation, maybe he's gay. The hell if I know." Biff shrugged once more. "All I know is that she left something, and we were both in the area."

"What is this 'something'?"

"I don't know." he shrugged again. "Tampons?"

The cop scoffed, "Be serious, please."

"I'm being serious!" Biff laughed. "This is so retarded. Look, we met dude in the parking lot because Agatha was getting her shit that she left. Some angry gangster dudes roll up and start shooting at each other, they take Agatha, and Jason chases them down with the sheriff."

"Okay."

"Yeah. So, what the hell is the point of this?"

"Just making sure we have all of our facts together."

"Sheriff Darwin?" asked an investigating Atlanta PD officer.

"Yep, that's me." Darwin replied, sitting patiently in the O.R. waiting room, sipping on some fresh coffee. He looked up, taken so off guard by the investigator that he almost spilled the cup.

"Do you always have an AR-15 strapped around your back?" she *had* to ask. It was the woman that he carried out of tower. He was startled by her beauty.

"One can never pack too much heat." Darwin said.

"Detective Folgers, by the way." she greeted. "Mind if I have a word?"

"Not at all." Darwin smiled. "Figured you'd be here. Folgers like the coffee?"

The detective sat down, "Protocol, and sort of. No relation."

"I know."

"Take a bullet?" she nodded towards the bloody patch on his shoulder.

"Nah." he shook his head. "Lucky for me, it was just a skin graze. How's the ankle?"

She smiled.

"Just twisted it a bit." she wiggled it for him. "Doesn't hurt nearly as bad as it did back in the building that you carried me out of. That was pretty noble of you."

"Just part of the job, ma'am."

"Cool, so let's get to it." Folgers set a slate on her lap, powering up the screen with her fingerprint. "We've pretty much got the situation down and covered, so I only have a few questions."

"Shoot."

Folgers scrolled through evidence files showing various photos.

"Well, we noticed you apparently stopping a man in that Jeep shortly before the incident happened on the security cameras. You know, the guy that got shot first, and now he's somehow still alive upstairs in the O.R.?"

"Yes." Darwin gulped.

Shit. If Darwin wasn't sweating before, he could feel the nervousness oozing from his pores. Was he guilty? Yes, but he was fortunately wise enough to stay out of the security camera's main view. Try as she may, Detective Folgers could only see the tail end of his police cruiser and the front end of the Jeep in the viewport.

"Any particular reason why you stopped him?"

"Looked suspicious." Darwin shrugged. "Man dressed in Gucci with a Rolex and a couple of diamond chains driving in an old Jeep."

"I see."

"I don't know. He kept driving around in circles as if he was waiting for someone, but when he saw me he got really goosey and started driving stupid. Almost hit a few cars when he saw me pull out of my spot and he tried to speed away."

"When you pulled him over, what happened?"

"I asked him for his license and registration." Darwin lied. "He showed both. I remember the name 'Tyshawn Booker' on it. Plates on the car and everything matched the registration and the addresses matched, too. The guy didn't look like a 'Tyshawn', and he said he was meeting with family in the garage."

Folgers nodded, keeping her eyes locked with Darwin's, only for a moment to emphasize.

"Alright, I see." she jotted the information down. "Did you notice that the tags on the license plates had expired?"

"Yes. So with me being an out-of-state, small town Sheriff, I wasn't even going to intrude into the big-city Atlanta PD method of business. I took a peek in the back of the SUV, noticed nothing but a bunch of blankets and I just let him go until I saw the rest of them guys rolling up in the garage towards the Jeep. Then I plugged in the plates into my computer."

"Uh huh."

"It's an old model, but I was able to wirelessly connect to the Atlanta PD network. Ran the plates, and it turns out the damn car was stolen."

"Yes, it was."

"So, after figuring that the guy had gone inside the building, I went in after him to tell security before radioing in the call."

Folgers smiled, "How'd you know he was in the building?"

Darwin shrugged, "Had a hunch. I figured he knew them guys were coming for him, and the only place to run was the building."

"Sources at my end say that the guy vanished from security footage shortly after entering a restroom on the 40th floor. And then someone got access to the maintenance room, it's funny because the access card was registered to a guy that didn't show up for work today."

"Oh? Is that right?"

"Yeah." the cop chuckled. "That's right."

"That's really odd."

"Uh huh." Detective Folgers smiled. "Tell you what."

"What?"

"How about you and I take a walk down my squad car? A little bit more privacy to continue our discussion here."

"Why can't we continue in the waiting room?" Darwin put down his coffee, trying to figure out what Folgers was trying to pull.

"People are here," Folgers motioned to the Underground members sitting in the chairs around them, "and this is police business."

"Alright." Darwin got up, his mind weary of the idea.

Folgers stood up, too, leading the way to the parking garage.

-The Underground Kings-
Deluxe Edition

EPISODE NINE

"Team Players"

-2:02PM-

Game time. This would be settled once and for all.

Carlos and his boys rolled up to the hospital, knowing the perpetrators were inside. He was a practitioner of *plausible deniability*, knowing well the legal doom of approaching their targets directly. Instead, he honed the very reason that minions existed, for times like this, where espionage and strategy became key. Their mission wasn't to kill—at least yet—but it was designed to scout out a proper opportunity to do so. Upon orders, however, they could finish the deed if provided a perfect getaway.

These were super minions, hitmen in training, per say.

Mafia business was dirty, and sometimes it required drastic measures. Enter two groups of these gentlemen, one with three men and the other with nine, walking towards the hospital through the main entrance and the parking garage. If anyone was going to be killed, it would have to be silently, so Boss and Carlos strongly advised against the usage of firearms. The leader called Carlos after reaching the front entrance.

"They aren't giving out information, sir." he said in Spanish.

"Privacy laws. Head to the ER or the trauma place." Carlos waited in his Porsche, two blocks away from the hospital.

"What makes you think that?"

"Haven't you watched any episodes of 'ER' before?"

"No, why?"

Carlos hissed, "Just get in there. Send the fighters up to the ER, Boss says one of the guys we are looking for can fight."

The gangster smiled, "No problem."

Good. Carlos figured they wouldn't have too much trouble that way. If they did, though, he'd be two blocks away. Plausible deniability.

....

"Whew!" Darwin whistled when he saw her car. "Nice ride, Detective."

It was a jet black 2003 Mercury Marauder, an old, but hopped up version of a venerable American icon: the Ford Crown Victoria.

"Thanks, glad you like it."

"Always wanted one, but never had the money to find a mint condition example. I guess that 'detective' upgrade also upgrades your pay grade?"

"Correct." she nodded. "And this car is inherited. My grandfather was always into old Fords"

"Good man!"

"Indeed, he was."

"Any particular reason why we had to come out to the parking garage?" Darwin kept his arms folded. Folgers popped the trunk, showing a trio of heat-scathed leather bags.

Darwin gulped, recognizing it as the bags he stashed in his cruiser.

"Found this on the highway." Folgers opened it. "Came out of the back of your cruiser, I guess, when it got stuck between the trailers."

Darwin recalled Agatha jumping off the trunk lid, and though he knew it stayed closed throughout the chase, he never paid attention to what happened *after* she made the jump and was successfully in the car. Somewhere in the mess, it obviously fell out.

Dammit. He was running low on creativity.

"So, we got about a-hundred-fifty-grand and a, uh, very well-wrapped glass slipper in the bag. It didn't even shatter. Amazing, eh?"

"Was gonna return those back home, ya know?"

She folded her arms and scratched her frizzy hair.

"I was hoping you'd say that." her voice was strong, feminine. "Looked up how you showed in Marietta to extradite some guys that committed some crimes in your town."

"Yeah, speeding and what not."

"You sure?" she seemed manipulative. "Because I was told you claimed a possible theft."

Shit. Darwin had to think quickly.

"Uh huh, had a guy in the national park file a report of break in. Apparently, someone came in, and you know, 'lifted' some stuff from his cabin."

"A glass slipper?"

"Yes." Darwin tried not to fidget. "Got it out, checked it and the box; which they matched according to the report that I have with the serial number of the box on it. That was spelled out by the owner of the cabin himself. A guy at the local gas station back in Porter knows him."

Folgers nodded, pushing her glasses up on her nose.

"Okay." she said, preparing for the hook and sinker. "Got yourself cleared of that one, but can you explain the hundred-fifty grand in the bags?"

But Darwin didn't respond. During her sentence, he noticed something odd in the surrounding area. The garage was quiet and mostly desolate save for a few cars and AVs. It was a hospital, not a shopping center, and in the five minutes that they had talked, he saw not a single person—except for what he thought was someone ducking behind a car. Instinctively, he pushed Folgers back towards her police cruiser, drawing his weapon in anticipation.

"Stay back there." he said.

"What?" she was completely thrown off by the sudden change in topic. "What is going on, Sheriff?"

"Just call me Darwin," he stepped cautiously, "and I think I just saw someone creeping through the garage."

"Lots of people walk through the garage." Folgers stood up and peeked around the corner to see. "It's a hospital, Darwin."

"Well do they duck behind a car when they see me looking at them?"

"No."

"Precisely, so stay back there."

She drew her weapon, finding herself a bit offended by his controlling statements.

"Mind you, Darwin, but I *am* a police officer too."

"Yeah," he nodded, "but you're a pregnant one, no offense. Stay behind the police car, please."

"I'll call for backup."

"Do it quietly."

⋯⋯⋯

"We've got the cop guy in the garage, sir." said one of the gangsters on the phone with Carlos.

"Is he alone?" Carlos responded nervously.

"No, there's some pregnant lady with him. She looks like a cop, too."

Carlos sighed and punch the steering wheel,

"Don't take a shot unless you know you can get him and get out."

"We can't take a shot, anyways. Gotta wait till he turns around, because I think he saw one of us or something. He's got his gun and shit out. The loco cop walks around packing serious heat."

"Just get out of there."

"But we can kill them, sir. I have the silencer on my gun."

"Get out of there!"

Carlos hung up. The minion was angry, itching to get another kill on his rep sheet. Amid his frustration, he stood straight up.

-2:19PM-

Darwin saw his gun, prompting him taking aim.

"HANDS UP!" he shouted. "Drop the weapon!"

"Shit." the minion knew he was done, acting as if he intended to sit the weapon on the ground, only to throw it to his buddy.

It was a perfect catch, the minion buddy taking aim, and firing off a few shots. BANG.

He fell onto the ground gasping for air, likely due to a collapsed lung. Darwin shot him in the chest, purposely away from the heart.

"Freeze!" Folgers found another guy that had stepped out from behind a car when Darwin walked past. "Put the weapon down! Don't try anything cute, or you'll end up like your friend bleeding on the ground right there!"

He put his hands up, watching his buddy struggle to breathe. Police sirens were getting closer to them. Darwin kicked the gun away from the wounded minion and kept his pistol pointed at the original gunman. This time, with another officer tagging along, he figured that he'd have to play things exactly by the law. He got the handcuffs out of his back pocket with his left hand, tackling his target onto the nearest car.

After the cuffs were good and tight, Darwin spoke again.

"You're under arrest." he said.

They guy laughed.

"Do think this is funny? You think trying to shoot a cop is funny?"

"It's what happens when you shoot my boys." the minion growled in the struggle. "Eye for an eye, homie."

"Welp, looks like your assassination attempt failed." Darwin laughed and then looked for Folgers. "You got the other guy?"

"Yeah." she already had the cuffs on the third guy. "Pregnant ladies can handle themselves too."

They wrestled him into the police car and radioed for help with his wounded friend. Remember: this *had* to be handled by the books.

"Aren't you going to read me my rights, officers?" taunted one of the minions.

"No." Darwin pointed to the Atlanta PD officers approaching the scene. "They will, though."

"Eye for an eye, man." the minion kept laughing. "You ain't the only target, homie."

Dammit. The kids.

Darwin burst into full sprint, the realization hitting him like a tsunami. He tightened the hold on his weapon, turning towards the garage entrance doors to the hospital. Folgers jumped to her feet and tried her best to keep with him, limping on her ankle that truthfully still hurt.

<hr>

Darwin and Folgers stormed the building with a team of Atlanta PD officers, their collective dashing for the elevators. He stood there, anxiously pressing the call button until he accepted that this method would be far too slow. Directly above the buttons was a sign. It read:

IN CASE OF EMERGENCY, USE THE STAIRWAY.

Good advice.

He ran as fast as his feet could carry him, trying to guess how many more minion had been sent upstairs for dirty work. Bursting from the stairwell, he marched in, pistol first, scaring a few people in the hallway but he did the police thing,

"Get down!" he shouted, making his way through.

"Atlanta PD!" Folgers backed him up. "Move! Move!"

They reached the waiting room, seeing nothing more than a group of surprised Underground contestants. Coincidentally, Jason and Biff were in the waiting room, escorted there just minutes ago following their interrogations. The escorting officers saw the commotion and did the 'cop thing,' drawing their weapons.

"What's going on?" one of them asked.

"Yeah." Biff put his hands up. "I thought the bullshit was over, Sheriff."

"It's not!" Darwin ran over to the service desk. He hunched forward, his face just millimeters from the pretty receptionist's behind the desk.

"Yes, sir?" she was scared too, shivering with chills.

Darwin shouted, almost at the top of his lungs.

"A group of rough looking dudes, gangbangers, have you seen them?"

"What? Who?"

"A GROUP OF GANGSTER GUYS WITH RDM TATOOS ON THEIR WRISTS!"

"Uh—uh—." she couldn't respond.

"What the hell is going on?" Jason looked around, seeing more cops file into the surrounding area.

"Some more of them RDM gangster guys just tried to off me and Officer Folgers here down in the garage. One of them said there were more guys in here somewhere. You seen any?"

"*Detective* Folgers." she quickly corrected him.

"I just left a really stupid interrogation with the cops." Jason answered as he put on his Cubs hat. "Haven't seen anyone like that."

"Same here." Jenkins agreed. "How can we help?"

Yet the help wasn't necessary. Seconds later, five men appeared from the ER hallway entrance, greeted by cops and anxious members of the United Underground behind them. Darwin locked eyes with the first guy, pointing his pistol towards him, the others obviously threatened by the police presence. They were unarmed, left with no choice but to run.

Too bad the only escape route was filled with people.

"These those guys you looking for?" asked an Underground contestant. Jason recognized him. He owned a pristine 2003 Mercedes-Benz SL55—as if that mattered now.

The man curled his fists, the tension building in the room as more Undergrounders stepped up to form an impenetrable wall.

"They fit the description." Darwin replied.

"Are you trying to get out of here, guys?" asked another Underground elite.

"Doesn't look like they have any weapons, gentlemen." Folgers noted.

"Well, I think these men here," Darwin nodded towards the Undergrounders, "have a bit of beef with them, since they screwed up their competition and took a well-known club member hostage on a wild police chase."

A mutual understanding bonded them.

Darwin lowered his weapon. Folgers did, too.

The other officers holstered their guns, pulling their tasers instead.

"Maybe you guys can do some civil duties. You know, help us apprehend these men should they try anything stupid, which they very well might."

Folgers nodded to the officers standing nearest to them.

"Go head, take them in." she said.

There was long pause, a rift in time where no one could move a muscle. Ambient hospital noise hovered above the silence, the sounds of medical equipment in the distant hallways, door latches clanging into socket, the subtle hum of wind hissing through the air vents.

It was but a guess of who would make the first move.

The lead minion's eyes checked the holster on each cop, confirming that their guns were momentarily an ill threat. Chances were slim, but non-zero. In their line of employment, legacy bred power and respect. To go down a bitch was little different than suicide, so in a flash, they took the road less travelled by: tackling cops and whoever else stood in their way.

A battle brewed. United Underground vs. Red Devils Mafia.

Blitz. That was a better word for the first moves, which in all shared the surprise felt by the first officer to lose his balance. One second he reached to grapple and cuff, wherein the next he saw nothing but the ceiling, his inner ears registering a hit akin to a school bus.

His partner panicked and fired the taser, deploying little "fangs" that hosted capacitors capable of 50,000-volt bursts. They flew but a few feet before lodging into the skull of an Undergrounder, sending him toppling to the ground. Oops.

"Aaaaghgh!"

"Shit!"

"What the fuck!"

"You asshole!"

The minion pushed him away and took off behind his buddy. He took five steps towards the door before catching the first fist, thrown by a small woman holding a baby. She worsened the blow with a follow through to bind his neck into her elbow, turning the stunner into perhaps worst clothesline move in modern history.

Reaction forces took hold, spinning him backward so fast that both of his shoes disembarked as if they were thrown. He paid prime cash for those Air Jordans, such a shame to see them protest his behavior so wildly as to remove themselves from his feet. His wide eyes caught them mid-flight, one hitting the wall, the other landing across the face of the pretty desk clerk. She screamed bloody murder. Yes, that would be another assault charge added to the list.

Dammit.

"Get him!"

Yes, it wasn't over. His backward spin continued, his face subjected to three more punches—each by different people—all before his body had the chance to hit the ground. Well, another hit changed his vector, so maybe a chair whose pointy armrests jabbed into his side like stingers.

"Oowwww!"

"Motherfucker!"

Oh, the paralysis of 50,000 volts. Clearly, the second taser shot didn't miss. Now, he was *thrown* to ground, left to watch his four buddies fight what quickly became a losing battle. People swarmed them like fast-moving zombies, zeroing in to double, triple, and even quadruple team each leftover minion into submission.

"Look out! Look out!" an officer shouted.

The crowd split. Capacitors charged.

"Taser! Taser!"

"Hit him!"

POW! Sizzle. Hum. A minion thudded to the floor.

"Oooooh!"

"Daaaamn!"

"Grugmphmphmph!"

"Got him!"

POW! Sizzle. Hum.

"Aaaaahghghgh!" and another minion fell.

POW! Sizzle. Hum. Thud. POW! Sizzle. Hum. Thud.

They dropped like dominos. Poor guys.

-2:33PM-

It dawned on him. Jason never got around to calling his parents.

Man, they *had* to be ready to kill him by now, but there were bigger fish to fry. He hustled through the waiting room battle and into the hallway leading to the ER. The minions came from that direction, but he couldn't shake the strange feeling that there was more. What was their goal? Revenge? If so, what if they already succeeded?

Oh, no. Agatha!

"Who the hell are you?" he heard her ask someone.

He reached the room moments later, noticing the unexpected visitor. Agatha braced herself, preparing to launch from the bed on warning. Then she saw Jason, the look of confusion on her face changed instantly into a smile. It surprised the visiting minion, who turned around shocked by Jason's sudden adversarial appearance.

Everyone froze, until the minion wielded a knife.

"Assholes!" Jason shouted, arming himself with the nearest object.

The ordeal was brief, the minion taken down by the smashing hit of a defibrillator box. When he tried to recover, Jason bopped his head again, totaling four bops between initial attack and surrender. Once the guy was down, he kicked him to make sure.

"You okay?" Jason asked.

She nodded, "Can I ask a quick question, for the second time?"

"Sure."

"How did you always manage to get your ass kicked so much before," she was honestly confused, "but now you can suddenly fight?"

"Uh," Jason was still trying to catch his breath, "last time I didn't have a defibrillator to hit the other dudes in the face with. Or maybe I just morphed into the Hulk? Hulk-mode?"

"*Beast*-mode!" she shrugged, hopping to her feet as if she was getting used to the action. "Let's go!"

"Yeah, it's an important aspect of street fighting that I've figured out over the past two days. Hulk-mode and blunt objects. I learned from the best."

"Well, keep a hold of that defibrillator." she stood close to him, her hand clutching his sides. "Are they sending more guys to get us now?"

"If you asked Captain Obvious that question, he'd likely say yes."

Darwin barged in, wielding his pistol. Biff was behind him.

"FREEZE!" he shouted upon entry. "Everything okay in here?"

"Now it is." Jason nodded towards the knocked-out man on the floor.

"Darwin!" Folgers shouted from the hallway. "We got another suspect making a break for it!"

They exited the room as a group. Squad.

"How many guys did they send?" she was aghast, seeing the four defeated RDM minions on the floor. The cops were busy arresting them now.

"Quite a few." Biff answered. "We handled it."

Then came more of the old. As usual with the sight of her, the Underground boys smiled, except this time, she didn't smile back. She didn't need their attention. It was no longer important, no longer vital to her. She took lead, with Jason and Biff trailed behind. They eyed a few Undergrounders, smiling as they went.

Jason loved every second, knowing well that he had found life anew on this trip. This journey was his moment, finally his coming of age that was long delayed.

Beast-mode. It had a ring to it.

Uh oh. Then he noticed that Agatha was gone, running full speed down the hallway. He looked over at Biff, his face strewn with frustration.

"I swear to god, this woman!" Biff shook his head, defeated.

"I know," Jason sighed, "I know. It never ends with her."

Yeah, talk about bull-headed. They took off after her, judging the distance after they reached the stairs.

"Agatha!" she hollered down the flights. "Agatha! What are you doing?"

"I just saw the guy running down the steps!"

"Wait for us!"

"Wait for who?" Biff was already out of breath. "Me? I'm not running down those steps. Let the police get those dudes."

"BIFF!" Jason ordered. "COME ON!"

"This is some bullshit!"

They reached the second floor of the lobby, running towards the large windows that overlooked the entrance. Spotted: Agatha Peters in pursuit of the minion perhaps fifty feet ahead, closing the distance with the speed of a thoroughbred. Her feet lunged quickly, so quickly in fact, they were barely discernible to the naked eye. Seconds after she hit the sidewalk, Biff swore she broke the sound barrier mid-sprint.

The girl was *fast*. Like, Forest Gump fast. Even with fractured ribs.

"Damn!" Biff couldn't breathe. "No way we're catching him."

"Yeah we are." Jason held up the keys. "We'll take the car!"

....

Agatha was locked on target, her feet barely gracing the ground at full sprint. Her speed was a gift of genetics, a heralded geometric advantage of long, powerful

274

legs. Yes, she could run, nearly fast enough to set national records in her glory days of high school, but that was long gone. Briefly, her mind flashed back to the dreams of the Olympics, the prospect of being good enough to compete on the world stage, yet she had ruined it for greed.

Damn, she was the queen of horrible life choices.

Okay, well except for hard drugs. There's a plus.

Clouds rolled in through the afternoon, solely responsible for the annoying drizzle that didn't cool the air so much as make it more punishing and humid. Still, she focused, smiling at the relative ease she experienced closing the gap between them.

Running was a cake walk, even if the busted tendon.

The minion, on the other hand, was at the peak of his struggle. He realized within seconds that an exercise regimen should very well be part of the Red Devils Mafia training program, but it wasn't. His lungs burned. His throat desiccated. His eyes shed tears of pain. Truthfully, it looked like he was about to die crossing the street filled of dense Atlanta traffic. He held his hands up, attempting to notify motorists of his position as they zoomed towards him. Tires squealed, their emergency safety systems engaged to swerve, barely missing the gangster a few times. Nevertheless, he made it across, taking off again towards a nearby parking lot where Carlos had taken refuge.

Agatha wasn't more than ten feet from him now. She zoned in, grunting for the final effort when a loud shriek urged for her attention. Shit! Immediately, Agatha braced for a hard impact.

"Owww." she groaned, rolling off the hood of a vehicle unable avoid her.

Did it hurt? Well, yes, but she'd be toast were it not for the large airbag cushion that rapidly deployed from windshield base, spreading its blanketed protection to keep her from piercing through.

The driver, an older woman, got out of the car crying.

"Oh my god! Are you okay?"

"Owwwww. I'm fine. Sorry!" Agatha limped back into a sprint, grabbing her ribs to catch her breath. "Thanks!"

No time for accident reports.

She ran onwards after the minion in the distance, hearing police sirens wailing behind her. The guy hopped into a classic Porsche—what appeared to be a 996 chassis 911 Carrera C4S. *Nice.*—and was currently arguing with the driver, a terribly angry fellow she hadn't seen before. It was obvious that he wanted no part in it, but when the minion pointed towards Agatha, the driver took off.

Then she heard *the car*. Her badass old GTO.

"Need a lift?" Jason smiled as she rolled up beside him.

"Yeah." she was winded. He opened the driver's door and hopped into the passenger seat.

"You can drive." he insisted.

"No," she shook her head and clutched her ribs, "you got this."

Fair enough. So, he sent the rear tires up into smoke again, fishtailing around a parked truck in one of his favorite maneuvers. He understood the old brute of a car, with its brash, but punchy personality proving to be desirable as ever. Maybe this whole 'American muscle' persona was starting to get to him—well, the engine was American, not the car itself.

Thanks, Australia and the dear Holden, one of the early victims of the Carpocolypse. Rest in peace, mates. Together, the squad swore they once produced astoundingly good vehicles.

"Hey! Jason, are you going to be buying me new tires when we get done?" Agatha asked, holding onto the door handle. The GTO was very squirrelly on the wet pavement.

"Maybe." Jason said in the most matter-of-fact way, searching the immediate area for the Porsche. "You know, if we make it through this okay and all."

"Man," Biff noted, "this guy's got a damn nice car."

"I know, right?" Agatha agreed. "996 C4S. Damn nice!"

"If it ain't 997, we aren't—"

"Look out!"

"Aaaah!"

"Whoa!"

Near miss, yet another one out of hundreds so far. The GTO hopped over the curb and onto the sidewalk before Jason steered it back into the street again. Stabilized and in control, Jason checked the situation, finding that he'd nearly been broadsided by a black sedan the size of a battleship.

They looked over, seeing Darwin riding shotgun, a smile as bright as Vega on his face. The Detective wheeled along, waving a passive gesture of apology for the close call.

"Assholes!" Agatha flipped her off.

Jason swerved again. "Almost messed that one up!"

"Man." Biff shook his head after a near miss with an innocent pedestrian. "This shit was cool to watch on TV, but I'm not sure about the whole thing in reality."

"Shut up!"

These vehicle types weren't well suited for the rain. They were large-engined, rear-wheel-drive hooligan barges, their center of mass distributed far forward of the occupants. Modern cars and their skateboard architectures provided an uncanny stability that the classics rarely had, and every performance enthusiast knew this. Old cars required skill and finesse, as applying power was almost impossible without sending the rear end of the car sideways, but maybe that was the fun in this setup. Jason was cautious, opting to follow the leader in this case. Law enforcement had the right of way, so he motioned for Darwin and Folgers to take the lead.

He did, using the police sirens to clear the road of traffic. Folgers radioed the call to the surrounding area, hoping to get some back up and end this chase before it grew ugly with the rain.

"You sure you got this thing under control?" Darwin asked, a bit of nervousness in his tone. "Are you sure you should even be driving like this?"

Folgers gripped the wheel, whirling it back and forth with a finesse indicative of skill honed long ago. Yes, she was a lover of the classics, a wielder of vehicle control mastery, just like the others.

She scoffed, "I know how to drive, Sheriff."

"Well, again," he was trying to be nice, "you're pregnant. Don't want this thing crashing and you hurting that little baby in there."

"It's my son." she said, keeping her concentration on the road, "And I believe I'll be fine. I try to sit pretty far from the wheel and stuff, ya' know?"

"Yeah." Darwin laughed. "And I'd also hate to see this pretty ass car messed up, too!"

Folgers cracked a smile, "Don't you like high speed chases?"

"Yeah, only if I'm driving."

"Oh, so is that your way of telling me that I should let you drive and show me some of your manly motoring skills?"

"Pretty much."

"Not a chance in hell." Folgers whipped the big sedan around a corner. "Get your own car."

"I had one!"

"Yeah, and some hoodlums stole it and crashed it into a wall."

"In the line of duty." Darwin looked down at the radio. "Do you like music when you're giving chase? It helps keep me relaxed and focused."

"Sure!" she whipped another corner. "Turn it on."

50 Cent came on the stereo. Old school. Darwin recognized the song, '*Heat*'.

"♫If there's beef, cock it and dump it, the drama really means nothin'. . .To me I'll ride by and blow ya' brains out. . .♫"

Darwin laughed.

"Heck damn!" he cheered. "*Great* song!"

"You think so?" Folgers briefly looked over. "One of his best! Kind of makes me want to shoot people. Gets me in the cop mood."

"Well I'll say!"

-2:39PM-

Boss hissed, holding his breath in anticipation of what he hoped would be good news. The wrist computer buzzed intently, Carlos' name blinking about the screen.

Success? Finally, a close to this action-packed peril?

Well, no. None of that, actually.

He answered the call, hearing a direly frightened Carlos shouting above a racing engine as he shifted gears. Horrible news awaited, prompting Boss to sulk. Questions streamed through his head.

Why were simple tasks so difficult?

And why were his efforts to calm them only making it worse?

"Carlos!" he bellowed. "Carlos, what is happening?"

But there was no answer. Instead, he heard his panic.

"Stupid!" Carlos repeated. "Stupid! Stupid! STUPID!"

"Carlos! ANSWER ME!"

"Boss?"

"Carlos!" Boss was getting into his Escalade, his door opened slowly by a minion as to not damage the hinges. "Dammit!"

"Sorry, Boss, but the men are down!" Carlos checked his mirrors but wasn't very good at multitasking.

"What do you mean the men are 'down'?" Boss turned on his Nintendo again. "This was *simple*, Carlos! You weren't supposed to move in until it was clear!"

"The men slipped up! I send them in when they say the coast is clear, and suddenly they come out in handcuffs. It wasn't my fault!"

"Cállate la boca, Carlos!" Boss fumed. "*You* were in charge, and these were *your* men!"

"Look! Boss, I'm sorry! The police got the rest of the men! One of them got out and ran to the car, but the police and that bonita were following him!"

Panic was a contagion. Incubation took mere seconds, the symptoms of high stress prompting decisions that often required deep thought, all at the wrong time. This is when doom was recognized, where desperation overtook the need for humility and logic. Carlos was his right-hand-man, Boss' trusted confidante for years, but time had thinned for him. In the comfortable leather captain's chair, Boss yanked his own hair, wishing it could pull it out by the root.

This wasn't going to easy, but sometimes business wasn't.

"Then lose the police! Ditch the car, but you better not set your foot on *my* property without your ass clear of them! I'm *not* going down because you cannot handle a simple task!"

"Boss!"

"Carlos! It's done! I gave you a simple assignment, and you have demonstrated you cannot handle that!"

Carlos knew what came next, yet he leaned on drastic reactions to prove his loyalty, pulling out his pistol and blasting his minion passenger. He slowed down to open the door, pushing him out onto the street as tears flooded his face. Yeah, he wasn't proud of it, but it was necessary.

The door closed and he continued, speeding away while checking the mirrors to gauge his odds. Fortunately, the police were still a few blocks behind, opening the opportunity to make a getaway.

"The stupid guy is gone now, Boss." Carlos growled. "Dumped him out of the car. None of them have an ID or anything because I told them to leave it, just in case!"

"Good." Boss snarled. "Taking action is what you should've done in the place, so ditch the car and get out of there!"

"Yes, Boss. I'm sorry!"

"Save the apologies, Carlos. Don't want to hear it."

Boss hung up. The sirens were closer, echoing through air around him. It was too quiet, too calm, too unreal. He wiped his eyes, clearing the tears away before shifting gears.

He just needed out of here. Simple.

Suddenly, from dead ahead, Folgers swerved her Mercury in front of him and slowed to a stop. It was a bully tactic, a bold one for anyone provided the speed of Carlos' Porsche, but it worked. Carlos panicked, attempting an avoidance that skidded the Porsche into a nearby pole. Old school rear-engine dynamics and abrupt weight transfers didn't help his case.

RIP, dear classic Porsche 911.

The wreck disoriented him, yet he found the strength climb out of the car and limp away. Nearby, he spotted a shopping mall. Figuring that he could lose the cops in the big crowds, he ran in.

They watched the Porsche crash from a distance, its driver unknowingly right in the path of responding Atlanta PD officers. He wouldn't last long, and they knew. Slowly, Folgers cruised along, listening to the music.

"♫My heart bleeds for you, nigga, I can't wait to get to you / Behind that twinkle in ya' eyes, I can see the bitch in you / Nigga you know the streets talk / So they'll be no white flags and no peace talks. ♫"

"Whoa!" Darwin said, pointing to the man dumped from the Porsche. "Dead man in the street?"

She saw him, but he wasn't dead.

"Looks like our guy that ran!" she put the transmission into park.

They got out and checked the scene. It involved lots of blood.

"Damn!" Darwin covered his mouth. The guy hollered in pain, sounding like a sound bite from an old horror film. "Looks he tried to shoot him in the head but missed."

"Shit." Folgers agreed. "Looks like he'll need a new set of teeth on that side of his mouth."

"Talk about 'eating a bullet'."

"Oh god!" Agatha leaned out of the window and gagged. "What the hell happened to him?"

"Looks like his friend in the Porsche turned on him, shot him, and dumped his ass."

"I'll call for an ambulance."

Jason and Biff were stunned. Folgers was busy radioing the situation in to dispatch.

"Did you see which way he went?" Jason asked. "Dammit, I was hoping he wouldn't crash that car. It was beautiful."

"Sure was. But, look guys," Darwin leaned into the window, "I got love for y'all but, we got Atlanta police in the situation now, you guys have to back off for real."

"What?" Agatha was offended. "What do you mean 'back off'? We can catch this guy!"

"You guys *aren't* cops!" Darwin explained. "Now, you got my phone number so if you see this guy, give me a call. Try to stay on him and we'll get some police on his ass."

"Well, damn, I was just trying to help." Jason snorted.

"I know you are." Darwin whispered. "And I'm just saying that I have to play by the rules here now. Rules are we can't have civilians playing cops with us."

"Oh yeah, that's right. They bitch at you for that in the real world."

"Yes." Darwin smiled. "To say the least, so hang back and let us handle this one."

"Fine."

Darwin and Folgers drove away in the Mercury, leaving the GTO sitting in the street.

"Well, that was short lived." Jason relaxed. "I was kind of getting used to this action-filled lifestyle."

"I'd rather have them chase the guy anyway." Agatha dismissed with a smile. "It lessens my chances of death from your driving."

"Oh, so I can't drive now?" Jason turned the GTO around and headed back for the hospital. "Your squad came through for you on the highway. Had me as the wheelman, dodging cars, AVs, trucks with grease spilling on the pavement and shit. Biff hopped up on a trailer, pulling some *Mission Impossible* stunts, and you still try to roast on the squad."

"Jason, it's *very* hard to drive one of these cars in the rain, especially fast. Making mistakes is understandable. I'm here for you if you need more coaching."

"Whatever." Jason rolled his eyes. "I still had it under control."

"Shit, I don't know about that at all." Biff laughed. "It just looks like you just got *lucky* a lot of times."

They stopped at a red light and watched police cars blow through the intersection at full speed.

"Maybe it's luck, or like, maybe it's skill." Jason shrugged with a smirk. "You never know."

He put the car in neutral, letting the engine idle. Finally, he relaxed, feeling a flow coming on strong. His baseball cap titled a bit to the side, his head bobbing to the imaginary beat.

"So, I use my skill, movin' in for the kill. With my crew on my shoulders, these gangsters never gon' hold us. Pushin' the whip like a beast, you haters havin' a feast."

"And your rap skills are whack," Agatha interrupted, "just to say the least."

Jason stopped cold and focused on her. His smile made her straight face curl into a grin.

"That's really funny." he said. "Really funny."

"Bud, are you looking to make a career out of Dealmart?" Biff asked. "Just curious."

"Wow, haters!"

But the laughter wouldn't stop. Agatha hadn't seen anyone this funny in quite some time. Like, genuinely entertaining.

"I'm just joking, but man, I'm tired." Biff rubbed his forehead, breathing in long striations. "This has been like the longest two days of my entire life."

"I think everyone in the car agrees." Agatha stretched her legs.

"Your ribs killing you?"

"Yeah." she played with her hair. "Hairline fracture and bruises. Doctor says he'd recommend me laying off wearing bras for a while. Push up time, I guess."

"That's a real shame." Jason murmured without thinking.

He was a fan of her sprightly chest in the tank tops, or better yet, any shirt. A sports bra would dull it down a little.

Bummer.

"I don't like it when they're all bouncing around." she used her finger to swipe her frizzy hair out of her face. "We're doing a lot of running and stuff, chasing after these bad guys, collaborating with crooked cops, eluding the Mafioso hit men, getting into car chases, shootouts, leaping off of cars and semi-trailers, and other miscellaneous badass shit. I need to be comfortable in action, you know?"

"Agatha," Jason had to ask, "did they give you pain medication at the hospital?"

"Just a little Tylenol, with Codeine, though."

"You take some already?" Jason grinned.

"Yeah," she was curious, "why?"

"I could tell, mostly because you are saying really dumb things, but they're actually funny for once."

"Want to see my boobs?"

"Wait. What?"

"Man," Biff shook his head, "I swear, if you offer another threesome, I will kick you out of this car while it's moving."

Then came the uncontrolled laughter.

"I'm not sure if I should be offended." she tried to remain serious. "You're never going to let me live that down, will you?"

"Nope." Jason instantly replied.

"Nah." Biff agreed. "Never."

"Fine. So, are we going back to the hospital?"

"I was thinking about it, why?"

"Nothing else to do." Biff shrugged, working up the courage to admit, "Besides, we lost the items."

"What?!" Jason was shocked.

"Yeah, I forgot to mention that they were booked into evidence. Sorry, guys."

A few more cops flew by. Agatha shrugged.

"I say we follow the cops instead." she suggested. "I'm in for some more action."

"You like his cop drama, don't you?" Jenkins asked.

"I must say," she admitted, "it *has* been a pretty badass weekend."

Jason looked back at Biff to get his opinion. He held his wrist computer in camera mode, obviously still recording. Until now, it had gone unnoticed.

He seemed lackadaisical, "I agree, maybe just to watch. You know, you can get quite a bit of points in The Odyssey by getting epic shit on camera."

"How long have you been recording?"

"Since the fight in the hospital, dog. This shit is epic." he smiled. "I even got like fifteen minutes of footage from us catching up and following you guys during the chase."

"Wait." Agatha turned around to face him. "Do you have footage of me jumping off the back of that police car without a shirt on?"

"I think the entire world has footage of that, Agatha."

"Did I mention this particular wrist computer has a high-definition camera with a 20x zoom lens? Swear, I can see Neil Armstrong's footprints on moon with this bad boy."

"Lies." Jason recoiled.

"You douchebag!" she snarled. "If you don't delete that, I will literally murder you. I'm done being a movie sensation!"

"Dude, I'm not a horrible person." Biff said. "Don't worry."

Green light. Suddenly, the car lurched forward. Jason did another burnout and drifted the GTO around the corner. Holding his foot down, he made a pretty spectacular smoke show with the rear tires in the first three gears on the wet pavement.

"Jason!" Agatha screamed. "I'm *serious* about those tires!"

"You mad!"

-3:32PM-

They heard dispatch call over the radio.

"Did she just say what I thought she said?" Folgers asked with a peculiar smirk.

"I think she did." Darwin picked up the radio. Fortunately, the rain was clearing up.

Dispatch relayed the message again.

"*We have a 10-33 in progress at the Atlanta Cove Shopping Center. Security forces requesting immediate assistance from police, claiming subject is possibly attempting suicide. Repeat, possible 10-56-A.*"

"That's right up the street." Folgers noted. "You think that can be our guy?"

"Possibly. Maybe he called his boss and got his connections cut off when they figured out that we have all his men."

"Well, that makes sense. It sucks when you're cornered." and out of the blue, she said, "Oh, and speaking on cornered, while we're on the way, maybe you can feed me another bullshit excuse about them bags of yours I have in the back of the car."

Darwin froze.

"Why didn't you turn the bags into evidence like you were supposed to?" he asked.

"The same reason you took the bags and put it in your car." she was honest. "These assholes run around with this kind of money all the time, and if I turned it into PD, all they would do is just feed it into the Chief's yearly bonus stipend."

"Now I'm just trying to figure out whether or not you're setting me up on a sting mission. Awfully friendly and talkative for someone who suspects me of abusing my badge."

She laughed as if she was offended.

"Aw!" her eyes grew large. "Seriously? I've got a baby to feed, honey. And between you and I, my department gets 'extra payment' from these guys on a regular basis."

Darwin's eyes widened in surprise. After a moment to collect himself, he simply nodded.

"If you get my drift." she added. "I mean, I'm sorry if I come off as hitting on you, like you're an attractive man, but c'mon. Who's going to pick up the single pregnant lady?"

Darwin didn't care, "Yeah, I get your 'drift', Folgers."

"My first name is Maggie."

"Alright then, 'Maggie'."

———

Jason, Agatha, and Biff approached the shopping complex slowly, their eyes in awe of Atlanta PD cars strewn through the parking lot splayed like dominos. The strobe lights pulsed, alternating between red, blue, and white, the dozen officers grouped together looking up towards the roof above the giant 'Ulta' sign. A man stood, pacing back and forth, holding his wrist up to talk on the phone.

Crime TV. Live.

It didn't get any better than this.

"Is that the guy?" Agatha squinted. "Why the hell is he up there?"

Jason squinted to see, "I think it's safe to say that he's either going to kill himself or he's just trying to get an insanity charge when the police finally catch him."

Biff laughed, still recording as they exited the car.

"You know," Agatha made sure she stayed beside him, "there's no need to be a total asshole to me all the time. I almost died, ya know."

"Yeah, *almost.*"

Folgers and Darwin rolled up in the Marauder, blasting rap music from the speakers. Old school, before it all turned to garbage.

Clipse, "Kinda Like A Big Deal."

"♫They whisperin' about us/ I know you haters doubt us/How you count our money we ain't even finish countin'/Pardon me, I must say, I'm kinda like a big deal♫"

"What up?" Darwin did the nod that was common with young people. "How you like the whip?"

"Sweet." Jason laughed. "Got a new car already?"

"Nah, it's the lady's here. I love these things."

Folgers leaned forward with a smile, "I don't believe we ever officially met at the hospital. Detective Maggie Folgers. Atlanta PD."

"Jason Weathers."

"Agatha Peters."

"Biff Jenkins."

Folgers killed the engine, leaving the police lights in strobe mode to fit in. Darwin slowly got out, taking time to stretch his legs.

"Welp." he stretched. "There's our asshole atop the building."

"What do you think he's going to do? Jump or try to get an insanity plea?" Agatha asked as she looked up. "Asshole sent people in to kill us, didn't he?"

"Uh huh." Folgers nodded. "Why don't you kids just sit back and watch like everyone else in the mall, here?"

Folgers motioned towards the crowds of mall goers that had gathered around the scene along with a couple of news drones. Like a band of teenagers going to wherever the action was, the rest of the Undergrounders rolled up.

"Looks like Underground is here again." Jason put his hands on his hips.

"This is going to make for an interesting new thread." Agatha mumbled. "Kinda like my sweet sex tape."

Then, they saw the infamous duo.

The duet of douchebaggery, a distinct old Camaro and a Corvette.

"Speaking of that, here's the douchebag in the flesh." Jason growled, watching Justin and Chase exit their cars.

Undergrounders seemed thrilled to see them. How surprising?

"Oh my god. I can't go over there." Agatha shielded herself. She knew they were talking about her.

"It's cool." Jason reassured. "Just stay cool."

Darwin and Detective Folgers had wandered off towards the building. Police business, they reiterated.

....

Carlos dialed again and again, desperately trying to get a call through to Boss. This was unusual, a sign of excommunication at time when he needed it the most. Normally he answered every single call, but by sad coincidence at this moment, this rule no longer applied. He paced back and forth, waving his pistol in the air before pointing it back towards his head,

"Answer you punta!" he raged and redialed.

"What is the deal?" Boss finally answered the twelfth call. "Why do you keep calling, Carlos?"

"You told me to call you when I ditched the car." Carlos was trembling. "And I ditched the car just like you said, Boss."

Boss sighed and cleared his throat. He was, for once, at a loss of words. Again, business was sometimes colder than Neptune.

"I tried calling some more boys for some backup, but no one seems to be answering my phone calls!"

Boss ruffled his hair, "Yes. I told them not to answer you."

"WHY!?" Carlos broke down. "But *why*!?"

"You're a liability, Carlos." Boss said. "Every single operation that I've put you in charge of for the past week has shown your incompetence. *You* were in charge of the Atlanta piece of my operations, but I turn on the TV, and see that it has all gone to shit!"

"Boss!"

"I told *you* to get some new recruits, but these kids are stupid! They try to steal cars from people in Tennessee up north, but still have their IDs on them?"

"Boss!"

"I tell *you* to send people to get those kids that screwed it up in a park in the middle of the damn night! But you can't even do that right. So, I have *my* men getting arrested left and right, and now the situation is even worse at the hospital and the tower downtown!"

"Boss. C'mon."

"So, what do you expect me to do?" Boss was sincere. "You want me to jeopardize myself, all of my clients, and the other men that work around us all?"

"Boss, I'm sorry but everything was fine until—"

He was cut off. Boss was tired of this.

"Everything *was* fine!" he snapped. "*Was*, and that is the point! Nobody messes with my money, and my peace. You and your leadership have screwed up *everything*, so I am forced to say that I can no longer support you."

- The Underground Kings –
Deluxe Edition

FINALE

"Going the Distance"

-4:11PM-

Detective Folgers and Darwin followed the hierarchy, combing through each police attendee until they reached the lead officer on deck.

He seemed bored, holding a loudspeaker in his hand, and a bagel in other just in case. But superiors had to show face, especially when the news was on scene. Guaranteed promotion. Period.

"Any luck with negotiations?" she asked him. "We've been out here for over an hour."

"Nah." he chomped on the bagel. "Asshole was spotted in the mall trying to buy clothes with blood all over him. Security checked it out, noticed he had a gun, and the guy went ballistic. He ran onto the roof and won't let anybody even close to him."

"You got a file on him yet? Facial recognition?"

"Uh huh." the officer took another bite. "Guy's name is 'Carlos Mencia'."

"As in 'Carlos Mencia,' rumored head of the 'Red Devils Mafia' gang sector in Atlanta?"

"Yes," the officer replied, "though he was recently put in charge of expansion to the north. Our sources say he deals with newcomers and their training per the RDM's efforts to clean up their otherwise terrible track record."

"Looks like they've been doing a great job at that lately."

"So, that is who this guy is." Darwin butted in. "*This* is the numskull that has been sending his recruits up into Tennessee to vandalize my town?"

"We believe so." Folgers replied. "He's been running money through the town for years now by selling that 'poonshine' shit. We've tried getting him, but he always finds some legal loophole to get through. Every time he sues and gets a bunch of dumbass officers like us fired."

"Sounds like a bunch of bullshit."

"Yeah." the superior agreed. "Lately we found out that he's got a lot of connections in the justice system that keep him out of the ring, but it's kind of hard to get out of this one."

"Got him on video with his gang trying to execute the money drop guy and fleeing the scene. Not to mention aiding and abetting the guy he brought to off those kids back there, before shooting him in the jaw, *and* dumping him out of the car—all while fleeing from police."

The superior squinted, "Aren't those the kids that caused all that bullshit on I-75 this morning?"

"Uh huh." Folgers patted Darwin's shoulder. "Oh Sergeant, this was the sheriff with the sharp shot, picking those assholes off one trigger pull at a time."

The superior pawned his half-eaten bagel to a low tier officer, wiped his hand on his pants, and then stuck it out towards Darwin.

"Second Mexican-American War veteran?" he asked.

Darwin nodded, "Yes, sir, I am. Semper Fi."

"Well, damn that makes two of us!" he smiled. "Everyone watched that whole thing unfold. The chief was like, 'that's one hell of a cop there!', and shit like that."

Darwin blushed. He rarely got the credit.

"I try." he tried to shrug it off. "Just part of the job."

"We need to get more of you small town cops on the force." the superior laughed. "A couple teams with guys like you could get these morons out of Atlanta for sure, mhmm."

Folgers batted her eyes at Darwin. Pregnant or not, he found her irresistibly hot.

"Well, thank you, sir." Darwin shook his hand.

"You want to take a stab at talking him down?"

Darwin thought about it and looked up, seeing Carlos breaking down fast.

"Looks like he's going to jump or shoot himself." Darwin observed. "Whoever he reports to is on the phone telling him to fuck off."

"Well, if he jumps we've got a fancy net for that."

"What about the gun?"

"You got a sharp shot," the Sergeant grinned, "don't you? Switch to the stun rounds on that sidearm and pop him. Zap his ass!"

Excellent idea. Darwin cracked his knuckles and righted the weapon. He adjusted the focus on the scope and took a deep breath.

———

"You can no longer support *me*?" Carlos was crying like a baby. "*I* gave you my entire life for your 'operations' and I only messed up badly just *once*."

Boss laughed, inspecting the black slate computer his new second-in-charge gave him. A minion said that it was the one taken from the little red car in Tennessee. He wondered what was stored in its memory, as it apparently belonged to one of the kids he was so desperately trying to hunt down. The karate kid with the red hat.

"You only need to screw up one time to bring us *all* down." Boss sneered. "I'm trying to *grow* the Red Devils, not destroy them. Now I only have *one* option to get us back on track!"

"I'm sorry, Boss—I really am."

"Screw your 'sorry', Carlos." Boss finalized. "You're done. So, can you do one thing for me? Just one thing?"

"Yeah, Boss, I'll do anything."

"Fuck yourself."

"Boss!"

"Goodbye."

"Boss!"

Nothing. The line was dead.

Now he was truly all alone. No allies, and nowhere to go. This was the end of the road, and he knew it. Taking a deep breath, he drew the gun up to his temple. Still crying, he worked up the guts to pull the trigger.

POW! Sizzle. Hum.

But he wasn't dead. In that moment that he was finally ready to go, he felt the introduction of 50,000 volts. His knees buckled, his arms flailing wildly as he toppled forward and waited for the concrete to end his life.

Too bad he found a net instead.

Carlos opened his eyes, seeing Darwin peering down with a huge smile on his face,

"Hello, asshole." he greeted. "You've just booked yourself a one-way ticket to your friendly local penitentiary, where I'm sure your rival gangsters will have tons of fun with you."

The surrounding cops restrained him and took him into custody.

"That sure as hell is a sharp shot." Folgers complimented.

"It's what I do."

They walked away from the commotion, heading towards Maggie's car. Unexpectedly, they were greeted by Justin and Chase lounging on the hood.

"Any particular reason why you're all over the lady's car, here?" Darwin put his hand on his weapon.

"Yeah, I'd like to figure that out, too." Folgers crossed her arms. "I hope you didn't dent my hood."

Chase laughed and hopped off the hood. Like a true bro, he flexed his arms before stepping directly in front of Darwin. He seemed aloof, probably drunk, or maybe he was *that* stupid. Jason saw the ordeal and grabbed the attention of his friends.

"Look who showed." he said. "You guys ready?"

"I was born ready."

"If we're going to take them," Biff said, "we take them together."

They looked at one another, each giving a collective nod of approval. Together, they approached as Biff still filmed.

"Should I turn this thing off now?" he asked.

"No." Jason answered. "Leave it running."

"Denting your hood is the last thing I'd be worried about, officers." Chase taunted with his typical sly grin. "You should be worried about how much we're going to sue your asses for."

"Sue whose 'ass'?" Folgers was taken by surprise with this.

"Him." Chase pointed straight at Darwin.

Darwin raised his shoulders, "What brings you here, boy?"

"Same thing that brought everyone else here." Chase pointed to the mall. "That guy trying to kill himself. See, we got our car back from the police impound and all that, then we heard about these fiery police chases and your 'heroism' with everything."

"Alright?"

"Yeah, we decided to show up and let everyone know how much of a little bitch cop you *really* are."

Darwin was nervous now that a crowd had gathered.

"How you going to do that, boy?"

"By telling them all of that illegal shit you did back there."

"Oh?"

"Yeah you know, not to mention your phone conversations that we overheard with you talking about using our property for the exchange of some video 'evidence' you so badly wanted."

Darwin didn't reply. Chase continued, "Yeah, and you told your little buddy to call Biff faggot ass, because they apparently had your 'evidence'. So, you arrest me and my buddy Justin, here, take us away for holding some items that you wanted, and then you drop us off when you're done."

"What the hell did you just call me?" Biff seemed serious for once.

"Son, I dropped you off because it turns out that I had gotten the wrong men."

"Don't you normally do that at a police station?" Justin chimed in. "And you gave us money to keep quiet! Remember that?"

Darwin rocked back and forth on his heels, badly wanting to beat the hell of the kid, "Can't quite say I do, boy."

Chase laughed, "What is with you and calling me 'boy', dude?"

"That's all you really are." Darwin said calmly. "Just some stupid boy trying to start some bullshit with the wrong crew."

"No, I'm just letting you know that we're planning on suing."

"For what?"

"For wrongful arrest if anything." Chase stood as tall as he could. "Not to mention that we're key witnesses to you calling Biff here and asking him for that video evidence in exchange for those supposedly 'stolen' items that you took from Justin's car."

Darwin froze, knowing that the kids could probably fry him at any time. His end of the deal had not held up, and he knew that people couldn't be trusted. Jason wanted to finally have his chance to duke it out with Chase, but Agatha stopped him.

This was *her* battle.

"What 'evidence'?" she put her hands on her hips, looking at the camera and then at Biff, trying to draw a response from him.

"I don't have no damn 'evidence'." Biff chimed in. "What are you talking about?"

"Well, let's see your wrist computer, it'll show that you've been talking to him."

"And?" Agatha got snappy. "It wasn't about evidence. We had stopped by in Porter on our way down here, and I talked to him because I left something of value there."

"Oh, and damn," Biff let out a fake sigh, "look at that! The memory card on my phone was accidentally erased! Oh no."

Chase knew it was all bullshit.

"Oh really?" he folded his arms. "And what was that?"

"The diamond ring that my mom gave me. Left it in the bathroom of the general store."

"Do you expect anyone to believe that shit? And how would he find Jenkins' number?"

Jason spoke up just as more police officers approached. They were department friends of Detective Folgers.

"My car got stolen outside of that town, but it was recovered." Jason said. "My phone was in it and he knew that Jenkins, Agatha, and I were friends. So, he called Biff's phone and got a hold of us."

Chase erupted into laughter with Justin, "Ha! Ha! How long did it take you to think of this bullshit story guys, really?"

"Oddly, it doesn't sound any dumber than yours."

"Yeah," Agatha added, trembling with rage as she fought away tears, "and if you want a *real* story, then how about we talk of how I woke up in my car with all of my shit gone, Chase? What about that? You took my keys, my wrist computer, my slate, and everything? What, were you just going to leave me there by myself?

In the middle of nowhere? Do you always videotape your girls and then turn around to release it without their consent?"

Chase had to save face, "Okay. First, I don't know what the hell you're talking about with 'consent,' considering that it was your idea to drink the shine and to bone. You said you liked how it made you horny and how you like to be bent over and rammed." he laughed, somehow with a level attitude despite the topic. "Plus, you were pretty coherent the entire time. Mhmm, you sure knew how to work it. As for the video, c'mon, you've done it plenty of times before. Don't try to act shy. You're a porn girl. 'Stacy Vixxen,' eh?"

Responses came from all directions. Voices mixed.

"Whoa!"

"Dammmmmnnn!"

"Are you kidding me?"

Yep. That was the final straw for Agatha.

Who needed 50,000 volts when a kick to the gonads did the trick?

He quickly fell to the ground. Justin didn't lunge for anyone in particular, but Jason punched him anyway. When he got back up to his feet, Biff punched him again and he fell back down. Two hits to the face steered his decision to sit on the ground instead.

"You're so full of shit, Chase, it's unreal!" Agatha leaned down, snarling inches from his face. "I thought you were just a ladies man. I thought you had the testosterone to backup all of that talk."

"You did all of the 'backing up'," he groaned in pain, holding his rapidly swelling man-parts, "if you don't recall."

"Dude," Biff couldn't help it, "that video lasted for about five minutes. That's some *real* stamina you got there, bro. It would be best if you just stopped trying to defend yourself. It's pathetic and you embarrass me. Dog, you are a disgrace to anyone with a johnson."

Darwin and Folgers were speechless. Still, Maggie stepped forward.

"You know," she said to Agatha, "it's a crime to film and distribute material like this, *especially* if the woman didn't consent."

Agatha folded her arms. The tears came anyway.

"Yeah." she said angrily. "I know, but it doesn't stop them from doing it anyway."

"Dude," Justin defended, "you did porn like a year ago! What the hell do you expect?"

"Like that matters?" Agatha recoiled, on the verge of yelling. "You think that just because *I* did something on my own will, Chase and everyone else has the right to just see me whenever they want? To invade *my* privacy? To treat *me* like this?"

"It was already out there!"

"Dude, what the hell is wrong with you?" Jason interjected. "That doesn't give you the right to treat people like garbage, but that's your thing. You and your boy. That shit ends now."

"Shut up." Chase said, pushing his body to a seated position. "You're just mad because you're a broke ass loser. What, are you in love with her?"

Yeah, he was. Jason said nothing. Agatha. Biff. They all said nothing. Instead, they stood as one, subconsciously grouped closer in the realization that their friendship was greater than any insult.

Chase continued, standing to his feet "You think that being friends with her is going to change that, bro? A girl like *her*? A train wreck? Dude, a few of my boys literally ran train on her three months ago. She gets herself plastered, and when she's drunk, she'll do anything."

Agatha folded her arms, her grin sly, her glare lessening to an expression of sorrow. She wasn't angry with him. What he said was the truth. The mistakes she could never undo. The times of being an attractive eighteen-year-old connected to the wrong crowd, doing the things like liked best: drinking and having sex. At times, she was even paid to film it.

Agatha waited for this moment, thinking of all the things she'd say and do, all of the insults and attention she'd deflect by kicking Chase's ass in front of the Undergrounders—but it all faded. It was gone, replaced by a reality that she hadn't felt until she realized the sum of her value.

She looked down at Chase, her eyes as dazzling as marbles in the tears, "I'm a person." she said. "Did you now know that? I'm a person, too, and I don't deserve to be treated this way. You're an awful man. A pitiful excuse of one."

"Not my fault you're a hoe." he said. "Look in the mirror."

Sorrow replaced anger. Remorse replace animosity. She felt sorry for him, sorry that he felt the need to act this way because he was obviously missing that important sense of human value.

Oddly, tensions reached a ceasefire as quickly as they had flared.

Jason unclenched his fists, shifting his attention to Justin, who was smiling as if he'd won.

"Well you're a sorry loser in the friendzone," he said, "and I can't wait to ban your ass as soon as I get back online. You think you're cool with your two dumbass friends, but I bet you've never watched any of the *VideoVixen's* limelight, have you?"

Agatha and Biff held their breath.

"No." Jason said. "I haven't."

"Well, it'll change your 'friendship' with those two, I'd bet."

"I'll pass."

The Undergrounders stopped. In their tenure, automotive fandom trained each member to identify specific vehicles based on nothing but the sound of their engines. The crowd split in two, their ears pulsating from rhythmic thump of a V8 engine rumbling through the parking lot. It was raspy, with a deep baritone note, growling as if it could inhale anyone that dared to challenge. They turned towards the sound, their eyes bright blue 2005 Ford GT rolling up to the group and coming to a stop.

Underground's owner and ruler:

[*Wrath* (A-5)]

"Here comes the Wrath." Biff said, as if everyone didn't already know who he was.

Wrath was displeased. He was four steps behind the contestants by now, wondering how and why the United Underground made the local *and* national news. They were brash and proud of their classic car hooliganism, yet fiery car chases were a stretch. Notoriety had to be controlled, and now, Mr. Wrath had no control.

Underground was mostly autonomous, which was the exact reason for the leadership structure designed to manage key functions. Because of this—and the fear of looking incompetent, the elites tried to handle it without him. Normally he'd be checked into a hotel or one of the checkpoint depots, but matters escalated beyond reprise.

Now, it was time to deal with it. Face to face.

Wrath walked toward the crowd, his steps heavy with frustration. He wasn't nice, or privy with greetings. There was little time to waste on that.

He spoke, to anyone in the vicinity with the gumption to answer him, "What the hell is going on here?!"

Everyone grew quiet. Wrath stepped forward, between the police officers and the douchebag-duo. Chase and Justin shrugged, opting to refrain their response. So, Wrath turned to Agatha.

"Oh, nothing." she said sarcastically. "Just informing everybody about how much of a two-timing piece of shit Chase is. Have you been on Underground recently to check the blogs?"

"I own and run the club." Wrath replied with offense. "So, yeah. I'm on it every day."

"That means you know about that fantastic video that Chase was awarded a shitload of points for?"

"Just saw it, unfortunately. And that's another reason that I've been looking for a particular elite and his admin friend."

"I was just following the rules." Chase pleaded. "Followed the guidelines and got a very good item."

"After posting an explicit video of me on the internet without my consent." Agatha noted. Jason and Biff stood patently beside her.

"You told me that you didn't mind me taking photos."

"Dude," Jason butted in, wielding a bottle from the back of the GTO, "she was wasted on horndog drugs, and that doesn't mean you can post the videos. Surely that wouldn't stand in a police investigation or in a court of law."

Wrath picked up the cups and shrugged.

"How am I supposed to know that this is drugged?"

"Well." Folgers stepped forward. "I only have a little bit of this story here, but I can take it back to the station for a few tests if needed. We've seen a considerable increase in pregnancy rates around here with this 'poonshine' stuff. If both parties drink it, it's a guaranteed deal."

Jason laughed at Chase.

"What kind of a man are you?" he said angrily. "And even still, you stand there smiling like there is actually something funny here. You're lucky I'm in a good mood, but I know you saw what I posted earlier. You've already crossed the line that I drew long ago, and I promised I'd deal with that when we were face to face."

"Yeah?" Chase manned up. "And? What the hell would you do about it? If you even brought up charges, I'd have them thrown out in about ten minutes. You won't find shit because I didn't do any of those things that you described. So, please, step up to the plate."

"Agatha." Jason never let his eyes leave Chase's.

"Yes?" she replied.

"Hold my hat, please. I paid fifty dollars for that."

She gladly held it for him.

"What, are you going to try to fight *me?*" Chase laughed. "What are you kid, seventeen?"

"Just turned nineteen two months ago, asshole, you scared?"

"Am I scared?"

Jason curled up his fists. He figured he couldn't bitch out now when everyone was watching, including the camera.

"You heard me." he said, preparing to square up.

"What are you going to, freestyle me to death?" Chase mocked. "I heard some of your garbage music on YouTube. Sometimes I listen to it whenever I need a good laugh."

"Bro, really?" Jason smiled and held his hands out. "Her idea to drink or not, you made a video of yourself having sexual relations with a girl knocked silly on some wet-wet opiate-laced crunk juice. Sweet skills with the ladies, man. Should I continue, or should I get the cops standing right here to start reading your rights *after* I fracture your fucking face?"

Chase took a moment to respond, probably because there was nothing to say. As the conversation had progressed and more people "investigated" the video, he could see his potential allies bailing one by one.

"Chase, so, she was high when you did that?" asked another Underground member.

"That's pretty messed up if it's true." said another. "Like I heard rumors that you could get bonus points for getting a video of her, which was off-the-wall in the first place, but getting her drunk her, too? Let me guess, you pretended to drink, didn't you?"

"It was *her* idea to drink! She brought the drink, for crying out loud!" Chase pleaded during his retreat.

Questions continued from the crowd.

"So it was okay to post the video and throw her under the bus like that?"

"It was only okay until people questioned him about it."

"The definition of a Class-A creep."

Then the chanting started.

"Creeper! Creeper! Creeper!"

"Fuckboy! Fuckboy! Fuckboy!"

Darwin started to find the situation a bit funny. He adjusted his hat and leaned forward towards Chase, checking to see his friend Justin still on the ground holding his bleeding lip, silent as a dead bird.

"Well, it looks like everything is starting to go a little south for you." Darwin whispered to him. "Fuckboy."

"So, what, I'm supposed to turn down a girl using poonshine to spice us both up, man?" Chase hissed and turned back towards Agatha. "It wasn't a lot, I mean, at least for me, and it's not like you didn't *want* to have sex, anyway. You even said that it made you feel good."

"Hey, you mother—!" Jason lunged, only to be stopped by Agatha.

"This is *my* fight." Agatha demanded, before turning to Chase to finish her response, "Hold on." Agatha couldn't believe it. "What'd you just say?"

Chase froze, his mind hung up on wordplay. Yeah, there was clearly no way out of this. Even his best friend grew cold feet,

"Yeah, dude." Justin took a step back from his prior position. "Are you saying you *did* drug her?"

"For the last f-ing time," Chase shouted, "I didn't 'drug' her! It was *her* idea to drink the poonshine because she wanted to bang!"

"But instead, you waited until *I* was drunk, not you, because you purposely didn't want to spoil anything for yourself." Agatha summarized. "So instead, once I was inebriated, you got me to drunkenly consent to a sex tape that you posted on the internet to help you cheat in The Odyssey. Okay. We understand, now. You're still a piece of shit."

Chase looked around, seeing the puzzled and disgusted looks on everyone's faces.

"Chase." Justin asked again. "You said she was down for it, dude. What the hell?"

"Dude." Chase wobbled a bit. "She was down for it."

"C'mon, Chase, what the hell. I didn't watch the video, but that's messed up, dude."

Chase shrugged, "She did it willingly."

"So, is that a confession?" Darwin stepped forward. "I mean, we have the video that we could prove you participated in, not to mention the cups and an empty bottle that you mistakenly left in the back of the GTO when you were trying to hurry up and leave her stranded on the side of the road in the middle of nowhere. Whether or not it was her idea to drink the poonshine, you're still in bad water over the video and arguably the sex act if she were to decide that it was nonconsensual."

Chase was silent.

"Nothing to say?" Agatha tried to contain her anger. "Maybe you should stop drinking."

"Public intoxication is a crime, too, you know?" Darwin added, laughing all the while. "You're just racking em' up."

"Can I go ahead and fight him now?" Jason still on defense, his fists curled and ready to go. "You're kind of ruining the moment, you know."

"I mean, if you want to punch him, that's fine with me." Darwin shrugged. "I don't care."

Wrath interrupted everyone, stepping between the two. He waved his hands back and forth, shaking his head in protest.

"Whoa, whoa, whoa here!" his voice was serious. "So, you mean to tell me that you're admitting to waiting until she drunk off of a spiced drink, and videotaping it, not only because you're an asshole, but also to cheat?"

"Well—uh."

"Yeah." Folgers answered for him. "He admitted to it."

"And who the hell put this 'video' on the list of prizes anyways?" Wrath looked around at the group of members surrounding him. "Why would this be on the list? Are you guys serious? Do *any* of you have any goddamn couth?"

"The only person that is capable of editing the item roster is an elite Major Administrator, I believe." said someone in the crowd.

"I read it and thought it was a joke."

"A 'joke'?" Wrath was livid. "A damn 'joke'?"

No one answered. Wrath walked up to Justin, standing closely so he could properly understand how serious this situation was.

"See," Wrath was beginning to quiver, "*this* is the kind of shit that takes this all clearly too far. I allow tons of freedom in our club and appoint you as elite administrators to keep order and make sure that the line of 'impunity' that we have doesn't get crossed."

"Dude." Chase rolled his eyes. "We're out here driving like idiots on a 'scavenger hunt' for shit and *you* are talking about a 'line of impunity'? Is that like an oxy—uh, an oxy——."

"Oxymoron, moron." Darwin helped him out.

"Yeah." Chase nodded. "That."

Wrath paused, sizing him up for a moment, before he lunged forward and slammed Chase onto the hood of Folgers' car. He held him down by his neck and got close to his face,

"Look here you piece of trash." Wrath growled. "However you decide to go about getting all of the items is on you, but when you post up stuff like that video on *my* club website that I worked hard to build, you put the crosshairs on *me* and everyone else that's part of that site. I don't even want to get into how heinously immoral it is to do such a thing to a woman."

The other police officers went to move in to alleviate the tension in the situation, but Darwin and Folgers asked them to hold off.

"Let the man talk." Darwin nodded. "From what I hear, he's the one that runs things."

Wrath looked up a Justin.

"And *you*." he scowled. "You were part of this?"

"Look, man." Justin held his hands in the air. "I had no part in the whole drugging nonsense and all that. Chase just told me he was going to get the video and we could share the points!"

Chase felt betrayed, "Justin, come on, man."

"No, 'come on' nothing, dude." Justin backed away. "You said she was 'into you' and you were just going to get those points. Man, you didn't say shit about drugging, and leaving her in the middle of the road alone and all that."

"Dude, don't try to play to innocent here." Chase was mad. "How the hell do you think I got the items, man? How do you think that got put on the item roster, by itself? No, you put it on there."

"I didn't know that you left her out in the middle of road!"

"Man, just stop."

Justin kept shaking his head, eventually turning to Darwin and Folgers.

"I'm not with that at all, officers."

"Either way." Darwin shrugged calmly. "You had a part in the video of a drugged and essentially sexually assaulted woman."

"I didn't have a part in that! I didn't know anything about the drugs!"

"Should've inquired about that before you went along with sharing the 'points'."

There was silence, aside from the collective whispers between those surrounding the huddle. Wrath let Chase stand up and looked at the police officers. He was torn. A woman was violated, plain and clear, yet his selfishness thought of Underground. His head hung low, knowing what was next. Investigations would be thorough, the entire site opened up to law enforcement compromise. He stood and looked at the group.

"So, what's next?" he asked quietly, direction his question to Agatha. "What he did to you was *wrong*."

"I know it was." she said. "But I don't know if I want to open up a can of worms. I don't want to do that to everyone."

"Agatha."

"It's fine."

"No." Wrath stopped her. "He shouldn't get away with that. Not in a lifetime should he be allowed to do that."

Fair point.

"What would happen?"

"I don't know." Detective Folgers walked forward. "Obviously, I could arrest mister 'Chase' here and his little buddy, Justin, but it'd take a little investigation because I have a hunch that more people would be getting arrested in this whole thing. FYI."

Wrath wanted to be forward, "I removed the video from the site as soon as I found out about it."

"Well, if I arrest these two gentlemen here, we'll need to have a formal investigation, which will mean that you'll probably have to open up your 'club' to our people. The problem we've seen with this 'poonshine' stuff is that court trials are awfully hard to get a good conviction from."

Folgers saw her Sergeant walking up, so she finished just before he arrived, "Something tells me that this club and its website conducts a lot of illegal stuff like street racing and sales of possible stolen goods. So, if we dig around and find more stuff, then more people are going down, likely including you, uh, 'Wrath'."

"What the hell is going on over here?" asked the Sergeant. "Someone tells me that we got some kind of rape, or something being uncovered."

"Yeah," Folgers answered honestly, "but that's only if she decides to press charges. I mean, judging by the video, it could be rocky, but I'm not a judge or lawyer. He posted it online without her consent, which is a Class One Misdemeanor.

"Hear that?" Darwin taunted. "That's up to twelve months in jail, asshole."

"Depends on the conviction." Folgers clarified, "Either way, this Chase guy is a piece of shit."

"Dammit." said an Undergrounder in the crowd. "We're all screwed now."

"Can we just get in our cars and leave?" asked another.

"No." said the Sergeant. "If we have to investigate, you're staying right here, depending on where this incident took place."

"In the rural areas of southern Tennessee." Agatha mumbled, her face flushing with humiliation, but she had something different.

She had the courage.

She had the willpower.

She had the capability to be honest with herself, and now others.

"But Detective Folgers is right." Agatha's teary eyes locked onto Chase's. "I wanted to do it with him, at least initially, but I never thought he'd turn on me. I never consented to a video, though."

"Agatha," Jason put his hand on her shoulder, "you don't have to—."

"Yes, I do."

"Well, that would put the jurisdiction in your hands, Sheriff Loveless."

"Well, damn," Darwin leaned into Chase, his mouth roughly an inch from his ear, "sounds like you're mine. And that happened within the city limits of Porter, so you know what means. Guaranteed conviction, maximum sentence. Son, you could bring the best lawyer in the world, and nobody in Porter, Tennessee will give a shit. Fuckboy."

Everyone looked to Agatha. She hated her position; the sad victim, standing with folded arms, trying to control a temper just short of boiling over. Her eyes locked with Chase, filling with tears as he stared back, trying his sinister act now that his drunken plan backfired.

She thought deeply about her choices. Was it worth it? Was it worth seeing Chase get what he deserved? All at the expense of the entire club full of people that had nothing to do with any of it?

Or did they? Of all them, who knew?

Agatha searched, blindly routing through the crowd in search of guilty faces. It was tough. Tough to weed out the culprits, as at this point, she had very little trust in anyone. She'd always been that way, a shadow of her true self, an artificial construct of a woman that hid behind a pretty face. This was why.

"Agatha." Jason said, but she didn't respond.

She looked at their leader. Wrath's skin grew cold, the blood retreating to his body in the onslaught of uncertainty. Sure, he had loads of money; so much money, in fact, that he had millions allocated to deal with any type of legal skirmish, but that inherited risk. Exposure was never a goal, but here it was, staring him in the face. It bogged Agatha's mind to a halt, as for all she knew, he was a pretty nice guy. He was a founder. He built Underground into its modernity from the ground up, with many of its members flocking there for happiness and tranquility. Automotive bliss. A place of admiration for a dying work of art: the self-driven, fossil-fueled car. Lots of friends, sisters, brothers, dads, sons, and average decent people that would suffer with Chase. Think of the biggest Underground street racing club bust *ever*.

That couldn't be on the hands of her drugged night. The concept of sexual assault and the destruction of her dignity remained pinpointed in her mind, but she didn't want a court to fight the fight for her. She didn't want expensive lawyers to battle with petty words, but she wanted to do the battling *herself*. She wanted to erase the thoughts in her head that had originally convinced herself that spending a drunken, nude night with him was a good idea, just like she had done with her selection of other gentlemen in the past, but she could only see forward.

Finally, for once, she felt empowered to change this.

She had her team behind her. She wasn't alone.

Not in this fight, but there was a message to send.

"Yes." she said after a few tense moments of nothing.

"What?" Folgers didn't understand. "'Yes', what?"

"I want to press charges."

"Don't worry about your people." Darwin assured. "He's on my turf, so it's covered. I know how much this club means to you."

"Thank you."

Chase gasped as Agatha walked up to face him, "Everyone knows how low you'll go for notoriety, but now it ends with *me*. It's *my* choice," she looked to Darwin, "what was that you called him? 'Fuckboy'?"

"Yeah. Something they called his kind back in my day." Darwin smiled. "You know, the scum guys that can't make a good decision to save their lives. That kind."

"I like it."

Chase was astounded. "C'mon! You can't do this to me! It was a joke! Yeah, maybe we took it too far."

"Who is 'we'?" Justin shook his head. "Don't even throw me in the mix!"

"Shut up!" Chase quieted his 'friend,' turning back to Agatha to further his pleas. "Look, I'm sorry. Okay? I'm really, *really* sorry. You have to believe me. Don't go too far with this. Please."

"You sound so sincere." Agatha grinned, still withholding her tears. "But it's kind of sad, though. Now I don't know whether to be mad at you or feel sorry that you're this way. Everyone gave you so much credit for always getting laid, being 'the man', running up your tally, but if this is how you treat your ladies after your five minutes of glory, tell me, sport, how does it feel to be a piece of shit?"

A few people laughed. Chase looked at the ground.

"You should honestly be castrated, but I'll be nice, and I'll deal with you myself."

She curled up her fists and stood beside Jason and Biff. Folgers looked at Chase and then back at Agatha. In the throbbing of her jaw, Folgers could tell that the girl wanted blood.

"You guys can't fight here unless it's okay with my Sergeant."

"You mean to tell me that everyone found out that this kid waited on that girl to get drunk in order to get some?" the Sergeant wanted to laugh at Chase. "*And* he videotaped it without her permission? *And* he released it?"

"Yeah, pretty much."

"Well, shit." he walked up, cocked back his right leg, and sent his steel toe boot into Chase's groin. "I'll help you out. How's that steel toe feel, fuckboy?"

Chase collapsed onto the ground, groaning and flailing like he had been shot. A steel toe to the testicles had that power, that same demeaning, and degrading influence upon every man watching the event. Each of them could imagine the pain, yet very little shared the empathy.

"Damn!" Biff couldn't stop laughing. "*That* was pretty degrading."

"Yeah." Jason kneeled to see the look on Chase's face. "I don't think he'll be having any children now."

"Agatha." the Sergeant greeted her. "While the news cameras are over there filming the gang-banger guy being arrested, if you want to get a few kicks and hits out on the guy squirming on the ground, feel free. I'll tell my boys to look the other way."

She looked to Wrath.

"I'm not going to stop you." he said, surrendering.

"Whoop his ass." Jason said. "Or I will."

"I mean," Biff added, "let me know if a brother can get a few hits in. Dude is a bitch, for real."

"Lord knows I'm not the classiest girl that's ever lived." Agatha said. "People have heard enough about me over the years, but I'm worth more than that. So, I'm one-hundred-percent positive. I'd never be able to legally do this otherwise and it would eat me up forever. I got this, guys."

"Very well, then." Wrath took a step back to give her and her team some room.

She smirked, eyed Jason, and then looked at Biff.

"You got that camera rolling?" she asked.

"Yeah, baby." he nodded. "Recording for everyone's viewing pleasure."

"Good." she grabbed Jason's hand and whispered to him. "I know you've wanted to do this for so long. I know you've wanted to face up to him. Jason, he's tormented you since we were in grade school, but *please*, let me handle this. For once, I can handle this myself. Just this one time."

Jason looked into her eyes, wanting so desperately to kiss her, but the courage never arose. Instead, he smiled and took a step back.

"She's going to handle this." he told Chase.

"Everyone," Agatha declared, "allow me to kick his ass, please."

"Don't hurt him too bad, now." Biff seemed skeptical. "No murder charges, please. We all know you're a newly found gangster."

"Meh." Darwin broke up the serious moment with laughter. "We've got an ambulance right there. He'll be okay."

"Agatha." Chase looked up at her, still holding his groin. "I don't hit girls."

"Oh yeah?" she wound up. "Well, I hit low-life fuckboys that claim to be men."

-4:31PM-

The crowd was awe-stricken, paralyzed by this new, never seen, alternate apeshit Agatha. Chase stood no chance, submitting reluctantly to the ass-beating of a lifetime—as if he had a choice. She kicked as hard she could, jumping on him, stomping on him, all before ducking down to take care of his face with every punch she could muster before tiring out.

"Huh!" she blurted between hits, "How does—*that* feel? Or—*that*?"

The crowd seemed to get joy out of the rampage.

"Oooooooooooh!" they would cheer every time she would deal a good hit.

"Oh, daaaaaaamn!"

"You piece—" kicked him again in the gut. "—Of worthless—shit!"

"Oooooooooooooooooooooh!"

The cops found all of it funny, too, but Jason eventually stepped in to keep her from crossing the line. Sure, Chase was an asshole, but this needed to end on a high note for Agatha, specifically *without* her beating Chase into a coma. It took a bit of effort, as she initially tried to resist, but he calmed her.

"Alright." Jason locked his arms around her. "Alright, that's enough."

"Mmmph!"

"That's enough, Agatha. Relax."

Chase did nothing but squirm, coughing from the hits as small traces of blood seeped from his split lips and busted nose. Biff scanned the scope of damage. Critically wounded? Nah. Embarrassed? Yes.

Agatha released her tension all at once.

"You okay, now?" he wanted to make sure before he let her go.

"Yeah, I'm fine if you'd just get off me!"

"Alright, then." He released his grip.

She shoved him away and gave Chase one more kick.

"Oooooooooooooh!" the crowd awed.

"Okay." she surrendered. "I'm done now."

Folgers leaned down to Chase and handcuffed him.

"Now that she's done, we'll take you in for public intoxication."

"Ggggrrrmph." he couldn't speak.

"I know you're probably hurting right now, but look at it this way: You should really thank Agatha and Darwin for that, because jail time in Atlanta would be considerably worse."

Chase managed a nod, "Mmhmm."

"You better make sure that you read him his rights." Darwin said sarcastically. "It's easy to forget in the heat of the moment."

⸻

Wrath walked back to his Ford GT and retrieved his slate, running on nothing but a hunch. His idea was bold, one that would easily accomplish what the club

311

needed: a coup. He logged into Underground, using his administrative powers to change a few things. Once he was done, he re-approached the group and specifically directed his first statements at Detective Folgers,

"Anyone mind if I make an announcement?"

"Not at all." she stepped back.

He sat his slate atop of her car's hood and linked it to a piece of electropaper in his hands to port the display to the public, drawing a few negative responses from her body language.

"Don't worry," he smiled at her. "I'm sorry about the dent I put on your hood. I'll write you a check and you can buy a new Marauder if you want."

That was enough to change her mood. Going under assumption by seeing his extravagant car, Folgers didn't doubt his statement at all. She stepped back and gave him the room to speak.

Undergrounders were quiet and ready to listen.

"Alright, people." he spoke just loud enough for the gathering to hear. "We've got some new rules here. First one, no one will *ever* do that bullshit again."

He was serious.

"If I *ever* see any videos or photos of some girl that you had to drug on *my* website, I will send the link to the police and give them all the information I can get on your sorry ass. I have a daughter, and I know of many members with friends and family that are women, sisters, and mothers, so I can personally attest to the fact that if this happened to her, I would be wanting to kill the son-of-a-bitch that thought it was funny."

"I could also imagine that Agatha's father—"

Agatha cut him off, "He's dead."

He regrouped and continued.

"Well, if he were here today," he shook his head, "he'd likely feel the same. No one puts this club in jeopardy, because you know we get enough flak from the police anyway."

Wrath then looked at Justin.

"Anyone who is an accomplice to anything like that will be banned, and handed over to the police, too. That also includes my elites."

Justin was standing alone by his car. He sighed.

"Come on man!" he pleaded. "We go way back dude."

"Still doesn't mean you aren't banned." Wrath glared. "Rules are rules. Also, the points gained by this nonsense go to Agatha and her team."

Chase, in all his cheating, had amassed 384,000 points. Yeah, an actual game changer. Agatha didn't know what to say. Neither did Jason or Biff who was still recording.

"Alright, well, because I'm still in a relatively good mood," Wrath's frown grew to a smile, "I think I'll do something a bit radical and fill the empty elite and admin spaces with a few young novices to create some more drama. Screw the elite space, I'm going to admins."

Wrath positioned himself directly beside Agatha, Jason, and Biff.

"I'll start with Agatha," he continued, "not only because she just taught me that a person can be spiritually strong enough to think about the goodwill of others despite a giant wrongdoing, but her popularity among her nut-huggers on the website. I think it'll be a nice change to see every guy on there make even *more* of a fool out of themselves once she's got some pull on things."

Agatha was overcome with speechlessness. Her, an administrator?

"And to Biff Jenkins," Wrath patted him on the shoulder, "Just because he's a broke ass ricer that everyone makes fun of, and the fact that he managed to get *all* of this on tape."

The last announcement completely threw everyone for a loop. Biff Jenkins, the kid who never owned anything more than a collection of old raggedy Hondas had been appointed to the rank of admin? Most people laughed, because it was funny, but there were the few people that had their objections.

Well, a key objector was Jason, but he tried to remain as humble as he could to hide his hidden anger. Jealousy fought within him. Comparing and contrasting their actions only made it worse. What did Biff do that was so special? Did he chase down gangsters? Outmaneuver a slickster cop? Drift a car through the streets of Atlanta? No, and *he* got the appointment to admin? Jason found it hard to hold a steady face and not display the anger and disappointment that he was feeling. Wrath noticed it, though, wrapping his arm around his neck playfully,

"What's wrong with you, Jason?" he teased. "Angry about the new nominations?"

"Not, 'angry'." Jason tried to keep his wording calm. "Just 'surprised,' I guess?"

"Psssh. You mad, man?" Wrath laughed. "I couldn't make you an admin *that* easily. All you've done is not only prove to us but prove to the entire world that you're Underground's biggest ricer by drifting Agatha's old 5.7 GTO around the Atlanta, Georgia highway system like it was your f-ing day job. That's good enough for an entry level elite, I suppose."

The crowd erupted in laughter. Jason scrunched his face up, unable to hide embarrassment, especially when he saw Agatha and Jenkins laughing at him, too.

"Like, honestly." Wrath continued. "I didn't even know it was remotely possible to kick the rear end out and burn *that* much rubber in a car with only like 340 horses at the wheels. You, my friend, have proved to us that despite its negative definition, being a ricer is sometimes a *very* good thing. Bravo, my Underground Kings, bravo. Jason Weathers is seriously my new hero."

The laughter continued as Wrath did.

"Even the local police can thank you for that!"

....

"So," Folgers spoke to Darwin after the crowd had dissipated, her voice soft, "should I even bother to ask if any of that stuff Chase was talking about is true?"

Darwin sighed, finally feeling a bit relieved.

"I'm just going to say 'no'." he said.

She laughed.

"So, what's on the plate now?" her eyes twinkled.

"Hopefully no more of those gangster guys."

"Oh, they'll always be there somewhere."

"Don't spoil it." he looked out at the sky. "But what's on your plate now? You still have all that shit in the back of your police car. I assume you'll, uh, be keeping that for yourself?"

Sergeant smirked and looked away.

"Nah." she smiled. "Sergeant will get his cut, and a few of the other higher guys."

"Well, I guess you can kiss that hundred-fifty grand goodbye."

"What do you mean 'hundred-fifty grand'?" the smile on her face grew even larger. "Take a look in the trunk again."

314

She popped the lid with her remote. Darwin looked around to check for anyone watching and then he peeked in,

"Holy hell." he shut the lid. "God damn."

"Yeah, turns out that there were *twelve* bags filled with fifty stacks each in that Jeep."

Sergeant took over.

"The official report says that the shootout occurred because apparently the guy assigned to drop the money for the 'Red Devils Mafia' had a Jeep loaded with four bags in it. Who's left to disprove that?"

Darwin was giddy, trying to keep himself composed, "Are you son-bitches trying to nab me?" he had to be sure. "Because this is unreal."

Folgers looked at her superior officer, who snickered a little and handed her a piece of paper.

"See that?" she pointed to a signature and stamp. "That's the Chief of Police signing and authenticating the report into the records. It's already filed, so how could we possibly screw you over?"

Darwin held the paper up to the sky just to check. It was complete with the watermark, so yes, it was authentic.

"So is this why you love them gangbangers so much?"

"Yeah," Sergeant laughed, "precisely. Chief agrees, too, so if anything, he told me to give you a share just to assure that you'll uh— keep your mouth shut."

"Oh, is that right?"

"How's one bag sound to you?" Sergeant offered. "No strings attached. Seventy-five for you. Call it a 'finder's gift'."

"Well." Darwin took a moment. "Alright, then."

"Might allow you to replace that police cruiser you lost, unfortunately."

"Just might."

Sergeant shook his hand and walked away.

"So, Sheriff, you're free to go if you wish." Folgers looked sad. "Nice knowing you."

"You expect me to just walk off like that? Or are you using your woman powers to put some guilt trip on me."

She cringed, but then smiled.

"Maybe I'll lean more towards the last option." then she shrugged. "But I wouldn't expect you to want to 'kick it' with the lady who's three months pregnant with another man's child."

Darwin stood up straight and cleared his throat.

"Well, I wouldn't be so sure about that, ma'am." he stuck his hand out, "I've only known you for a few hours, but you seem to be the type of woman that don't take no funny business. So, with all due respect to you, that child growing in your stomach and how that happened doesn't give me any right to place judgment on you."

"That's noble."

"No, that's honesty." he took off his hat, finally letting his thinning hair blow in the wind. "I know I'm not to most well-rounded or attractive man on the planet, but I know when I see a woman that fits that description, pregnant or not."

Folgers blushed, "You seem plenty attractive to me."

"Maybe we can 'cop' a bite to eat or something." Darwin was excited, "I guess that's how kids say it these days."

"I think I'll take you up on that offer, sir." she seemed satisfied. "You must *really* trust me, huh?"

"No." Darwin nodded toward his wrist computer that he had just purchased earlier in the day. "I can work on the 'trust' thing, but until then, I had one of my boys back in town record every goddamn word you and your sergeant said a few minutes ago."

"Wow!" Folgers fluffed her hair and fidgeted a bit. "Always watch your back, don't you?"

"I try to whenever someone has dirt on me. Get an equal amount of dirt back on them to keep things 'mutual' and stuff stays diplomatic. You know, 'eye for an eye'?"

"You bastard." She shook her head, fighting the smile.

"Still on for that date?"

"Uh huh."

"Well, let's get going. Gonna have to take your car though, until I use my seventy-five-grand to buy my own. Maybe we can stop by the hospital on the way, just to make sure my buddy ain't being too naughty with the nurses."

Folgers giggled, looking him in the eye as if she still doubted reality. Why couldn't she have met him four months ago? Where was he when she fell into a bottomless pit of bad luck? Was this real, or a front?

Then, she realized that she didn't care.

"You drive." she said, sitting down in the passenger seat of her own car, ready to feel the wind against her skin.

"Yes, ma'am!" Darwin started the engine.

The big Mercury drove away.

Closing:

Jason found a reclusive spot in the suburbs and tried to work up the courage to dial home. What would he tell them? What was he going to say? They were probably worried sick by now, his mother likely a broken mess and his father likely in the same shape. What had he done? How could he be so stupid to think that—by some stretch of his fouled imagination—his parents had morphed into monsters he avoided like the plague?

Maybe it was the feeling of overwhelming shame, the shame that he had dismissed them both, never realizing how *good* his life was, despite the faults. Agatha Peters' parents died before she was even old enough to remember them. Biff never met his, despite them both presumably still alive. *Both* parents, and here he was whining because his mother never stopped riding his ass about screwing up, or that his father kept pushing him to work more hours or look closer into the local community colleges and universities.

They *cared.* They were there, right in front of him.

As the guilt boiled inside of his conscience throughout the past few days, he made excuses as to why he couldn't contact them. The original plan was to hold out until he either succeeded or failed, both of which would be somewhat obvious given the circumstances of the point tallies. He wanted to fix it. That's all he wanted to do, but everything went so horribly wrong that it still seemed hopeless, despite the happy ending to car chase and police ordeal.

Finally, after standing there for five minutes, he held his breath and dialed his home number. It seemed to ring forever, until finally he heard the receiver register a connection.

"Weather's residence." he heard his father say.

His voice nearly made his heart stop.

"Dad. . ." was all he could muster.

"Jason?" his voice suddenly flooded with life. "JASON?"

"Yes," he nodded as if he could see him, "it's me."

"Jason, WHERE ARE YOU? WHERE HAVE YOU BEEN? I— WE'VE BEEN SO WORRIED! YOU JUST DISAPPEARED!"

"Dad. . ."

He kept ranting, but this time he let him. Sometimes, a person just needed to talk, to get it out, to convey their angst. If anyone understood, it was Jason. As he finished his wildly panicked statements, Jason gradually shushed him.

"Dad, listen to me." Jason led. "I'm okay. Do you understand that?"

"Jason, what's happened to you?" he heard his sniffles, the sound of hi tears enough to wither away his strength. He had never seen his father cry. "Why won't you talk to me? Why won't you listen? Jason, *PLEASE*!"

"Dad. . ."

"Did you know—" his father started.

"Dad, calm down." he said, but his father refused to stop.

He kept crying, harder now, his sobs rolling in rhythm with the ends of his sentences. "Jason, did you know what the doctors told your mother?"

"Dad, please."

"Listen to me." his voice was soft. "Just listen, this one time. Please?"

"Okay. I'll listen." he wiped his eyes. "What did the doctors tell her?"

"They told her—" he sobbed. "They told her ever since she was a teenager that having a baby would be impossible. Did you know that?"

"No." Jason smiled. He had to love the random rants about the past. "No, I didn't, Dad."

"And she went her entire life thinking that she would never have the ability to make the one thing that mattered the most to her. She'd never be able to make a family. She couldn't reproduce. She was hopeless, you know?"

He sobbed again and continued, "It took her years to tell me that because she was scared, but I married her anyways. I cared about her, you know? I said that we could adopt, or by a dog, because I love dogs, but it just would never leave her mind and I could tell. But something happened to her. I don't know what it was, but something worked. One day, she felt sick, and they told her that she was pregnant. We couldn't believe it."

"Dad. . ."

"Do you know how much you mean to me, Junior?" he asked. "Do you know what I would do to make sure that you were safe? You are *my* boy, Jason. *You* are my proof that when someone tells you that it's 'impossible' and that you shouldn't try, it's nothing but nonsense."

"I'm sorry, Dad." Jason tensed up. "I'm so sorry."

"And even still, they told us that it would be 'highly unlikely' that she'd be able to carry you to term. They recommended that we 'terminate' you, but I wasn't having that. We talked one night, and she asked me if I wanted to do this. I said 'yes', and then I worked *three* jobs to make sure that she didn't have to lift a finger for five years. And I remember how she wondered about why I needed three jobs, but I didn't tell her until the day we pulled up to our house."

He laughed a little during the recollection, the heavy tears were subsiding, "I wish I could tell you how it felt when they said that I was having a little boy. I've never been so damn happy and determined in my entire life. I told her that you needed your own room because our one-bedroom apartment wasn't going to 'cut it'. You're our baby. You're our miracle. I know things have been rough around here, and it hasn't been easy for any of us, but you can't run away, Jason. *We* are a family. We are the only thing that is holding this fragile house together, and right now I'm scared. You ran away. After the first night, your mother wasn't sure that she'd see you ever again. She's a wreck"

"Is she home?" Jason fought the tears away by closing his eyes.

"No, I convinced her to go to work."

"Well, I'm scared to talk her." Jason's throat was clogging. "She'll reach through the phone and kill me."

He and his dad laughed.

"She just wants the best for you. So do I." his father said. "All I have are my two hands, and that's *it*, but you have a brain. You sure as hell didn't get it from me because I'm dumber than a box of rocks, but it's there. I hate to see you waste it. God, I do."

"Dammit, Dad, I'm so sorry." Jason finally broke down. "I've been thinking the past few days about everything, and I just wish it would go away. We're losing the house, we're losing everything. I don't know what to do. I couldn't think of anything."

"Junior, that's the last thing you need to be worried about. You've got your entire life ahead of you. You *have* to be better than I am!"

"That's impossible." Jason shook his head, the tears streaming down his face now. "I can't even put my car together right. Everything I touch, I destroy, but I'm done with that. Now, there's just one thing that I have to do."

"Son," his dad's voice stayed so calmly reassuring that it chilled Jason's spine, "please come home."

Jason sobbed a few times and covered the mouthpiece of the wrist computer as he gathered himself. Instantly, he remembered to remove his hat, which he sat atop the GTO.

"I can't." was all that Jason could say.

"I don't care where you are. I'll come get you. Are you in jail? Are you in trouble? *Please*, please talk to me! I will *save* you."

"Dad, I just can't. I'm fine. I swear that I am, but I have to do this! I have to save *myself*."

His father started crying again. He could hear the echoes of his sobs in the background.

"Jason, it doesn't matter. I won't be mad. I won't be upset, I swear to God. I just want my boy back. We'll figure everything out at home, I always have."

"I might be able to fix it."

"Fix what?"

"Everything, but I can't come home."

"Will you tell me why? Son, you don't have to do anything stupid! C'mon!"

"Remember when I was a little boy, and you'd take me to my baseball games?"

"Yes."

"I'd strike out every single time, and I mean *every* time, and I hated it. I wanted to be like Babe Ruth so badly, but I couldn't even hit the damn ball even after all of that practice. You'd take me to the batting cages and I'd swing, and swing, and swing until I finally hit it, but I couldn't do it in a real game. They'd have me bat last—"

"—But you still wanted to play."

"Because one day, when I was five or six years old, you were teaching me how to ride my bike and I wanted to give up because I kept falling off." Jason's smile was bright, despite his reddened and tear-flooded cheeks. "I wanted to give up, but you looked at me and you said, 'Junior, it's all about the light at the end of the tunnel, son, not how far away it looks.'"

His dad immediately remembered and finished the statement, "It's about having the courage to keep chasing it. That's life."

"And I didn't give up until I could ride it. I never gave up swinging at those pitches, despite how much everyone told me that I couldn't do it. Everyone on the team made fun of me every day, but I would remember what you said and suddenly I could keep going. And when I finally hit the ball for the first time, my homerun, it was amazing. You never got discouraged in my abilities. You stayed there to show me that the light was at the end of the tunnel."

"Yes."

"And right now, dad, I can't come home because of it." Jason sobbed. "But I am okay. I swear to you that I am fine. Just know that I'm not going to give up, okay? I'm not going to stop this. I've gone too far already, and I might just be able to fix everything."

"Junior—"

"I know it sounds stupid, and I know it doesn't make any sense to you, but I promise I'll explain everything when I get home. Just know that I can't quit. You never quit, and I'm so sick and tired of quitting. It's all I've ever done, but I have two people that I barely knew two days ago, but they were willing to stand beside me, and I can't let them down. You should see these people, Dad. They are my friends."

"Is it the girl you told me about?" his father asked. "The beautiful one? The one you love?"

"Yes." Jason nodded.

"Have you gotten around to telling her?"

"No." Jason admitted. "I can't."

"Why not?"

"I—I can't do it right now." Jason was now at least a safe distance from the car. "I'm scared. I'm afraid she won't love me back, so I won't tell her yet."

"But you will when the time is right. You know how your mom was, kid. She couldn't stand me—at least at first."

"God, dad, I know!"

"Sorry."

"But, yes, she's here, and my other friend. They have risked everything for me. They've fought with me and fought for me. I can't let you down either, and most importantly I can't let myself down. I can never stop driving. That's the number one rule, here. Never. Stop. Driving. And, Dad?"

"Yes?"

"Will you trust me?" Jason wiped his eyes and sniffed. "Will you trust me enough to believe that I'm okay? I know I haven't been the most honest kid in the world, but just this one time?"

His father inhaled deeply, fighting away a powerful sob before answering.

"Yeah, son." his father forced a laugh. "I'll trust you, but I swear to God that you don't need to worry about a thing."

"No, you tell that to mom when you see her."

"She won't believe me, so you'd better call here later and tell her yourself."

"I'll make sure of it." Jason nodded, contemplating whether or not he should just open up and tell him to entire story, but he didn't want to jinx it. "Dad, can I ask you one question? Just one honest question?"

"Yes."

"If you had to do one thing, just *one* incredibly challenging thing that could possibly fix it all, what would you do?"

"I'd give it hell, Junior." his father laughed through the sobs. "I'd stand up on my two feet, and I'd give it hell. Just like I've always said."

Jason's face filled with complacency. His eyebrows relaxed, the wrinkles on his forehead flattening out with the retraction of his worried demeanor. In that moment—that instant that his father's voice gave him the final reassurance that he hadn't made a mistake in taking the biggest risk of his life—Jason Weathers found peace.

Jason Weathers found drive.

Jason Weathers found the motivation.

"I love you, Dad." was all he said. "I love you."

"I love you too, son."

That was the first time that he had ever heard him say it.

Maybe, just maybe, that was all he'd need.

"Are you seriously angry, Jason?" Agatha had to tease him a bit more. Jason returned to car in a mood that showed neither dismay, or outright happiness. "Cheer up, will you?"

"Shut up." he dismissed, getting back into the GTO.

Eventually, he re-affixed his red Chicago Cubs hat.

"Aw, man." Biff climbed into the back seat. "It's not *that* big of a deal."

"You shut up, too."

"Now you can't talk crap to me anymore, Jason." Agatha fastened her seatbelt. "Or else I'll ban you."

Darwin and Detective Folgers rolled up. He lowered the window to see them both grinning.

"Are you two a thing now?" Agatha asked.

"I got a date." Darwin nodded. "So that's my chance to work my charm."

"Glad to hear." Jason smirked. "Plus, I heard that there were a few nonexistent memory cards that a couple of law-defying nineteen-year-old kids mentioned a while ago to reverse-blackmail a small-town sheriff in Tennessee."

"You've got to be shitting me!" Darwin growled, his smile briefly vanished, only to return a second later.

"You told me that teenagers are good at lying." Agatha shrugged. "Do you honestly think that we would have a random set of memory cards just lying around in the GTO waiting to be used?"

"You little bastards!"

"Sorry." Biff couldn't help but laugh. "You mad, bro?"

Then there was silence, as Darwin had to work himself up to say it.

"No. Not one bit, however, I must admit that you're pretty damn clever." Darwin shook his head, the smile growing bigger. "But I, uh, wanted to uh, thank you all for saving me and my buddy's asses back there. I'm going to head back and check on Waldorf. You know, make sure that he's not groping the nurses and all. "

The Three Kings were humbled. Pure respect. Pure mutuality.

"I told the boys in Porter about what you did, and you can come back and get your car anytime you'd like, Jason. The impound fee is free of charge."

Jason rolled his eyes and let out a brief laugh, "Alright, Sheriff."

Folgers leaned forward and revealed them in the window, "Plus, I happened to find a couple things on their way to evidence today. A nice little glass slipper all bubble-wrapped inside of a plastic box, and a highly valuable red, white, and blue glass prism. Sounds like they should be returned to their rightful owners, eh?"

"Yeah," Biff agreed, "uh, I wasn't going to mention that until later. You know, when shit cooled down and all."

"It's in a bag next to eight thousand dollars that should more than get you through your journey."

"That, along with the announcements at your club meetings should easily get your point count back in the lead." Darwin winked. "And if you ever want to play 'cops and robbers' with any *real* cops, feel free to visit Porter, Tennessee at any time. I'll have a new cop car by then, and I'll sure as hell get a bit bored."

In unison, they share a moment of happiness and laughter.

"Damn." Jason's grin couldn't be held back. "This is pretty badass."

Agatha playfully blew a kiss.

"Coolest cops *ever!*" she said.

"Heck dang!" Darwin revved the Marauder's engine. "Ain't that 'tyte', fellas?"

"Naw," Biff leaned forward, "that's '*mad tyte*', man."

Eventually, they parted ways, the black GTO chugging happily along the highway into the horizon. Headed south, they would see Florida's welcome sign appear within the next three hours.

"Jason?" Agatha suddenly spoke. "How'd the call go, with your parents?"

"I talked to my dad." he seemed content.

"I still need to get the balls to call mine." Agatha joked. "I have to be the worst adopted child ever right now."

Biff simply laughed, "Just tell your parents a nice story." he said, wishing he had his own.

"A wild story." Jason agreed.

"What wild story should we tell them?" Agatha asked, the sun twinkling off her tanned skin in the open window. "We need something really convincing."

Jason gazed, wondering if he'd ever have the courage to confess.

Admiration fueled him. She was otherworldly beautiful, her smile so enchanting, her voice so sultry, her hair blowing in the wind as if God himself was carefully lifting every strand. To stare was to fulfill an urge so powerful, he likened it to drug addiction. Agatha Peters. This woman made him feel *alive*, his emptiness fueled by the euphoria of her companionship.

Unrequited love: an all too familiar feeling.

Sure, it sucked, but only if he let it.

"Jason?" she snapped him from the trance.

"Yeah?"

"Help us with the story!"

"Oh! Right! We'll, uh, just say that we left home and we continued onward because we haven't finished this." Jason said. "We're not done. There is light at the end of the tunnel, and today, we decided to keep chasing it."

Agatha smirked, her eyes bright with acceptance.

"We'll tell them that we left to become kings." she declared.

"The ricer kings?" Biff chimed in, the slate computer in hand, its GPS map loaded.

"No." Jason smiled from ear to ear. "*The Underground Kings.*"

Zooming out, their old black car headed due south, pushing through the vastness of the South Georgia horizon. It was summer, the thick of it, the humid haze, the sun kissed skin, the boundless sky.

For they had youth and ambition—together an unstoppable set.

And this would do, for now, considering the many tests ahead.

- The Underground Kings –
Deluxe Edition

The Underground Kings

I poured my soul into this.

Project Mad Tyte completed: 13 June 2009. 5:13PM.
Publishing Revision 2 completed: 1 July 2012. 9:33PM.
Publishing Revision 3 completed: 14 May 2013. 8:00PM.
Final draft completed: 27 June 2014. 12:18AM.
Final edit draft completed: 22 July 2014. 10:44PM.
Final edit Release completed: 17 February 2018. 12:01AM.
TUK Rev2 completed: 6 December 2018. 11:13AM.
TUK Deluxe competed: 29 December 2018. 10:40AM.
TUK Deluxe Release complete: 17 February 2020. 8:38PM

THE

HANDBOOK

Just in case you're wondering. . . solve your curiosities here:

(Deluxe Edition)

WINIVERSE SETTING

Calendar date(s):
2037CE
Present date(s):
Friday 12 June 2037 (day 1);
Saturday 13 June 2037 (day 2);
Sunday 14 June 2037 (day 3)

MAIN CAST

Jason Floyd Weathers Jr., [Hero_tits (G-4)]

DOB: 4 April 2018
AGE: 19yrs. HEIGHT: 6'0" WEIGHT: 174lbs
TYPE: Human. HAIR: Blonde. EYES: Blue.
PRIMARY VEHICLE(S): 2001 Honda S2000; Car #12-GTC2B

DESCRIPTION—

Queue the loner cliché. Yeah, the one that's all too familiar. He's depressed, just another distraught young man struggling to find his way in life. He's a recent high school graduate, the kind that specialized in applying minimal effort. Jason is just young, dumb, and broke. Adulthood isn't a faraway land anymore. It's already here, and it sucks enough without his caring, yet somewhat overbearing parents trying to help.

They only want the best for him: a good life, a stable career with growth prospects and other adult-like charms that Jason has little interest in. He's lost, in a world of classic muse. Old-school cars are a given, the majority of his knowledge "wasted" on their legacies. His mind hones skills in hip-hop, rapping with glee, dreaming of the day where he can leapfrog life and step into riches doing the things he loves. Oh, what a dreamer, his naive and powerful imagination refusing to conform to what the world wants from him. Poor guy. He only wants what everyone wishes for: happiness.

Agatha Lily Peters/Garcia, [NinjaVixen (G-4)]:

DOB: 11 May 2018
AGE: 19yrs. HEIGHT: 5'4" WEIGHT: Classified.
TYPE: Human. HAIR: Brown. EYES: Brown.
PRIMARY VEHICLE(S): 2004 Pontiac GTO 5.7; Car #12-GTC2B

DESCRIPTION—

Ah, the struggle of being young, beautiful, and desired.

She's a dreamer, another inspired member of her generation. Like her peers, she carries the burden of its upbringing like an anchor. Agatha is a byproduct of negative feedback, her childhood controlled by media, advertisements, and of course, self-indulgence. There was little guidance in her youth, as the world always told her who and what she should be. Smarter. Prettier. Flirtier. Layers piled atop a fragile little girl who understood one thing: it's difficult to know who you are, if you never knew who you *were*. So she evolved on her own, from an anchor baby, to an orphanage, and into a woman powerful enough to make men weep.

Rebellious? No. Call her "carefree," a wild spirited unicorn in need of guidance that even her adoptive parents can't instill. Beauty, though obvious, is the least of her merits. She's a fighter, a lover, a self-taught guru of automotive mastery with a thirst for speed, respect, and legitimacy. No more apologies. She's done with that.

Biff Earl Jenkins, [ThunderD (G-4)]:

DOB: 1 March 2018
AGE: 19yrs. HEIGHT: 6'2"" WEIGHT: 168lbs.
TYPE: Human. HAIR: Brown. EYES: Brown.
PRIMARY VEHICLE(S): 2008 Honda Civic EX; Car #12-GTC2B

DESCRIPTION—

Roles aren't universal, but his is very clear.

He's the stability in this group, the rock and foundation of a hot-head and a dopey cynic. Survival instincts come in many forms, but for him, calm pays dividends unheard of in his world. Anger and turmoil destroyed his neighborhood long ago. It was the same sad story, told time and time again, but he refused this destiny. His parents fell victim to trouble, yet Biff lives to defy the stereotype, of his age, of his background, of his color.

He sees things anew, his optimism untouchable, his resolve unquenchable. In a life filled with trials and tribulations, Biff steps forward with humor, instead choosing to "laugh through the storm" rather than fear it. Friends struggle with adjectives to describe him.

Composed. Intelligent. Gentle. Kind.

But he doesn't see it. Choosing to describe himself in the mirror draws stark contrast. Adjectives? No, plurality yields to just one word that haunts his every move:

Scared.

Darwin Peter Loveless

DOB: 6 May 1994
AGE: 43yrs. HEIGHT: 6'2"'" WEIGHT: 211lbs.
TYPE: Human. HAIR: Brown. EYES: Blue.
PRIMARY VEHICLE(S): 2002 Ford Crown Victoria Police Interceptor

DESCRIPTION—

Think old-school western, but instead in Porter, Tennessee. We're talking the lawmen that used their guns to negotiate, the ones that met the challenge of a foe headfirst, face-to-face in the prairies. If the itinerary includes gunfights, consider Sheriff Darwin a subject matter expert. Car chases and blackmail? Well, that puts him in a pickle, one that he'll happily accept with glee.

He's a military vet, proudly Semper Fi. He's seen war, and he's seen pain. Infantrymen are battle hardened, but cunning subjects bring about a softer side. Darwin is no different. He holds strongly to history, to loyalty, to love, to legacy. Maybe it's the reminder that beneath his hardened skin, he's as human as ever. So, he drives his old classic Police Interceptor, keeping his friends close, and his town in his palms. Shame on anyone that dares to break those bonds, because they'll have one hell of a foe—or friend, depending on fate.

Heck dang.

Factions

United Underground (UU or "double-you")

It's their own little world, the lovers of relics, the vehicles of times past, the ones that required effort and mastery to pilot. Yes, the majority of their fanfare follows illegal activities like street racing, law evading, and region-spanning scavenger hunts, but the 8,200 members mean well. They only seek to love the last of what society has shunned—the art of driving.

Scene View Deluxe System - The native program that forms the backbone of UU, giving its members unfettered access to everything related to automobiles. User access is granted by a Technical or Major Administrator only after that member qualifies via background check, interview, and a complex vetting period. Notable features include the ability to use the member's computing device as a host server, providing a highly secure network that is constantly monitored by Underground's IT forces. This botnet makes UU's structure incredibly difficult to infiltrate and track.

The most recent edition of Scene View Deluxe, version 13.0.1, includes a secure browser, navigation capabilities, police scanner, and a communicator program. Elites and Admins have additional capabilities unlocked versus non-elite subordinates.

Ranking System - All members are sorted through a ranking system designed to keep a constant tally of "reputation points" that are awarded positively or negatively by others. These ranks are separated into two classes according to their power in the organization, "elites" or "grunts." Rank promotion is done through yearly evaluations hosted by the elites, who use special reports detailing member conduct combined with a voting system to promotes eligible members to the next highest rank.

"Elites"

[E-4] Owner/Diety – **WRATH**

[E-3] Major Administrators – **Dolly, GrimReaper, OMGARGO**

[E-2] Administrators- **whiptacular, etc. . .**

[E-1] Technical Administrators – **06Bruiser, TTZ33, etc. . .**

"Grunts"

[G-1] Members/Ricers – too many to list. . .

[G-2] Supporting Members – too many to list. . .

[G-3] Overseers – **Herotits, NinjaVixen, ThunderD** too many to list. . .

[G-4] Technical Moderators – too many to list. . .

[G-5] Moderators – too many to list. .

[G-6] Major Moderators – **Rosy, Deuces Nukem, etc. . .**

Odyssey 2037

Overview:

The "Odyssey" is an annual ritualistic scavenger hunt that covers large areas of the United States. Odyssey 2037 is special in the fact that it celebrates the 35th consecutive year of the event, highlighting that its popularity has started threatening it existence. Members register, vet themselves, and prove their worthiness to compete before setting off in teams (or in some cases, individual teams) of retro vehicles to locate and accumulate hidden items.

Each participant can strategize their trip, using a "bread-crumbed" GPS map to find the hidden treasures, collect them, and tally them at designated checkpoints depending on their time allotment. Obviously, the goal is to acquire the highest point tally possible before the finish line. Point totals vary by difficulty and importance, and can be earned by performing various tasks such as: "Epic Points" for doing extraordinary things along the journey, "Monument Points" for reaching certain declared national monuments, or simply collecting "Item Points" by retrieving the hidden glass figurines.

Qualifications/Eligibility:

Due to the high population of Underground, stringent requirements along with an entrance exam must be taken before a member is eligible for entry. The most important qualifications are as follows:

[1] Rank – In order to be eligible for entry, a member must at *least* carry a ranking of G-3 and above (see "Underground Ranking System" in the above section).

[2] Contributions – On top of the ranking requirement, an eligible member must exceed a minimum amount of representation or "rep" points that provide quantitative figures on a person's physical, mental, and moral contributions to the club. The minimum rep-point requirement for the Odyssey 2037 is currently at 9500 points, a figure that takes at *least* 2-3 years to meet if not more.

[3] Postings/Activity – While most argue that this should be conjoined with the "contributions" sections of requirements, it remains a sole category due to the fact that while rep-points give a measure to the quality of your posts, actual post numbers and activity percentages give a clear idea of how dedicated you are to the site. Most "true" members spend roughly 9-10% of their total web browsing time on the United Underground Scene View Deluxe program, so the minimum requirement is 20%.

While many argue that this type of judgment is biased to those who have more free time, it has been clearly shown that contributions/rep-points have a direct correlation as a function of activity percentages.

[4] Background Check – each member that has managed to meet or exceed all other previous eligibility requirements must submit their personal information for a background check performed by some of Underground's IT board (usually referred to as "Major Administrators"/E-2s). Upon retrieval of a member's background, they must not have any outstanding warrants, court dates during the Odyssey event, past charged felonies, suspended licenses, and/or past due child support. Also (usually done covertly), an eligible member is investigated by means of computer espionage to ensure that they are not an active member of any law enforcement organization aiming to go "undercover" during the Odyssey (Scene View Deluxe turned the user's machine into a botnet computer which can at times allow backdoor access to the machine). While there have been a select few exceptions, these are normally due to a certain personal accord or vouch.

[5] Entrance Exam – After the background check has passed, an eligible member is required to take a selection of classes designed to educate and enlighten participants about the rules/stipulations and major points of the Odyssey. Here they learn various safety procedures that include a few key first aid procedures (CPR, basic stitching, emergency response, etc.) and a defensive driving course hosted by Wrath's racing team. This driving course also gives and hands on approach on how to deal with high speed maneuvers and control loss. These classes total 20 hours and are given in sets of 3 four-hour classes followed by the 8-hour defensive driving course. Upon completion of the class, a final entrance exam is taken by which an eligible participant must score higher than an 80%.

[6] Pre-event Vehicle Inspection – The final test of an eligible member's ability to participate as a contestant is a thorough vehicle inspection that entails a scrutinizing scan of a competing vehicle's operating equipment. Key things such as headlight/taillight/blinker functions are required, as are obvious safety features like working seatbelts/racing harnesses, working SRS systems, functioning brakes. Any vehicle originally equipped with a SRS system that has been removed must be fitted with a roll cage or 4-point harness of adequate specification. Tires must have 10/32s of tread and all tires must be DOT legal along with the requirement of at least one full size spare wheel and tire inside the vehicle. A first aid kit is required and an emergency repair toolkit is too. Each contestant must have a working cell phone and their Scene View Deluxe user account information like password and login name cleared from the saved directories of their computer and/or phones.

[7] Entry Free – The entry fee for the event is $600 (+ $90 per passenger with 2 maximum). While most consider this to be a steep price to pay for an overall very expensive event, it is noted that 95% of the contestants at *least* walk away with monetary awards equivalent or in excess to their entry fees. Also, considering that the grand prize is $50,000 (for each team), many consider the experience to be well worth the time, money and effort put into it.

Teams:

The Odyssey promotes and open-ended team structure, where all teams are voluntary and may consist of multiple vehicles. While most competitors tend to operate with multi-vehicle/multi-man teams, there have been cases where single-vehicle/single-man teams have been either equally or more successful. Team rules are also kept simple to ensure a mutual understanding between the contestants and the admins. They are as follows:

[1] Team Setups – Each team consists of United Underground members that have passed all required qualifications listed above. Teams may consist of up to six members and three vehicles total. Team modifications are only allowed ONCE throughout the competition and must be confirmed at a checkpoint within 24 hours of the team modification event. Any points accumulated before this 24-hour period by members not registered on the original team will be invalidated.

[2] Travel Log - Each team is given a slate computer with Scene View Deluxe installed. These slates include all functions necessary for the journey like: navigation, 6G wireless data, Scene View Communicator, emergency call capability, camera, NFC wrist computer link, and Scene View Travel Log required to complete the competition. All slates as of 10 June 2037 include 20TB of onboard storage, though this memory can be freed by uploading memory-intensive content to the Scene Cloud at each checkpoint.

[3] Check In – Each team is required to link their Travel Log into a checkpoint under the following frequencies:

1 car/1 person: 36 hours.
1 car/2 persons: 33 hours.
1 car/3 persons: 30 hours.
1 car/4 persons: 27 hours.
1 car/5 persons: 24 hours.
1 car/6 persons: 21 hours.
2 cars/2 persons: 24 hours.
2 cars/3 persons: 20 hours.
2 cars/4 persons: 16 hours.
2 cars/5 persons: 12 hours
2 cars/6 persons: 8 hours.
3 cars/3 persons: 22 hours.
3 cars/4 persons: 17 hours.
3 cars/5 persons: 12 hours.
3 cars/6 persons: 8 hours.

Competition:

The main portion of the Odyssey involves the glass items. They vary greatly in point value, directly correlating with their relative ease or difficulty to locate along with their quantities. For example, high-value items are rare, extremely difficult to find and are usually available in low numbers (1-3) while the lowest value items are in contrast, plentiful, easily found (or bought), and routinely accessible through ordinary means.

In total there are approximately 900 items included in the Odyssey 2037 placed in very well-hidden location by members of Wrath's greater entourage. Each item is pinpointed by relative location on a digital map viewable only on a machine equipped with the latest secure version of Scene View Deluxe. The item locations marked with a circle beacon that has a variable coverage radius solely depending on the value of an item. For example, a low point value item can have a location radius as low as 1 foot while the highest point value items can have location radii as large as 30-40 miles (making them *much* harder to locate).

During the event, each team is responsible for checking into a checkpoint station to log their total traveled miles, hours and current point tally. Normally, a team was required to check into a checkpoint in eight-hour intervals, but this rule was amended to help much smaller teams (for example, Jason's single-man, single-vehicle team) in compensation for their greatly reduced searching power. Whereas a team of 3 vehicles with 3 occupants each is required to check in every 8 hours, a team of 1 vehicle with one occupant is only required to check in every 36 hours. However, this is rare due to the tendency of people to prefer teamwork over solitude when the fact of the Odyssey's massive coverage area is taken into account.

Overall the entire competition/journey takes between 7-10 days, with ten being the maximum allowable before the final checkpoint in Queen City. While the distance covered is entirely variable dependent on each team's planned routes, it is not uncommon to see the total amount of distance covered by one 3 car team to exceed 6500 miles. At the end, during the award ceremony in Queen City, Wrath and the team of Underground "Elites" give the award commemorations and the collage of photos and data received by each vehicle's GPS logs.

Point System:

Over time, the point system has grown quite complex. Because the competition seeks to encourage the use of older, retro vehicles, the rules have been tailored around this, including a set of variables to keep things as fair as possible. This is sort of complex, so be warned.

Total Points (TP) - the final allocated point value after correction

$$TotalPoints = FPV - (FPV(Tax))$$

CF (Correction Factor) - calculated started with 1.9 as beginning number added to a log f(x) of in K$ with a base of the computed tax. This creates a logarithmic growth curve that expands point benefits as a function of price and model year age. Why 1.9? Well, I went back through some math with an idea of the outputs I wanted. I wanted the curve to favor increased vehicle age in an attempt to encourage the usage of older "classic" vehicles. Of course, this is a textbook exponential growth formula depending on value, with the FPV growing in respect to increased age. The 1.9 value seemed to help the curve a bit as well as ensuring that the tax values had a nice negative to positive flow as well. I pretty much toyed with the numbers until I got the tax value to intercept x=0 right around ~$20,000. Works well enough.

$$CF = 1.9 + log_{0.0375}(K)$$

Tax - calculated by subtracting 1 minus the CF (which is a varying base log function) and multiplying by 100. As it follows the CF calculation, you will see the tax benefits start hugely in favor of inexpensive vehicles and grow greatly positive with increasing value. This way, we don't have a shitload of rich douchebags buying fancy high value classic cars and taking all the winnings. Also, this follows basic car rules. It is nearly impossible to find an old car, with a high percentage of authenticity, in good working order, that is very cheap. We need this to be competitive, and throughout the narrative, there will be hints telling how the formulas were modified depending on results and mishaps of previous Odysseys.

$$Tax = 1 - CF$$

FPV (Final Point Value) - the final value of allocated points calculated by the PF*PAVar.

$$FPV = PF * PAVar$$

PF (Point Factor) - calculated by using another exponential function that takes the base allocated points plus the square of the vehicle age in model years. The final PF accounts for the percent authenticity of the vehicle, basically multiplying the PF by this percentage. Why? Because I said so. Seemed legit enough. Like all exponential functions, it increases in as age and percent authenticity do as well. Worried about it being potentially rigged? Try having a vehicle that's old and also 100% authentic, reliable, and cheap.

$$PF = Age^2 + Points$$

Value Tax Chart - below is an example chart showing the tax percentage trend versus appraised vehicle value (in K$)

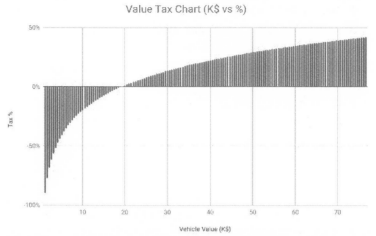

FPV Chart - below is an example chart showing FPV vs Vehicle Age

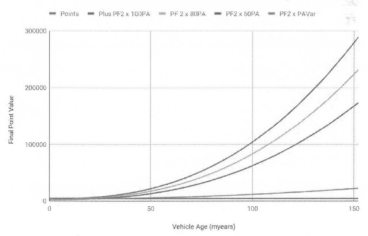

Notice that with both charts, the curve is biased to a certain "target region" by design. For the *Value Tax Chart*, the best takeaway is that vehicles with an appraised value higher than $19,500 begin to see a positive tax for every item point earned in that vehicle. However, in the *FPV Chart*, each item point's final value is positively affected by the vehicle age (in model years). The older the vehicle, and the more authentic it is (as in, the vehicle has more original parts) in *Percent Authenticity*, the higher the *Point Factor*. Notice that the 100% PA curve grants far more points than a 60% PA curve, for example. Strategizing a good mix of these two key points can help a contestant "tune" their ability to compete.

So, with all that said, the target vehicle would be between 10 and 30 years old, with an appraised value beneath $20,000, and the highest PA value possible. Any deviation from this target zone will require a contestant to find ways of offsetting negatives.

In teams, most contestants will max the team car quantity (three cars) and use the following strategies:

STRATEGY A {Rich Douchebags}

[CAR #1] - Between 10 and 50MY old. Rare. High Appraised Value (AV > 50K$). Used primarily for Epic Points, as there are more opportunities to use the car for eye candy in blog posts, attracting celebrities, etc.
[CAR #2] - Between 10 and 30MY old. Common. Low Appraised Value (AV < 19.5K$). Used primarily for collecting Item Points, biasing team FPVs towards the car with the least amount of taxation.
[CAR #3] - Between 0 and 10MY old. Common, newer vehicle. High Appraised Value (AV < 19.5K$). Used primarily as a support/staging vehicle, not used for anything else.

STRATEGY B {Smart Plebeians}

[CAR #1] - Between 10 and 30MY old. Common. Low Appraised Value (AV < 19.5K$). Used primarily for collecting Item Points, biasing team FPVs towards the car with the least amount of taxation.
[CAR #2] - Between 10 and 30MY old. Common. Low Appraised Value (AV < 19.5K$). Used primarily for collecting Item Points, biasing team FPVs towards the car with the least amount of taxation.

[CAR #3] - *Between 8 and 15MY old. Common, economy car. Low Appraised Value (AV < 19.5K$). Used primarily as a support/staging vehicle, not used for anything else.*

STRATEGY C {Dumb Ricers}

[CAR #1] - *Between 10 and 30MY old. Old. Poor condition. Low Appraised Value (AV < 19.5K$). Used primarily for collecting Item Points, biasing team FPVs towards the car with the least amount of taxation. Breaks down frequently, probably won't make it through the competition*

[CAR #2] - *Between 20 and 40MY old. Common. Poor condition. Low Appraised Value (AV < 19.5K$). Used primarily for collecting Item Points, biasing team FPVs towards the car because it is the only one that actually survives.*

[CAR #3] - *Between 20 and 40MY old. Poor condition. Low Appraised Value (AV < 19.5K$). Used primarily for collecting Item Points, biasing team FPVs towards the car with the least amount of taxation. Breaks down frequently, probably won't make it through the competition.*

Hopefully, that helps explain different ways to tailor teams. . .

Prizes:

At the award ceremony, each team is grafted into the competition calculator that takes into account things like item-point accumulation, miles driven, epic video content, blog posts, etc. While most of the competition is focused on the item-point system, the other factors are combined to give each team a total number of "Epic Points" with the highest determining the winner.

The awarded prizes are as follows:

[1] Grand Prize – awarded for the team with the highest grand total of both item and epic points. This winning team receives the $250,000 grand prize given to EACH participant. Amongst this grand prize, many of these winners are usually promoted to the "elite" rankings depending on their degree of success.

[2] 1st Place – awarded for the team with the highest total of item-point accumulation. This team receives the $200,000 monetary prize that is given to EACH participant. They also receive the "*Book of Rice*" with various gift cards and hefty discounts at local Cosmos tuner shops. Upon discretion of the elites, certain team members winning 1st place might be promoted in rank to elites.

[3] 2nd Place – awarded for the team with the second highest total of item-point accumulation. This team receives the $115,000 monetary prize that is given to EACH participant. Like the first-place winners, they too receive watered-down "*Book of Rice*" gift card booklets, but the coupons and discounts are significantly smaller. Upon discretion of the elites, certain team members placing second might be promoted to elite rankings, but this is extremely rare.

[4] 3rd Place – awarded for the team with the third highest total of item-point accumulation. This team receives the $75,00 monetary prize that is given to EACH participant. This is the lowest ranking place were the contestants receive the thinnest "*Book of Rice*" gift card booklets. Teams placing 3rd typically never receive any type of ranking promotion.

[5] Front Runners – these are (relatively) small prizes given to teams that failed to place within the top rungs but did show exemplary performances. They receive a gift card books (though not a *Book of Rice*) and have their places as Front Runners permanently attached to their online signatures. Recently, as of 2017, Front Runners are divided into 1st, 2nd, and 3rd place rungs too with each team's participants receiving $5, 3, and 2 thousand dollars each.

[6] The Successfuls – this includes everyone else that manages to complete the entire journey within the allotted time limit. Unlike the other placing systems, this basic system gives the driver of each automobile $300 (half the cost of vehicle entry) for simply crossing the finish line.

Vehicle Classes:

[1] Supercar (SUP) – ex: Lamborghini Zeus, Ferrari F80 Dio, Pagani Milite, Bugatti Krieger, McLaren Z1S etc.

A supercar is a very expensive vehicle capable of outlandish performance well in excess of lesser vehicle classes. They normally include state-of-the-art powertrain/drivetrain technology with extremely powerful engines, lightweight chassis construction with carbon fiber, magnesium and aluminum alloys, and suspension geometries representing the full engineering capabilities of the manufacturer. This combined with their low volume production makes them very expensive and rare.

//SUP1//
Price Range: $205,000-$500,000
Powertrain Type: Variable (Gasoline/Electric/Solar Electric Hybrid or Hydrogen Fuel Cell Hybrid are typical)
OEM Horsepower: 500+ HP Tolerance: +300/-75
EPA Combined Fuel Economy: 25-35mpg
//SUP2//
Price Range: $505,000-$1,000,000
Powertrain Type: Variable (Gasoline/Electric Hybrid /Solar Electric or Hydrogen Fuel Cell Hybrid are typical)
OEM Horsepower: 800+
HP Tolerance: +500/-200
EPA Combined Fuel Economy: 22-28mpg
//SUP3//
Price Range: $1,100,000+
Powertrain Type: Variable (Gasoline/Electric Hybrid or Hydrogen Fuel Cell Hybrid are typical)
OEM Horsepower: 1000+
HP Tolerance: +900/-100
EPA Combined Fuel Economy: 25-35mpg

[2] Classic Supercar (SUPC) - ex: Lamborghini Murcielago, Ferrari F40, Pagani Zonda, Bugatti Veyron, McLaren F1, etc.

See description for "SUP" class. At times, they have monetary values in excess of their non-classic counterparts, negating any price discrimination. To compensate, they are highly taxed and their

//SUP-C1//
Age Range: 20-25yrs.
Powertrain Type: Gasoline
OEM Horsepower: 500-699 (SUP-C1A), 700-999 (SUP-C1B), 1000+ (SUP-C1Z) HP Tolerance: +500/-75
EPA Combined Fuel Economy: 12-20mpg
//SUP-C2//
Age Range: 26-35yrs.
Powertrain Type: Gasoline
OEM Horsepower: 375-449 (SUP-C2A), 450-599 (SUP-C2B), 600+ (SUP-C2Z)
HP Tolerance: +400/-50
EPA Combined Fuel Economy: 9-17mpg
//SUP-C3//
Age Range: 36-55+yrs.
Powertrain Type: Gasoline
OEM Horsepower: 350-399 (SUP-C3A), 400-449 (SUP-C3B), 450+ (SUP-C3Z)
HP Tolerance: +300/-50
EPA Combined Fuel Economy: 9-17mpg

[3] Grand Touring (GT) - ex: Mercedes-Benz CLE, Ferrari 840 , Porsche 999, BMW 6 series, Bentley Corniche, Ford Mustang, etc.

- The Underground Kings –
Deluxe Edition

A grand touring car is fashioned in the mind of personal luxury, whereas it is designed to be comfortable over long distances as well as being capable of high performance in excess of more plebian cars. These cars are usually designed with a 2+2 seating arrangement, with two doors, long hoods, complex and powerful powertrains, tightly tuned suspensions, and relatively high prices.

//GT1//
Price Range: $25,000-$70,000
Powertrain Type: Variable (Gasoline/Electric/Solar Electric Hybrid or Hydrogen Fuel Cell Hybrid are typical)
OEM Horsepower: 200-399 (GT1A), 400-499 (GT1B), 500+ (GT1Z) HP Tolerance: +200/-35
EPA Combined Fuel Economy: 36-48mpg
//GT2//
Price Range: $70,000-$170,000
Powertrain Type: Variable (Gasoline/Electric/Solar Electric Hybrid or Hydrogen Fuel Cell Hybrid are typical)
OEM Horsepower: 400-499 (GT2A), 500-599 (GT2B), 600+ (GT2Z)
HP Tolerance: +200/-50
EPA Combined Fuel Economy: 35-44mpg
//GT3//
Price Range: $170,000+
Powertrain Type: Variable (Gasoline/Electric/Solar Electric Hybrid or Hydrogen Fuel Cell Hybrid are typical)
OEM Horsepower: 450-599 (GT3A), 600-799 (GT3B), 800+ (GT3Z)
HP Tolerance: +300/-50
EPA Combined Fuel Economy: 33-40mpg

[4] Classic Grand Touring (GTC) - ex: Mercedes-Benz CL, Ferrari 575 , Porsche 997, BMW E92 M3, Ford Mustang, etc.

See description for "GT" class. At times, they have monetary values in excess of their non-classic counterparts, negating any price discrimination.

//GTC1//
Age Range: 20-25yrs.
Powertrain Type: Variable (Gasoline or Gasoline/Electric Hybrid)
OEM Horsepower: 200-399 (GTC1A), 400-499 (GTC1B), 500+ (GTC1Z)HP Tolerance: +200/-35
EPA Combined Fuel Economy: 18-29mpg
//GTC2//
Age Range: 26-35yrs.
Powertrain Type: Gasoline
OEM Horsepower: 150-299 (GTC2A), 300-399 (GTC2B), 400+ (GTC2Z)
HP Tolerance: +200/-50
EPA Combined Fuel Economy: 15-27mpg
//GTC3//
Age Range: 36-55+yrs.
Powertrain Type: Gasoline
OEM Horsepower: 150-299 (GTC3A), 300-399 (GTC3B), 400+ (GTC3Z)
HP Tolerance: +300/-50
EPA Combined Fuel Economy: 13-30mpg

[5] Sports (SP) - ex: Nissan Z, Mazda Miata , Chevrolet Corvette, Jaguar E-Type, Ford Thunderbird, Ferrari California, Porsche Cayman etc.

A sports touring car is a vehicle specially designed for sporting intentions. There is little emphasis on room, and more focus on light weight, handling, and low center of gravity. While a sports does not have to be very powerful to fall under the classification, they do tend to perform better than average consumer vehicles. These cars are usually designed to hold a maximum of two passengers, with two doors, long hoods, usually potent engines, tightly tuned suspensions, and prices that tend to be extremely variable.

//SP1//
Price Range: $20,000-$70,000
Powertrain Type: Variable (Gasoline/Electric/Solar Electric Hybrid or Hydrogen Fuel Cell Hybrid are typical)
OEM Horsepower: 150-399 (SP1A), 400-499 (SP1B), 500+ (SP1Z)HP Tolerance: +200/-35
EPA Combined Fuel Economy: 42-50mpg
//SP2//
Price Range: $70,000-$170,000
Powertrain Type: Variable (Gasoline/Electric/Solar Electric Hybrid or Hydrogen Fuel Cell Hybrid are typical)
OEM Horsepower: 400-499 (SP2A), 500-599 (SP2B), 600+ (SP2Z)
HP Tolerance: +200/-50
EPA Combined Fuel Economy: 35-44mpg
//SP3//
Price Range: $170,000+
Powertrain Type: Variable (Gasoline/Electric/Solar Electric Hybrid or Hydrogen Fuel Cell Hybrid are typical)
OEM Horsepower: 450-599 (SP3A), 600-799 (SP3B), 800+ (SP3Z)
HP Tolerance: +300/-50
EPA Combined Fuel Economy: 33-40mpg

[6] Classic Sports (SPC) - ex: Honda S2000, Nissan 350Z , Chevrolet Corvette, Mazda RX7, BMW Z4, Aston Martin V8 Vantage etc.

See description for "SP" class. At times, they have monetary values in excess of their non-classic counterparts, negating any price discrimination.

//SPC1//
Age Range: 20-25yrs.
Powertrain Type: Gasoline
OEM Horsepower: 200-399 (SPC1A), 400-499 (SPC1B), 500+ (SPC1Z)HP Tolerance: +200/-35
EPA Combined Fuel Economy: 18-29mpg
//SPC2//
Age Range: 26-35yrs.
Powertrain Type: Gasoline
OEM Horsepower: 150-299 (SPC2A), 300-399 (SPC2B), 400+ (SPC2Z)
HP Tolerance: +200/-50
EPA Combined Fuel Economy: 15-27mpg
//SPC3//
Age Range: 36-55+yrs.
Powertrain Type: Gasoline
OEM Horsepower: 130-299 (SPC3A), 300-399 (SPC3B), 400+ (SPC3Z)
HP Tolerance: +300/-50
EPA Combined Fuel Economy: 13-30mpg

[7] Sport Compact (SC) - ex: Honda Civic Si, Nissan Sentra SER, Chevrolet Cordia SS, Mazda 3GT, VW GTI, etc.

A sports compact car is a vehicle specially designed for sporting intentions, though usually based off of an economic compact car platform. These cars tend to achieve a good blend of sprightly performance along with utility, fuel efficiency, and most of all, relatively low prices. In the enthusiast environment, this class of car tends to be the most prevalent.

//SC1//
Price Range: $19,000-$36,000
Powertrain Type: Variable (Gasoline/Electric/Solar Electric Hybrid or Hydrogen Fuel Cell Hybrid are typical)
OEM Horsepower: 150-199 (SC1A), 200-269 (SC1B), 270-350 (SC1Z)HP Tolerance: +200/-35
EPA Combined Fuel Economy: 44-50mpg

[8] Classic Sport Compact (SCC) - ex: Honda Civic Si, Mazdaspeed 3 , Chevrolet Cobalt SS, Nissan Sentra SER, Dodge Neon SRT-4, etc.

See description for "SP" class. At times, they have monetary values in excess of their non-classic counterparts, negating any price discrimination.

//SPC1//
Age Range: 20-25yrs.
Powertrain Type: Gasoline
OEM Horsepower: 150-199 (SCC1A), 200-249 (SPC1B), 250+ (SPC1Z)HP Tolerance: +200/-35
EPA Combined Fuel Economy: 19-24mpg
//SPC2//
Age Range: 26-35yrs.
Powertrain Type: Gasoline
OEM Horsepower: 125-159 (SPC2A), 160-199 (SPC2B), 200+ (SPC2Z)
HP Tolerance: +200/-50
EPA Combined Fuel Economy: 19-24mpg
//SPC3//

[9] Compact Economy (ECO) - ex: Honda Civic, Nissan Sentra , Chevrolet Cordia, Mazda 3, VW Golf, Toyota Prius etc.

A compact economy car is a vehicle specially designed to transport occupants in comfort, while maintaining excellent efficiency and a low price. Their powertrains are usually focused solely on efficient and reduced noise, while the suspension is tuned for ride quality. This is the most common car class in the world.

//ECO1//
Price Range: $14,000-$20,000
Powertrain Type: Variable (Gasoline/Electric/Solar Electric Hybrid or Hydrogen Fuel Cell Hybrid are typical)
OEM Horsepower: 110-159 (SC1A), 160-200(SC1B),HP Tolerance: +200/-35
EPA Combined Fuel Economy: 50+ mpg

[10] Classic Compact Economy (ECOC) - ex: Honda Civic, Nissan Sentra , Chevrolet Cruze, Mazda 3, Toyota Prius, etc.

See description for "ECO" class. At times, they have monetary values in excess of their non-classic counterparts, negating any price discrimination.

//ECOC1//
Age Range: 20-25yrs.
Powertrain Type: Gasoline (Gasoline/Electric Hybrid on occasion)
OEM Horsepower: 150-199 (ECOC1A), 200-249 (ECOC1B), 250+ (ECOC1Z)HP Tolerance: +200/-35
EPA Combined Fuel Economy: 25-45mpg
//ECOC2//
Age Range: 26-35yrs.
Powertrain Type: Gasoline (Gasoline/Electric Hybrid on occasion)
OEM Horsepower: 100-159 (ECOC2A), 160-199 (ECOC2B), 200+ (ECOC2Z)
HP Tolerance: +200/-50
EPA Combined Fuel Economy: 19-34mpg

[11] Family (FAM) - ex: Honda Accord, Nissan Altima , Chevrolet Bel Air, Mazda Attenza, VW Jetta, etc.

A general family car fits the same quality as a compact economy class car, being a vehicle specially designed to transport occupants in comfort, while maintaining excellent efficiency and a low price. Their powertrains are usually focused solely on efficient and reduced noise, while the suspension is tuned for ride quality.

//FAM1//
Price Range: $20,000-$40,000
Powertrain Type: Variable (Gasoline/Electric/Solar Electric Hybrid or Hydrogen Fuel Cell Hybrid are typical)
OEM Horsepower: 169-199 (FAM1A), 200-399(FAM1B),HP Tolerance: +50/-35
EPA Combined Fuel Economy: 47+ mpg

[12] Classic Family (FAMC) - ex: Honda Accord, Nissan Altima/Maxima , Chevrolet Malibu, Mazda 6, Toyota Camry, etc.

See description for "ECO" class. At times, they have monetary values in excess of their non-classic counterparts, negating any price discrimination.

//FAMC1//
Age Range: 20-25yrs.
Powertrain Type: Gasoline
OEM Horsepower: 150-199 (FAMC1A), 200-249 (FAMC1B), 250+ (FAMC1Z)HP Tolerance: +200/-35
EPA Combined Fuel Economy: 25-45mpg
//FAMC2//
Age Range: 26-35yrs.
Powertrain Type: Gasoline
OEM Horsepower: 100-159 (FAMC2A), 160-199 (FAMC2B), 200+ (FAMC2Z)
HP Tolerance: +200/-50
EPA Combined Fuel Economy: 19-24mpg

[13] Sports Sedan (SS) - ex: BMW 3/5 series, Cadillac CTS , Mercedes-Benz E class, Audi A4/A6, Lexus IS/GS, Tesla Model E/S/R, etc.

A sports sedan is a specialty passenger vehicle specially designed for sporting intentions. While there is a significant emphasis on room and comfort, there is a considerable focus handling, and vehicle dynamics. While a sports sedan does not have to be very powerful to fall under the classification, they do tend to perform better than average family vehicles. These cars are usually designed to hold a maximum of five passengers, with four doors, long hoods, usually potent engines, tightly tuned suspensions, and prices that tend to be extremely variable.

//SS1//
Price Range: $20,000-$70,000
Powertrain Type: Variable (Gasoline/Electric/Solar Electric Hybrid or Hydrogen Fuel Cell Hybrid are typical)
OEM Horsepower: 150-399 (SS1A), 400-499 (SS1B), 500+ (SS1Z)HP Tolerance: +200/-35
EPA Combined Fuel Economy: 42-50mpg
//SP2//
Price Range: $70,000-$170,000
Powertrain Type: Variable (Gasoline/Electric/Solar Electric Hybrid or Hydrogen Fuel Cell Hybrid are typical)
OEM Horsepower: 400-499 (SS2A), 500-599 (SS2B), 600+ (SS2Z)
HP Tolerance: +200/-50
EPA Combined Fuel Economy: 35-44mpg
//SP3//
Price Range: $170,000+
Powertrain Type: Variable (Gasoline/Electric/Solar Electric Hybrid or Hydrogen Fuel Cell Hybrid are typical)
OEM Horsepower: 450-599 (SS3A), 600-799 (SS3B), 800+ (SS3Z)
HP Tolerance: +300/-50
EPA Combined Fuel Economy: 33-40mpg

[14] Classic Sports Sedan (SSC) - ex: BMW 3/5 series, Cadillac CTS , Mercedes-Benz E class, Audi A4/A6, Lexus IS/GS, etc.

See description for "SS" class. At times, they have monetary values in excess of their non-classic counterparts, negating any price discrimination.

//SPC1//
Age Range: 20-25yrs.
Powertrain Type: Gasoline
OEM Horsepower: 200-399 (SSC1A), 400-499 (SSC1B), 500+ (SSC1Z)HP Tolerance: +200/-65
EPA Combined Fuel Economy: 18-29mpg
//SPC2//
Age Range: 26-35yrs.
Powertrain Type: Gasoline
OEM Horsepower: 150-299 (SSC2A), 300-399 (SSC2B), 400+ (SSC2Z)
HP Tolerance: +200/-50
EPA Combined Fuel Economy: 15-27mpg
//SPC3//
Age Range: 36-55+yrs.
Powertrain Type: Gasoline
OEM Horsepower: 130-299 (SSC3A), 300-399 (SSC3B), 400+ (SSC3Z)
HP Tolerance: +300/-50
EPA Combined Fuel Economy: 13-30mpg

[15] Sport Utility (SUV) - ex: Ford Explorer, Cadillac Escalade, Mercedes-Benz ML class, Toyota Hilander, Porsche Cayenne, etc.

A sport utility vehicle is a car designed with added utility in mind that often includes a larger body, higher ground clearance, larger engines for towing, and reinforced chassis for high load carrying capacities. Like the sport sedan class, the sport utility class is greatly varied in its offerings with rugged off road vehicles and vehicles capable of performance rivaling that of sports cars.

//SP1//
Price Range: $20,000-$70,000
Powertrain Type: Variable (Gasoline/Electric/Solar Electric Hybrid or Hydrogen Fuel Cell Hybrid are typical)
OEM Horsepower: 150-399 (SS1A), 400-499 (SS1B), 500+ (SS1Z)HP Tolerance: +200/-35
EPA Combined Fuel Economy: 33-40mpg/93-120mpge
//SP2//
Price Range: $70,000-$170,000
Powertrain Type: Variable (Gasoline/Electric/Solar Electric Hybrid or Hydrogen Fuel Cell Hybrid are typical)
OEM Horsepower: 400-499 (SS2A), 500-599 (SS2B), 600+ (SS2Z)
HP Tolerance: +200/-50
EPA Combined Fuel Economy: 30-34mpg/89-100mpge
//SP3//
Price Range: $170,000+
Powertrain Type: Variable (Gasoline/Electric/Solar Electric Hybrid or Hydrogen Fuel Cell Hybrid are typical)
OEM Horsepower: 450-599 (SS3A), 600-799 (SS3B), 800+ (SS3Z)
HP Tolerance: +300/-50
EPA Combined Fuel Economy: 33-40mpg/93-120mpge

[16] Classic Sports Utility (SUVC) - ex: Ford Explorer, Cadillac Escalade, Mercedes-Benz ML class, Toyota Hilander, Porsche Cayenne, etc.

See description for "SUV" class. At times, they have monetary values in excess of their non-classic counterparts, negating any price discrimination.

//SUVC1//
Age Range: 20-25yrs.
Powertrain Type: Gasoline
OEM Horsepower: 200-399 (SUVC1A), 400-499 (SUVC1B), 500+ (SUVC1Z)HP Tolerance: +200/-65
EPA Combined Fuel Economy: 10-26mpg
//SPC2//
Age Range: 26-35yrs.
Powertrain Type: Gasoline
OEM Horsepower: 150-299 (SUVC2A), 300-399 (SUVC2B), 400+ (SUVC2Z)
HP Tolerance: +200/-50
EPA Combined Fuel Economy: 8-22mpg
//SPC3//
Age Range: 36-55+yrs.
Powertrain Type: Gasoline
OEM Horsepower: 130-299 (SUVC3A), 300-399 (SUVC3B), 400+ (SUVC3Z)
HP Tolerance: +300/-50
EPA Combined Fuel Economy: 7-20mpg

- The Underground Kings -
Deluxe Edition

Stay tuned for future editions, sequels, and online media coming soon! – Bryan

www.winiverse.com

Immerse. Envelope. Imagine.

Made in the USA
Coppell, TX
15 May 2020

25758064R00206